Praise for

The Deer Kings

"Deer saints, darkness and the strangeness of family ties; Wagner effortlessly mixes football and folk horror in this terrifying new novel." —Angela Slatter, award-winning author of *The Bitterwood Bible and Other Recountings*

"In Wendy Wagner's masterful *The Deer Kings*, past and present are interwoven in a dark tapestry of occult mystery, small-town secrets, and mounting dread. This is a compulsively readable novel with strong characters that live and breathe on the page and a richly detailed and evocative Pacific Northwest setting. This story will sink its claws in you from the first word and won't release you until the last, and it will haunt your imagination long after you finish reading. One of the best books I've read in a long time, highly recommended!" —Bram Stoker Award®-winning author Tim Waggoner

"What Stephen King has done for New England, Wendy Wagner does for the Pacific Northwest. In *The Deer Kings*, Wagner captures the hidden magic and terror of coming of age in in her own specific, unerringly authentic voice. Exploring the unique horror of how the special and supernatural can be corrupted into the crass and everyday, *The Deer Kings* is a grand, gorgeous, and—at times—gory wonder." —Gordon B. White, author of *As Summer's Mask Slips and Other Disruptions* and *Rookfield*

"A novel of fog-shrouded towns and dark secrets, of corrupted youth and shadowy barns, and of insidious cults and rituals taking place beneath the veneer of a seemingly ordinary Oregon town, *The Deer Kings* is a novel by an author at the top of her game. With an evocative sense of place, flesh-and-blood characters anchored by long shadows to the sinister events of the past, and a narrative punctuated by jolts of startling horror, this compulsively readable novel has solidified Wendy Wagner's place as one of the most exciting writers in the genre." —Kealan Patrick Burke, Bram Stoker Award®-winning author of *Kin* and *Sour Candy*

"Not just a novel of cult fanaticism and sinister fears, but an enduring search for redemption: Wendy N. Wagner's *The Deer Kings* is a beautiful coming-of-age tale of friendship, sacrifice, and horror, when the monsters created from our youth prove not to vanish in older years." —Eric J. Guignard, award-winning author and editor, including *That Which Grows Wild* and *Doorways to the Deadeye*

THE DEER KINGS

WENDY N. WAGNER

ISBN: 978-1-950305-97-1 (sc)
ISBN: 978-1-950305-98-8 (ebook)
Library of Congress Catalog Number: 2021943604

First printing edition: August 27, 2021
Published by JournalStone Publishing in the United States of America.
Cover Design and Layout: Mikio Murakami & Scarlett R. Algee
Edited by Sean Leonard
Proofreading and Interior Layout by Scarlett R. Algee

JournalStone Publishing
3205 Sassafras Trail
Carbondale, Illinois 62901

JournalStone books may be ordered through booksellers or by contacting:
JournalStone | www.journalstone.com

Dedicated to Heidi Wagner, for never missing a chance to scare me.
This is probably all your fault.

The Deer Kings

PART I: The Line of Scrimmage

Football is unconditional love.
—Tom Brady

Grant me, O Lord, a steady hand and watchful eye, that no one shall be hurt as I pass by. Thou gavest life, I pray no act of mine may take away or mar that gift of Thine. Shelter those, dear Lord, who bear my company from the evils of fire and all calamity. Teach me to use my car for others' need; Nor miss through love of undue speed. The beauty of the world; that thus I may with joy and courtesy go on my way. St. Christopher, holy patron of travelers, protect me, and lead me safely to my destiny.
—The Motorist's Prayer to St. Christopher

CHAPTER ONE

GARY: 2018

THE CROWD SURGED upward, the bleachers groaning under the sudden shift in weight. Kim slammed her shoulder into Gary's, laughing as he stumbled through the chant. They clapped and stomped in sync with what had to be the whole damn town, the noise vibrating up from Gary's sore butt and into his teeth. His fillings hurt.

"Aaaand the teams return to the field! The Kingston Bucks are up six points after halftime, but the Gold Beach Panthers look ready to turn things around."

A girl soared up over the other cheerleaders, her golden ponytail a victory streamer. No one had ever looked as happy as she did at that very moment, and Gary felt suddenly, impossibly old.

"I'm going to take a leak." He had to lean close to Kim's ear to be heard over the cheering.

She gave him a playful swat on the chest. "You should have peed at halftime. You'll miss all the action!"

He ducked under the brim of her Bucks hat to steal a kiss. Her mouth tasted like Big Red gum. "If the line for nachos hadn't been so long, I would have."

Her face went thoughtful. "Maybe I should have Mr. Nakamura review the cash-handling protocols again. I told him not to let the drama club run the concession stand the first home game. At least one of those kids is in remedial math."

"They did fine." He winked at her and squeezed around the bulk of the woman next to him, making for the stairs. The woman narrowed her eyes at him, possibly a look of recognition or else a glare—it was impossible to tell, as her red-and-white face paint had swallowed the rest of her features. He didn't remember face paint being a thing back when he and his sister were attending Bucks games.

He wished he was at home with Zack. Back in Portland, Kim would have never expected Gary to attend a football game, but as the new high school principal, she had to put on a show.

A group of girls pushed past him, giggling hard enough to slosh the soda in their paper cups. The knot of giggles could have been lifted straight out of his own teen years. In fact, the girl at the end of the group even had Jessica Weissman's white-blond curls and acid-washed jeans. Anywhere else, it might have been a coincidence, but there was always the chance, here in Kingston, that the girl was one of Jessica's relatives—or hell, her kid. The thought felt painfully strange. He'd never wanted to come back, never wanted to again be a part of the incestuous, thick-rooted society of Kingstonians, and now here he was. Jessica Weissman, after all, was his third cousin.

The crowd thinned as he worked toward the concession stand and the cinder-block bathrooms. If up in the bleachers the crush of humanity overpowered, then down here the loneliness felt equally oppressive. The volunteer at the booster club's merch stand looked like the last survivor of some kind of apocalypse. Gary picked up the pace, and when he finally got through the bathroom door, he was almost disappointed he had the place to himself.

The mascot opened the door while Gary was washing his hands.

For a moment, the big brown buck looked nearly real, its glass eyes gleaming like a deer's eyes caught in high beams. The skin on Gary's neck crept at the sight.

But then its plush antlers caught on the door lintel, and the spell was broken, the silliness back in place. The kid inside the costume had to keep his neck craned backward so he could see out the gaping muzzle, and he had the hoof-gloves tucked into the buck's ridiculous red and white belt. His human hands sticking out the end of the furry costume looked uncannily like skinned paws.

"Hey, mister. You got a light?"

"Aren't you a little young to smoke?"

The kid shook his head, the buck's ears and antlers wobbling. Gary thought he could just see the kid's eyes behind the black mesh of the mascot's mouth. They were probably rolling. "Nobody *smoke*-smokes anymore. It's for the fourth quarter mascot burning."

Gary had forgotten about burning the mascot. Did they have that ritual at other high schools, or was it just Kingston? He tried to remember the last time he'd been to a game at CHS and came up blank.

"Right. Yeah." He felt in his jacket pocket for Kim's lighter. "Here you go."

"Thanks. Stop by at the end of the game, and I'll give it back to you."

Kim wouldn't want anyone to see the kid passing them a lighter; smoking was her guilty little secret. Gary shook his head. "Keep it. I mean, you'll need it for the next game, right?"

"Yeah. Good idea."

Gary dried his hands and pushed open the bathroom door.

"Thanks, Gary."

How did the kid know his name? He turned around to ask, but the boy had already vanished into a stall.

The fog had started to come in off the bay while he'd been in the bathroom. That and the wind made Gary wish for a heavier coat. It was always damp, this close to the ocean. He picked up the pace for warmth, but then let himself pause a moment beside the field house, watching the boys on the bench. He would have been one of those boys if he'd given in to his father's dream that he play football. When he'd graduated high school, he'd weighed one hundred and twenty-three pounds—if he'd been caught in a particularly nasty rainstorm. Coach Dusseldorf wouldn't have even let him step out on the field.

A boy caught him looking and gave a weak smile. The kid's heart was out there, on the gridiron, the field of combat. Even as just a nerd on the track team, Gary had understood that the boys on the football team were a different kind of human, the kind who lived and died and dreamed of a kind of glory that only came from muscle, grit, and a certain kind of balletic grace that left the human body once it hit the age of thirty. That glory suffused not just the players but also their school and their town. A town with a winning football team stood taller than the towns around it, no matter if they had lost their lumber mill or their strip malls had closed. There was more to the life and meaning of a town than just economics, and football was just as important as the church, a good bar, and a decent police chief.

Gary turned away from the field and hurried back to his seat. The crowd had begun to chant, "Go Big Red!" and the pep band was really blasting along. He resisted the urge to plug his ears.

"Took you long enough," Kim griped when he sat down beside her.

He put his arm around her. In just her Bucks sweatshirt, she was probably colder than he was.

"Hey, I had a great idea while you were gone. You ought to help with the track team this spring. You went to state, didn't you?"

"Yeah," he admitted.

"You have so much to offer, Gary. It'd be good for you. And for Kingston."

"I'll think about it," he said. "I might be on deadline during track season."

She beamed back at him, her smile as blinding as one of the cheerleaders.

He unwound his arm from around her shoulders and thought to himself: *I'd rather chew off my own foot.*

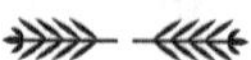

STACIE: 2018

Stacie Clinton woke up on her couch, gasping for air and shouting for someone she hadn't seen in nearly thirty years. She forced herself to silence and then remembered the breathing exercises she'd picked up at yoga class a few months ago. *Breathe in blue*, she told herself. *Breathe out pink*. It sounded like bullshit, but it worked. Mostly.

When her muscles had stopped trembling, she sat up and blinked at the lights still blazing in her living room. The television flickered quietly to itself, some Netflix original she couldn't remember turning on in the first place. Her cat padded into the room, jumped up on the couch, and nestled against her feet.

She had been dreaming. It had been weeks since she slept in her bedroom, so it wasn't a surprise that she had fallen asleep in front of the TV, but she wished she hadn't. Only in dreams did she see the flames, the antlers, the man with the snake tattoo.

Thank goodness the lights were still on. Stacie hugged her arms around herself. As a little girl, she had suffered from night terrors, but this kind of fear felt nothing like that. A night terror struck hard and then seeped gradually away in lamplight. Whatever she'd dreamed seemed to press closer and closer with every blue-to-pink breath.

It would pass, she reminded herself. The dreams came back every year at the end of summer. Once the leaves began to fall, they faded into nothing.

She took one long breath and then reached for the remote and turned up the volume. Whatever stupid show she'd left on, it had to be better than falling asleep.

She fixed her eyes on the television. If she could, she'd go right back to 1989 and shoot Vincent Vernor before any of it ever started.

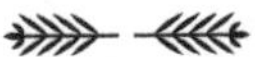

GARY: 1989

On the groaning front porch of the Big House, Gary knocked on the door frame. Only the screen door was closed, the green paint flaking, the wood warped enough to leave a gap at the bottom corner. A smell floated out of the old house—a dank stink of stale beer, cigarette smoke, and something nasty that Gary couldn't quite place.

A shadow shuffled toward him through the darkened living room. It might have been a man or a woman, old or young. Gary hadn't seen enough of the new neighbors to know who all lived inside the old farmhouse. The shadow cursed softly, and Gary's skin prickled despite the heat. He had seen things in that house too many times not to be a little afraid today.

A face appeared behind the screen. "You want something?"

The voice was so rough it took him a second to recognize it as a woman's. Her face floated behind the screen, the eyelids thick and pink where they weren't smeared with yesterday's mascara, her mouth swollen. She brought her cigarette to her lips and took a drag. "Yeah?" she said, exhaling into his face.

He held up the toolbox, his skinny wrist wobbling. "My dad needs this."

The cigarette glowed between her fingertips, the tobacco hissing as she inhaled. That too-puffy face made him want to step backward.

Smoke rushed out into his face again. "So why didn't he bring it with him in the first place?"

There was no way to explain this to a stranger. "He's got two toolboxes," he said.

She unlatched the screen door. "Fine. Whatever."

He had to squeeze between her and the wall, his shoulder pushing into the spongy mass of her enormous breasts. He thought he heard her laugh. If she hadn't, he might have stopped and stared around himself, overwhelmed by the difference between the house today and the way it had been just a few months ago.

His dad had been the Bermans' caretaker for almost two years now, ever since Mr. Berman had open-heart surgery and his doctors told him to start taking things easy. Dad liked being a help to the old man, and the rent break didn't hurt any. Working in the woods wasn't getting any more lucrative.

When the last family had moved out of the Big House—always capitalized in Gary's head, even when he just glanced across the winding driveway and expansive lawn that separated their own smaller cottage from the white farmhouse—Gary had helped his dad clean out the place. There was the usual haul of forgotten kids' stuff (Gary had discovered a battered red D&D manual he couldn't wait to read through this summer) and mismatched socks, but the Donderos had been fairly tidy tenants, and overall the clean-out had been painless.

Well, not painless. Not for Gary. Not when the Big House filled itself with patches of shadows that moved when they shouldn't and whispered to itself in voices that oughtn't whisper. It had been a very long weekend for Gary—maybe the longest. The skin on his neck had prickled so much he thought it would run away.

It prickled now as he made his way through the debris of empty beer cans and wads of what he was pretty sure were dirty diapers. Things crunched under his sneakers that he knew he didn't want to see. The toolbox banged against his leg with every slow step, the sharp corner threatening to jab right through his jeans. His mouth went dry as a small heap in the middle of the floor gave a wriggle and a twitch.

"Watch out for the baby, moron," the woman snapped. She pushed by him and stooped over. Her thin nightgown suggested she hadn't bothered with underwear. He tried to look somewhere, anywhere else.

"You're a stinky little shit," she complained. She eyed Gary. "Any chance you change diapers?"

"No," he said quickly. "I, I—"

"Gary?" His dad's voice cut him off. "That you, son? I need my metal-working toolbox. Can you go get it?"

"I got it," Gary shouted.

The baby let out an angry squall. The woman glared at Gary. "He's on the stairs," she growled, waving her hand toward the room's second doorway.

Gary hurried away. The living room opened on a narrow hallway, a staircase making up one wall. To the other side, the dark maw of a bathroom gave off the stink of old pee. The hall ended on the back door, but a mess of disassembled railing guaranteed he wasn't going any farther than the end of the stairs.

His dad sat on the next-to-last stair, rubbing his bad knee. He jerked his chin at the mess on the floor. "Had to take down the entire banister.

Can you believe it? Ought to be rebuilt with all new wood, but Berman would never pay for that."

Gary used his foot to clear a path forward and put the toolbox down at the end of the stairs. He shook out his wrists. "So why do you need the metal-working tools?"

His dad pulled his readers down from the top of his head and studied Gary's face through the lenses. "I'd say the real question was how you knew I needed them before I did."

Gary shrugged.

His dad sighed. It wasn't the first time he'd asked Gary something similar and gotten no real answer. "Gotta cut some of the old nails," he explained. "Don't want that little baby scratching herself once she starts going up and down those stairs, right?"

"Right," Gary agreed. He opened the toolbox and took out the wire snippers. "Think these'll do it?"

The back door groaned opened, pieces of old wood clattering against it as the neighbor man strode in. Gary had never seen anyone look so much like a movie villain: the long blond hair and battered jean vest belonged on a Hollywood mercenary or motorcycle gang member. The blue tattoos crawling out from under the dirty sleeves of his thermal shirt and up his neck looked actual-creepy, though. And he did ride a real Harley.

The man shifted a toothpick into the corner of his mouth. "Landlord finally sent someone to take a look at that railing, I see. Death trap, don't you think?"

Gary's dad stood up. "John Sheldon. I handyman for Mr. Berman sometimes." He hooked his thumb in the direction of the driveway. "We live across the way."

The man's pale blue eyes settled on Gary, traced over his face, down the scrawny length of his chest and hips. Their transit left Gary feeling squirmy. "What about the kid?"

"Mine," John laughed. "Carried over some extra tools."

"Huh." The toothpick, seemingly of its own volition, turned over in the man's mouth, then settled back in the corner of his lips. He put out a hand and stretched across the ruins of the banister. "Vincent Vernor," he announced. "My old lady's around here somewhere. I call her Gwennie."

"Vernor, huh?" John smiled. "Like the soda?"

"Like the soda." Vincent laughed.

Gary's dad nudged Gary forward. "Go on, son. Introduce yourself."

Gary put out his hand. "Gary Sheldon."

Vincent clasped Gary's hand in his own. The knuckles looked

chapped, and there was a thin line of black grease under his nails. His palm was almost uncomfortably hot. "Nice to meet you, Gary Sheldon."

Behind him, the shadows pooled and wriggled. Gary had to swallow twice before he could reply.

"You, too, sir."

The shadows squidged off down the hall, but Gary could still feel the darkness squirming beneath Vincent Vernor's boots.

CHAPTER TWO

GARY: 2018

AT THE FRONT door, Kim pulled her keys from her purse, the keychain-photo of a kindergarten-aged Zack catching on the zipper. Gary caught her hand on the second tug, and then gave her a long, tongue-twining kiss—the kind they used to indulge in ten or twenty times a day when they'd first met.

They broke apart, both giggling, and she unlocked the front door. "Kid, we're home!"

The house didn't really have an entryway foyer, the door opening directly on the front room like the house was in a hurry to show off their fireplace. The aroma of the evening's take-out made Gary's stomach growl.

"Hey." Zack waved a hand, then quickly returned his fingers to the video game controller. The blue beanbag rustled and grumbled beneath him, and a few Styrofoam balls oozed out of a burst seam. He lacked only the bag of Doritos and empty two-liter of Mountain Dew to complete the gamer stereotype. "How was the football game?"

Gary shrugged off his jacket. "Kingston won."

Kim kissed the top of the Zack's head, then beelined for the kitchen. "*We* won, you mean. Show some team spirit!"

"Exactly." Gary dropped onto the floor beside his son. Boxes flanked the television. He really needed to get serious about unpacking. "*Mirror's Edge*? I thought you'd still be sniping dudes with Jayden."

"He's got a lacrosse game tomorrow, so his mom made him go to bed early."

Gary glanced at the only decorative item that had made it out of a box, a rosewood carriage clock Kim's parents had given them for their wedding. "Before ten? That's draconian."

Zack laughed. The figure on the screen plummeted off the side of a building. "Crap." The controller chirped as he began shutting down the game.

"Hey, don't quit on my part. You know I love Faith and her parkour powers."

Without any of the awkwardness of most kids his age, Zack laid his head on Gary's shoulder. "Nah. I kinda just want to hang out with you."

"I hear ya, buddy." Gary lowered his head until his ear touched Zack's hair. He knew better than to kiss the side of Zack's head; Kim could get away with that kind of thing, but Gary would be pushing his luck. Not that he didn't feel lucky—most high school freshmen didn't tolerate even hugs. Gary did sneak a deep breath, drawing in the scents of sweat, dandruff shampoo, and stale cotton, the same boyish smells Zack had been emitting since fifth grade and the discovery of regular showers. As long as he kept smelling right, he had to be doing okay.

"Were you just *smelling* me?"

"Of course not." Gary lifted his head, his face carefully schooled in innocence.

"Because that would be weird, even for you." Zack sat up, his nose crinkling. "Speaking of weird, you smell funny. Did you go to a bonfire or something?"

"Bonfire's not until homecoming!" Kim shouted from the kitchen. The top of a can cracked open in there. "You want a rum and Coke, hon?"

"Yes. Please!" Gary called back. Then he plucked at his shirtfront and sniffed the fabric. Smoke, mellow and tangy, with a hint of scorched hair. "Oh. They burned a papier-mâché panther. Weird Kingston tradition."

Weird, indeed. They certainly hadn't broken out the pyrotechnics at Kim's old school. Of course, back in Portland, burning the likeness of an animal probably would have caused a protest. He doubted if anyone in Portland even went hunting. Half the cars in the Kingston High parking lot tonight had gun racks in the back. Empty, nowadays. He'd started high school the first year they'd stopped allowing guns on campus. Hadn't stopped most of the kids, not during hunting season.

Jesus, this town.

Zack poked him in the side. "Dad?"

Gary blinked at him. "Huh?" He had the feeling that wasn't the first time Zack had called his name.

"You doing okay?" There was a seriousness to Zack's question. Kim was still too high off landing her first principal gig—her dream job—to pay much attention to Gary's coping skills, but Zack never stopped looking and listening. He'd always been more attuned to other people's feelings than most kids. His aunt Jill maintained he was an empath. She sent him a rose quartz every year on his birthday to "protect his heart chakra."

"Yeah, I think so." Gary leaned back against the couch, studying the popcorn texturing on the living room ceiling. He'd spent high school in a house just like this, an ordinary ranch house on an ordinary cul-de-sac in this small, fucked up town.

"But you didn't want to come back to Kingston."

"I never said that." He folded his arms across his chest with affected nonchalance. "Your mom has a dream, kiddo. That's more important than staying in Portland."

Zack put the controller on the arm of the couch with great care. "But you wouldn't even let us drive through Kingston. Not even the time we camped our way down the coast."

Gary sighed. "It's not that big of a deal anymore. Really."

Kim popped her head around the corner. "Hey, your dad has every right to have bad feelings about this place. He lost his parents. That's dark stuff, Zackariah. Don't give him a hard time."

"Yeah, I know. I just—"

"Hey, what time's your thing with Skyler tomorrow?"

"Skyler?" Gary looked from Zack to Kim. "Who the heck is Skyler?"

"A kid in my class."

"A kid who invited you to hang out," Kim corrected. She'd taken off her ball cap, but a red mark remained at the top of her forehead, as if she'd put on the kind of ultra-skinny headband she'd worn in college. For a moment, Gary lost himself in a flash of memory: Kim, her dark ponytail framed by a pink headband that matched her terry cloth shorts. Oh God, those shorts. If he kept thinking about them, he'd get chub.

"What do you think, Gary? Will ten minutes be enough time to get over to Ranch Road?"

It took him a second to realize that as the former resident of Kingston, he was now expected to give driving directions. And of course, he still could. Twenty-two years away from the place, and the roads were just the same, the landmarks mainly untouched. The hoagie shop up the street from the high school had become a convenience store, and the steakhouse had been torched for the insurance money, but otherwise the same collection of antique stores and diners held the same places on the town's main street.

"Ten minutes is more than enough."

"Still, you'll want to take a shower in the morning, Zack. We don't want Mrs. Oakley to think you grew up in a barn."

Zack climbed out of the bean bag. "*Sam*, Mom. She told me to call her Sam."

"In my day, we never called our friends' parents by their first names." She put her hands on her hips in an unconscious imitation of her own mother.

Gary stood up, rubbing his back surreptitiously, and realizing as he did it that he was aping *his* mother. "That's because your parents were super-Catholics, not because you were raised in 1905."

Zack snorted. "Grandma Clark's house is more like *18*05. She doesn't even have a smart phone." He hugged his mother. "I'm going to bed."

"Good boy." She patted him on the cheek and watched him head into the hallway. "1805. Jeez, he's right."

"You're telling me." He followed her into the kitchen. "Drinks on the patio?"

"Bring my cigs?"

He stopped in his tracks. "Oh, damn it. I gave your lighter to the mascot."

Kim put up her hand to stop him. "I don't even want to know. Can you just…? Shit." She rubbed her eyes. "I can't even guess where the matches might be. We have got to start unpacking this place. It's been three weeks."

"It's okay. I'll just run up to the corner store and pick up a new lighter."

She softened. "You'd really do that?"

He pulled her to him. "If it means being the principal's pet, then of course."

"Do you need a special treat when you get back?" Her hips swiveled against his, her eyes mischievous. Sometimes he still wondered how he'd gotten such a hot chick to hook up with him.

He blew her a kiss as he grabbed his jacket. "I'll be back in a flash."

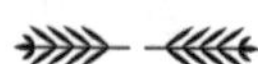

JILL: 2018

Sometimes when she was painting—not often, and usually only after smoking some particularly good flower—the world lost its grip on Jill and she returned to the vision place, the place she used to enter so easily as a child, but that these days she had such a difficult time finding. As her hand swept red paint across the top of the canvas, she felt herself leave her body and float on the edge of a vast, dark plain, lit up with one tiny spotlight. For a moment she hovered above that bit of light and then she plunged into it, the sounds turning into colors, the colors traveling out of her astral body and into her hand.

She floated in the sounds for a long time, and when she came out of them, she stared at the painting she'd made. A seascape, definitely a seascape. A boy hung half-in and half-out of a sailboat, his arm seized in the maw of…a sea lion? A shark? Her draftsmanship, during these vision times, broke down into only the vaguest suggestion of shapes. But she didn't need details to know the boy tumbling out of the boat was her nephew Zack. Her very brush strokes were infused with his personality.

Her legs wobbled, and Jill put down the paintbrush. The visions always left her exhausted. She wiped her hands on a cloth and sat down on the couch beside her big golden retriever. Merlin twitched in his sleep but didn't move. Sometimes she thought he became more sleepy when she had her visions. Miguel claimed it was a sign of their spiritual connection.

Miguel was the only one who appreciated her visions. As kids, her brother had—but after all the shit with their parents and their fucking uncle, he'd turned his back on all the things that had made him special. He took his pills. He made his snarky posts on the internet, slamming "new agers" and "religitards" equally. Then he wrote his smug little books and acted like the things they'd seen in the past were just the work of overactive imaginations.

Jill rolled her neck and reminded herself she no longer lived with Gary, but she did live with Miguel. And he understood things like clairvoyance and auras and tarot cards. Hell, he was a fricking Reiki healer.

Still.

Gary was her brother, and they had been through some shit together. Some serious shit. She reached for the St. Christopher medallion she always wore and gave it a squeeze. And she more than understood why she would have visions about Gary's family. It had been a long time since she had thought about Kingston, Oregon, but once Gary had mentioned Kim was looking at a job there, she hadn't been able to *stop*. It wasn't just her parents' car accident. It was a lot of things.

Her fingers pressed against her throat, remembering the collar of her button-down shirt twisting into her flesh.

She forced her hand to her side. She hadn't been able to wear a shirt with a collar ever since the godawful night she'd babysat for Vincent Vernor.

She petted Merlin and saw the tremble in her hand. She was too upset to keep painting.

With a sigh, she picked up her phone. She wouldn't be good for anything until she talked to Gary.

JILL: 1989

Jill pushed aside the plate of fries and grabbed Stacie's hands. "Don't look now, but that's our new neighbor."

Stacie squeezed her fingers. Fry-salt crystals dug into Jill's skin. "The blond guy by the pool table?"

Jill sat up taller to see over the booth. Now Stacie's pink scrunchie blocked her view of the man—Vincent Vernor, Gary had told her—but she could still make out the other men loafing around by the jukebox and pool table. Nadine, the waitress-slash-chamber maid, had just delivered them a pitcher of beer, and now the guys were laughing and pounding it back. Jill recognized most of them as regulars, logger-types who lived farther up Calhoun Lake: Dave Coates and his greasy high school dropout of a son, Brian; Earl Anders, who had spent last summer working with Jill's dad fighting fire; and Mike Jones, who had just graduated at the bottom of his class. Outside of Dave, they were all young men, the kind of rowdy guys who were always putting quarters in the pool table or a video game.

Vincent Vernor stepped around Dave Coates and took a pool cue off the rack. The others were big, barrel-chested men whose cut-off Hickory shirts and Romeo slippers marked them as woodsmen. Vernor looked like a rock 'n roll mechanic in jeans and black motorcycle boots. He was skinny, but that didn't make him look any less tough. Maybe it was the tattoos or the ugly silver skull ring glinting on his right hand, but Jill thought he looked like he could kick any one of those loggers' asses. He slipped between them like a weasel sneaking through a crowd of bears, and broke the rack with an enormous crash.

"His hair is almost the same color as yours, Jilly," Stacie whispered. "And as long as mine."

Jill found herself hugging her arms to her chest. "He gives me the creeps."

Stacie took an abstemious sip of her Coke. Her mother had threatened to switch her to Diet if she gained even a pound this summer. "Why? He's no worse than any of the other guys. He doesn't even chew tobacco like Bryan and Earl."

"He was out by the mailbox yesterday morning, doing something with his motorcycle." Jill's arms tightened themselves. "Just the way he *looked* at me."

Stacie pulled Jill's hand free of her side and squeezed it. "I know what you mean."

Jill risked a glance at Vernor again. She wasn't sure Stacie could understand. There was something spooky about the man's nearly colorless eyes, something empty and hungry that made her mouth go dry and her feet want to run.

Gary had seen it when he'd met Vernor at the Big House. He might be her little brother, but he understood things. Even her dreams, the ones that didn't feel like dreams and sometimes came on when she was awake.

She realized she was still gripping Stacie's hand and released it. "Did I tell you what Gary and I made this weekend?"

Stacie shook her head.

Jill grinned. This was a lot more interesting than her white trash neighbor and the greaseballs playing pool. "Have you ever heard of a Ouija board?"

"Like in the movie *Witchboard*? Far *out*, Jill! Did you use it yet?"

Jill couldn't help noticing Vincent Vernor moving away from the pool table, his hand on Mike's shoulder. He pushed the younger man toward the pinball machine as he held out something small and shiny—like a tiny Ziploc bag, full of what looked like salt. Mike snatched it from him, his face going red. What were those two up to?

Vincent spun around, his eyes fixing on Jill's. A finger of ice ran between her shoulder blades.

"Earth to Jill? Did you even hear my question?"

Jill scooted down in the booth so she wouldn't see Vincent any longer. The Ouija board seemed like kid stuff now. "We're taking it to the barn tonight," she said. "Gary's pretty sure there's a ghost out there."

Stacie's brown eyes widened. "What about you?"

Jill opened her mouth and then closed it. She and Stacie had been best friends since third grade—since the first day Stacie had walked into Mrs. Ternahan's class wearing galoshes the same shade of pink as Jill's. But Jill had never once told her about the pictures she sometimes saw when she was falling asleep or painting. It was nothing like what Gary lived with, but Jill knew it made her weird. Maybe even crazy, like her Grandma Sheldon had been.

Unless the Ouija board proved she and Gary were totally sane.

"I can't wait for tonight," Jill admitted.

She covered her mouth with her hand to stifle the excited laugh bubbling up in her throat.

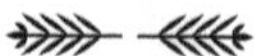

GARY: 2018

Gary almost wished he'd grabbed his headlamp for the trip to the 22nd Street Market. Fog obscured the houses on the far side of the road. The mist carried a chill up from the sea and spread it over the town. The steep hump of Peshak Head stood between the ocean and Kingston, but the hill meant nothing to the fog. The stone and spruce was as easy for it to scale as the sand dunes a few miles south. The fog's dampness slipped through their branches like it slipped through his windbreaker.

He turned up his collar and tried not to shudder. As a child, the fog had scared Gary. At night, it seemed like the fog strangled the light out of the streetlights and hid the stars. By day, it was no better. A fog bank looked like a slab of cotton unrolling over the landscape, swallowing up details like the lumber mill and the lighthouse, cutting off the town from the rest of the world.

It was worse when they'd drive up the lake to visit his grandparents. No matter how carefully his mom drove or how many times they took the trip, the drive had terrified him. Riding their bikes was worse—hell, even Jill had been frightened of that bike ride. The fog mouthed up to the very edge of the highway, a road clinging to a cliff face that some intrepid settler had decided was wide enough to drive on. He and Jill had seen no fewer than four car accidents in their travels to and from their grandparents' house, so they knew firsthand that Calhoun Lake Road was always hungry.

And then it had swallowed their parents.

As if summoned by his memory, Jill's ringtone sounded from his pocket, the first two bars of "Freebird."

"Gillian," he breathed, relieved and comforted to know that even in Petaluma, California, his sister knew he was having a hard time.

"What the *fuck* are you doing in Kingston, Gary?"

"Yell at me, please. It makes me feel like you're really here."

"I ought to come up there and kick your ass, except that would require setting foot in Kingston."

The lights of Main Street—Highway 101, really—glinted ahead. Gary leaned against someone's privacy fence. Jill hadn't been to Kingston since the day his parents drove into Calhoun Lake. He'd managed to avoid the place up until the move was utterly unavoidable.

Zack was right. He hadn't wanted to come back to Kingston. But if he was going to survive living here, he was going to have to face what had happened to his parents.

"I wish I really knew what happened that night on Calhoun Lake Road, Jilly. Why Mom and Dad died."

"I told you about my vision. I told you they committed suicide."

"But why? I was getting sick, but everything else was finally good for them. After years of struggling, they actually had their shit together."

"Because of the deer saint."

"That was just kids playing!"

Her voice crackled with anger. "You always bought into the stories Uncle James told us. That the 'stress of losing our parents' made us flip out. I'm the one who spent two years on the funny farm, but you're the one who thinks we're crazy."

"I know you're not crazy. I just… God, I don't know."

She huffed a long sigh. He hadn't been to her place for a while, but he could see her perched cross-legged on her papasan, a cone of incense sending up smoke from the end table beside her. The his-and-hers bongs she and Miguel had made in their glass-blowing class resting on the table in the place of honor. Her dog, Merlin, snoring on the couch.

"I know you won't believe me, but I did one of my paintings, and I think it was a warning."

"What was it?" He bent his knees to loosen them. He'd given up telling Jill what he thought about prophetic dreams years ago, but she already sounded too pissed for him to remind her.

"It felt really metaphorical, but it was clearly Zack on a boat, getting attacked by some sea monster."

"A sea monster?"

"It's a metaphor, Gary. You moved to the fucking coast." She paused. He could almost hear Merlin's ears flap as she reached over to rub the mutt's head. "Our parents were normal until they got caught up in Kingston's shit. That town is whack."

"Yeah." He tried to think of a rational response and came up empty-handed. He cleared his throat, which felt uncomfortably tight. "Yeah. I think you're probably right."

She made a little sound that could have been a gasp or a sigh or a sob. "I'll get Miguel to cast a protection on you three. Okay?"

He nodded and remembered she couldn't actually see him. God, he was actually encouraging her witchy nonsense. That's how much this move had unnerved him. "Okay."

Maybe if she felt like she was doing something to help, she'd feel better. And maybe if she felt better, he'd feel better. Because he was probably in no more danger here than he'd ever been in back at Portland, despite the creepy fog and small-town insularity.

"Look, Jill, I've got to go. I'm really glad you called me."

"You're the only family I've got left," she said, her voice cracking a bit. "You take care of yourself, Monkey Boy."

"You, too, Jilly Bean."

The phone went silent. Gary kept its warmth pressed to his ear another minute, as if he could absorb just a little more of his big sister's comforting presence through the line. As if she could keep him from thinking about the fog, and Calhoun Lake Road, and the summer before his parents stopped being themselves.

CHAPTER THREE

GARY: 2018

AFTER RINGING IN the handful of dimes from the week's copying fees, Gary tucked the key to the copy machine inside the battered tackle box kept just for this critical library miscellany. The box also contained a sewing kit, the key for the hose bib by the front door, and a set of Allen wrenches. As far as he knew, every library had a box like this. It was the first-aid kit of a library's physical establishment, and the building would certainly be shabbier for the lack of these funny bits. He tucked the box into the filing cabinet behind the front desk and turned around to find his boss's nose nearly an inch from his own.

Gary managed to repress a startled shriek. "I didn't know you were coming in today, Shawn the Stealthy." The volunteer manager had dubbed Gary "Scary Gary" for the number of times Shawn Magruder had made Gary jump in just the two weeks since he'd started at the library. It was one of the reasons he was glad Shawn—and the volunteer manager—had Saturdays off.

Shawn smiled. He had a surprising gap in his otherwise perfect teeth. He pushed up his glasses, the same oversized plastic frames as Gary's, but in a bright blue that complimented his much darker skin. "I just stopped by to see how things were going. Your first Saturday shift on your own."

"Well, Jeannie was here until an hour ago. But thanks." Gary glanced at the clock. "I'd better start closing up."

"I'll help."

Without discussion, Shawn made his way into the children's room while Gary made a quick pass of the bathrooms and the meeting room. Gary could hear the twin toddlers—near-daily visitors—bellowing happily as he headed into the adult fiction area.

When he was in the stacks, the ache went out of his shoulders and he could breathe more deeply. The town outside had gotten more battered, the lumber mill had closed, but the library had barely changed since he was an after-school volunteer shelving books under the watchful eye of Mrs. Steiner, down to the same fake flower smell of the carpeting. It smelled like safety.

He stuck his head around the corner to peer down the back hallway of science fiction and westerns. An old man stood with his back to Gary, his scrawny figure tall and spare in jeans and an orange hunting vest. His beat-up Hickory shirt looked like the ones Gary's grandpa wore when he worked in the woods. In fact, for a second, the old codger looked just like his Grandpa Thompson.

"Sir?" Gary's voice came out scratchy and small.

A page turned in response, a dry rasp of paper against skin.

"Sir," Gary tried again. "The library's closing."

The old man slowly turned around, still engrossed in the book in his hand. Gary's heart sank when he saw his own face looking out of the back cover.

"If you're ready to check out—"

"Welcome back to Kingston, Gary Sheldon." The old man lowered the book. His bald head gleamed in the fluorescents, but his eyebrows were black shark fins above his eyes.

A pendant hung from the old man's neck, a white disk strung on a leather cord. An illegible shape, something like a rune, had been burned into the material. For some reason, it made Gary deeply uncomfortable, as if he had seen it before and had encouraged himself to forget it.

"Do you remember who I am?"

Gary forced his attention from the pendant back to the man's face. He couldn't imagine forgetting those eyebrows, but yet Gary couldn't quite place him. Or didn't want to place him. Years of public service warned him that this guy was trouble.

"You always did have your head in the clouds. You weren't a half-bad writer, though."

Then the years contracted, and Gary was fifteen again, listening to JV football players sing the fight song while he tried to read *Slaughterhouse-Five*. He could almost smell the bubblegum and discount body spray, sophomore English all over again.

"Coach D?" he whispered. Time had ravaged the man's physique, drained muscle down to the bone, drained color from the flesh. Even the eyebrows had changed—an unmanaged thyroid condition must have shrunk them.

"Come on, Mr. Dusseldorf." Shawn's voice was kind yet firm. "We're closing for the day." He put his hand on the man's shoulder and steered him toward the front door.

Gary had to lean on the science fiction shelf. Coach Dusseldorf might have overlooked the shenanigans of his football players, but he'd always encouraged Gary's writing, in his upbeat and yet terrifying way. It pained Gary to see him so aged—but he had to admit the old guy was still intimidating.

"Hey." Shawn dropped Gary's novel on top of the bookshelf with a thud. "Come on back to the staff room."

Gary followed him, his mouth seemingly disconnected from his brain. He wished he could call Jill and tell her what had just happened.

"You can't let those old farts get to you," Shawn said, reaching for a black reusable Safeway bag on the floor by his desk. "Half of them should be in adult day care."

"Yeah," Gary managed.

"I think you need this more than I do." Shawn pulled out a six-pack. "Last sixer of Hopworks in the whole town."

"Oh man." Gary took the beer. "Thank you."

"No, thank you." Shawn began folding the bag. "When Frances had to move to Seattle, I thought I'd never get anyone to cover Saturday shifts. You coming to town felt like a little miracle."

"It was good luck for both of us."

"Better luck for me, I think." Shawn leaned in conspiratorially. "Virginia and Jeannie are terrific, but let's face it—a man can only listen to so many stories about grandkids and cat videos before he begins to wonder if he went into the wrong line of work."

Gary laughed. The knot in his stomach eased a little. It was true that librarians up in Portland were a younger bunch than the crew who worked here. At least Gary had known before he'd sent in his resume that Kingston's cultural scene veered toward the white-haired tribe. Shawn had never set foot outside Oregon's metro area.

If he had, he might have reconsidered moving to the coast. More often than not, Gary felt out of place in such a conservative area, but at least he wasn't Black. Oregon's legacy of sundown towns and KKK interference made faces like Shawn's uncommon in its rural precincts.

On the other side of the room, Gary's phone buzzed. He hurried to grab it from his cubby of personal things. "Hey, Zack."

"Hey, Dad. I can't get ahold of Mom. Can you pick me up at Skyler's?"

"Yeah, I'm just locking up here. Text me the address, and I'll be there in fifteen." Gary hung up.

"That Zack? I can finish locking up here if you need to pick him up."

"Are you sure? I mean, it's not even your day to work."

"Yeah, I don't mind. Go home and knock back a beer or two. You deserve it."

"Thanks, man. I owe you one."

Gary gathered up his things and hurried toward the back door. Just as he was pushing it open, Shawn appeared in the hallway.

"Gary? Remember what I said about the old guys. Don't let them get to you."

"Right." Gary gave him a wave and a smile, and then stepped outside. Here in the sunshine, the discomfort he'd felt facing Coach Dusseldorf evaporated like dew. It was silly to be so worked up about an old man with a funny necklace. It was just more of the same anxiety he'd felt since the day Kim decided to apply for her job.

He squeezed shut his eyes and took a deep breath. He was only anxious because of the past, and the past could only hurt him if he clung to it, he reminded himself. He just had to be logical about his feelings. Logical.

Letting out a long breath, he pulled his keys from his pocket and stepped toward his battered gray Saturn. And stopped.

There, under the windshield wiper, someone had tucked a single filtered cigarette. He knew before he picked it up that it would be a Marlboro. The brand his dad started smoking when he started working at the mill. The Deer Kings' brand.

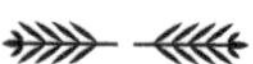

STACIE: 1989

Stacie swallowed the last bite of her Pop-Tart, put down the library's slightly battered copy of *Alanna: The First Adventure*—she didn't care if it was for kids, she couldn't start summer without giving it a re-read—and checked the clock by her bed. 11:45. Her mom would start moving around in the next few minutes, if she wasn't up already. Stacie cocked her head and listened, but the apartment was silent.

She got up anyway. On the days her mom closed the lodge, it was easier just to get out of the house than to be as still and quiet as her mother demanded. The whole house stank on those days, her mother's jacket and shoes and even her hair giving off stale cigarette smoke. Stacie's mom usually went out on the porch when she smoked at home, but sometimes, when she worked the night shift, she didn't bother. Stacie hated the way her eyes and nose would itch whenever her mother lit up. But she would never complain. Her mom had it hard enough without Stacie riding her ass.

She pulled on her outfit and wondered how it could only be the second day of summer break. She was already bored. But over the last few summers Stacie had learned a few tricks for surviving the long days without school. The first trick was to spend as little time at home as possible. She crept into the kitchen to sort out some kind of lunch and beverage to get her through the afternoon. Last year, she'd mostly stuck to peanut butter and jelly, but a few months ago she'd decided she liked ham better. Ham and mustard. Somehow her mother had brought home a jar of Grey Poupon, and now Stacie couldn't get enough of the combination. Maybe it was just those ads with the shiny silver dome and the stuffy people, but she'd never had a sandwich that tasted so good, even on plain white bread.

She refilled a 7-Up bottle with water and tossed it in her backpack with the sandwich. She wasn't sure where she'd spend the day. Jill's, maybe. Jill's parents never minded having an extra kid around. Jill's little brother could be a little weird, but he wasn't so annoying now that he was on Ritalin.

Her mind set on the Sheldon house, she ducked into the bathroom to scrub her teeth and put on another layer of deodorant. Jill lived half a mile outside of town, and there was no way Stacie was going to get there stinking and sweaty like she used to when they were little. She pulled her brown hair back in a ponytail and made a face at her freckles. Jill didn't have freckles. Jill was never sweaty or stinky. Her curly blond hair always bounced perfectly around her like a shampoo ad. If she wasn't Stacie's best friend, that hair might have been good reason to loathe her. But she was, and had been since the day Stacie's mom arrived in Kingston, freshly hired to manage the Calhoun Lake Lodge. Freshly divorced, too, but Stacie didn't like to think about that. It was better to just pretend she'd never had a dad.

She shut the medicine cabinet and left the bathroom, hurrying now. Her mom would be up any minute.

"Hey there, gummy bear. Where you off to?"

She turned around, forcing a smile. Her mother sat on the couch in her old leopard-print bathrobe. She was already smoking a cigarette. "Hi, Mom. You sleep okay?"

"Could have used an extra hour or two. Did you hear the neighbors and their damn dog? Someday that dog is going to turn itself inside out barking."

Stacie held her breath as she gave her mother a hug. "I wish they'd let me walk it. It's not its fault it's so miserable."

"It's not mine either." Her mom looked her up and down. "You headed out?"

"Yeah, I thought I'd hang out with Jill today. Make our plans for the summer. She knows some people who might need babysitters."

Her mother beamed. "Not a bad idea to make a little extra cash. You'll need some new clothes for high school." She pulled Stacie toward her and licked a finger, which she then used to scrub at the corner of Stacie's eye. "Baby, you're a mess."

Stacie tried to wriggle away. "I just washed my face."

Her mother patted her cheek. "You ought to take more pains." She reached for the hem of Stacie's pink button-down and undid the bottom three buttons before tying the tails in a knot. "Show off that cute little figure of yours!"

Stacie managed to free herself. "Sure. Thanks, Mom. I'd better get a move on."

"Stop by the lodge for dinner!" her mother called after her. "You'll be right there."

Stacie waved noncommittally. The only bad thing about spending the day at Jill's was that her house was just down the road from the lodge, so Mom always expected Stacie to pop in for a visit before she went home. Which wasn't entirely lousy. Mom always gave her free sodas, and dinner there was better than stirring up a box of macaroni and cheese or something. But her mom was always so *cheerful* while she was at work. Cheerful and fake. And at her cheeriest, she liked to march Stacie around the place and introduce her to the regulars. It felt weird, being looked at like that. They were always old men or loggers who had just crawled out of the woods or hunters on their way to some way-out hunting camp. Always men with their eyes like tiny fingers running all over her.

She closed the door on her mother's cigarette smoke, and then she was outside, in the clean, tree-smelling air with sunshine pouring all around, and she could untie the knot in her shirt and smooth out some of the wrinkles. She buttoned it back up, put on her backpack, and unlocked her bike. She half-expected her mom to open the apartment door and tell her fix up her shirt again, but the door stayed closed. Stacie had started a big pot of coffee about an hour ago, and her mother was probably drowning in that.

It was an uncharitable thought, so she pushed it away. She did love her mom. She really did.

Her bike practically flew out of the apartment's little parking lot, and then she turned onto Camp Road. If she had turned to the right, she'd head toward the new subdivisions with their big new houses. But she turned left, following Balfour Drive to where it narrowed into a one-lane track that paralleled Highway 101. You didn't have to be smart to know that riding a two-speed down 101 was a very stupid idea.

She almost never saw anyone on this stretch, but up ahead, two boys sat on an ancient, half-crumbling tractor, their bikes flung down haphazardly enough that Stacie nearly ran into them. She braked so hard her bike turned almost sideways.

"Hey, you shouldn't block the shoulder of the road! Where am I supposed to ride?"

"Sorry," the one boy said, leaping down from the tractor seat with a book under his arm. "Sorry," he repeated, dragging his bike onto the grass. "Sorry!"

She recognized him a little. He was a year behind her in school, a skinny little weirdo whose bangs threatened to eat his face.

The other boy just stretched and yawned, as if he could not be more bored by Stacie or her complaints. He was in her grade, she knew, but maybe he'd been held back—he looked a lot taller than the other eighth grade graduates, and when he gave another stretch, his shirt rode up, revealing a thin line of fine brown hairs connecting his belly button to the top of his boxer shorts.

David. That was his name. New last year.

"Oh, yes, this road is *so* busy. You're in so much danger," he said, rolling his eyes.

Stacie's face went hot. "I guess it's no big deal," she mumbled.

David unfolded himself from the back of the tractor. "Girls are always flying off the handle."

She narrowed her eyes at him. Three years ago, she probably would have punched him in the nose for being an asshole, but now he was big and she was no longer a scruffy little tomboy with fists of steel and speed like a sugar-hyped otter. Being a real girl sucked.

"Oh damn, I bent the corner," the other boy muttered, and then Stacie saw the book he was holding and forgot all about punching people.

"*Witches and Mediums*? Far out! Can I look?"

The boy's eyebrows shot up on his face. They were the same brown color as his freckles, and a bit darker than his floppy hair. "You're into this stuff?"

"Why wouldn't I be?"

He looked her from head to toe—or rather, from green polka-dotted scrunchie to pink button-down to bleached white Keds. His eyebrows contracted and shot up again.

He himself wore a plain white t-shirt and jeans. She put her hands on her hips. "You don't exactly look like a necromancer yourself."

David laughed. "You two kids are cute." He had moved closer to Stacie while she wasn't looking, and now he tweaked her ponytail. "But Jordan does have a point. I've never seen a more wholesome little girl than you."

She took a step away from him, keeping her attention on the boy he'd called Jordan. Jordan swiped his bangs out of his eyes and gave Stacie an uncertain look.

"Where'd you get it? Not the library."

He shook his head. "My mom won't let me have a library card."

"What?" She stared at him in horror.

Even David looked shocked. "What else is there to do if you don't have satellite?"

Jordan's cheeks flamed. "We spend a lot of time at church." He thrust the book toward Stacie. "I found it at a garage sale. They had a couple other volumes in this series too."

Stacie took it out of his hands with reverence. "I always wanted to be a witch."

The words fell from her mouth without even thinking about them. The second they were out, she felt herself scrambling for a way to make them into a joke, to distract the boys from her ever speaking them, to sink into the ground and vanish.

But Jordan was nodding. "Me, too," he whispered.

David didn't say anything. He didn't laugh or roll his eyes either.

The book had fallen open to an illustration of a woman sitting at a table, a strange shape rising from her mouth as a group of black-clad people stared at her. Stacie had watched enough horror movies to know it was ectoplasm and the woman was a medium.

She looked from Jordan to David. She didn't really know either of them, and she had never liked David's loud mouth or mocking manner. But despite all that, she was certain fate had brought them together for a reason.

She licked her lips. "Do you know Jill and Gary Sheldon?"

"You mean that hot blonde you hang around?" David asked, at the same time as Jordan said, "Gary the Geek?"

"They've got a Ouija board," Stacie said. "And Gary can use it."

Jordan grabbed his backpack off the tractor seat. "What are we waiting for?"

CHAPTER FOUR

GARY: 2018

GARY PULLED UP in front of Sam Oakley's house. It looked even more ordinary than his own house, the lawn a small square of neatly mowed green, the shrubs a neat mustache of azaleas around the open mouth of the front stoop. A man and a woman stood on the brick pathway leading up to the house, and both heads swiveled to take in Gary as he got out of the car.

"You must be Mr. Sheldon." The petite redhead strode toward him. In the cool green of her shrub-framed porch, she looked like a five-foot-four flame, her floral top and her lipstick the same artificial shade as her pixie cut.

"Gary." He put out his hand. He couldn't tell if the pair was together or not. The big man was so bland as to be nearly unreadable.

"I'm Sam, Skyler's mom. And this is Mitchell Kane. His son Hunter's in back with the rest of the boys."

The man's blue button-down matched the siding on the house. He had the same rectangular blond head as every dad Gary had ever seen at a sporting match, and he stood a good four inches taller than Gary did. He didn't return Gary's smile.

Sam must have noticed Mitchell's disinterest. "Zack's dad," she explained to him.

"Oh! Zack!" The man stuck out the meaty square of his hand and pumped Gary's arm vigorously. "Hell of a ball handler you got there." He jerked his head toward the open front door, and Gary finally saw through the heart of the house to the French doors in back.

The back yard must be more than double the size of the front to fit so many kids in it. Even on the far side of the house, he could hear shouting and laughter. Just at that moment, Zack streaked by the French doors, legs pumping so high Gary could see his yellow Adidas, a football tucked under his arm. He shouted over his shoulder and then vanished from sight as a bigger boy passed in front of the glass.

"Football?" Zack had done track last spring, but he'd never shown any interest in team sports.

"Kid's a natural." Mitchell clapped Gary on the shoulder. "I was watching them from my deck. Bucks'll be lucky to have him on the team."

"Mitchell's my back door neighbor," Sam added. "Skyler and Hunter both play junior varsity."

"Oh." Gary had half-forgotten the tiered system of high school football and that JV squads were a thing. Then again, his dad had to bribe him with Star Wars novels to run track.

"You know, I was just going to serve lemonade and snacks. Would you like some?"

Mitchell was already stepping inside, and Sam's smile looked like it wouldn't accept a no.

"Sure. That'd be great."

The front door led straight into one of those open living spaces, a cream rug marking the living room off from a spacious kitchen space. The French doors connected it all to the outdoors like something out of *Sunset* magazine. The Oakley family had definitely found a more modern home than he and Kim had.

Although perhaps the Oakley family was just Sam and Skyler. The portraits beside the French doors featured only Sam and a Latino-looking boy, and the decor leaned far from a masculine aesthetic. The fabrics were purples and florals, with at least six throw pillows on the lavender couch. Nothing you couldn't find at Target, except the wall paintings with Asian motifs, maybe. They looked nearly authentic.

"This is a great house, Sam."

She reappeared from inside the stainless-steel refrigerator, pitcher in hand. "Thanks. I'm not much of a decorator, but I like to collect stuff."

That explained the bookshelf filling up the wall at the end of the living room. Little Thai figurines perched on the shelves between the books and a few framed snapshots. He ran his finger along the shelf. Bullfinch, Campbell. Starhawk and Crowley. The King James Bible. The New Standard Revised Bible. A photo of Sam in a graduate's robe smiled out from between a copy of the Koran and *Zen and the Art of Motorcycle Maintenance*, the robe's neckline trimmed in scarlet.

"Where'd you go to school?" He sat down at the island beside Mitchell, who was already reaching for a sandwich from the stack in front of them.

"OSU for undergrad, Duke for divinity school."

"Are you a minister?"

"At Faith and Unity, down by the elementary school. You should stop by sometime. We're a young congregation, very fun, very open. And the youth group is growing like crazy."

"Hunter loves it," Mitchell added through a mouthful of sandwich. "He says Sam's the best thing that ever happened to church."

"Oh, please." She blushed, the pink stains in her cheeks shedding most of the stuffiness created by the matching hair and lipstick.

Gary decided not to mention his personal opinion of organized religion and merely nodded.

"Would you like some lemonade?" She put a glass down beside the plate of sandwiches. "I'd better get some out to the kids too." She hoisted a tray stacked full of sandwiches and turned toward the French doors.

Mitchell put down his sandwich. "You going to let Zack join the team?"

"Isn't it too late to sign up?"

"We're not *that* serious, Gary. We're trying to teach the kids what's fun about the sport, not design a championship team."

We. "Are you one of the coaches?"

"Just an assistant. Doesn't mean I'm not totally committed, though."

Gary forced himself to pick up his lemonade. The expression in Mitchell's eyes made his skin crawl. Gary had tried tee-ball for one short season, and he still remembered the parents' faces, just as serious, just as intent, their teeth bared as they pushed their way onto the field to shout at the umpire. It was the last time he'd willingly joined a team.

"It's up to Zack, I suppose. He's still getting settled at school."

Mitchell pushed the plate of sandwiches toward Gary. Sam came through the doors and took a seat across from Mitchell. "There's no better way to settle into Kingston than getting involved in the football program," Mitchell urged. "It's the heart and soul of the town."

Gary raised his eyebrows. "Are you allowed to say that in front of a minister? Heart and *soul*?"

She reached for a sandwich. "He's not wrong. I learned not to schedule choir practice on Tuesdays—the booster club meets that night—and we never schedule anything on Thursday or Friday nights. Until spring season, of course. No one really cares about baseball."

"Hey, baseball's not so bad."

She nibbled off a corner. "It's a football town."

"Go Bucks," Mitchell intoned.

"Hey, Dad!" Zack stole the lemonade out of Gary's hand, his shoulder hot and damp against Gary's arm. A sea of boys washed in around the table, chattering and laughing with the loudness of happy teens. "It's our night to cook dinner. Remember?"

"Yeah, we'd better get going." Gary got to his feet, suddenly eager to be done talking about football. "Thanks for having Zack over today."

"Any time." She put down her sandwich to reach for Zack's hand. "It was great having you, Zack."

"Thanks, Mrs. Oak—I mean, Sam." The boy grinned at catching himself.

Gary steered him toward the door.

"Hey, Zack! If you change your mind about the team, we sure could use a runner like you," Mitchell bellowed.

Gary pushed Zack through the front door before the boy could answer.

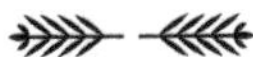

GARY: 1989

Gary was sweating a little as he walked up to the great hollow shell of the barn. He'd spent a good hour just bashing through the woods, following the old logging road up the hill until it washed out and the brush wove it back into forest. It was the last place on Earth his sister would come looking for him, and a part of him had wanted to stay up there. But it would be lunch soon, and he was hungry, and hot, and if he stopped at the barn right now, maybe he could steel his courage together to ask her to come back and try things again.

In daylight, this time. He was never coming back to the barn in the night ever, ever again.

Back when this place had been a farm, the Big House had been the farmer's house, and Gary's family's cottage had been the bunkhouse for the hired help. The barn in those days had sheltered the work horses. But the farmer had sold out twenty years ago, and Mr. Berman had given up looking for a farm tenant. He sold off the barn's enormous sliding doors to a contractor building some advertising agency's offices, and Mr. Berman had stripped the plank floor for his own palatial spread in the Portland suburbs. Now the barn smelled of dirt and mice and the rusty equipment the farmer had left behind.

The barn scared the shit out of Gary. It always had, and now it felt even worse inside.

Once you walked into its big open front, the temperature dropped a good ten degrees and the shadows began shifting in their dark corners. Gary forced himself to balance on one of the rough crossbeams that had once held up the floor, and then he picked his way to the crate.

The crate drew him to the barn at least once a week, scared or not. He had measured himself against the enormous thing since they'd moved into the cottage: First, he'd had to climb up on the narrow band of wood that framed the bottom of the crate to even peek inside the gigantic box; then, he had stood on his tiptoes; and now he stood flat-footed, the dusty, cobwebbed wood pressing into his chest as he leaned against it, waiting for his eyes to adjust to the dark.

Every inch of the crate was filthy and mysterious. The faded red letters stamped onto the boards formed impossible words, and the occasional bit of script that was actually in English only made it more exotic. He could remember turning pages in the atlas at school, wondering just where the Philippines were and how long it had taken the crate to get from those distant islands to boring old Kingston, Oregon.

Gary's dad had told him that before Mr. Berman was rich or even a landlord, he had gotten a job at an Asian import company. Back then, he'd traveled all over southeast Asia rounding up wonders. Now he'd worked his way up the corporate ladder until he owned, as Gary's dad would say, the *whole shitaree*. The crate was a legacy of that curious, acquisitive young man; the crate's presence in the barn was a warning that once you had the whole shitaree, you might forget about the value of wonder.

Because that was what the crate held inside it.

Deep inside the crate's dark, filthy core, an enormous oyster shell stood. It was nearly four feet tall, and significantly wider, and if anyone had taken the time to remove it from the crate, Gary would have easily been able to curl himself up inside it. When he was littler, he'd dreamed about doing just that—crawling into the shell and lowering himself into the sea, where it was blue and cool and quiet like no place above the water.

He stared into the oyster shell and wondered, yet again, what that enormous creature had seen and heard when it lived on the ocean floor. How long had it rooted itself to the bedrock of the South China Sea, sipping at the salty waters and slowly accreting the pearl that would be its doom?

"Gary?"

"What, Jill?" He didn't look away from the great emptiness of the shell. He was still embarrassed about what had happened out here last night.

"Some people came by."

He turned around. The four of them were just silhouettes against the white noon sun. He recognized Stacie's shorter shape beside Jill's, but the other two figures were completely strange to him.

No one said anything. The sun blazed down on the kids outside and the sweat turned cool between Gary's shoulder blades. His head had lost contact with the rest of his body, somehow floating just above and slightly to the right of his actual neck. A disembodied thought. A dis-en-thinking body. The ridiculousness of the thought made him grin.

One of the figures stepped up into the doorway of the barn. Gary thought he recognized the skinny boy by his floppy hair.

"Hey," Gary said. It didn't come out as friendly as he meant it to. He cleared his throat. "You were in Mr. Abel's class this year, right? I remember you from the cafeteria."

"Jordan," the boy said. "I remember when you jumped on the table and started playing that Van Halen song on air guitar."

"Def Leppard," Gary corrected.

The boy shrugged. "My mom only lets me listen to Christian rock."

"That's got to fucking suck," the other boy said.

Gary recognized him now, and he couldn't believe his sister would bring David Washburn to their barn. The kid had gotten suspended for giving Allen Campbell a wedgie in gym class. Allen had screamed so loud and so long he lost his voice, and he didn't come back to school for a week. Someone told Gary one of Allen's nuts had burst, but Gary wasn't sure a wedgie could have that dramatic an effect.

Still, David Washburn. He looked like a thug, and he walked like a thug, and he made everyone around him feel tiny and afraid.

"I like classical," Jordan said. "Some of it's got Latin names, so my mom thinks it's all right."

"I like classical, too," Stacie said. It was the first thing Gary had ever heard her say that wasn't about school or boys or nail polish. He had to stare at her for a minute. She went a little pink as she realized everyone, even Jill, was looking at her. "There are these composers that make music that sounds like horror movie music. It scares me, but it's peaceful too. I like it."

Jordan bobbed his head. "That makes perfect sense, yeah."

David sighed. "I didn't come out here to talk about boring music with little kiddies. Strawberry Shortcake over there"—he jerked his head toward Stacie—"says you and Blondie have a Ouija board."

"Yeah," Jill said. "We do. We made it this weekend."

"Does it work?"

"Yeah!" Jill had come to Gary's side, and now she put her hand on his shoulder. "We wouldn't have made it if we didn't think we could use it."

David laughed. "Tough words for a little lady who still wears a necklace that says, 'Daddy's girl.'"

Jill's hand went up to her throat. Gary had never thought about the necklace. He could remember Jill getting it for her eighth birthday, and he didn't think she'd taken it off since. "Look, David—"

Jordan stepped between them. "There's no reason to argue," he said in his soft voice. "We all want to use the Ouija board."

"Together," Stacie added.

"The Ouija board?" A lump choked Gary's voice down small in his throat. "Jill, did you…"

He couldn't force himself to finish the sentence. He couldn't stand the thought she might have told someone, anyone, about what had happened in the barn last night.

"No," she said. "But, Gary, if we had all of us together, and we tried it during the daylight, maybe it would be different."

He pulled away from her. "Maybe it wouldn't." His hands had balled themselves into fists. He thought he could still smell the hot stink of his piss soaking into the wood. He couldn't believe how scared he'd been last night. He wasn't going to feel that scared again, not ever, not if he could help it.

Jill's mouth turned down the way it did before she started crying or shouting. "I need to try it again. I need to see if this stuff is real. You know why."

Jordan put his hand on Gary's shoulder, warm and light as a bird landing on a branch. "I don't know what happened to you guys last night, but if we do this, I promise we'll stop the second anything scary happens."

"Yeah," Stacie said. "The very second." Her smile wobbled a little. "It's one thing to watch a movie about Ouija boards, but I don't want to get too scared in real life."

But it was David who decided it. He slung his arm around Stacie's shoulder and flashed them a crooked grin. "I'll kick that Ouija board's ass if it tries anything."

Gary laughed. Maybe David wasn't such a jackass after all.

"Okay," he said. "We'll try."

GARY: 2018

"How was your day, Dad?" Zack asked as he buckled his seat belt.

Gary replayed the events of the last hour in his head, past the awkward conversations about church and football, past the distressing presence of that cigarette tucked under his windshield wiper, past Coach Dusseldorf's weird way of welcoming him back to town. "Not…bad."

Zack couldn't have known about the unique challenges of a day in Kingston, but he was all-too familiar with the foibles of working with the public. "Let me guess: an old libertarian lady got in your face about paying her fines." He reached for the volume knob on the stereo. "Level 24? What, did she pull a gun on you?"

Greg laughed. His need for aggressively cathartic music was a running joke in the family. "Something like that."

"Well, my day was great. Skyler is totally cool. I'm going to see if he wants to play *Call of Duty* with Jayden and me."

Gary braked to let a girl and her dog cross the street. Sam's end of town had a lot more kids in it than theirs did. "Skyler's into video games, too?"

"Dad." Zack rolled his eyes. "Casual gaming is like watching TV was back in your time. There's nothing nerdy about it anymore."

Gary pulled up to the intersection of Highway 101. A red-and-white banner hung between two lamp posts, proclaiming the schedule of the Bucks' home games for residents and tourists alike. For a Saturday afternoon, the roads were dead. The closest car in sight was a black Nissan pickup pulling out of the parking lot of the Dunes Diner. The left turn signal showed a steady red.

"How was the football game?"

"Fine." Zack opened the glove box. "Any snacks in here?"

"Didn't you just have a sandwich at the Oakleys'? And you looked like you were having a great time."

"Well, it's a pretty fun game, I guess. Especially when you're playing with people who know what they're doing. No offense, Dad," he added quickly.

The light finally changed. "None taken."

If Gary hadn't given Zack a micro-second glance, he would have never seen the pickup shoot through the red light. As it was, he only had time to open his mouth, to begin to shout a warning, when the side of the car imploded in a rain of safety glass and broken plastic, and then his field of vision filled up with white.

CHAPTER FIVE

STACIE: 2018

STACIE SAT AT her desk, Amon Amarth murmuring from her speakers. People didn't expect the head of a nonprofit to blast Swedish death metal in her office, but if they had her inbox, maybe they'd understand. She reached for the volume control but let her hand fall to her desk. She was also thinking about Jordan. Of course.

David had been the metalhead in their little group, and he'd taken his job "educating" the others with a seriousness he brought to nothing else, at least, not that summer. Stacie had been a mostly straight-up pop listener; Paula Abdul, Milli Vanilli, that sort of thing. If she got lucky at the library, she listened to a little Penderecki or Schoenberg. Electric guitar solos went right over her head.

Jordan took to metal like a duck to stale bread. He would sneak David's cassettes into his bedroom and listen to them late at night, his mom's cordless phone lying on his pillow so he and Stacie could listen to the same song at the same time. Had there ever been anything more intimate in her whole life than lying half-in and half-out of sleep, Jordan breathing in her ear, his occasional soft *wow* resonating through the bones of her head?

There had been nothing sexual in it, not between the two of them. Never between the two of them.

She pressed her palms over the sockets of her eyes and felt them go hot and damp. After she moved back to Corvallis—after that horrible summer—she put all of them out of her head. She never called Jill with her new address or phone number. She forgot Gary and David almost entirely. But Jordan, he had tracked her down. It was a small town, after all, and he had cousins there to help. Every month or so she'd get a postcard, at least until they went off to college, her heading north to the anonymity of Seattle, and him following in her footsteps, settling down at Oregon State like a thousand other Oregon boys. He hadn't belonged there. Could never have belonged to a cow college with a dozen fraternities.

Stacie wiped her eyes on the backs of her hands and looked at her computer screen. She couldn't remember what email she was supposed to be sending. The cursor sat in the empty white "to" box, blinking heavily.

It looked nothing like the heart-shaped planchette Gary had cut out of old plywood, but it made her feel exactly the same: as if she was waiting for a message from someone she wasn't even sure existed. As if she sat in mystery, her breath held.

For a second, she was sitting on the narrow strip of wood floor that still remained inside the Sheldon's big ancient barn, her back straight, her legs folded Indian-style (*They don't say "Indian-style" anymore,* some still-normal part of her brain reminded her), her kneecaps pressing into Jordan's and Jill's. Everything was silly and ordinary until Gary's eyes changed, the surface slicking over in rainbow clouds, a puddle on oily pavement.

And when the rainbow flickered, something electric traveled up from the plywood heart, buzzing through her fingertips, vibrating in her wrists, rushing through her arms in pins and needles and the prickling, terrifying sense of *other*.

Gary and Jill had made a Ouija board, and somehow out in the old barn, it worked.

It worked.

She forced a deep breath, the air rattling down her throat as she rocketed back to reality. She didn't dare remember any more than that, because *that*? That had been only the beginning.

Her office door swung open. "Stacie? Are you all right?" Her assistant stared at Stacie, their face worried beneath their spiky blue hair.

Stacie brushed trembling fingertips to her eyes. Maybe Kiernan couldn't see the tears. Maybe she didn't look entirely like a mess.

"I'm fine. Thanks, Kiernan."

They frowned. "Do you need some water or something? You sounded like you were choking."

"Tea would be great."

Stacie's playlist shifted from metal to Nirvana. She reached for the speaker's knob and snapped it off. There was no way she could listen to Nirvana on the anniversary of Jordan's overdose. Kiernan was still looking at her.

She forced herself to smile. "I guess I'm a little spacey today. Better make it coffee."

JILL: 1989

They yanked their fingers from the planchette like one person. Jill could feel the shudders coursing through David's shoulder where it pressed into hers. Not a one of them could look away from Gary.

He had been frozen.

That was her first thought. His fingers had come off the planchette, but his hands remained outstretched, ready to drop into place in an instant. They didn't shake or even wobble. And his face—she could barely stand to look at it. She had seen his eyes go slippery before, but this time the weird shininess seemed thicker and heavier than usual, like some kind of oily cataract.

"What did you see?" Jordan asked. "Gary? What did you see?"

"I felt it," Stacie whispered. "In my arms. Something electric."

"Something huge," David added.

Jill could only stare at her brother. He still hadn't moved.

She couldn't take it any longer. She lunged across the board and grabbed his shoulders. "Wake up. Please wake up."

He gasped and went rigid. She pulled him toward her, crushing him into her arms. He was shaking horribly.

"You okay, man?" David asked. He patted Gary's back.

Stacie and Jordan scrambled to Gary's side, patting and stroking him, murmuring soft words of comfort. Gary coughed and sniffed, then pulled free of Jill's grip.

"What did it say?" he asked.

"I—I don't know," she admitted. "I couldn't keep track."

"It moved so fast," Stacie explained.

"It was our names," Jordan said. "But, like, our whole names." He looked at Jill. "Is your middle name 'Louise'?"

"You couldn't have known that," Stacie said. "I mean, you've never even talked to Jill before."

"But do *you* know?" David snapped at her. "Because you could have been moving it."

"Is your middle name 'Jay'?" Jordan asked. "Because I didn't know that and I'm sure no one else did either."

"Shut up," Gary mumbled, rubbing his eyes.

"Who knows what everyone else actually knows about us? What if one of us saw our records in the school office?" David was getting up now, his face reddening. "I don't even know any of you except Jordan, and he's—"

"He's what?" Jordan shouted, leaping to his feet.

"Shut up!" Gary screamed. He jumped up too.

Jill and Stacie stood up, slowly. Jill hated the feeling crackling in the air, like the days when they'd first moved to the cottage and her parents were still fighting all the time. Fighting even when they weren't saying a word. Her stomach squished in on itself.

"No one was moving anything," Gary said. "This barn…" He rubbed his eyes again. He didn't look eleven anymore. He looked like a very small old man, all pinched and tired. Jill reached for his hand, but he pulled away. "This was different from last night. Worse, but better."

David took a step backward to lean against the big crate. "What happened last night?"

Gary opened his mouth and then just shook his head.

"Sometimes I have dreams," Jill said.

Everyone looked at her.

"Sometimes I'm not even asleep," she said, scared to say this out loud to anyone but Gary. "But it's like I'm dreaming, dreaming in sounds. Sometimes when I wake up from the dream, I remember the sounds and they *smush* into pictures." She shook her head. "It doesn't make any sense when I say it, but when it happens, it's just normal. I'll draw a picture when I wake up, and I realize it's a picture of whatever I was hearing in my dream."

Stacie had crossed her arms. Jill wasn't surprised by the hurt look on Stacie's face. She had never told her about the dreams. "What does any of that have to do with last night?"

"The board didn't make words last night," Gary said. "It made sounds. Every time the planchette"—he caught David's confused look—"the heart-shaped thingy—moved, it kind of sang."

"And Gary started singing along," Jill interjected. "And then something started moving in the back of the barn."

They all turned to look. How could they not? The light from the barn's open front faded as the barn stretched out, the shadows growing thicker in the open spaces between the joists that once held up the floor, the heaps of ancient machinery drawing their own patches of darkness. A tiny hint of daylight beckoned in the back corner, where the outline of the barn's human-sized backdoor beckoned faintly. It was a green and aquatic light, the sunshine fighting years of blackberry vines and seedlings to make its way to Jill's eyes.

There had been no light last night. The glint of moon and stars had refused to penetrate the dark heart of the old barn. Jill had stood her flashlight upright beside the old crate, and its beam had clawed its way up to the vaulted roof, a thin and milky finger of brightness that only made her feel smaller as she looked at it.

The memory made her reach for Stacie's arm, but Stacie was too far away to touch, and if she saw Jill's hand, she didn't reach out for it.

"It was probably an animal," David said.

"Right." Jordan patted Jill's arm. "I mean, you guys were already scared because of the Ouija board, and you obviously have some pretty weird…talents. But whatever you saw? Probably a raccoon or a porcupine."

"Guys?" Stacie shifted to stand closer to David. "Do you hear that?"

They all froze. Gary's eyes nearly bulged from his head. Jill couldn't help remembering the way he'd peed himself the night before. She was half-surprised she hadn't.

"I don't hear anything," she whispered.

Then it sounded again. A ripping noise. A scraping, ripping noise.

"What the fuck is that?" David whispered.

The door in the back of the barn shook.

Stacie screamed and pushed past Jill, racing for the safety of sunshine and the open field outside.

"Wait!" Jordan shouted, racing after her.

"Stacie!" Jill shouted, but Gary yanked her toward the others. David was still running.

Stacie and Jordan had stopped in the field, staring at something in the overgrowth behind the barn. They didn't look any less scared.

"What the hell are you kids doing out here?"

Gary's hand clenched on Jill's. They both recognized Vincent Vernor's voice. They turned to face him.

If they had looked earlier, they might have noticed the tunnel he'd slashed through the brush, but they hadn't looked. Why would they? Only an idiot or a crazy person would have any interest getting through all those blackberries and weeds. No one had used the old east field since before Mr. Berman had even bought it, and twenty years of neglect had turned it into something wilder than even the forested hills.

Now Vincent Vernor stood at the end of the brush tunnel with a machete in his hand, shirtless and panting. An American eagle spread its wings across his chest, the ink blue and whiskery. A rope of purple scar wriggled through one of the wings like a snake sunning itself on the rock of his chest. In one claw, the eagle held a syringe; in the other, a cigarette. Just beneath the cigarette, a skull vomited bullets down his side.

He grinned at them. *He ought to at least have a gold tooth*, Jill's brain prattled. All the movie bad guys had a gold tooth.

"You like playing around in that old barn?" He cocked his head, looking from one kid to the next. His eyes slid down Jill's front, and he smirked. Then his head snapped up, his eyes narrowing at David. "Aren't you a little old to be playing games?"

David said nothing. He had looked so big when Stacie had brought him up to his house, so grown-up and tough, but now he looked like just another kid. Vincent Vernor was not a large man, but he was a grown man, after all. A dangerous one.

And that made Jill realize: she had drawn this. Just this morning, she had found her pencil scooting across the back of the Chex box and the recipe for Chex mix. She had drawn a snake with wings, and she had known, drawing it, that it was what she had heard the night before in the barn. Blood had dripped from the snake's fangs. Well, maybe venom, but probably blood.

Vincent took a few steps forward and glanced inside the barn. He smirked and strode toward their board.

"No, please—" Gary started to say, but Jill yanked his arm as hard as she could to silence him.

There was an actual snake tattoo going up Vincent's arm, a big blue snake with a rattlesnake's rattle and a cobra's hood. Whoever had drawn it had twisted its head so its fangs seemed to sink into the meat of Vincent's shoulder.

Oh yes, he was a snake.

He held up the Ouija board. Jill had only painted the one side, and now the cheerful yellow of the cereal box showed itself embarrassingly. "Cute, kiddos."

Stacie and Jordan were looking at Jill. She wanted to sink into the ground in embarrassment. Had she really believed a handmade Ouija board would let her talk to ghosts? Would reassure her that the voices she heard in her dreams were spirits and not some kind of mental breakdown?

Vincent threw the board into the air and slashed out with his machete, laughing. The machete barely made a sound as it cut through the cardboard.

Vincent kicked the cardboard scraps out of his way and hooked his thumbs into his belt loops. The machete swung beside his leg, and the skull on his belt buckle jutted out at them obscenely.

"You kids stay out of this barn if you know what's good for you." He spat on the ground. The yellow goo hit their planchette. "Stay out of this whole field."

"But—" Gary began.

Vincent's arm moved in a blur. The machete pointed right at Gary, the blade unwavering. "You heard me!"

"Yes, sir," Jill said. "Come on, guys."

She turned around, waving for the others to come with her. Stacie squeezed in close, her shoulder against Jill's.

Jill could feel Vincent's eyes on them as they walked away. She knew that if she turned around, he would be watching her in particular, watching and grinning, his face cold and hungry, like a snake's.

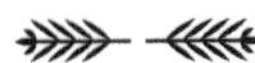

GARY: 2018

Gary gripped the edges of the exam table. "I already told you. Other than the plastic *stuck in my face*, I'm fine. Where is my son?"

The doctor passed him a tissue for the blood trickling into his eye. "The paramedics got the worst of it, and I don't want to take off the field dressing until I finish this medical history."

Gary wiped his face. "Zack? My son?"

The doctor laughed. It made the gingery curls bounce on the sides of his head. "One-track mind, I see." He raised a hand to stave off Gary's next protest. He had to be five or six years older than Gary, but a massive school ring still glinted on his right hand. "Hey, I get it. I've got kids myself. Outside of the cuts on his face and hands, your son looks terrific. But we can't be sure until they wrap up those head CTs. His side of the car took the brunt of the damage."

Gary nodded. Just thinking about Zack's side of the Saturn made him queasy. The fire department had to cut Zack out through the roof. That was when they made Gary let go of the fingers of Zack's left hand—the one bit of Zack he could touch—and get out of the car. He'd nearly thrown up then.

He remembered then that they weren't the only part of the accident. The black pickup truck had fared far worse than the Saturn. "Any word on the other driver?"

"En route to Sacred Heart. But I wouldn't mind if he didn't make it all the way to Eugene."

"What?" Gary lowered his tissue. "You're a doctor. Aren't you supposed to wish people good health?"

"It's a free country, isn't it?" The doctor tapped the tip of his pen on his form, pointedly. "Any pain in your neck?"

"You already asked. Didn't you take an oath to help people?"

"Sure, if they show up in my ER. If you're some jackass doing seventy through a commercial district, you don't get the benefit of my goodwill. Especially if you're a jackass from Plymouth who I treated for a broken ankle last year and who then tried to forge my signature on a stolen prescription pad."

"Bad egg, huh?"

The doctor shrugged. "Trevor Hyatt couldn't think his way out of a paper bag. Had two DUIs before he was even sixteen. But until that injury, he was Plymouth's starting running back, and their team led the league." He ran his hands down Gary's sides. "Any kidney or digestive conditions I should know about? Your abdomen feels good to me."

"No. You're a football fan, I take it?"

The doctor moved behind Gary to press the icy circle of his stethoscope between Gary's shoulder blades. "I played for the Bucks in high school. Kept my eyes out for a position here so my son could have the chance to play for them."

He moved around to face Gary. The gold school ring made more sense now.

"Did he? I mean, did he want to play football?"

The stethoscope played over Gary's ribs. "He's quarterback this year for the JV team. He's only a freshman, but the coach says he might make varsity next year. Hell of an arm on that boy." The doctor glanced at the intake form and frowned. "Leukemia? When was that treated?"

Gary sat up straighter. "I was fourteen."

"You should have mentioned that first thing. There are a number of later-life implications to childhood cancers." The doctor probed Gary's throat. "Your thyroid feels pretty good, though." He made a note. "How's your overall health?"

"Pretty good. My cholesterol was reasonable, last time I had it checked. My wife's a vegetarian, so that probably helps. And my son and I like to go running together."

"Well, keep that up." The doctor pocketed his stethoscope. For the first time, Gary noticed the name stitched over the man's heart. Rothschild. Frank Rothschild had been a tight end the first year Kingston went to state, the year Gary was in ninth grade and the whole town got Bucks fever—never to recover, apparently.

Adhesive crackled as Dr. Rothschild peeled back the dressing the paramedics had pasted over Gary's shredded forehead. He reached for some tool off the cart beside him. His free hand pressed dry gauze firmly to Gary's eyebrow region.

"You could have gone anywhere after med school, and you picked Kingston?"

A squirt bottle wheezed cold over Gary's hairline. The gauze turned sodden.

"Is there any better place? The ocean, the trees, the dunes? Even the people are different here. I think that when John King settled this place, he found a place blessed by God."

A damp trickle forced Gary to close his eyes. Even if he believed in God, he doubted he would have called Kingston "blessed."

"Gary, thank goodness you're okay!"

Kim whooshed through the exam room door in a fug of coffee and cigarettes that folded itself around Gary like an olfactory hug. Rothschild grumbled, and she shifted her grip. The skin under her eyes had gone gray, either with worry or tears or both. Gary squeezed her hand and wished he could get up off the exam table to give her a real hug.

"Zack's out of CT. His scans look great," she said.

Gary closed his eyes, his body going soft with relief. Zack was okay.

"I'm going to put in a couple of sutures," Rothschild said, but his voice came from a place that was very far away and that mattered very little. Zack was all right. That was all that mattered.

CHAPTER SIX

GARY: 1989

HE JUST WALKED.

The others followed him. Gary knew they would, even though he half-wished they'd leave him alone. Alone to think about what had happened back there in the barn, both today and last night, the faces he had seen while his fingers rested on that planchette, the sense that something enormous and powerful had reached out and touched the very core of his being.

He swiped his arm across his face, drying away snot and sweat. Gravel crunched under his feet. He wasn't sure where he was going. He couldn't lead a group of strange teenagers into the house where right now his mom was getting ready for her shift at the 7-Eleven. His feet steered him to the orchard at the back of their house. Branches caught at his hair and grass swished around his knees. No one had mowed back here since last summer.

"Where are we going?" Stacie whispered. Gary had always figured she was a strictly indoor girl.

He threw himself down on the remains of a gravel pile. Maybe someone had meant to make a little sitting area beneath the big plum tree, or maybe someone had just finished working on the driveway one day and lazily dumped a load of gravel back here. Whatever its origins, the patch of gravel made for a nice flat space on the edge of the grassy wilderness.

Jordan sat beside Gary, hugging his knees to his chest. He was chewing the dry skin on his thumb, a little blood already showing on his lip.

David stood for a moment, studying the trees and then the narrow brook that separated the orchard's tame trees from the forest beyond. He plucked a long strand of grass and stuck it between his teeth as he dropped to a sit. "Nice yard."

Stacie and Jill huddled together, looking smaller than two high school girls ought to look. A few strands had come loose from Stacie's high ponytail, and now they hung around her face like the ears of a lop-eared rabbit. The analogy nearly made Gary smile.

Jill caught his eye. "Are you okay?"

Was he? He wasn't sure. He forced himself to sit up and thought about shrugging. It seemed like a lot of work.

"That was your neighbor, wasn't it?" Stacie asked. "The one we saw at the lodge."

"Yeah," Jill said. "He was creepier today, though."

"Creepy's one word for it." David pulled the grass stem out of his mouth and twisted it in his fingers. "The guy's a nut job."

"Definitely," Jordan agreed. He shot a glance at Gary. "Do you actually know him?"

"I was in his house about a week ago." Gary thought about it for a moment. "My dad and I…talked to him. But we don't really *know* him."

Jill's head shot up. "I wouldn't want to know him. He's a snake."

"Too bad about the Ouija board," David said. "I mean, I'm sorry your neighbor's a dick, but the board's the real loss, isn't it?"

Jill flung a piece of gravel toward the stream. "It was just cardboard. Just homemade."

Jordan took off his backpack and pulled a book out of its depths. "Maybe that's why it worked so well." He held up one of those coffee table books—*Witches and Mediums*. The cover was red cloth with a color illustration of a woman in a black cloak and a cauldron glued into place. The folds and gaps of the cloak suggested she might be naked underneath. "You have visions, Jill. And Gary? I think you're like a real medium or something. When you made that board, you put a lot of yourselves into it."

Gary looked, really looked, at the other boy. Behind the too-long bangs, his grayish eyes were piercing as he held Gary's gaze. No one had ever studied Gary's face so intently.

"So?" Jill snapped. "It's gone now. And I don't know if I want to make another one. I got really scared back there in the barn."

Jordan shook his head. "Yeah, but that barn's like super spooky. We could try going into the woods." He began flipping pages in the book. "And if you didn't want to make another board, we could try other stuff." He turned the book so other people could see it. "Automatic writing, maybe."

"That's not a bad idea." David leaned forward, his eyes fixed on the picture of a girl holding a piece of chalk to a small slate. "We could meet up by the lake sometime. Bring a chalkboard."

"Wait." Gary pushed himself back from the group, his legs scraping across the gravel. "What are we saying? That we want to keep talking to whatever is out there? Ghosts, spirits, whatever you call them? Look, I've done this twice, guys, and neither time was any fun."

Stacie stared at him. "But don't you want to know?"

"Know what?"

"What's out there!" She got up and started to pace around the edge of the gravel. "You're a smart kid, Gary. Maybe the smartest kid in Kingston." She made an apologetic face at Jill. "I've seen the way you read. Even before you started taking Ritalin, you read faster than anyone I know. When something interests you, you learn everything about it."

"So?"

"So you're curious! And I am too." She stopped, like maybe she'd said too much, but the words wouldn't let themselves stay bottled up. "I know I'm not like most of the kids here in Kingston. I'm not going to graduate high school, then just shack up with some logger and crap out a bunch of kids. I'm not going to join the Deer Kings and raise money for the football team. I want to learn about what's real in the world. I want to help other people. Other weirdos."

The look on her face was so fierce Gary could only stare at her. How many times had he wished Jill would hang out with someone who cared more about books than lip gloss and boys? He'd only seen Stacie's matching outfits and her perfectly bleached sneakers, and completely ignored what lay beneath her surface.

David patted the ground beside him, urging Stacie to sit down. He put his arm around her when she did, and her face turned the color of an overripe tomato.

"Okay, the cool girl's with me. What about you, vision chick?" He raised his eyebrow at Jill.

She looked at Gary and then quickly away. "I—I want to."

"Jill!"

"It's what Stacie said, Gare. We have the chance to learn something *real* about the world. I know you can talk to ghosts. I know you see things that other people can't. You could give us all something nobody could ever take away."

"Not even your psycho neighbor," Jordan said. He smiled at Gary, and it was like an invitation to someplace new. "What do you say?"

Gary looked around at them. David, Stacie, and Jill, all starting high school in the summer. He and Jordan, still marooned at Hewlett Middle School. None of them normal, not really. Jill didn't just see visions and spend her free time drawing pictures of monsters—she cut her hair short and let the curls do whatever they pleased. She never wore any color besides green, and sometimes he caught her talking to trees. Stacie was secretly a nerd. David had moved to town last year and hadn't made a single friend besides the PE teacher. And Jordan? Who knew anything about him besides the fact his mom put a crucifix in his lunch box? He was so quiet he was practically a ghost.

They all needed something. And maybe this summer, he was what they needed.

"There's something here in the woods," he said. "It's lonely, and angry, and I think it's the ghost of somebody that died a long time ago."

"Maybe it's John King!" Jill blurted.

Gary shrugged. "Maybe. I guess there's one way to find out."

David leaned in. "Meet me at the Eagle Cove campground tomorrow night at seven. I have an idea."

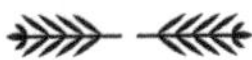

GARY: 2018

Gary took down a glass from the cupboard. It wasn't yet seven o'clock, and he wished he could have stayed in bed another hour. Zack had gotten him up three times in the night, once for pain meds and twice from nightmares. But Gary'd had enough of his own unpleasant dreams to pull him out of Kim's warm spoon-curve.

With a sigh, he padded to the sink. Even though they'd only been in their house for three weeks, he moved quickly in the near dark. Their kitchen layout could have been lifted from his parents' house here in Kingston. Just another tract-style ranch, the kind of place he'd always hoped he'd seen the last of. But there weren't any cute Craftsman bungalows in this town. A few Victorians had managed to hang on in the historical district, but the town's early period had seen too many floods and fires to keep houses around for very long. Here on the better side of town, nothing predated the fifties.

He ran the water a minute to clear the tap, blinking tiredly out the window over the sink. He liked the way it faced the wilderness on the edge of their lot, a thick patch of forest that set the town off from the flanks of Peshak Head. In the early morning gloom, the forest presented only as a dark mass, the trees and bracken as indistinguishable from each other as faces in a mob. The real estate agent had promised them plenty of wildlife viewing opportunities.

Gary put down the glass and leaned over the sink to get closer to the window. The real estate agent hadn't lied. A deer stood at the very edge of the yard, its body half-shielded by a scraggly azalea.

Breath held, he crept into the dining nook, where the sliding glass door offered a better view of the timid animal. It took a tentative step out of the azalea. Another deer had appeared behind the first, its ears swiveling with caution. Gary pressed his forehead to the glass, wondering at their presence. They'd never gotten deer back in Portland. He'd almost forgotten how wonderfully slim their legs were, the stem-like ankles ending in such dainty little feet. He couldn't imagine balancing on anything so small.

The second deer took a few steps toward the patio. The creature's face turned to face him. Gary's limbs froze stiff. Did it see him? Could those huge round eyes see into the darkness of his unlit kitchen?

"What is it?" Kim whispered. She padded up behind him, putting her arms around his ribcage.

"Deer," he breathed.

"Oh, pretty."

They stood quietly for a moment, the man, the woman, the animals. A finger of sunshine made its lazy way around the south side of the house. It all felt peaceful and miraculous, a much-needed moment of quiet beauty. Gary's forehead pressed harder against the cold glass, as if he could press it into his brain indelibly, as if it could overwrite yesterday's nasty memories.

"They're different when they're up close, aren't they?" Kim mused. One of the deer's ears twitched, but the other didn't even seem to notice the noise, munching placidly on lawn grass. "Up close, you can see all the things that make them real animals. Like this one's got a notch in her ear. And I think the other has a tick on her face."

"Maybe that's the real reason they're crepuscular. Daylight melts away their glamour. Like a faerie."

Kim laughed and the spell was broken. The deer slipped back into the woods.

"Crepuscular. Honey, you are such a nerd."

The doorbell rang. Kim frowned.

"Who the hell would be here this early? I hope they don't wake up Zack."

"I'll get it." Gary hurried into the living room, hoping to interrupt the doorbell before it rang again. He pulled open the door.

The man on the stoop looked too large for his blue police uniform. Everything about him seemed out of proportion: his hairline crowded the lines on his forehead, nearly driving them into the thick bar of his eyebrows; his ears stuck out like handles on a Grecian urn; his nose threatened to spill across his cheeks, as if broken two or three times and never set. And yet, overall he gave off a pleasant handsomeness, perhaps boosted by his relaxed smile.

"Gary Sheldon?"

Gary nodded.

"Sergeant Brian Danse. May I come in?"

"Absolutely." Gary stepped inside, waving the policeman toward the kitchen dining nook. Kim had flipped on the light and was already busy in the depths of the kitchen.

"I was just making coffee, officer. Would you like a cup?"

"That would be nice, Mrs. Sheldon."

She flashed her professional smile. "Please. Call me Kim."

Gary took a seat on the bench side of the upholstered booth, the house's only nod to uniqueness. Danse took a seat on the chair across from him.

Danse turned his own professional smile toward Kim. "You're the new principal at the high school, aren't you?"

"I am. Do you have any kids there, Sergeant?"

He shook his head. "My wife and I haven't been blessed yet." He turned his gaze back to Gary and his face changed, his friendly expression folding itself away like an unnecessary t-shirt. "How's your son, Mr. Sheldon?"

"He'll need a follow-up exam in a few days to be sure, but the ER docs said he's as healthy as any teenage boy. Minus a few cuts and bruises, of course."

"And you're fine, too?"

"I guess the safety features on our Saturn were as good as they claimed to be." Gary forced a chuckle. "The car's totaled, though."

Danse just looked at him. His non-smiling face was impossible to read. Gary began to regret the chuckle. He gave his glasses an unnecessary push up his nose.

Kim set a tray of coffee mugs and fixings on the table and sat back down, reaching for Gary's hand.

"How's the other guy?" Gary asked. Kim passed him a cup of coffee.

"By the time life flight landed in Eugene, he'd been dead eight minutes."

"Shit." Gary covered his mouth. He could almost hear Dr. Rothschild's voice: *Trevor Hyatt. Plymouth's starting running back.*

"Serves him right." Kim dropped the coffee carafe on the table hard enough a little coffee sloshed out. "He could have killed you and Zack."

"It was an accident," Gary reminded her. *Plymouth's starting running back.* God, he wished Rothschild had kept his big mouth shut.

Danse reached for the notebook in his shirt pocket and flipped it open. "The other driver was doing"—he double-checked something on the page—"seventy-five miles an hour when he went through that light. Considering he had just pulled out of the lot at the Dunes Diner two blocks away, that's an impressive feat of acceleration."

Gary had no idea what the appropriate response to this set of facts might be. Did Danse mean to imply that Trevor Hyatt had *tried* to ram Gary's car? And if so, what did that mean about Trevor?

"They took my statement at the hospital," Gary managed to say through a mouth gone dry. "I only caught a glimpse of the pickup. And I'm new to town. I definitely don't know anyone from Plymouth."

"But you're from the area, aren't you? Originally, I mean." The big police officer raised one of his crooked eyebrows.

Gary made a noncommittal face. "Yeah, I was born here and lived here until I was in high school. When my parents died."

"In a car accident, right?" Danse filled his coffee cup and reached for the sugar bowl. He stirred a spoonful of sugar—not the disciplined touch one would expect from such a fit-looking man, but a heaping spoonful—into his mug.

"Yes, in a car accident." Gary shook his head. "What does that have to do with this situation?"

Danse took a sip from his mug. "Mighty fine cup of coffee, Mrs. Sheldon. Thank you."

Her attempted smile lacked the vitality of the first one she'd given him.

"I'm just trying to finish this report, Gary. Dotting the i's and crossing the t's, so to speak."

At some point, Gary had gone from "Mr. Sheldon" to "Gary," and the smile had come back out of the place where Sergeant Danse kept his expressions. Gary wondered what had triggered the change, and if it meant something good or bad.

Gary reached for his mug. "That's good of you, Sergeant Danse."

"I take the safety of this little town awfully personally," Danse said. He took a long drink from his mug. "*Mighty* fine cup of coffee." He put it down and got to his feet. "Here's my card. Call me if you think of any details you might have forgotten in your original statement."

Gary got to his feet. "I'll walk you out."

"That'd be great." They made their way to the front stoop in silence, and then the big man raised a finger. "Oh, I almost forgot. I've got your jacket in the car. You left it as the hospital last night."

Gary followed him to the cruiser parked at the curb. He could have sworn he saw movement across the street as someone quickly flipped their curtains back in place. He hadn't met any of the neighbors yet, but he had no doubt this little visit would set tongues flapping all across town.

Danse unlocked the passenger side door and pulled out Gary's raincoat. "You'll need this by the end of the day."

"Thanks." Gary glanced at the skies. Blue reigned above their corner of the world, but a strip of gray lay out to the west. "You sure that's headed our way?"

"The weatherman is." Danse leaned toward Gary. "Gary, are you sure you don't know Trevor Hyatt? Maybe you or your family had dealings with his back in the day?"

"I never met the guy. But my parents—I couldn't say."

The officer went around to the driver's side. "Okay. Like I said, if you remember anything, give me a call."

Gary waved as the man pulled out into the street. The phone he'd forgotten in his jacket pocket began to ring.

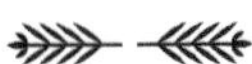

JILL: 2018

Jill gripped her cell phone so hard she felt the rubberized case deforming in her grip. The other line rang in her ear, a long unfolding question mark. Was there anything worse than waiting for someone to pick up their phone when you had to hear their voice—desperately had to hear it?

"Pick up, Gary, pick up," she hissed.

A woman browsing the pottery display shot her a disapproving look. Jill resisted the urge to tell her that her aura looked sick. That Prada handbag meant a possible sale, after all. Sally Jane's astrological ceramics didn't run cheap.

"Hey, Jilly Bean."

She snapped her attention back to the phone. "Hey, Monkey Boy."

She smiled at Chloe, the Sunday sales clerk, and nodded meaningfully toward the Prada woman. Maybe with a little attention she'd take the bait. Then Jill slipped into her office. "Are you okay?"

He hesitated.

"I knew it. I painted the damn boat again, only this time—fuck, Gary. What is going on down there in Kingston?" Jill paced to the window behind her desk and then back to the door. It was a small office. The gallery itself demanded all the floor space.

"Zack and I were in an accident."

"And is he all right?" Her voice climbed to a near-shriek. She forced a deep breath. "He's okay, right?"

"Yeah, just some bumps and bruises. But it was bad, Jill. They had to cut him out of the car with jaws of life." His voice trembled. She could almost picture him, pressing the side of his hand into his eyelids, stoppering tears. He had never been afraid to cry as a kid. It was only after the accident that he had learned to bottle them inside.

"It wasn't a regular car accident, was it?"

"What the hell does that mean? Every accident is a regular accident. People do drugs, or they just don't pay attention, or they're tired. Accidents *happen*."

Not to our mom and dad, she thought, but she knew better than to say anything.

She picked up a piece of rose quartz and turned it in her fingers, feeling its warm pink register in her skin. "What about you?" she managed to say. "Are you all right? Should I fly up?"

"No, I'm fine." An engine growled somewhere in the background. She knew without asking that he was standing in his front driveway, a short stump of a drive that led up to his perfectly ordinary garage. It was a green, early '60s ranch, nearly a twin of the house they'd moved to when Dad went to work at the paper mill. Gary had never sent her a picture or even described the place, but she knew.

She waited.

"Okay, I'm not fine." A metallic squeak—he was opening and closing the black metal mailbox. Even medicated, Gary needed to fidget like she needed to breathe. "I got one little scratch. Our car was *totaled*, Jill. Like the passenger-side-fucking-imploded totaled. Like the other guy didn't even make it through the life flight."

"Scary."

"And I was just coming from a total stop. The kid driving…" He sniffed, hard. Still not crying. "It reminded me of that accident on Calhoun Lake Road. You remember that one? We were on our way back from Grandma and Grandpa's?"

Jill put down the rose quartz. "I'll never forget it."

But she wished she could.

CHAPTER SEVEN

GARY: 1989

GARY SLUNG THE picnic basket into the hatchback of the car and looked over at Jill. She put the wet towels in the bucket Mom had brought for just this purpose and then noticed he was waiting for her.

"What?"

He hesitated a second. "Are we really going to the campground tonight?"

"Yeah." She waited for him to step back and slammed shut the trunk. "Right?"

It wasn't that he didn't like Eagle Cove. At least half a dozen times, his dad had taken him fishing at the campground's tiny beach, and last fall he'd earned pocket money delivering firewood to a group of hunters down from Eugene. But the woods felt heavy around the place, heavy and noisy with a presence less welcome than wildlife. It wasn't outright spooky, not like the barn, but it had a lot more potential for trouble than, say, the marina.

"I guess. It wasn't as bad in the barn this time," he admitted. "I think having the others with us helped."

"I know it did." She poked him in the arm affectionately. "Let's go say goodbye to Grandma before she talks Mom into another cup of coffee."

They ran up to their grandparents' wraparound porch. Every summer Gary could remember had been spent mostly on that porch. Mom would load them up in the car and drive the twenty minutes up Calhoun Lake Road to get to Aspen Valley, the barely-a-town where she'd grown up. There was no post office, no stores, and only a two-room elementary school for the kids. She'd learned to drive so she could get to high school in Kingston.

To Gary, the village's remoteness made it a secret paradise. Here, no one knew he needed pills just to sit through math class. No one knew it took him three hours to get through his homework, even though he knew the material backward and forward. Here he was just another kid running through the woods and diving in the creek. Everybody was loud and wild out here. It was the place where wild things belonged.

His mom was already standing up, a bag of homemade bread dangling from her hand. "Finally! Everything loaded up?"

Grandma Thompson got up. "Want some fudge for the drive?" She held out the plate. Gary had already eaten six huge squares, but he took another one.

"Sorry about the walnuts," Grandma said with a wink.

"My favorite!" Jill said. She took two pieces.

They all exchanged hugs and kisses, and Grandma pressed another piece of fudge on everyone, including their mother. Then they climbed into the silver Ford Fiesta and started out the rutted dirt road. Gary had helped his dad gravel the drive a few years ago, but no one had gotten a chance or money to do it yet this year. Money was always short at the Thompson and Sheldon households.

He pressed his forehead to the window, letting his skull bounce to the rhythm of the rough drive. If he could change one thing about the world, he would get rid of money. He hated seeing his parents worry and fight about the stuff—even more than he hated seeing things and shadows in places there ought not be any. They both made his stomach turn into a pretzel, but at least he didn't see that shit every month when the bills came.

Their tires crunched on gravel as they entered Aspen Valley proper, passing the little white school and then the fire station, the thudding against his forehead pounding less and less until the Fiesta turned onto the smooth pavement of Calhoun Lake Road. They were now only ten miles from Kingston, and in a few moments, he'd see the narrow fingertip of Calhoun Lake, barely wider than the creek that ran through his grandparents' backyard. It got bigger, though, its flat waters widening into a gleaming playground for those with free time and free cash. He had stopped noticing the whine of speedboats since about the first of May.

The car stopped so hard his head skidded across the glass and then smacked into the back of the seat in front of him. Pain rushed down his neck.

"Jesus Christ!" His mom was already throwing open her door.

"Shit," Jill breathed. She opened the passenger door and then remembered her seat belt. "Shit," she repeated, unbuckling it without taking her eyes off the road ahead.

Chaos filled the two narrow lanes of Calhoun Lake Road, steam and broken glass and plastic parts jettisoned by tremendous force. It took Gary a moment to identify the smaller vehicle as a gray Datsun, its nose half-devoured by the blue pickup in the southbound lane.

Gay found the button for the lap belt and got it undone. It was hard to take a real breath. Their car had stopped barely two feet from the rear side panel of the Datsun, testament to his mother's good reaction time. They had only just gone around the corner of Skep Rock. The accident had been invisible on the other side of the curve.

Jill stepped out of the car, not bothering to close the door. "Is everyone okay?"

Their mother raised a warning hand. "Stay by the car. Or God, no. Gary, go to the shoulder of the road. Jill, can you turn on the flashers?"

Their mom took a cautious step forward. She normally looked so sturdy, like she could do anything, manage anything. But today in her yellow t-shirt, standing between the two smashed cars, she looked nearly as scared as Jill did.

Gary got out of the car as the passenger door on the pickup opened.

"Are you okay?" his mother shouted.

A man stumbled out of the pickup. Blood streaked down the side of his face. "They came out of nowhere."

Gary's mom hurried to him, pulling a handkerchief from her back pocket. "Put this on that cut. Jesus, an inch lower, and you would have lost that eye."

He held up a pair of pink sticks it took Gary a moment to recognize as flares. "Gotta set these out."

Gary ran to grab them. "I can do it."

"Gary—"

"Mom, I can help." He ran down the center lines, hoping like hell there were no log trucks coming.

He thumbed off the flare's cap and struck it on the pavement. It hissed into vibrant life, and he threw it down in the middle of the two solid yellow stripes. The jutting curve of Skep Rock looked down at him, warning him that at any second a car full of speeding tourists could power around that blind curve and smash him and his family into a thousand motes of red goo.

He ran back to the cars, sweat making his glasses slide down his nose. The muscles in his butthole had clenched themselves tight.

"I can do it," Jill said, reaching for the second flare, but he pushed past her, squeezing beside the gray Datsun. He could see the driver out of the corner of his eye, slumped over the steering wheel. Didn't want to look closer, because no one could sit like that if they were just fine, no one. He put all his strength into tossing the second flare out in the road.

The Datsun's radiator made a sad hissing as he turned to face the disaster. The man from the pickup was crawling back into his rig. Jill stood in the middle of the broken glass, biting her lip. His mother was moving toward the driver's side of the Datsun.

He didn't want to go to his mom's side and see what she was seeing, but he had to. His feet were already steering him toward her, like someone in a horror movie who couldn't resist going down the basement stairs no matter how loudly you shouted at the screen not to.

"Get back, baby," his mom said, but she barely noticed him. "Are you all right?" she called, reaching for the door handle. The window had broken in about a hundred places.

Jill pressed into Gary's side. "We should go for help," she whispered.

They were about two miles from the lodge. Gary could run it if he wanted. But he couldn't stop staring.

"Are you all right?" his mother asked again.

The woman in the car—Gary wasn't even sure she was a woman at first, just a heap of fuzzy blond hair hunched over the steering column—didn't respond. Gary's mom opened the door. The woman wore a flimsy tank top with spaghetti straps, and broken glass coated her skin like glitter. Gary's mom made a sound like a whimper.

The woman flopped backward, her breathing a gurgling whistle. Blood streamed from her nose and mouth where she must have smashed it on the steering wheel. He couldn't see a seat belt.

"Gary," Jill breathed. She pointed to the passenger seat, where the woman's purse had barfed out napkins and tampons and an open Cheetos bag, orange bits strewn everywhere. But Jill's gaze was fixed on the funny glass pipe with a tiny plastic bag stuffed in its mouth.

Consonants gurgled in the woman's throat. The skin of her chest was a livid purple, the shape of the steering wheel strong and clear.

"Don't talk. We're going to go call an ambulance," Gary's mom reassured the stranger.

He could hear the crackle of a CB radio coming from the blue pickup and realized the other driver was already calling for help.

The woman's hand shot out, closing on the front of Gary's shirt. She gasped and spluttered—talking, maybe, the sounds like rocks in the bottom of the creek.

"Deer," she gasped. Red outlined the rictus of her mouth.

He tried to pull away, but her hand spasmed tighter.

"Gary!" His mom grabbed his shoulders, but the woman held him tight.

"Was a deer," the woman hissed. Her eyes bulged in her head as she stared at him. "Deer!"

Black bubbled up on her lips and sent a spray of blood across the windshield and the side of Gary's face.

GARY: 2018

The very act of adjusting the Camry's seat made Gary feel guilty. Ostensibly, Mondays and Tuesdays he did nothing but write. His editor had already given him an extension for this book, the second in a long-hoped-for trilogy, and he hated the thought of disappointing her. More importantly, after all the expense of the move—anyone would think a house in an economically depressed town in the middle of nowhere would be cheaper than its counterpart in the Portland suburbs, but the facts denied such logic—they needed the next payment toward his advance more than he'd like to admit.

But not even twenty minutes after Zack left to catch the school bus, Gary found himself in the driver's seat of his wife's car, dressed in his running gear and so tense his teeth hurt. All night he had been dreaming of blood and terror and his sister's face streaked with paint. Over and over he had heard her voice warning him, begging him to be careful. She had known something was going to happen and sure enough, something had.

It was stupid to get in a car when his nightmares had been filled with car accidents, but once he reached the end of their cul-de-sac, he found himself breathing more normally, the hunch going out of his shoulders. As a kid, a good long run in the woods had always set him straight when he was worked up about stuff. Sometimes, as an adult, his run needed a wilder environment than a suburban-style subdivision. He aimed the car south. Toward the beach.

He rolled down the windows, letting the cold air slap him in the face. It wasn't really raining, but the car's speed turned the drizzle to little needles. They prickled his flesh just enough to sting.

He needed this. Hot damn, he needed this.

Since he'd come to Kingston, everything had wadded up inside his brain. Ten years ago, he wouldn't have worried about any of Jill's stupid dreams. They'd put that crap behind them after his parents died and Jill had her little breakdown. She had always been crazy. *He* had been crazy. Their aunt and uncle were the ones who had finally gotten them the care they'd needed their whole lives. He didn't know how his parents could have ignored all the signs their kids had come unhinged. The Ouija boards they'd painted right at the dining room table. Jill's insistence on doing a painting before anyone made any kind of big decision, like Ronald Reagan consulting his astrologer before drawing up national policy. Gary's endless, constant nightmares. And then that summer the lodge burned down. Surely they must have seen the way their kids were falling apart that summer.

But no. Not only did they do nothing, they let themselves get sucked into Kingston's cliquish little clubs and rituals. Back when they'd been lakies, living on the edge of town, spending more time at the lodge than any business in Kingston proper, at least they'd *cared* about Gary and Gillian. Once his parents joined the Deer Kings, how often did they even have dinner together as a family?

He slapped his signal light and made the turn for Beach Access Road without even slowing. Christ, he needed a run.

Zach had nearly been killed. The car was wrecked. And Jill—Jill nearly had him believing her mystical bullshit.

He parked the car at the second beach parking lot and opened the door. The wind battered his face and ears, and he started to reach toward the backseat for his ball cap before he remembered he'd driven Kim's car. He slammed the door shut, faced into the kelp-stinking breeze, and made his way down to the beach.

Spray and sand ground into his face. It hadn't been this miserable back at the house, but then again, it was always nastier at the beach. He did a little stretching. The air stank of fish and salt and some rich, buttery smell he always associated with the sea. He put his head down and began to run.

He had no idea how far he went. From this stretch of the Oregon coast, it was possible to follow the beaches all the way to Charleston, at least at low tide. He didn't run that far. But his sneakers pounded on the tide-packed sand, crunched on broken shells, slid on sheets of torn seaweed. It didn't matter. He ran until the salt scoured the lining of his lungs. Gary ran until his legs burned and wobbled, and the world between his ears shrank into something manageable. Kim's late hours at work: not such a big deal. Zack's request to join his new friends on the football team: good news, surely. The ever-encroaching deadline on Gary's stupid novel: totally and completely feasible. Maybe.

He ran faster until he could actually believe the last one. A flock of tiny little birds burst into flight.

Gary let himself slow. Living up north, he'd missed this kind of beach. Even on weekdays, the sandy stretches around Cannon Beach and Astoria never got this empty. To his left, a few signs reminded him of humanity's presence. The inevitable scrim of rubbish marked the high-water line: empty bleach bottles, shredded fishing nets, a lonely, once-white sneaker. But the water stretched out to his right, gray and empty, whitecaps dotting its surface.

Christ, he'd missed this. The dull roar of all that water moving over the belly of the world, the hiss of each individual wave spinning itself down to foam. The weirdly fresh smell of it, despite the rank stink of dead seaweed and who-knew-what. To live on the coast was to stand in the face of the enormity of the ocean and never dumb it down with a beach umbrella or a sandcastle or a Frisbee. To face the grandeur and simply be.

He stood on one foot and slid off sneaker and sock, repeated the process. He closed his eyes. His toes curled in the sand, the grains sliding over his skin and catching in the hairs like tiny ice cubes.

A seagull screeched and his eyelids shot open. He bent his knees a few times and then jogged a few feet forward before returning to a walk. His feet weren't tough enough yet for beach running. The sand looked smooth, but he'd cut his feet on broken shells too many times not to learn caution out here. All those old half-forgotten nuggets of knowledge were coming back, things he'd forgotten he'd ever known rising to the surface of his mind like those Japanese glass floats—once nearly garbage, and now surprisingly valuable.

A circle of driftwood caught his eye. He and Jill had loved to build fires on the beach. Driftwood, if you could find any dry pieces, added strange colors to the flames, a kind of subdued fireworks. He could imagine a group of high schoolers coming here on the weekend, friends hoping to do some quiet drinking or couples hoping for a romantic make-out session. The first time he'd ever gotten to second base had been on the beach, and sometimes when he slipped his hand under Kim's bra, he still thought of the sea and a fire and the cool kiss of a pilfered beer.

But if the people who had made this fire had been kids, they were much more resourceful than he and his friends had ever been. Two good-sized rocks had been dragged to the land-side of the fire, a gray slab of driftwood laid across to form a low table. Dark stains blotted the surface—probably spilled wine or juices from some midnight feast.

He picked his way across the sand to look at the makeshift fire pit. A seagull flew up from picking at something invisible in the sand, and settled on the ring of driftwood, eying him balefully. He took another step forward, curious.

Something black stuck out of the sand. Just the furry tip, a familiar but still-strange shape Gary's brain couldn't quite place. The seagull gave one of their chivying cries.

He fumbled in the sand for a stick and gave the black thing a poke. It flexed a little, the weight of the sand holding it erect despite its innate flexibility. It looked so familiar. He worked the stick into the sand, prying.

Stop it, Gary, some little voice whispered. He tried to ignore it, like the shadows swirling in the corner of his left eye. There were no shadows. There had never been any shadows.

The stick slid down the rough length of something until it found the bottom of the mysterious find. He worked the stick beneath the thing. Was it really furry, or was it just his imagination?

It popped free of the sand: black and furry and caked in sand. It took him a second to make out the shape of the paw pads. Another second to see the red meat sticking out of the fur.

He flung aside his stick and doubled over. A dog's paw. A dog's paw and the bottom three or four inches of its leg.

Fuck.

What kind of sick fuck cut off a dog's paw and buried it on the fucking beach?

The seagull shrieked. Gary stood up, but it had already snatched the paw, and now it leaped into the air. Its grizzly find dangled from its claws as it rose into the air.

"Screw you!" he shouted. He grabbed for a shard of shell in the sand and threw it after the bird. "I hope you choke!"

The shell landed on one of the big rocks with a clank. He looked at them, the rocks, the long slab of driftwood. The stains, red and clotted and dark.

He pressed his forearm into his mouth. Someone had done more than cut off that dog's leg. Someone had killed it on that driftwood slab. No: on that driftwood *altar*.

He broke into a run. He had to get home.

CHAPTER EIGHT

GARY: 2018

UP AHEAD, THE light at the intersection to Highway 38 turned green, and on instinct, Gary made a right. After what he'd just seen, he needed a donut, damn it.

Gary had lived in Portland for more than twenty years. He'd eaten a habanero jelly-filled at Voodoo Doughnut at three in the morning and sampled Blue Star's decadent horchata-glazed brioche ring mere moments after it had come out of the deep fryer. From gourmet shops to tiny diners, he'd checked out donuts across the Pacific Northwest in search of just one that could compare to the ones he'd grown up eating. But Murphy's Bakery brooked no contenders.

He pulled into the parking lot and headed inside. A chainsaw-carved bear greeted him, a straw hat perched on its rustic head and a stack of Kingston postcards resting in its thick paws. The golden smells of hot oil and vanilla glaze swept him past the ice cream counter and the pie case, straight to the counter display of row after row of tender pastries.

"Gary Sheldon, is that you?" The diminutive black woman behind the counter beamed at him. She kept her hair in the same short ball of curls she always had, but white had overtaken most of the black. Other than that, she hadn't seemed to have aged since 1995.

"Mrs. Murphy! You remembered me."

"Of course. How's Gillian? I haven't heard much from her the last few years."

He'd forgotten that Jill's first job had been here at the bakery. Three days a week, she would leave the house two hours before school to decorate donuts, and she never failed to come home without a bag or two of day-olds. "She's good. The gallery has really taken off the last few years. But I'll make sure she calls you." His eye wandered to the maple bars and he forced it back. "How's Deondra?" He'd always had a bit of a crush on the older girl. Looking back, he had to imagine that as one of three black kids in Kingston High School, Deondra Murphy's years there had been hellish.

"*Really* good. She had to hire another resident this year, her practice is growing so fast. Plus, she and Bill are expecting their first. I'm going up in a couple of weeks to help set up the nursery."

The light in her eyes gave Gary a pang in his gut. Would his mother have looked so happy if she had lived to see Zack into the world? The chance to see that joy had been stolen from him.

The bell over the door chimed. Mrs. Murphy's face closed down. "What can I do for you?" she called.

Gary glanced over his shoulder. Two boys in letterman's jackets pushed past the bear. The shorter one flicked the chainsaw bear's straw hat with a finger. It fell to the floor.

Gary's fingers curled angrily into his palms. Teenagers hadn't acted like this when he'd been in high school.

"Got any day-olds?" the tallest demanded. If Gary had to guess, he'd place this one at maybe age sixteen, younger than the shorter one. Each of the boys probably outweighed Gary by forty or fifty pounds. Their crew cuts glistened in the bakery's fluorescent lights.

"Sorry, we're sold out."

"Dominique always gives us a free maple bar if you're out of day-olds." The shorter one leaned on the counter, his teeth showing. The ring finger on his right hand was set in a splint.

"That's not store policy, and Dominique knows it." Mrs. Murphy didn't stop smiling, but the expression looked forced.

Gary rapped his knuckles on the counter. "Shouldn't you boys be in school? It's 9:30." It was a lame attempt at a distraction, and he wished he'd thought of better the minute it came out of his mouth.

The short boy's eyes rolled slowly over to Gary. "Fuck off."

The younger, taller one leaned toward his friend. "Dirk, that's the principal's husband." He gave Gary a nervous look, and Gary recognized him from the game: the boy on the sidelines who had smiled at him. Now Gary noticed the knee brace clamped over the boy's jeans. "The *principal's* husband!"

"Mr. Sheldon," Gary added pleasantly.

"Study hall," the tall kid explained. "Nobody cares if we miss it."

Dirk's cold eyes slid back to Mrs. Murphy's face. "Right. Sorry about the confusion." He pulled a five out of his pocket. "Six maple bars, two milks."

"Can I get a cup of coffee, too?" the tall kid added.

"Sure." Mrs. Murphy rang it all up. "That'll be $6.85."

"Well, shit," Dirk said. "Alex, you got any money?"

"Shit. I mean, crap." The tall kid cut a glance at Gary. Gary could feel Kim's power radiating out of his body like a science fictional laser ray. "I left my wallet at home. I guess I don't need that coffee."

"Don't worry about it," Mrs. Murphy said. "Just don't worry about it." She was already filling a white paper bag.

"Well, that's right kind of you, Mrs. Murphy." Dirk clapped Alex on the shoulder. "Ain't that nice of the lady?"

"I don't need the coffee," Alex repeated.

"Get your coffee," Dirk ordered. He took the sack of donuts off the counter and paused at the refrigerator beside the ice cream. "Did I say two milks or three? Must have been three." He hooked three cartons of 2% out of the fridge and walked out the door.

Alex paused beside the chainsaw bear. "I'll pay you back for the coffee." He swept the straw hat off the floor and plunked it on the bear's head, and then hurried after his friend.

Mrs. Murphy waited until the door swung completely shut. "I hope those little fucks get in a car accident."

Gary couldn't blame her for saying it. He watched the boys get into a dented pickup truck. The wilted remnants of white and red crepe paper crisscrossed the bed of the pickup. "Does that happen often?"

"Often enough. Kids start out all right, but a year or two on the football team seems to go to their heads. Town would let them get away with murder, I swear." Mrs. Murphy narrowed her eyes. "Somebody ought to stand up to them."

Gary's palms had gone cold. Was that going to happen to Zack? Was he going to head into football practice this afternoon a nice kid and come out some kind of raving asshole?

He cleared his throat. "Why don't you do something? Call the cops or the school?"

"And do what? File a complaint? Press charges? I can just see how that would play out. I'd be run out of town for ruining the futures of two of Kingston's finest."

"I'll talk to Kim. Maybe she can urge the football coach to do something."

She put her hands on her hips. "Gary, did you ever ask what happened to the previous principal?"

"I assumed…" He broke off. "Retired? Or test scores weren't

working out, maybe? I'm sure Kim knows."

"Maybe you should ask her about that." She brushed off her apron. "Enough of this ridiculousness. You came in for a donut, didn't you?"

He nodded. "I think I'm going to need more than one too. And a cup of coffee."

She began extolling the virtues of the different pastries, but both of them kept their bodies angled toward the door, as if watching for the boys to return for more trouble.

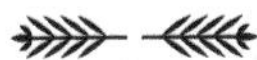

JILL: 2018

She was out walking Merlin when Grandma Thompson called. Anyone else but family and she wouldn't have picked up. She clamped the phone between her shoulder and her ear—so much easier with a real phone than a cell—and listened to her grandmother take an ear-achingly loud slurp of coffee. It never mattered who she was calling or when, Grandma Thompson had to have a cup of coffee in her hand to talk.

"That you, Gillian?"

Her grandmother had never once begun a phone conversation with "hello."

"Hi, Grandma. How are you tonight?"

"I'd be better if those son-of-a-bitching Huskies had won their game. Now I owe Sue at the senior center ten bucks." Grandma gave a dry bark of laughter. "You'd think I'd have learned by now!"

Jill risked taking one hand off Merlin's leash while he snuffed around the base of someone's shriveled lilac bush. She took hold of the phone and rolled her neck a little. Stupid cell phones. "How's Sue doing these days?"

"Oh, suffering again. Her husband lost his foot to the diabetes, so I'm going to go into town tomorrow to help her clean house. Gotta cheer her up a little."

As far as Jill could tell, Sue At The Senior Center was nearly twenty years younger than Grandma and Grandpa Thompson, but such details never bothered either of her grandparents. They weren't letting their eighties get the better of them, no way.

Jill yanked the leash when Merlin began pawing at the dirt beneath the lilac bush. She grabbed his collar and steered him on to the next yard, nearly dropping the phone in the process. "What was that, Grandma? I missed it."

"I said that I found a box of your parents' old stuff." Grandma gave another slurp. "Must have gotten shoved behind some of your grandpa's projects, and this summer when we were cleaning out his studio, there it was. Lot of stuff from that town group they were so fond of."

"The Deer Kings?"

Merlin glanced at Jill like he could hear the disgust in her voice. She leaned over to pet him, wishing she could forget about the club. Leave it to Kingston to miss out on the Elks or the Moose or any of the other normal community groups. John King and his family had started their own semi-exclusive club of municipal do-gooders, and anyone who had ever been anyone in that stupid little inbred town had been a member. In the span of one summer, her parents had gone from mocking it to joining it.

"Yep, that's the one! It sure was nice for your folks, wasn't it? They never had many friends before that."

Jill had to suppose that was true. She couldn't remember her parents ever having anyone over or going out. They had each other, and that had always been enough—at least until her dad got the job at the mill and her mom started meeting the new neighbors.

A cat sprang out from beneath a car and Merlin sat down, watching it morosely. She stroked his head. Her grandma was slurping again.

"So shall I mail it to you?"

"Me? Why not just give it to Gary?"

"What do you mean?"

Jill stopped mid-pet. Merlin pushed his head against the palm of her hand, urging her to continue. She dug her fingers into his thick fur, her stomach sinking. "Haven't you heard from Gary?"

"Heard what? He's not much for this old stuff, Jilly. I think he'd rather just forget all about Kingston."

Merlin started walking again, and Jill stumbled trying to catch up with him. "But, Grandma, he just moved to Kingston."

"No, he didn't. He would have told me." Grandma paused. "He would have told me, wouldn't he?"

"I would have thought so."

A man stepped out of his house and glanced oddly at Jill. He had long blond hair and wore a jean vest, and for a second her heart stopped, certain she was seeing Vincent Vernor again. "Fuck."

"What?"

The man took the mail out of his mailbox and turned away. He was probably almost ten years younger than Jill, younger maybe than Vincent Vernor had been when he first came to Kingston. And this man was much sturdier in build, much shorter. He looked nothing like Vincent.

"Nothing, Grandma. I just tripped, that's all. And yes, I'm sure Gary's been meaning to call you. Kim got a job at Kingston High School. It's a big change, and I know they've had a hard time of it."

"He's right here in Kingston and he didn't tell me?" Grandma Thompson's voice had gone thin and strained. It was the first time Jill had ever heard her nonplussed, even when Jill's mom had died.

"Maybe you should call him," Jill said. "I'm sure he'd love to hear from you. He could probably use a friendly conversation."

"He didn't tell me," Grandma repeated.

Merlin gave a sudden leap and his leash pulled free of Jill's hand.

"Oh, no!" Jill shouted. "Grandma, I've got to go. Good luck with Sue and Gary!"

She raced after the dog and caught him just as he threw himself at a garbage can overflowing with loose trash. She spent a solid five minutes picking up Styrofoam meat trays, and nearly forgot to feel guilty for hanging up on her grandmother. She almost missed the last package, which Merlin pawed out from under a recycling bin. She wrestled it out of his grasp and then caught a glimpse of the chewed label.

Venison. It had held venison.

She flung the tray in the garbage with revulsion. She had gone vegetarian after that summer—not the one where her parents died in the car accident, but the summer before she'd started high school. Even now, she could not look at a deer without thinking of the thing they'd seen in the woods all those years ago.

She found the hand sanitizer in her fanny pack and squirted half the bottle on her palms. Later that night when she washed her face, she would swear she could still smell meat on her skin.

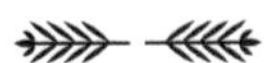

STACIE: 1989

11:30! Stacie jumped out of bed and grabbed a scrunchie. There was so much to do still, and the day was practically shot.

She hadn't meant to sleep so late, but after everything that had happened yesterday, there had been no chance of falling asleep, not when her mom was working late and it was just Stacie and the television and the occasional outburst from the neighbors. She'd stayed on the couch as long as she could, watching old episodes of *M*A*S*H*, and then she'd gone to her bedroom and laid there with the light on for an hour or two. She'd tried re-reading her favorite Dean R. Koontz novel, but even the friendly dog and its adventures couldn't distract her from the memories of Jill's Ouija board and that horrible Vincent Vernor.

He hadn't looked so scary, back at the lodge. But standing there shouting at them and waving an actual machete—Jesus, she understood why he freaked Jill out so much. Insanity practically dripped off the guy. She ran her hairbrush through her hair, ignoring the snapping sounds as the teeth struggled through the knots, and then pulled her hair back. Red scrunchie today. She had a red polo shirt that would be good for a warm day.

There was barn dirt on her Keds, so she put them in the laundry hamper and brought out her second pair. It took a lot of work to keep them as white as she liked, but she thought it was worth it. When she and Jill had watched *Dirty Dancing* last summer, she had noticed how white Baby kept her shoes. They made her feet look tiny and dainty, but practical and agile at the same time. They had watched that movie over and over, and Stacie had even borrowed it from Jill for a weekend. How perfect Baby was, always smart even when she thought she was being awkward. On her, brown hair looked nice. More than nice. Stacie wished she could spend her summer with someone like Baby. They wouldn't need to dance or anything like that. They could just sit together and talk about books, sitting side by side beside the lake with their shoulders touching.

She pushed the thought away and slipped on the polo shirt and jean shorts. Her mom managed a shitty restaurant with a bunch of cabins and an RV park. There wasn't money for luxuries like summer camp. She was being an idiot.

She grabbed her backpack and headed for the kitchen. The living room stank more powerfully of cigarettes than normal.

The door slammed and she froze mid-step. Why was her mom out on the front porch? Was everything okay?

And then she saw who her mom was standing with, the blond hair and the denim vest. She couldn't move. Couldn't breathe. Hadn't Gary said Vincent Vernor was married? That he had a toddler and everything? So why was her mom putting her arms around him, putting her mouth on his, clinging to him even as he walked away from her?

Stacie's stomach rose up and threw itself back down. Her mom was crying out there. Stacie could hear her sniveling and sniffing, and for Christ's sake, she was standing out there in just her dressing gown.

Stacie spun around and hurried into the kitchen. She couldn't stand the thought of seeing her mother like this.

The door opened and closed.

Stacie grabbed a pouch of Pop-Tarts out of the cupboard and shoved it in her bag, praying her mother would just go back to bed. She looked blankly at the cupboard and then closed it. Maybe she'd pack an apple. An apple would be good. Her brain kept looping back to her mother standing there, her arms around that creepy psycho.

"Hey, baby."

She had to turn around. The smile on her face felt as fake as spray cheese. "Good morning." She gasped. "Oh, Mom!"

She rushed forward, pressing her fingers to her mother's swollen face.

Her mother twisted away, hissing. "Careful, sweetie." The cut on her lip had opened up, and a drop of blood ran down her chin.

"What happened?" Stacie remembered how good ice felt on a bruise and went to the freezer for a package of frozen peas.

"I was stupid," her mom said. She took the peas and put them on her chin and bottom lip. "You've got to treat a man right, baby. You say the wrong thing and they, they just gotta show you what you did wrong."

Stacie shook her head. "What?"

"I was mouthing off." Her mother's eyes glistened. "He's a good man, though. Always tips good."

Stacie took a step backward. "Did…"—she couldn't bring herself to say his name—"…that man hit you?"

"You saw him?" Her mom lowered the package of peas. "You were spying on us?"

"No." Stacie shook her head again. "No, of course not. I was just coming into the kitchen."

"And you thought you'd spy on me. I see how you are." Her mother looked her from head to toe and then smiled. She winced and touched her lip. "Can't blame you, baby. You were probably thinking about how much you'd like a man like Vincent. He's a handsome one, isn't he?"

Stacie sidestepped her mother's approach. "I've gotta go, Mom. Jill's expecting me."

She didn't run out of the house, but she wished she had. She wasn't even out of the driveway before she was crying, wiping the tears out of her eyes as she pedaled, barely staying on the road. She was halfway to Jill's house before she remembered Jill and Gary were going to their grandparents' house that day.

She stopped her bike in the middle of Balfour Drive. "Shit!"

"Stacie?"

She turned around. She had just passed the old tractor. She hadn't even seen it, she was crying so hard.

"Hi, Jordan."

He rushed out of the long grass. "What's wrong?"

She got off her bike and walked it toward him. "Nothing." She leaned the bike against the tractor. "Everything."

Jordan took her hand. "Come on." He led her away from the tractor, into the trees. She had never noticed the tiny house set back from the road, but she saw it now and realized it must be his house. There was a neat little garden and a stand-alone porch swing with ripped yellow cushions.

They sat down on the porch swing. Its springs creaked and groaned, but it held.

He crossed his legs beneath him and turned so he faced her. He was wearing a blue "Oak Grove Church Camp" t-shirt that looked about four sizes too big for him and a weird yellow scarf like the one Fred wore on *Scooby Doo*. But his smile was kind. "You can tell me."

She stared at him. The way his bangs hung over his eyes made him look like a thin, fervent sheepdog, and maybe because of that, she felt oddly comfortable sitting with him. Like maybe she could tell him everything, all the weird stuff that twisted and turned inside her head.

"My mom slept with Vincent Vernor," she said, and then she told him all about her morning.

By the time she had finished, she had leaned her head against his bony shoulder and he'd given her the scarf for a handkerchief.

"I see why you were crying," he said.

She sat up and blew her nose. "It was really gross."

He bit into one of his cuticles, even though it already looked swollen and raw. "Can I tell you something, Stacie?"

"Absolutely."

"You can't tell anybody else."

She shook her head. "I wouldn't. Not even Jill."

"Okay." He took a breath. "I think all of that stuff is weird. Kissing. Sex stuff. I don't ever want to do it."

She wrinkled her nose. "You're only twelve, Jordan. You'll probably change your mind."

"You wanted to kiss someone when you were twelve, didn't you? You had crushes."

She looked at him. He was dead serious.

"Yeah," she whispered. "But—"

She stopped. She couldn't say anything more. She'd never even told Jill. She wasn't even sure she understood what she wanted to say.

"It's okay," he said. "We don't have to talk about it."

He shifted so he could push his toes into the ground. The porch swing creaked as it swung backward.

The seat hung in the air a moment, the way the words Stacie hadn't said hung there, waiting for her to know just what she meant.

"Let's talk about music," Jordan said.

And then the swing rushed forward, and the early summer wind tugged at her ponytail, and little details like crushes and kissing didn't really matter anymore.

CHAPTER NINE

GARY: 2018

GARY MASHED A banana into his cornflakes, wishing he was already tucked into his office. After yesterday's little nightmare at the beach, his timeline for the new novel looked irreparably damaged. The sounds of Zack and Kim moving around the house in their morning routines prickled under his skin. The sooner they left, the sooner he could concentrate on work.

Zack rushed by the dining nook, sack lunch in one hand, toothbrush in the other. He was only wearing one shoe.

Gary took another bite of cornflakes. If the kid really needed help, he'd ask.

Kim bustled up to the table. "Can you zip me?"

Gary found the minuscule tab and whizzed it up the blue sheath dress. The outline of her figure eased some of his morning irritability. "Wish my principal had dressed like this."

She made a face. "There's a lunch meeting at the City Club, and Harrington wanted me to go." She shrugged into her matching blazer. "Wining and dining some bigwig from Keridan Bridge Company. I could really use the help of a local cultural luminary like yourself."

Shit. Just what he didn't need: a boring lunch with a bunch of town big-shots. "I can see why the superintendent would want you to go. You're the jewel of the Kingston school system."

"Don't butter me up just to get out of this. I need you there. This is Keridan Bridge. The future of this town and my career. Plus, did you hear? Apparently Plymouth is in the mix now."

Speculation about the Keridan Bridge Company had even made it into the *Register Guard*, the region's biggest newspaper. Kingston's old lumber mill site held the most promise, but the distant hamlet of Aberdeen and now, apparently Plymouth were competing too. Even the school district was crapping its pants about the thing. That didn't mean he had to.

"I'm just really behind on this book."

"And whose fault is that? No one made you go to the beach yesterday." She found her purse on the kitchen counter and ripped it open. "You could be a little more supportive. After all, if the town lands the contract, the school district is expected to double in size."

"I'll go, of course." He shoved aside the cornflake bowl. "Jesus, Kim. You nearly tore a hole in your purse. Pissy much?"

Kim threw open the fridge, knocked something over with a clang, and slammed the fridge shut. "You know how I feel about this political stuff."

"You knew it was part of the job when you decided to go back to school for it."

"Oh, screw you, Gary. Now I don't even *want* you to go." She dropped a yogurt into her purse. "I'll see you tonight, if you're not too busy. And make sure Zack gets on the bus in time. Remember, we only have one car now."

She vanished into the front room. He heard her shout a goodbye down the hallway at Zack, and then the front door slammed.

Four minutes and a replacement lunch sack later, Zack made his own exit.

Gary sat silently at the table for a long moment. Goddamn, Kim was on her high horse this morning. Becoming a principal had been her dream, not his. He hadn't wanted her to become a political animal, hadn't wanted her to rip them up by the roots and dump them out in the middle of nowhere—no, worse than nowhere: here. His stomach knotted up and for a moment he thought he would spew cornflakes and banana across the table. He had come to Kingston because of *her*.

He could hear himself breathing, shallow and snorting, and he forced a long deep breath. Things had maybe gotten a little out of hand the last couple of days. He was letting his fear get the worst of him.

Slowly, he unpeeled his palms from the vinyl surface of the table and cupped them over his eyes. Of course he was freaked out. Coming here was never going to be easy. And the accident—well, hell, his parents had *died* in a car accident. No wonder he was freaking out. His innards were twisted up because of purely natural sensations, honest reactions to old memories and deeply ingrained fears. Those things had him taking Gillian's ridiculous dreams seriously, had him jumping at beach picnic sites, seeing Satanists in every dropped cigarette and weird stain. He couldn't explain the dog's paw he'd found in the sand, but it didn't have to mean animal sacrifice. Made no sense to think it did. It had nothing to do with his accident or the things he had seen in the woods as a kid.

He knew all this, and yet he had let this place get to him.

He took another long, shuddery breath and dropped his sweaty hands to his knees. Logic, that's all he'd needed. Dr. Monroe had taught him that.

He slid across the booth until he could reach his phone on the counter to shoot off a long series of apologetic text messages. He'd go to this stupid lunch and be a role model husband again, damn it.

Then he washed his cereal dish and poured a second cup of coffee. He let the taste of it sweep away the morning, his son, his wife. For now, it was time to write.

GARY: 1989

They rode their bikes down to the Eagle Cove campground in silence, Gary's hair still wet from the shower. He had stayed under the spray until the hot water ran out, scrubbing his face with Lava soap. He still didn't feel clean. That woman—he saw her face every time he blinked. The smell of her blood had lodged in his nose.

When they came around the sharp curve of Trans Am Corner—another blind curve, and even more dangerous than Skep Rock—Gary's palms were damp on his handlebars. It always made him nervous to ride his bike by the lake, but he'd never been this scared before. He'd been holding his breath ever since they passed the Calhoun Lake Lodge. Jill must have felt it, too, because she kept speeding up, pushing faster and faster until the Eagle Cove sign appeared.

The campground was empty. By midsummer, the small clearing with its hard-packed sites would be packed with tents, maybe even an RV or two, but for now the tourists were satisfied by the fancy flush toilets and hot showers down at the Bureau of Land Management's main campground. This spot was better for hunting camps, anyway. In the fall, it was packed with bow hunters who appreciated the trails connecting Eagle Cove to the surrounding hills. Gary might come back this fall and try selling firewood again. It had been pretty good pay.

Jill leaned her bike against the shingled wall of the pit toilet. "We beat the others."

"Yeah."

She glanced back at the road. She didn't say anything, but he knew she was thinking about the accident. They were only about five miles up the road from Skep Rock.

He took a step away from her. No way was he going to bring it up.

Then out on Calhoun Lake Road, voices echoed off the cliffs in possibly the worst rendition of Bobby McFerrin's "Don't Worry Be Happy." David's singing voice came closer to howling than actual singing. The song changed to a whoop as he caught sight of Gary and Jill.

"Hot diggety dog!" David bellowed. He gave his bike a burst of speed and streaked toward Gary, pulling short at the very last second in a spray of gravel and debris. "Wasn't really sure you'd show up."

Gary gave him a look. "Why not?"

David shoved his shoulder, but not in a mean way. "You weren't that into the idea when I first brought it up."

"Neither was I," Jill said.

Stacie got off her bike. "Are you two okay? You look funny."

"There was an accident," Jill began, but Gary cut her off.

"We don't want to talk about it."

"Okay." Stacie gave Jill a quick hug. "You can tell me later if you want. You can always tell me anything."

Gary thought Jordan made a face at that, but he couldn't imagine why. Stacie and Jill were best friends, after all. They told each other everything, even what kind of tampons they liked. Sometimes being around them was downright disgusting.

David threw down his bike. "Let's find a place to set up." He charged off toward the edge of the campground.

"What are we doing, exactly?" Jordan asked. "The Ouija board got ruined, remember."

"I brought candles," Stacie said. "They always have candles in the movies."

"My grandpa used to take me here."

They all turned to look at David. He stood at the trailhead on the far side of the campground, looking up into the canopy of the massive overhanging maple tree.

"We'd set up our fire right here, under this tree. After we had dinner and maybe roasted a few marshmallows, I'd just lay on my back and watch the smoke go up into the leaves. I always figured that's what heaven looked like."

"A tree?" Jordan asked.

"A tree with smoke in its leaves." David stared up at the leaves for another second, and then, with a clap of his hands, turned to face them. "Wanna set up right here?"

The others hurried forward, digging in their backpacks for a picnic blanket or candles or whatnot, but Gary just stood there looking at David. His eyes were too bright, the two spots of red in his cheeks too red.

"You want to talk to your grandpa, don't you? His spirit, I mean."

David hesitated a second before he put his hands on his hips. "Yeah. Is that so wrong?"

Gary took a few slow steps toward the other boy. Jordan was smoothing out the picnic blanket Jill had packed, and Stacie had arranged a circle of candles all around it. It looked nice. Cozy, even. Welcoming.

"How long has he been dead?"

"Two years?" A muscle flashed in David's cheek. "Maybe closer to two and a half? That's why we moved here. After he was sick, we couldn't keep his trailer. There were just too many bills, and my parents—" He stopped. His face had gone tight and mean, and Gary had a feeling that if he asked another question, David would punch him in the nose.

"It's okay," he said, quickly. "I don't think time makes a big difference. I'm just not sure about this place."

"I like it," Jordan said.

"Yeah, it's pretty," Gary agreed. "But this fall when I was out here, I saw some weird stuff in the woods. I think maybe people have died out there."

David went and sat down by Jill. "Grandpa said there used to be a coal mine here on Calhoun Lake. He said this was where they loaded the trucks."

The *rightness* of what he said resonated inside Gary's chest. He stumbled into the center of the blanket, his eyes not really seeing. "Fourteen men," he murmured. "Fourteen men and a Shetland pony."

Jill reached for his arm. "Gary? What are you saying?"

He put out his hands blindly. "Take my hands, take my hands!"

The warmth of their fingers ran up his arms. The green of the woods fell away in dark clumps, gray mist and smoke swirling in to replace it.

We told him to shore up the entrance, someone whispered, and he felt the words creep out of his mouth an instant after they entered his head.

The coal was runnin' out, someone else said, their voice pure Georgia peach. *Weren't hardly worth digging anymore.*

I told my wife I'd cut a load of wood before dinner, another said, the consonants crackling hard and Germanic. *Who's going to cut that wood now?*

My little boy will be so cold.

"Grandpa?" David whispered. "Grandpa, are you there?"

Smoke forms slammed into Gary's body. He gasped for air as they twisted down his throat.

"*Davey?*"

Gary knew it was his throat, his mouth speaking, but it was not his voice. Smoke filled his mouth as the voices fought for control of him.

They were going to take him over, rip him open, burst every last seam of his body. His whole body shook at the invasion of it.

Fingernails dug into his arm, and the terror lessened. This was his skin. This was his body. He could do this with his friends' help.

He focused on one smoky curl and pulled it up into his mouth.

Davey, you were the best thing that ever happened to me, and don't you forget it. I wish I could have had more time. Wish I could have sent your good for nothing ma and pa packing.

"Can you stay with me, Grandpa?" David whispered.

The smoke forms condensed into a sudden wash of cold.

It's coming!!!

It wasn't one voice but all of the voices, tearing out of Gary's mouth in ice and fire. The smoke boiled out of him, rushing into the woods, the green and brown of the world returning too fast, scorching his eyes. But behind it all, in the deepest of the shadows: something.

"What the hell is that?" Jill shrieked.

Spirits whispered and hissed. A pair of eyes gleamed blue-green in the shadows, its body's shape a mere suggestion. A deer? A man? A man with antlers? It looked at them for an endless minute.

It looked at them and *saw* them. Gary could feel his mind unfold for it to see, his every hope and wish spilling out for its delectation.

The deer-man took a step closer, its edges rippling and swirling.

Jordan slapped at the nearest candle, breaking the circle of flames. "Gary! Wake up! Gary!"

The deer-man held Gary's eyes, then charged forward, leaping up and over the group like they were only rabbits or ferns or something. Hooves clattered on the gravel. Gary blinked at it, its rack so enormous he could barely believe it could hold up its head. He had never seen such a big buck.

The white pickup truck slammed into its side and sent it flying.

The truck's tires screeched on the pavement. With a little shriek, Stacie rushed forward, and Jordan ran after her. Gary took an uncertain step forward. He didn't want to see another mashed and mangled body, even if it was just a deer.

It wasn't just a deer, something whispered in his ear. *There's never been a deer like that in all the world.*

The pickup's door opened. "Motherfucker!" the man growled. The normal part of Gary's brain recognized him as Earl Coates.

Stacie and Jordan stopped at the edge of the road, staring at the deer's enormous body lying on the ground. Gary forced himself to take another step forward. Shadows rippled and flowed over the beast's flanks, slipped and slid over its antlers. A dozen whispering voices echoed in Gary's ears. David and Jill were leading him toward the others.

This is a bad place, a man whispered. *A cursed place.*

The deer jumped to its feet.

"Holy shit!" Earl shouted.

The deer took a stumbling step forward and then leaped, jumping right out onto the beach. It broke into a run, charging into the brush along the water. Branches snapped and crashed as it ran.

Then, silence.

"What the hell just happened?" Earl asked. He got into his truck and slammed the door.

A breeze blew ribbons of shadows up into Gary's face. He doubled over, coughing and gasping. His throat ached like the time his mom let him try one of her cigarettes.

"What was that?" Jill sobbed. "What was that?"

"A deer," David said, too quick. "It was just a deer."

"Right," Stacie agreed. She had taken Jordan's hand. "A deer."

The dying woman's face flashed in Gary's mind. *Was a deer*, she cried. *A deer!*

He stumbled away from the picnic blanket and vomited in the ferns.

CHAPTER TEN

STACIE: 2018

THE RECORDED VOICE announced the next stop, and Stacie began to push her way through the rush-hour commuters. Mass transit stunk, but there was no way she was going to pay the outrageous parking fees at any of the downtown lots.

She squeezed around an enormous man in head-to-toe Seahawks gear who refused to look up from his phone, tripped over a woman's golf umbrella, and finally managed to extricate herself from the packed train. Someone was already playing electric guitar on the opposite street corner. A woman had spread out a blanket and was hawking jewelry and bags made from woven plastic bags. The air was thick with the smell of Portland's coffee addiction.

She shifted her messenger bag over her shoulder and started walking. It galled her to admit how much she missed Clarissa's BMW. How pleasant it had been, zipping down the freeways, her backside cradled in a sleek, self-heating leather seat, her stainless-steel mug of tea snug in the cupholder, some kind of soft jazz crooning in the background instead of whatever noise the buskers dished out. Although to be honest, the jazz had always felt a little pretentious. Clarissa insisted Stacie's lack of appreciation for her musical taste was half the reason their relationship had crashed and burned. Stacie had let her think it. It was easier than explaining how awkward Stacie felt every time she passed the concierge in the lobby of Clarissa's condo building or how painful it was to see Clarissa pick up the tab at any restaurant fancier than a burrito joint.

She stopped before the glorious old building which housed Our Living Room. The ornamental exterior hid sloping floors, groaning pipes, and a service elevator that threatened to stop working every three days, but the landlord gave the organization a steep discount on rent, and the downtown address could not be beat. Stacie had seen OLR grow from two grant writers working from an actual living room to an established nonprofit with a hip board of directors, an entire crew of excited volunteers, and four paid employees coordinating LGBTQIA+ youth outreach across Oregon and SW Washington. Sure, Stacie hadn't given *herself* a raise in three years, but then again, she also still clipped coupons for office supplies and refused to pay for an office Spotify account. Every penny they had, she wanted to go to serving kids as confused and scared as she had been.

A car honked at her, and she realized she had been standing in a parking spot staring for a good two or three minutes. She rushed across the street and let herself into the building. The stairs creaked as she bounded up them. Taking the train might not be as glamorous as driving a BMW, but at least once she got to the office, she wanted to be there.

As usual, her assistant had beaten her to the office. In the central work area, they had the kettle bubbling and were already refilling the paper tray in the copy machine.

"Morning, boss!" Kiernan called. "I brought in a new kind of tea. Delia says it's a new fall blend!"

Kiernan's girlfriend worked at a small Ayurvedic-inspired tea company founded by a pair of white girls who claimed balancing their chakras had improved their prowess at snowboarding and surfing. Stacie couldn't tell her heart chakra from her solar plexus, but she certainly wasn't going to complain about free caffeine.

"Awesome, thanks." Stacie hurried into her office, hung up her coat, misted the air plant, and turned on her computer. The dry erase board with its to-do list loomed over her desk. There were meetings at ten and one, an email interview to finish up for a local high school newspaper, and a few thank you notes to send to this month's donors. *If* the thank-you cards had come in. She frowned and picked up a dry-erase marker. Maybe Kiernan could call the printers and see what was up with their order.

Kiernan stuck their head around the corner. They'd buzzed off all their hair but one stripe along the left side, which today was dyed blue. Their face had gone dangerously apologetic.

"So I just checked the voicemail. Do you want the message now or after you're caffeinated?"

Stacie braced her back against her desk. "Lay it on me."

"Robin Takas has to have emergency surgery tomorrow. She'll be on bed rest for at least a week afterward."

"Oh, crap." Stacie sagged. "I really wanted this check presentation to be special for this group. How am I ever going to find another speaker willing to go all the way to Coos Bay with so little notice?"

"It really sucks."

Stacie nodded emphatically. "Kids down there are awfully short on heroes. Robin Takas is somebody they can look at and say, 'Hey, look at this amazing gay woman! She came from here. She's an award-winning graphic novelist. It really *does* get better!'"

"Robin is an amazing artist," Kiernan agreed.

"And now what? We just put the check in the mail and let the local PFLAG have a normal, boring awards dinner? The money's important, but a big part of what we're doing here is providing inspiration. Hell, we send these kids hope!"

Kiernan bit their lip. Stacie recognized that look on their face.

"Are you coming up with one of your genius ideas?"

"Well…" They trailed off. They were looking awfully closely at Stacie's face. "We do know someone who grew up down there who has a really great career."

Stacie shook her head. "I can't think of anyone. Our entire board is originally from California or the Midwest." Her voice sounded strained even to her own ears. She didn't want to be this upset, but anything that close to home—to the southern Oregon coast, she corrected herself—brought out her anxiety.

Kiernan crossed the room and carefully patted Stacie on the shoulder. "What about someone who started up an amazing nonprofit that helps connect queer kids to each other and to amazing queer mentors?"

Stacie opened her mouth. Closed it.

"Your life story is totally inspirational, boss. I mean, you changed my life."

Stacie forced herself to smile. "That's an option I hadn't considered. Good idea, Kiernan."

Their smile was nearly blinding. "Well, then, that's solved! Are you ready for your tea now?"

"That would be great," Stacie managed to say.

It wasn't until Kiernan stepped out the door that the shivering began. Stacie rubbed her hands over her forearms and felt goosebumps prickling across her skin.

Coos Bay was only thirty miles from Kingston.

GARY: 2018

The parking lot at the Landing was full. Kim passed it, the car's tires rumbling as they rolled slowly down the boardwalk. A girl with green streaks in her hair, probably a sophomore skipping driver's ed, leaned against the side of the t-shirt shop smoking a cigarette, watching them disinterestedly. Oregon state law discouraged smoking so close to the entrance of a business, but the odds of a customer setting foot in the place were so low, Gary couldn't fault the store's owner for letting the delinquent be. He wouldn't have been able to stand up to her.

Kim gave the girl a double-take and shook her head. Kingston's graduation rate was one of the worst in the state, and better attendance was one of her pet projects.

"So this lunch thing is about…that bridge deal?"

"Keridan Bridge Corporation. Their VP of something-or-other has come down to meet with the 'business interests' of Kingston. And since Aberdeen started waving every possible tax break at this company, Superintendent Harrington wants us to put on our best dog and pony show."

Gary knew enough about school funding to know that landing a new big employer meant the world to a small-town superintendent. "I thought Plymouth was trying to land this company." He pointed ahead. "There's a spot right in front of John King."

She slapped her turn signal. "Yeah, them too. And God help all of us if Plymouth beats Kingston in this deal." She pulled the Camry up until its nose nearly touched the bronze statue of Kingston's founder. The great man—if a small-town grocer could really be called that—stared down at them, his countenance stern. The metal's patina outlined King's features in an eerie blue green.

Kim opened her door and carefully skirted a puddle. "Are you really related to this guy?"

Gary gave the statue one last measuring look as he got out of the car. John King's indented pupils drilled into his. "Oh, yes. Just wait—someone is bound to bring it up at the lunch. I'd wager a jalapeno popper on it."

She took his arm, and they walked down the boardwalk to the landing. "I can't believe how nervous I am."

"Well, it's your first time serving as a high muckety-muck. I'd be nervous, too, if I wasn't such an experienced cultural luminary."

Her little snort sounded genuinely amused. He had to admit he'd been on his best behavior since he'd arrived at her office. They'd never been the kind of couple to fight. They were talkers and people pleasers, and the awkwardness between them after any disagreement always felt like lemon juice rubbed on a road rash.

He cleared his throat. "And that's the place."

The restaurant sported all the appropriate nautical accouterments for an eatery on Highway 101: portholes for windows, glass floats hanging from the netting that framed the entry, and a lifesaver mounted on both of the double doors. What Kingston lacked in actual oceanfront property, it tried to make up for in posturing. He'd even heard that back in the sixties, the chamber of commerce had campaigned to dynamite a corridor in the side of Peshak Head, breaking through the big hill to open up ocean views and new developments. If they'd been successful, his new house would have been beachfront property.

Kim reached for the door handle and paused. "Hey, did I mention that you look terrific? That tweed jacket is grade-A novelist couture."

"Did I mention that you look great, too?"

She smiled. "Watch out, Keridan Bridge Company." She pulled her necklace out from beneath her dress. "Let's hope this new Buck Luck charm necklace works."

He was about to make a snide comment when he saw the thing, a half-inch circle of wood with some design wood-burned into the front. "What the hell is that?"

"This?" She held it up with two fingers. "They were selling them at the Bucks merch table. Somebody's dad makes them out of wood—see the deer antler design? It's supposed to be lucky. Everybody's wearing them, even the boys."

He remembered the pendant hanging from Coach Dusseldorf's scrawny old neck. Had he simply been wearing one of these ridiculous good luck totems? His memory flashed back to his mother, putting on her jewelry before a Deer Kings dinner. Was this just a low-key version of the old Deer Kings charm?

"Excuse me, folks," a man said, squeezing past.

"We'd better go in," Kim said, and Gary had to hurry to keep up with her, his questions unanswered and unanswerable.

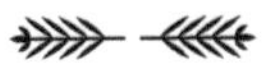

JILL: 1989

The sound of wood snapping startled Jill back into her body. She had to blink a few times before the gray emptiness of a trance fell away, and then she saw the shattered stump of the pencil in her hand. She had to pry it free of numb fingers.

She didn't remember sitting down to draw, but her box of colored pencils had been dumped out, the warm colors pushed to one corner of the desk. The blue-gray pencil was the one that had snapped. She brushed aside a few broken bits of wood and looked at the drawing she'd made.

Grays and blues. Hints of green around the edges. She brushed her fingertips over the pigment-smoothed paper. She hadn't drawn the deer-thing they'd seen at Eagle Cove, but the shadows and mists she had captured were almost more disturbing.

Her tongue clung to the roof of her mouth. She turned off the desk lamp and got up. Her alarm clock said it was only a little after eleven in the morning, but the forest butted up so tightly to the back of their house that it might as well be night inside her bedroom. Jill made her way to her door by sense memory and went out in the hall. Gary's bedroom door was open, but there was no sign of him. He wasn't in the living room either, not even curled up with a book on Dad's recliner beneath the sunset painting. The sunset painting looked back at her, the low orange sun sending out flames of loneliness across the painted sea.

She wished more than anything she could talk to Gary right now, or to someone, anyone of their group, but it was too early to call Stacie, and she didn't have Jordan or David's numbers. She didn't even know Jordan's last name.

"Hey, Jilly Bean."

Her mother sat at the kitchen table, her blond hair pulled back with a white plastic headband, a Nora Roberts novel by her elbow. She looked prettier than usual, and it took Jill a second to realize it was because she wore a pink t-shirt and not her green work uniform.

"Hi, Mom." Jill took a tentative step toward the kitchen. "Do you have the day off?"

"Strange, isn't it?" Her mother patted the table. "Want to sit with me a minute?"

Jill perched on a chair. It had been a long time since she had just sat down with her mother. She remembered how dry her mouth had felt and jumped back up.

"Do you want a drink of water? Or maybe some Kool-Aid?"

"Water would be nice," her mother said.

Jill brought them two matching glasses. The water smelled more powerfully of chlorine than usual, or maybe that was just how it seemed after spending the day at Grandma Thompson's. Sometimes little dirt specks came out of the tap at Grandma's, but even dirty, that spring water was the best thirst quencher Jill had ever tasted. Better than Pepsi, even.

"Any big plans for the summer?"

"Just hanging with Stacie and Gary." Jill gulped a long drink. It didn't taste as bad as it smelled. "Maybe doing some babysitting for the Dunnings. I could really use some cash for Beachfest."

"The Dunnings? I don't like it when you babysit all the way in town. It's such a long bike ride."

"Just three miles. Gary can do that in less than fifteen minutes."

Her mother raised an eyebrow. "Yeah, but how many candy bars would he eat afterward?"

Jill had to laugh. Then she chugged the rest of her water.

Her mother reached out for her hand. "What have you got all over your hand?"

Jill twisted her hand so she could see the side. One of the perils of being a lefty was always having a filthy side of the hand, and today was no different from any other. "Just colored pencil. I was drawing." Jill put down the glass. She remembered the sunset painting, so violently sad as she came out of her bedroom. "Mom?"

"Yes?" Something in her tone must have warned her mother Jill wanted to be serious.

Jill wasn't sure she wanted to actually ask the question on the back of her mind, but it was too late to stopper herself. "Did you ever meet Grandma Sheldon?"

Her mother looked surprised. "Yes. I mean, a little. She didn't get sent away until I was pregnant with you."

"We have one of her paintings, right?"

Jill resisted the urge to look back over her shoulder at the sunset painting. It was really a painting of a fishing boat, a trawler, all done in oils. The black outline of the boat cut across a furious sunset that refused to restrain itself to the sky. No sunset had ever looked so powerful in real life. So thick. So heavy. So true.

"Is that what's bothering you? Are you worried there's some kind of connection between her talent and what happened to her mind?"

"Well...yeah."

Her mother patted her hand. "You don't have to worry about that, sweetheart. Your grandmother had problems her whole life. Even as a little girl, she was always telling everybody her parents were going to get murdered or set on fire or some godawful thing. And when she was a teenager, she insisted all the weird animals she painted were real creatures she saw in the woods. She was broken, honey. If people had understood schizophrenia better, they would have locked her up *years* before she had your dad."

Jill wiped her palms on her jeans. "What did happen to Great-grandma and Great-grandpa Sheldon?"

Her mother took a drink of water. "I can't remember, baby. Some accident, I think. They were always going out in the woods."

But Jill knew her mother was lying. She had seen the article in one of her dad's scrapbooks. Her great-grandparents had shot each other when their daughter was only eight years old. And it sounded like Grandma Sheldon had known it was going to happen.

CHAPTER ELEVEN

GARY: 2018

CULTURAL LUMINARIES OR not, Kim and Gary did not merit seating at the top table. Their little four-top faced the larger one meant for the big kahunas, and Kim's eyes kept going from the empty seats to the door.

"Appetizer plate?" the waitress murmured at Gary's elbow.

"Please." His cornflakes had worn off before he'd even gone to meet Kim at the high school.

The waitress set a plate of jalapeno poppers and deep-fried mushrooms in front of him, then moved on to Kim.

The man across from Gary cleared his throat. "You're Gary Sheldon, aren't you?"

"I am." Gary put down his untouched mushroom and wiped his fingers on his napkin. "Nice to meet you. This is my wife, Kim."

"Jim Burns." The man pumped Gary's hand with the solid, leathery grip of an outdoorsman. Gary would have guessed him in his late fifties, maybe early sixties, and his jacket was the gray flavor of Gary's own. "President of the historical society." He stretched to shake with Kim too.

Gary had a vague memory of an elementary school trip to a musty building of uncertain provenance. "I think I visited the museum once."

Burns brightened. "It's really improved in the last three or four years. The state gave us a grant so we could bring in a real historian, get all of our artifacts straightened out. Plus, a group of volunteers refurbished the upstairs' bedroom. It's completely period-appropriate now."

With Kingston's alluring history, "period-appropriate" meant something like "trapper chic." The newly decorated bedroom probably reeked of donated homemade taxidermy projects, with a Pendleton blanket thrown in to class things up. "That all sounds terrific."

Burns beamed. "Big, big progress. And we're working on some really great stuff for Founders' Day. Speaking of which…" He cocked his head. "You're a writer, aren't you? And a direct descendant of John King, if I remember right."

Gary nudged Kim in the ribs, but she was already sliding a jalapeno popper onto his plate.

"That's right. His daughter Eugenia Ferguson was my great-grandmother."

"And you're really a writer?" Excitement reddened Burns' whole face, darkening to a purple at his receding hairline. He crammed a jalapeno popper into his mouth without taking his eyes off Gary's face.

"Well, being a librarian pays most of the bills, but I've written a couple of novels."

"Three," Kim corrected. She stood up. "There's Harrington. I'd better check in with him. You going to be okay over here?"

Gary nodded, but she was already on the move.

"Terrific, terrific!" Burns swallowed down the popper with difficulty. He gulped a little water and sputtered a second before adding: "This year's Founders' Day will also mark the one hundredth anniversary of the Deer Kings. You know, John King started the group. Kind of his way of making sure his legacy lived on in the area. Anyway, I was thinking it would be really special to write up a little pamphlet about the group, something people could buy for a dollar or two at the Founders' Day dinner. Make a nice souvenir, you know. And if we had a *real* writer—and not just a real writer, but a direct descendant of the man himself—write that little book? Wow, that would really be something."

Gary nearly said no. Work this morning…he wasn't sure he could finish this book. It wasn't just time and the move, it was *him*. Not for the first time, he worried that somewhere forgotten in the basement of their Portland house was a box packed full of his writing tools: imagination, intuition, a sense of wordplay.

"What do you think?"

Gary opened his mouth and then thought of Kim and their argument that morning. "Sure. I'd be happy to pitch in."

"That's great. That's just—"

Whatever else Burns might have said was cut off by a burst of applause.

Gary turned in his seat to make out the door of the banquet room. Kim stood poised and professional beside her boss, her hands pounding together just like everyone else's. A tall man held the door for a diminutive figure in a gray suit. Her carefully coiffed and highlighted hair announced her as the VIP from Keridan, although her pinched face belonged to an aggrieved meter reader. She stood in the literal and figurative shadow of the man holding the door for her. It wasn't just his height, although he had at least a foot on the Keridan rep, or the designer cut of his jeans and blazer. Charisma poured off him like scented oil. His smile, not so white as to blind, added a warm glow to the entire room.

"Coach Washburn," Burns breathed.

Coach David Washburn. Gary almost stood up. Of all the people to come back to Kingston, he would have never imagined it would be David.

Coach and VIP made their way to the top table, followed by business-looking types Gary didn't recognize and had no interest meeting. Kim sank back into her chair.

"That's the mayor," she whispered in his ear, pointing out a man with the beady eyes and pointed snout of a hedgehog. "The other two are managers at the paper mill."

The mayor began to talk, and although Gary tried to pay some kind of attention, most of the discussion did not compete with the appearance of salad (he was hungry enough not to care it was just iceberg lettuce and some pale orange cherry tomatoes) and then main dishes for the others and more salad for him and Kim. He wasn't surprised the Landing wasn't really prepared for vegetarian dining.

Harrington was just beginning to expound on the successes of the school system here in Kingston—his voice more strident than Gary would expect from a man holding part of a club sandwich in one hand—when the waitresses began to deliver dessert. Harrington broke off as a square of cherry-topped cheesecake appeared in front of him.

"Kingston certainly sounds like a fine community," the woman in the gray suit said. "As of this moment, your town is moving to the top of our list."

Kim elbowed Gary in the ribs, beaming. The entire room began to clap.

Gary pushed aside his plate. That sounded like good news to him. It had to be worth missing out on an afternoon of writing and eating a lunch made entirely out of iceberg lettuce.

A young waitress bent over his shoulder, smelling faintly of stale smoke and peppermint gum, and he recognized the green tips of her ponytail. The girl outside the t-shirt shop. Gary tried to make eye contact, but she was already walking away. He still couldn't tell how old she was or how young, how much the system had let her down. His pocket buzzed and he was glad for the distraction. He maneuvered the phone beneath the table, the soft blue glow lighting up the space beneath the tablecloth.

A text from Zack. He tapped it open.

Gonna be late. Football practice!!1!

Gary turned off the screen and gripped the phone tightly. The smell of canned cherry pie filling, metallic and too sweet, made his stomach fold itself around its lettuce leaves. The football team.

Kim was happy, of course. Gary wished he could be.

Jim Burns smiled at him, and Gary tucked his phone back in his blazer pocket. His left hand found the dessert fork and negotiated it into the quivering pile in front of him. Cheesecake had been his favorite dessert as a kid, same as his dad. Gillian had baked him one—a beautiful one, far better than this box-mix crap—the night he'd gone to the hospital. He could remember trying to pick up his fork even as his world closed down to a single dot of cherry in a long gray tunnel.

He put the yellow and pink glob in his mouth. It tasted like a scratch-n-sniff sticker.

GARY: 2018

He woke from hospital dreams and lay blinking and motionless until the darkness over the bed resolved itself into spackle and the outlines of a Home Depot-vintage chandelier. The cheesecake had done it, of course. Gillian had baked one the night he'd gone to the hospital, a reward for…something. Something forgotten and gone more nebulous than the shadows of his dreams.

Gary got out of bed and found his way to the downstairs bathroom. Kim would wake up if he ran the water in theirs, and the back of his neck was burning hot. He found a washcloth, wet it, and draped it over the scorching flesh. It had been years since he'd had the hospital dream, but it always ended like this, Gary in the bathroom, his neck stinging and his eyes full of grit.

His cancer had taken his family completely by surprise. He had always been an active kid, riding bikes, running in the fields, and although he'd gotten the usual childhood ailments, the worst had been the chicken pox at age ten: a week of itching, feverish misery, with green-oozing pustules in the spots he could scratch. But as a freshman in high school, he'd started getting tired. His dad had pushed and pushed, begging him to do some kind of sport—football, preferably, basketball as runner-up, baseball if he couldn't be bothered to do anything until fucking springtime. Gary chose track and field. He'd dragged his ass down to the clinic by Safeway for the physical, dreading the thought of hanging out with a bunch of jocks every day. If he hadn't had that physical…well, they wouldn't have caught the leukemia when they did, would they? Every time he went for a run he thought about that: how the physical he got for track and field probably saved his life.

Gary wet the washcloth again and laid it on the back of his neck. He could only remember snippets of what that time had been like: the long drive to Eugene to talk to a specialist, his parents crying at the dinner table, the night he'd passed out in Gillian's cheesecake. All he really remembered from that night was waking up with fire on the back of his neck.

The past swam around him, twined with dreams. The empty chair beside the hospital bed. The soft light of the hallway coming in through the open door. The warm, furry presence at his back, the heavy weight across his torso.

I'm free now, the dream-voice always said. Though it sounded tinged with a smile, the voice made the hairs rise up all over his body. *And you're mine.*

Then the pain began in the back of his neck, sharp and searing like a burn, a tiny fierce burn that threatened to eat through his skin and up his spine and all the way into his brain.

The light came on in the hallway. The real hallway.

"You okay in there?"

Gary pushed himself upright. "Yeah, just a little queasy. Must have been something I ate."

Kim stuck her head around the door. "I hope it's not norovirus. Do you want some ginger ale?"

His mouth immediately watered. "That'd be nice."

She paused. "Is your neck okay?" She took a step closer. "How'd you get this red spot?"

"Red spot?" He brought his fingers up to the sore place and found the skin raised, the surface taut and smooth and warm to the touch.

"It looks like a scar." She pushed his hand away to look at the mark more closely. "Like an old burn scar, maybe. But it's almost perfectly round."

Like the tip of a cigarette, Gary thought, and then remembered the smoke that always softened the edges of the hospital dream. A drop of water ran out from the washcloth, and he shivered as it slid down his spine.

"Let's get you that ginger ale." Kim steered him out of the bathroom, turning off the light behind them.

He hadn't had the hospital dream since before they were married. Since before he finished college.

She didn't bother turning on the kitchen light, but went straight to the fridge and the stash of half-sized ginger ale cans. Light spilled out, outlining her silhouette against the refrigerator and painting amber across the bottom of her face. She could have been anyone in that light, a stranger, a relative, even a man. He remembered the refrigerator his parents had kept in the garage when they lived in Kingston, the one just for beer and mixers. Had he ever seen his mother open it at night, her face lit up like this? And if they had a beer fridge, why did he remember so clearly pulling cold ones out of the square case of Hamm's above the vegetable bin?

He hadn't had the hospital dream since before he'd left Kingston.

Kim turned around. "Ginger ale will straighten out that stomach."

And for a second, he could have sworn there were horns coming out of her hair, which was somehow the same soft blonde mass as his mother's. The back of his neck burned hotter.

CHAPTER TWELVE

GARY: 1989

HE JOGGED IN the woods a long time that morning, up the old logging road and then down through the deer trails that skirted the little lake on the north end of town, picking his way through poison oak and vine maple, fern and just-blossoming huckleberry. He passed through a rutted clearing where someone must have just clear-cut their property, and an old man waved from the fence line. He ran on.

What else could he do but run? When he read, the deer-thing swam before the page, obscuring the words. When he lay down, the blue-green glow of its eyes lit up the whole ceiling. He'd gotten out of bed before seven and let his feet lead him where they wished.

Eventually he found himself on their own street, Balfour Drive, which old-timers still called Old Highway 101. He sat down in the grass of someone's unmowed field—it was too vast a stretch to be called a yard—and wished he'd thought to bring a bottle of pop or a sandwich, or better yet, both.

A shadow fell across him. "Hey, loser."

Somehow he wasn't surprised to see David looming over him. The older boy had his shirt draped over his shoulder, sweat glinting over his improbably brown chest. It was only the second week of summer break. How did anyone have a tan yet?

Gary put his hand up to shield his eyes from the glare behind David's blond head. "What are you up to?"

He shrugged. "Caught a football game in Highlander Park. Thought I'd head home for lunch. You?"

Gary made a noncommittal face. "Just trying out a new trail up by Lake Mary Elizabeth Park. Guess I was out longer than I thought."

"You ran all the way around town—through the woods?"

"Yeah."

"With no water or food?"

David held out his hand. "Come on. Let's find something to eat."

Gary let David haul him to his feet. His legs protested mightily.

David led him through the field, the long grass tickling Gary's wrists and forearms. A bird sprang up, its wings cracking the air as it rose frantically into the sky.

"You live around here?"

David nodded. "Keep your voice down, right? My folks work the night shift."

The brown double-wide looked like it had sat at the edge of that field since the European discovery of North America. Moss and algae had colonized the once-white roof, the walls leaned, and a fern grew out of the corner of one window. Gary put his hand on the wooden stair railing and felt the grain, weathered to a slight fuzz, prickle against his palm. The boards sagged beneath his feet.

David opened the door and the dull stink of mildew rolled out, undercut by cigarette smoke and the vaguely sour smell of old beer cans. The door crunched against something as David slipped through it. Two lawn-and-leaf bags full of cans, waiting to go to the grocery store for five cents apiece, took up most of the floor space in the little kitchen. In another room, someone gave a bark of snoring so loud it made Gary jump.

David already had the fridge open. "You like ham?"

Gary nodded, then realized David couldn't see him. "Yep."

"Cups are by the sink."

Gary hesitated a second. It was weird to be in someone else's house, especially someone he barely knew. But he was too thirsty to let himself stay nervous. He went to the sink, opened the cupboard on the right—full of dry goods—then the one on the left, and found a couple of aluminum cups. His mom had the same ones.

He ran the water in the sink a minute to let it get good and cold. Given the bags of cans and the bad smells, he half-expected the sink to be filled with dirty dishes and the stove to be caked in gunk, but the kitchen, scuffed and ancient as it was, looked immaculate. He offered David a glass of water and watched him gulp it down in one long, uninterrupted drink. David wiped his mouth on his arm and then swiped at a trickle going down his chest.

David waved Gary out of the way and found a butter knife in a drawer. "Miracle Whip and mustard okay?"

"Yep."

Gary could not take his eyes away from the care David put into the process of making two sandwiches. Gary had never used a cutting board while making a sandwich. He had never once spread mayonnaise up to the very crust of the bread and then neatly swiped away any overspill. He had never squirted mustard onto a knife, dabbed it in careful, equidistantly spaced dollops across the bread, and then smoothed it in an even golden layer. He wasn't surprised when David put the top piece of bread in place, set his knife, studied its angle, readjusted, and then made a perfect diagonal cut.

David plated the sandwiches, quickly scrubbed the cutting board and knife, wiped down the counter, and then picked up the plates. "You bring the water."

They went back outside and sat on the porch. Gary wasn't sure what to say to him. "You're neater than my mom" didn't sound like much of a compliment. But he thought he understood why the trailer looked so clean.

David took an enormous bite of sandwich. "Miracle Whip is the fucking best," he said, thickly. "Don't you think?"

"Yeah." Gary tried a more reasonable bite. "But my mom never buys it. She says it's too expensive."

"It's worth it." David reached for his water glass. "When I've got my own place, I'm only going to use Miracle Whip. And real cheese, too, not that waxy government shit."

A car turned into the driveway, a long, low blue Oldsmobile that Gary thought might be the ugliest car he'd ever seen. Red primer dappled its worn-out hood, and someone had smashed in the front grill. An enormous pair of fuzzy dice hung from the rearview mirror.

David put down his sandwich. "Who the hell is this?"

But Gary had seen the driver. "Shit," he breathed.

The car came to a stop and the door opened.

Vincent Vernor unfolded himself from the front seat and stood in front of them, smirking. He shifted a toothpick to the side of his mouth. "If it isn't the little neighbor fag and his new boyfriend. You kids having a nice lunch?"

David jumped to his feet. "What did you say?"

Vincent waved a hand. "Don't get your panties in a bunch, sweetcheeks. Where's your folks?"

David slammed his palms into Vincent's chest. "Fuck you!"

Vincent moved so casually, it couldn't even be called a blow. But his hand came up, and David went sideways, falling into the garbage can and crashing to the ground. He sat up, rubbing his side.

"Hey, knock it off!"

A big man stood in the trailer's doorway. Gary threw himself off the porch stairs, stumbling toward David, as scared of the man's angry red face as he was of Vincent Vernor.

"Morning, Larry," Vincent drawled. "Looks like you could use a little hair of the dog." He pulled a flask from an inside pocket and gave it a shake. It sloshed cheerfully.

"Hey, Vincent. My kid giving you some trouble?"

Vincent glanced down at David. "Just playing around. Right, boys?"

David's dad took a step backward, holding the door for Vincent. "Why don't you come inside, buddy? I'll see if I can wake up the old lady."

Vincent disappeared into the dark of the trailer, but before the door closed, Gary heard him say: "Oh, I've got something to wake her up all right. Let the *bon temps rouler.*"

David's hand closed on Gary's arm so hard it made the bones hurt. Gary didn't move. Neither of them moved until someone inside the trailer turned on George Thorogood, and then they were both on their feet, running hard.

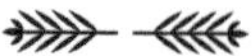

GARY: 2018

Gary dragged the heel of his hand across his eye and then took a long, too-hot swallow of coffee. The light changed and he crossed the street, unable to resist glancing south to the intersection where Trevor Hyatt had nearly pulped his son. He picked up his pace.

The high school took up a couple of blocks, a low beige structure with pleasant cornices around the red-painted front doors, the kind of neat details typical of a Civilian Conservation Corps project. His great-grandmother had been one of the first graduates.

Lack of sleep made his legs feel out of sync with the top half of his body. If he blinked too hard, he thought he might just drift off where he stood. The image of Kim-turned-his-mother kept flickering into his head, the living shadow of his nightmare. There'd been no way to sleep after seeing that.

The athletic fields stretched out behind the school, the grandstand marking off the far edge of the complex. The varsity team ran maneuvers out on the football field; the JV team had the green swath of the baseball field, their coaches calling instructions as foreign to Gary as Esperanto. A group of parents had gathered behind the backstop. The women were all blonde and the men all leaned into the wire mesh of the backstop, their focus on the field so tight they had to grip the mesh to stay upright. Gary took a stance beside the knot of women, glad he'd brought coffee.

A whistle sounded and the boys bounded toward the track. One of the mothers smiled at Gary. She might have been a year or two younger than him, and a clump of mascara stuck to one of her eyelashes. It looked like a bug leg camouflaged amid the rest. "They always finish with laps."

He nodded as if he had already known such a detail.

A hand tapped him on the shoulder. "Hey, Gary! I thought that was you."

Gary turned. "Jim Burns. Wasn't expecting to see you so soon."

The man beamed. He wore a brown blazer today, complete with historian elbow patches. "I try to catch practice a couple times a week. My nephew's second-string defense this year." He tipped his head toward the football field. "The team's looking great, isn't it?"

"Yeah, I made it to the first home game. Good stuff."

A whistle blasted, and the boys on the field stopped moving. One sat on the ground, clutching his face. Coach Washburn—Gary couldn't bring himself to call the man "David"—ran across the field toward him. Gary could feel every eye watching the man's movements. He crouched on the field beside the boy a moment, and then helped him to his feet, pulling a white handkerchief from his back pocket and pressing it to the kid's nose.

Another whistle sounded and the rest of the team moved into action again, obscuring the coach and the boy with the bloody nose. Gary craned his neck for a moment, seeing them finally standing at the edge of field, the coach patting the boy's back as the boy held his head tilted back.

Burns watched the field for another minute. A ball spun in a neat arc, soaring over thirty or forty yards to land in a tall boy's hands. A smile passed over Burns' face and then smoothed away, leaving an amiable residue. "You got one of your own out there?"

"Yeah." Gary pointed out Zack at the head of the JV pack. "He just joined the JV team."

"He's got fine form. Heck of a runner."

"He did track last year. We go running together sometimes."

Burns made a surprised face. "You're an athlete, as well as a writer? Man of many talents."

"It's good for the old bones."

Burns clapped him on the shoulder. "Well, I know I'm excited to see you down at the museum. You won't keep me waiting long, will you? Founders' Day needs your talents!"

Gary wondered if the man had found him just to bring up the King bio. "I'm really looking forward to it. In fact, I've got a half-day on Thursday. Planning on coming by."

Well, there went Thursday. Writing fiction had clearly given Gary a gift for white lies.

"Hey, Jim. Are you hectoring our resident author?"

Gary hadn't seen Samantha Oakley arrive, but he was glad to see her. Her red hair shone like a beacon. He took a step toward her.

"Oh, I'm just headed out," Burns announced. "I told Matthew I'd give him a ride home. But I'm looking forward to Thursday, Gary!" Burns gave them a little salute and set off for the football field.

Sam held out a Ziploc bag. "Cookie? I find I need a little sugar to wake myself up after I've been talking to Jim."

Gary took a dime-sized chocolate chip cookie from the bag. "He's not a bad guy."

"No, he's just boring. Football and history are about all that interest him." Sam tucked the cookies back in her purse. "Looks like the boys are headed back to the locker room. Perfect timing on my part."

"You don't like to watch practice?"

"What? I grew up on the stuff. My dad's Coach Dusseldorf. No, I'm just glad I'm not late. Skyler has it tough enough without dealing with that. Plus, we keep a pretty tight eating schedule—Skyler has diabetes, so it really helps."

"That sucks."

"It's just normal for us now."

She beckoned him to walk with her, and they made their way through the grass. He could feel the weight of a dozen mascaraed eyes against their backs. The husband of the high school principal and the minister, walking together.

"So you grew up here?" He glanced sideways, wondering if they had gone to school together. He would have remembered a Samantha Dusseldorf. He would have definitely remembered those blue eyes.

"My parents divorced, so I wound up doing high school in Coos Bay. Broken families are apparently a thing in my life."

"Skyler's dad?"

"In Texas. He hated it here, and leaving my dad wasn't an option." She pulled out the cookies again and popped one in her mouth. Gary waved away the bag. "Definitely not a big Latino population in

Kingston."

A sturdy boy bounded out the locker room door, his gear thrown over his shoulder. Zack couldn't be far behind him.

"I've always wondered why there are so few minorities in this town."

"I think it's probably intentional," she said. But if she had more to say about the matter, it was lost when Zack and Skyler burst outside, laughing and talking too fast.

Gary tried to remember what his friends had been like in high school. Had he laughed like that? Had he smacked his buddy in the head and pounded his shoulder in easy physicality, with nothing artificial or studied about the motion?

Samantha grabbed his arm and steered him out of the way as the first of the varsity team strode toward the locker room, all long legs and thick muscles. The football player's shoulder bumped Gary's, but he walked on, not noticing, or not caring.

The boys scampered around the older footballers and launched themselves at their parents. "Dad, can I go to Skyler's house for dinner? Or have him over? We've *got* to play PlayStation." Zack put his arm around Gary, smelling strongly of deodorant soap and damp beneath his t-shirt.

"Please, Mr. Sheldon? Please?" Skyler clasped his hands beneath his chin and made his brown eyes into puppyish orbs. Behind him, a group of varsity boys trudged toward the locker room.

Gary couldn't help but remember the two football players at Murphy's Bakery. How did such happy, innocent boys turn so cold? And how could he keep Zack safe from that shit?

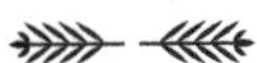

JILL: 2018

Jill glanced at the clock. Five to ten—so the long lithe bohemian standing at the gallery's shop counter had to be her morning appointment. She cocked her head and saw the bulging portfolio case resting beside their Josef Seibels.

"Are you Haley?" she called out, sweeping through the aisle like the very busy important gallery owner artists liked to see.

The artist nodded. Their fingers tugged at the fringed trim of their beaded vest. Jill had seen this painter's work hanging in a coffee shop in

Modesto and liked their approach to color. But it was apparent they were still new enough in the industry to be nervous of a gallery owner.

That was probably why they were on time, she thought sourly. But she only allowed a smile to show on her face. "Why don't you step into my office so we can chat? And I can't remember—what were your preferred pronouns?"

The artist sagged with relief. "He/him," he said in the smallest voice Jill had ever heard inside her own gallery. He picked up the portfolio. "Could I get a glass of water?"

Jill caught her assistant's eye. "I'll have some brought in. Do you need any tea or coffee?"

Haley shook his head. The tiny embroidered cap on the back of his head threatened to slide off. Jill turned away so he wouldn't see her smile. She could remember being this young and awkward.

The awkward years had all come after she'd left Kingston, though. Young Jill had never had any self-doubts. It was only after her parents died—no, after her aunt and uncle had her institutionalized for three months—that she had lost the confidence that had buoyed her through all her early years. College had been one stumbling, babbling torment after another.

Except in the studio. She had always known what to do with a paintbrush. If it hadn't been for the support of her art professors, she would have dropped out of college and probably turned into a drug addict.

She opened her office door and waved Haley inside. "Have a seat."

He sank into the chair facing her desk. She pulled her chair out from behind the desk and sat down facing him. "You don't have an agent?"

He shook his head, but it was a rhetorical question. No agent, not even the ones who worked with galleries like Jill's, would have let their client take such a big meeting by themselves. Or wearing that outfit. He was clearly pushing for an androgynous look, but instead, the poor dear simply looked like he had raided his grandmother's closet. If Jill signed him, she would have to introduce him to Comme des Garçons.

"Well, I'm very excited to see more of your work. Those studies of lilacs showed both impressive draftsmanship and a powerful sense of color."

Christie appeared with a bottle of Perrier and a glass of ice. She had found a perfect pink macaron somewhere too. She left the refreshments and vanished without a sound.

Haley unzipped his portfolio. "I'm working on a new series. Smaller in size, mostly." He brought out a 9x12 watercolor in a plastic sleeve.

"What do you think?"

She took the painting and went still. The strongly inked lines, the glorious depth of color, all of those were recognizable from the paintings she'd seen in the coffee shop. But the subject—

"Do you recognize him?"

Of course she recognized him, the man striding with his walking stick, the child on his shoulders. After all, she was the one who had found the Saint Christopher medal in that filthy cabin. She was the one who had worn it all that long, bad summer.

CHAPTER THIRTEEN

STACIE: 1989

TWENTY MINUTES AFTER finishing the lodge's famous French toast—a bribe from Stacie's mom—Jill and Jordan stood in the open doorway of the lodge's utility closet, looking more uncertain by the second. Stacie couldn't blame them. In the cramped space, the ammonia and Pine-Sol vapors made her eyes water. It was a good thing the closet opened on the outside of the building. Without the breeze, she'd probably suffocate in there.

She handed each of them a pair of yellow rubber gloves. "Thank goodness you two could come. I helped Mom clean cabins last year, just the two of us, and I thought I'd die." Somewhere out on the lake, someone gave a happy *whoop*, an unnecessary reminder of all the fun normal people were having on this perfect summer day.

"Isn't it totally illegal for Mrs. Clinton to hire us like this?" Jordan asked. "None of us are even fifteen yet." His mom ran the office for the Shell Station, so he knew a thing or two about this stuff.

Stacie shoved the plastic mop bucket out of the closet. "That's why it's under the table. Which is good news, since we all need cash for Beachfest."

Jordan raised an eyebrow. Stacie made a face. "What else is she supposed to do when someone's sick? It's not like there's an abundance of chambermaids out here in the woods."

Jill snorted. "'Abundance of chambermaids.' You're talking like Gary."

Just for that, Stacie handed her the gallon jug of ammonia. "Come on."

Stacie maneuvered the mop bucket down the sidewalk, its wheels bumping over every crack and ridge. The utility closet was built into the back of the lodge's motel wing, and whoever had built the sidewalk had obviously never expected anyone to use or look at it. The owner had added the four "honeymoon cabins" about four years ago and hadn't had the sense to imagine the daily trudge to and from the main building with cartloads of bedding and towels and cleaning supplies. Stacie's mom once told her she thought the damn sidewalk had caused more maids to quit than the owner's tight-fisted approach to overtime and pay raises.

She caught the bucket as it rushed down a sudden slope of broken cement. At least they weren't cleaning the motel rooms. Nadine was already rushing through them, changing sheets and replenishing towels at a pace no other maid had ever kept up with. The tall redhead had been working at the lodge since long before Stacie's mom had moved them to Kingston. The other maids hated her, but Stacie admired her. She didn't talk to anyone beyond the occasional yes or no response, and rumor was she had built her cabin out by the lake with her own hands and no power tools. Rumor also had it she sold pot out of the back of her VW van. All Stacie knew is that she had once walked past an open motel door and seen Nadine flipping a fresh sheet over a bed, her blue shirt riding up to reveal a tattoo of a rose on her lower back. She'd never seen a woman with a tattoo before. Sometimes she caught herself thinking about that red and green rose snaking across Nadine's pale, mole-speckled back and her cheeks would get hot and she'd have to think about something boring, like social studies.

Jordan rushed ahead of her to catch the mop as a rough jolt threatened to knock it out of the bucket. Stacie had given him the smaller bucket of rags and scrub brushes. "Did anyone else have bad dreams after…"

"Gary talked to the ghosts of a bunch of dead miners and then we nearly got trampled by a giant deer?"

He stopped walking, so they all did too. They were nearly to the cabins, which huddled around a u-shaped courtyard. Their cedar shingles had already turned gray with weather, and the pots of flowers growing by their front steps shouted false cheer.

"It was probably a mass hallucination, right? Or Gary was pulling our leg?" he asked.

"After what happened in the barn?" Stacie freed a hand and found the pass key in her borrowed apron's pocket. "Plus, Gary doesn't have a funny bone in his body."

"There was something weird about that deer," Jill said. She took the key out of Stacie's hand and pushed it into the keyhole of the first cabin.

"It didn't seem—"

Jordan grabbed her wrist. "Wait! Shush!"

They all froze. Then they heard it, and Stacie felt her cheeks go up in flames.

Jill covered her mouth with her arm, stifling a giggle. "Is that what I think it is?" she whispered.

Jordan's eyes went huge.

Jill grinned. "Come on," she breathed, already rounding the corner of the cabin.

Stacie and Jordan followed her around the side of the cabin, picking their way as quietly as they could over gravel and weeds. Jill stood crouched below a window. Seeing them, she grabbed the woodwork at the bottom of the frame and pulled herself up onto her tiptoes.

Stacie pulled Jordan along behind her and peered inside too. The window looked into the bathroom, but the couple had left the internal doors wide open, and the group could see right into the bedroom. It was a warm day and they obviously needed no blankets.

Stacie could not move. Not to look at Jill, whose shoulders shook in silent laughter, or to look at Jordan, who didn't even seem to be breathing. She could not take her eyes from the woman whose back was to the window: the smooth sweep of her spine, the curve and jiggle of her pale buttocks, the way her hair bounced and curled on her shoulders as she bucked and twisted and writhed. Stacie's whole body prickled with a strange heat.

Jordan yanked on her arm as he stumbled backward. He looked very nearly sick. "I've never seen that before," he said, voice shaking.

Jill laughed for real. "Well, they looked like they were having a great time. Both of them, laughing and smiling. I sure hope it's like that when I do it."

Stacie checked her Timex. "Check out was forty minutes ago. Why are they still here?"

Jill smirked. "We saw why."

"Let's start at the far cabin. Give them time to finish." Jordan broke into a run.

"Jordan—" Stacie called out, but he was already halfway across the courtyard. She wished she could tell him it was okay, that what they saw didn't matter, that nobody cared. But she wasn't sure she believed it herself.

The girls ran after him, the mop bucket sloshing and jangling across the uneven ground. Jill passed Jordan and leaped onto the cabin's steps, her cheeks not even pink. She took the key out of her pocket and then gave Jordan a quizzical look as he caught up with her. "You really never saw the deed before? Never walked in on your parents or saw it in a movie?"

"My dad's dead," he said. "And my mom won't watch anything rated higher than PG."

"Well," she said, and squeezed his shoulder, "nothing wrong with being a late bloomer."

His face flamed red, but Jill was already opening the door and didn't see.

Stacie took a tentative step toward him. "It's okay," she said in her softest voice.

"It's not okay, and you know it. I'm a fucking freak."

The cabin door popped open with a creak. Jill stepped inside and slapped on the lights.

Stacie's hand found his and twined her fingers through them. "I'm a freak too. So at least you aren't alone."

He pulled his hand away. "What's wrong with the door?" He brushed his fingers over a gouge in the door frame.

Stacie frowned. "Jill? Was the door actually locked when you opened it?"

Jordan tugged on the back of Stacie's shirt. "Wait a second—didn't your mom say no one used Cabin 4 last night so we didn't need to clean it?"

Stacie tried to remember. The French toast special had distracted her from her mother's droning instructions. "Maybe?"

Jill stuck her head out, gasping for air. "You two have got to get in here," she ordered. "You are not going to believe it."

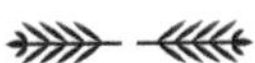

GARY: 2018

The house settled quietly around Gary's shoulders. Zack had finally settled on going to Skyler's for dinner, and Kim was still in some never-ending meeting. A tray of frozen lasagna in the oven gave off wonderful smells.

He could have squeezed in a few more pages, but instead he carried his coffee to the sliding glass doors. Twilight still stained the sky overhead, with darkness creeping up from the woods and over the backyard. If he slid open the doors, he would smell the ocean, its vapors rising over Peshak Head to tantalize the landlocked, and he would hear the trees, their branches softly moving in the breeze. His hand found the catch, urged on by his expectations.

He drew in a long draft of cold air. Ocean, and damp fir needles, and crushed fern, and just a hint of cigarette smoke. His nose crinkled. One of the neighbors must be outside smoking. He glanced left and right, but privacy fences obstructed the other yards too well.

He felt funny just then, his head cold and buzzy like it had gotten when he was kid, like the time his dad was fixing the stairs at the Big House and Gary's head went cold, and just like that he knew his dad would need his second toolbox. Back in the day he had called the sensation "getting one of his feelings." Back in the crazy days.

Gary drew himself together. He was probably just getting a cold or a sinus infection or something. He narrowed his eyes at the back fence.

Perhaps they should put up a more substantial fence along the back property line. He liked their nearly invisible split rail; it allowed the forest to come right up to the back of the house and say hello. But Kim was already talking about a garden. A garden would draw deer like free beer drew frat boys.

The smoke smell grew stronger. Gary squinted into the darkness. Had he seen, for one second, the dull red glow of a cigarette burning out there in the trees? So small and yet so bright, the cherry of a cigarette. He thought of cherry pie filling on cheesecake, and he made a face.

A twig snapped. Gary's grip on the sliding glass door tightened.

Two green-glowing orbs floated over the fence. Grass rustled. A patch of shadow resolved into the silhouette of a deer. Gary felt his heartbeat return to normal. Just a deer. He'd seen them outside just the other morning. Just a deer.

A flash of yellow flame, then. The brilliance of it lit up the underside of a hemlock's branch, then faded too quickly for Gary to make out more details. The red dot of a cigarette glowed again.

"Hey!"

The deer bolted back over the fence.

"You're on private property," Gary shouted. He wasn't actually sure who owned the forest behind the house, but this asshole probably didn't either. "You shouldn't be out there."

In reply, another twig snapped.

Gary put his coffee cup down on the table and stepped out the door. The pebbled surface of the patio jabbed at the bare soles of his feet.

Fuck, he was an idiot. Barefoot and alone with some stranger on the other side of his fence.

The cigarette brightened as its smoker inhaled. A dryness crept over Gary's tongue and made it press against the sides of his teeth. Could someone's tongue spontaneously swell to fill their entire mouth? Was it possible to choke to death on your own tongue for no reason but the fear you'd just picked a fight with a deranged redneck?

He took another step away from the house. The darkness gained a new texture out here, layers of gray on black, the branches of trees half-resolved in the last of the dying light. The deer had vanished completely, but he thought he saw the smoker now, a lean, long figure slouching against the biggest of the hemlocks near the fence line. Gary's leg refused the command to take another step forward.

The end of the cigarette bobbed as if whoever held it between their lips worked their jaw, like a man preparing to say something, or like a ruminant working its cud.

Gary remembered now that the ground dropped off beyond the fence, the process of homebuilding filling in the natural nooks and crannies of rocky country. The top of a man's head should just barely show if they stood on the roots of that big hemlock, but the end of the cigarette showed itself at nearly Gary's eye level. No one in Kingston was that tall.

"It's all right if you're just passing through." He hoped the smoker didn't hear the quaver in his voice. "Just be careful out there."

The cigarette nodded.

Gary turned around, his back prickling at its exposure to the figure in the woods, and hurried back inside his house. The sliding glass door felt like no protection at all as he slid the lock into place.

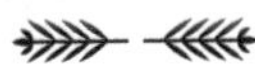

JILL: 1989

The smell filling the cabin—vomit and shit and rotting fish—nearly knocked Jill off her feet. She doubled over for a second, nearly losing her free breakfast (*oh, fuck you, Stacie's mom, I just earned every bite of eggs and potatoes*) before she bolted for the window and threw it open.

She drew in a long gasp of clean air before she turned around.

"You two have got to get in here," Jill ordered. "You are not going to believe it."

Jordan stepped inside the doorway. "Oh my God."

It took Stacie a minute to get the mop bucket up the steps, and when she did, her face twisted in disgust. "What is that smell?"

Jill pointed at the middle of the floor, where a brown mound had been sculpted on a bed of ropey fish guts.

"Is that a birthday candle on top?" Jordan whispered.

"Jesus Christ." Stacie kicked the mop bucket. "Who does this stuff? What the hell is wrong with them?" She yanked a black plastic garbage bag out of the caddy on the side of the mop bucket.

"At least it's on the linoleum," Jill said.

"We'd better check the rest of the cabin," Jordan said. He didn't move, though.

"I'll go." Jill practically pushed him out of the way. She'd been breathing that stink way too long.

"Jordan, can you get a stick or something?" she heard Stacie say behind her, but Jill had already entered the cabin's main room and found herself frozen.

She forced her eyes away from the bloody bed, but there was no place safe to look, not even the ceiling. She'd never have a birthday party again, that was for sure. Just looking at what had been done with that happy birthday banner guaranteed that. She had no idea how someone had threaded a fish between each colorful mylar letter, but it had been messy and they had done a thorough job of it. Her hand moved seemingly without her mind's intent to pull a birthday hat off of the stuffed jackalope on the wall. Her head felt funny, like she was in the middle of one of her special paintings.

"You okay, Jill?"

Something silver and shiny hung from the jackalope's other antler. She picked it up and stared at the little pendant. Something deep inside her told her it was important.

"You okay?" Stacie asked again. She put her hand on Jill's shoulder. "Jill?"

"What is this?" Jill asked, turning around to see Jordan, his brown eyes enormous beneath the shag of his bangs. "It's religious, right?"

He took the pendant and turned it between shaking fingers. "Yeah. It's a St. Christopher medallion. You wear one for luck. You know, because he's the patron saint of travelers. It's like you're keeping him beside you when you travel."

"I'm going to call my mom," Stacie said in a strangled voice. "I think she'll want to call the cops."

She took a step toward the phone and stopped. Jill couldn't blame her. The phone sat on the nightstand beside the bed. The bed with the fish tucked in like a row of sleepy little children, just waiting to be kissed. The bed with the stain, big and red and somehow clumpy, running right down to the floor.

"I can do it," Jill whispered, but Stacie had forced her feet into action.

She picked up the phone. Jill could hear the lodge's desk phone ringing all the way across the room.

"It's not like the movies at all, is it?" Stacie asked.

"Oh, Stacie," Jordan gasped. "Your shoe!"

As one, they looked down to see the syringe sticking out of the rubber toe of her Keds. The color drained out of Stacie's face.

On the other side of the bedroom wall, a toilet flushed.

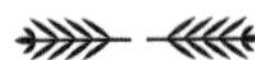

STACIE: 1989

They ran. Stacie kicked the syringe out of her shoe and tried to catch up, but she still held the phone in her hand and its cord yanked her backward. She threw it aside.

"What the hell?"

The man stood in the open bathroom doorway, his pants still undone. A white tank top stretched over the bulge of his belly, a streak of something red-brown striping the side of his chest "What are you doing here?" he growled.

Stacie launched herself toward the kitchen. She skidded on something slick and nearly went down, but kept moving. Her hip bounced off the refrigerator door handle with a bark of pain. The front door stood wide open, Jordan and Jill racing down the steps.

A hand closed on her wrist and yanked her around.

"Help!" she screamed. "Help!"

The man reeled her in. "What happened to Bob?" He gave her shoulders a sharp shake. "What the hell happened?"

"Get away from her!" Jill shrieked.

They had come back for her. Stacie couldn't believe it. Jill and Jordan stood in the doorway looking young and small. Then Jordan took a step forward.

He grabbed the mop from the mop bucket. "Let her go!"

The man pushed Stacie aside. "What did you do with Bob?"

"Stacie?" Mrs. Clinton called from somewhere outside.

"We're in here!" Stacie shouted. "Help!"

Mrs. Clinton burst into the cabin, Nadine on her heels. The two women stared at the chaos, unable to even speak.

Stacie flung herself at her mother. "Mom."

Her mother squeezed her tight. "Somebody start talking."

Nadine pushed past the kids. "Jeremiah, what the hell did you do last night? Weren't you supposed to be in Cabin 3?"

"You know this man?" Mrs. Clinton snapped. She let go of Stacie and pointed at him. "Do you know what kind of trouble you're in? The cleaning fee alone—"

"They killed somebody!" Stacie interjected. "And there are needles in the bedroom."

"We have to call the cops," Jordan said.

"No cops," Nadine said. She scowled at the man. "I thought you were going to stick to pot last night."

"Shit, Nadine." Stacie's mom threw her hands up in the air. "I thought you were done selling that garbage. You know the Kingston cops are on the warpath."

"It's those damn Deer Kings," Nadine growled. "Bunch of damn do-gooders…"

Stacie backed away from her mother. "What about the bed? This guy is a murderer!"

"We didn't kill nobody!" The man shook his head. "Except a whole lot of fish. You kids are taking everything wrong."

Stacie's mom beckoned to the others. "We can't call the cops," she said in a low voice, leading them out into the courtyard. "You kids shouldn't even be here, remember? And if we call the cops, Nadine will get in trouble, and she's my best maid."

Stacie's legs wobbled underneath her. Her French toast spun in her gut. "You didn't see it in the bedroom, Mom. You don't know how freaky it was."

They could hear Nadine scolding the man inside the cabin. A warm breeze blew the loose strands of Stacie's hair around her face. It felt like a perfect early summer day, the kind of day you ought to spend loafing around with your friends, enjoying every last second of freedom and sunshine. It was like an entirely different world than the stinking, filthy cabin they had just walked out of.

"Look, that guy is just a dumb fisherman who got so drunk and high last night that he and his pals forgot which cabin they were supposed to stay in. Nadine and I will sort him out." Her lips tightened. "Although I wonder just where he got the shit that messed him up so badly. Nadine's pot wouldn't do that."

Jill caught Stacie's eye. They both had a good idea who might have sold him those drugs.

CHAPTER FOURTEEN

GARY: 2018

NOTHING EVENTFUL EVER happened Thursdays at the library. The Kingston Garden Club met in the conference room; Linda led toddler book time; and Shawn had the day off. Neither the copier nor the two public computers needed repair, as if Wednesday had used up all their ailments and irritations. None of Gary's favorite regulars came on Thursdays, and of the true irritants, only Mrs. Brickle, the former librarian at the elementary school, stopped in on Thursday morning. Today she didn't even complain as she checked out her stack of Sue Grafton novels. He could only hope the rest of the series' alphabet would keep her as content.

It would have been the perfect day if he hadn't promised Jim Burns he'd stop by the historical society. As he unlocked the Camry's door, Gary wished he could grumble to himself like a hermit in one of his novels. The whole John King biography project felt like a waste of time. Everyone in Kingston knew his story. No archaeologist or historian had dug up new information about the man that would cast his life in new light. King had come to the Oregon coast, set up a general store, and lived in the woods until a bunch of idiots decided to build their houses around his shack. No drama, no gravitas.

He passed the bakery, resisting a stop only by great willpower, and headed up the little knoll where King's house sat. The original town of Kingston had sat directly on the banks of the Peshak River—King's grocery store had been built just a few feet away from the site of the Landing Restaurant. But King had the prescience to build his house up the hill from all that. When the flood of 1903 wiped out most of Old Town, he took in half the town until new houses could be built.

Gary shook his head as he pulled into one of the museum's four parking spaces. He had apparently retained a great deal more from that field trip than he'd thought he had.

Jim Burns had the door open before Gary was even out of the car. Gary paused a moment to find the notebook he'd stashed under the front seat and turned back to Burns half-prancing on the front step. The guy must really love his job.

"Come in, come in! We're closed to the public on Thursday afternoons, so it'll just be you and me. A private tour, so to speak."

Gary craned his head to take in the totality of the old Victorian. An attempt had been made to paint it in period colors, a surprising combination of green, burgundy, and mustard yellow, but cracks showed in the woodwork over the door, and the window frames flaked. "Looks like she could use a little love."

Something like a growl bubbled up in Burns' throat. "The damn Plymouth Historical Society!"

Gary raised an eyebrow. It felt awkward and affected, but he left it up a long moment to see if the gesture would elicit more information.

It worked. "They got the big grant from the Southern Oregon Institute—great group, helps fund a lot of good programs. Just stole it right out from under us. Claimed they needed to 'make seismic upgrades' to Ezra Watkins' house. Seismic upgrades! If there's an earthquake, that whole town is going down in a tsunami."

Burns stomped inside the museum. Mothballs and must assaulted Gary's nose.

"Who's Ezra Watkins?" The name sounded oddly familiar.

"The founder of Plymouth." Burns jabbed a finger at a sepia-toned photo. "He and John King came to the coast together. They built the original store on the Peshak, and then they had some kind of falling out. Watkins left and started a new store up in Plymouth."

Gary squinted at the two men, both magnificently bearded and dressed in dark suits. They looked alike as brothers, at least in the low quality of the ancient photo. "And the people of Kingston and Plymouth have hated each other ever since."

"Damn straight." Burns grinned. "Hey, you want a cup of coffee? I was about to start a fresh pot."

Gary's bad mood fizzled away. "That would be great."

"I might have cookies too." Burns pointed at a stack of photo albums sitting on a table. "I set those out for you, if you want to take a look at them while I'm in the kitchen."

"Great." Gary took a few steps toward the table and paused. The room must have been King's living room back in his lifetime. A fireplace sat dark and quiet beneath a simple mantle, and the door opened onto a smaller room with a few pieces of more ornate furniture. Attempts had been made to dress up the place, but it didn't take an architecture degree to see that the house had started out as a one-room cabin. The stairs and other rooms had the same half-thought-out quality as the gingerbread tacked up around the doors and windows.

He took a few steps into the parlor. King must have built this after he found a wife. The floor sloped to the left, so that Gary had to imagine every loose coin and wheeled toy the family had ever owned had rolled under the small, battered piano. A photo hung over it of a group of people. A middle-aged King stood in the center, arms outstretched, a beatific smile beneath his curled mustache. Prosperity had done him good.

A banner stretched behind King, and Gary tried to make it out. "Kingston's…Own." He stepped closer, his breath fogging the corner of the glass. One of the other men in the back carried a flag whose dark trim and strange text looked vaguely familiar.

"Do you play piano?" Burns called.

"I can barely play the radio." Gary glanced over his shoulder. Burns held a tray laden with creamer, sugar packets, and a bowl of chocolate-striped cookies. "What's this photo about?"

Burns put down the tray and patted the table beside it. "Oh, that's the first meeting of the Deer Kings! Good group—I was a member when I first moved to town. We used to organize beach clean-ups, fundraisers, things like that. Too bad it died out when the lumber mill closed."

"Why did it die out?" Gary took a seat in front of the cookies.

"I guess too many of its members moved away or died of old age and bad luck." Burns paused, then shook a finger. "That reminds me." He went to the bookshelf behind them and hunkered down, his knees popping like corn. "Yeah. That's what I thought." He groaned a little as he got back up, a heavy binder in his arms. He sat down beside Gary and reverently turned the pages.

"There." He pushed the tray away and slid the binder in front of Gary. "Have a look."

The 8x10 photo had been staged very closely to the one over King's piano: a big group of people, some holding flags, two stretching out the "Kingston's Own" banner between them. Though in color, the tones had the muted quality of images from the 1960s, and the fashions supported the hypothesis. Burns tapped a figure on the right, a man whose luxurious black mustache Gary had only seen a few times but remembered all too well. "Isn't that your grandpa?"

Gary took off his glasses and gave them an unnecessary polishing. “Yes. My dad’s dad. I had no idea he’d been involved with the Deer Kings.” He forced himself to take a deep breath and study the picture as if this fact hadn’t rattled him. His eyes paused on the flag carrier on the far left. They’d done a far better job carrying the thing than anyone else had. It hung down straight and smooth with no wrinkles to obscure the symbol embroidered in the middle.

He had seen it before, of course.

Coach Dusseldorf wore it on a pendant around his neck—and so did Kim. He had no idea why the booster club was using the Deer Kings’ old symbol, but it gave him the creeps.

Jim turned the page. “Oh, oops. I thought this was going to be a later Deer Kings photo. Guess not.”

Gary leaned in closer to get a better view and then pushed himself back in his seat. “What the hell is that a picture of?”

He couldn’t take his eyes off the photo of the fisherman posed beside an open net on a dock, two long, pale, bloated figures twisted together in a heap of seaweed and shells. One stared up at the camera with dark, empty sockets.

Jim made a face. “Two teenage boys that got brought up in a fishing net. They’d been tied together, their feet weighted. No one ever solved their murder.”

“Shit. When was that?”

“1922.” He turned the page. A train engine lay on its side, a load of logs spilling out across the ground.

Gary thought he could just make out the shape a human hand sticking out from beneath one of the logs.

“A lot of bad shit has happened here in this town, hasn’t it?” he asked.

Jim reached for another cookie. “Bad things happen everywhere,” he said. “We’re just lucky that in Kingston, a handful of people—people like John King—have stepped up to help their community when those bad things happen.”

His words should have comforted Gary, but they didn’t.

GARY: 1989

Gary handed Jill a bag of caramel corn. "Hey, you'll feel better if you eat this."

Behind them, an RV honked as a group of older high school students crossed the street without looking. Someone on the Tilt-a-Whirl screamed. A seagull landed at Gary's feet, watching the caramel corn—freshly popped from an enterprising stand at the edge of the parking lot—in case a kernel dropped.

She made a sick face. "How can I eat after what I saw in that cabin?"

"That was two days ago, and you sucked down a bowl of Rice Krispies just fine this morning." He pushed the caramel corn closer to her nose. "It's your favorite."

She grabbed a handful. "Yeah." She bumped his shoulder with her own. "Thanks."

They crunched together quietly for a moment, watching the boats pulling in and out of the Elk Harbor marina while the noise of Beachfest rattled and squawked behind them. Gary checked his watch. They still had a few minutes before the others were supposed to join them here on the edge of Elk Harbor's biggest day.

He had always loved Elk Harbor. While not *technically* part of Kingston, the little beach hamlet lay just on the other side of Peshak Head, and all the kids went to the Kingston schools. Still, Elk Harbor almost felt like another world. You could never smell the paper mill here by the water, and there were tourists nearly year-round, eager for whale watching and fishing trips or watching the view from the lighthouse. And, of course, every June there was Beachfest, all noise and fried foods and prizes to win. It made Kingston's stupid Founders' Day Weekend look like a trip to church.

"Hey, nerds." David rapped his knuckles on the back of their bench. "See any hot chicks out there?"

Jill threw a piece of popcorn at him. "You are such a pig."

He gave her a slow smile, and she blushed. Gary jumped to his feet, certain he could not watch his sister flirt with anyone, let alone someone who was sort of a friend.

"You ready to take over Elk Harbor?" He raised his hand for a high five.

David slapped it hard enough to make the skin sting. "I was born ready," he rasped in a fake-sounding voice. Gary thought it might have been a movie quote.

A brown station wagon pulled up beside them, and Stacie and Jordan scrambled out of the back seat. A wooden cross swung from the rearview mirror. Jordan waved at the round woman in the front seat and then hurried to catch up with Stacie. He had a camera slung over one shoulder.

"My mom sent me with an extra three bucks in case I run into any 'Christian fundraisers.' I don't think she really understands what Beachfest is," he said.

Stacie smiled from Jill to David and then back. "Hey."

"Hey," Jill said.

"So, did you all come together, or…" Stacie trailed off.

"Nah, I spent the night at a buddy's," David said. When they all looked at him, he shrugged. "One of those football guys I met the other day. His folks just got an above-ground pool."

"Enough talk." Gary smashed the empty caramel corn bag with a dramatic crunch. "Are we here to chit-chat or are we here to *Beachfest*?"

Jill leaped off the bench, grinning. "Hell yeah."

"Hang on!" Jordan raised his camera. "I want a picture of all of you."

They squeezed together, Gary with his arm around Stacie, Jill and David squashing in behind them. At the last second a woman walked by and asked Jordan if he wanted to be in the picture, too, and so they all managed to fit themselves together, somehow not giggling as the woman directed them to move in one direction or another and to say "fuzzy pickles." The click of the camera sounded improbably loud when she finally pushed the shutter.

Then they prowled through the stalls and the booths, shedding their hard-earned cash like jackets on a warm spring day. Nachos demanded tribute, elephant ears doubly so. Jill talked Stacie into getting their faces painted, and the boys waited for them outside the cramped and glittering tent, half-bored and half-entranced by the giggling inside.

David turned around first. "Hey, a dunk tank."

A tall man with the broad shoulders and narrow middle of a serious athlete held a megaphone to his face. "Step on up, support your local community! Dunk the Deer!"

Jordan elbowed Gary in the ribs. "That's Coach Dusseldorf."

The sun blazed off the man's polished bald pate. It took Gary a second to realize who Jordan meant.

"The football coach?"

Even David looked at him in surprise. "Who else?"

Gary shrugged. Jordan pulled three singles out of his back pocket. "Dunking the deer mascot sounds like a pretty Christian way to kill some time."

Gary glanced over his shoulder. Jill was still hunched over the book of designs. Whatever she was saying, the face painter looked pretty interested.

"Sounds great."

Jordan went first. Dusseldorf took his single and gave him three softballs. Whoever sat in the dunk tank wore a pair of knee-length swim trunks in a purple-and-black Hawaiian print. Their face was obscured, not by the Kingston Buck's fuzzy mascot's head, but a ski mask someone had sewn deerish features onto. The stuffed felt antlers sagged pathetically.

Jordan's first throw missed. Dusseldorf said nothing.

His second throw connected, but without enough force to launch the hapless buck into the tank.

Jordan's face contracted, his eyes tightening into serious little slits, his lips nearly vanishing. The ball shot out of his hand and hit the side of the tank hard enough to make the man inside jerk.

"Tough break, kid." Dusseldorf nodded at David. "You next?"

David paid and took the balls. He studied the man-deer inside the dunk tank, smiling the same smug smile he'd given Jill just moments ago. Then he lobbed the first ball. It thwacked the target on its bull's eye and sent the deer into the drink.

Dusseldorf laughed. "Oh, Wally, that was a good one!"

The man in the deer mask spluttered and climbed back onto his perch. "Nice shot!"

David threw the next ball and launched poor Wally back into the tank. David was grinning now, his teeth white and square in his tanned face. He could barely hold still as Wally, silent now, got back into his seat.

Whack!

The ball hit the target so hard the metal disk hit the back wall and leaped back into place. Wally made a small, furious sound Gary just caught above the enormous splash of his landing.

"Yes!" David made a victory fist. "That was awesome!"

"That was something else, all right." Coach Dusseldorf looked David from head to toe. "You starting at KHS in the fall?"

David went straight and yet somehow small. "Yes, sir."

"You ever think about trying out for the football team?"

David shook his head.

"You ought to." The coach pulled a package of Trident from his pocket and popped a stick in his mouth. "Arm like that? We'd be idiots not to put you on the team."

"Thank you!"

Jill appeared behind Jordan. "Hey, guys! Did you dunk the deer?"

Everyone turned to look at her—David, Coach Dusseldorf, even

Wally the man-deer. She wore white jeans and a black crop top, and now a series of red and gold firework sprays winked on her cheek. They looked pretty and wild, just like her. David couldn't even blink, he was staring so hard. But it was the look on the men's face that made Gary rushed forward and grab Jill's hand.

"I've got to have another elephant ear. Come on!"

"Hey," Jordan called, "wait up!"

"Slow down!" David bellowed.

They nearly collided with Stacie as she came out of the face-painting tent, her cheek a rainbow of tiny butterflies. "Where to now?"

"What was that all about?" Jill asked.

Gary just shook his head. He couldn't tell her what he had seen on the men's faces. *Men were pigs*. Where had he heard that? He had never wondered what it really meant, not until this very moment. Pigs were always hungry, weren't they? And they'd do anything to get to something they wanted to eat.

They walked back toward the elephant ear stand, although of course Gary didn't really want one. The smell of hot grease made his stomach turn over.

A cool hand squeezed his neck, and he looked behind him. Jordan didn't smile or say anything. He just nodded, and Gary knew he understood.

They got in line for elephant ears. Gary wished he could just go to the lake, dive into the water, and block out humanity entirely.

A baby gave a little squawk, pulling Gary back to Beachfest and the elephant ear stand. Stacie was counting her change to make sure she had enough for one. David was telling Jill a joke. And the man in front of them, who had just picked up three paper trays of elephant ears, stooped beside the still-squawking baby and pulled off a bit of sugary dough. "Hey, baby bundle," he cooed. "You're gonna love this." He popped the treat into the baby's mouth, laughing like any normal, happy dad, except he was Vincent Vernor.

"Aww, shit," David whispered. "Let's get out of here."

But Vincent Vernor had already stood up and turned around. His face had shifted from that softer-faced, happy man to something hard.

"It's the brat brigade." Vincent laughed, but not happily. "I feel like I can't go anywhere without running into you little shits."

He balanced the elephant ears on top of the red stroller. The woman with him—his wife, Gary realized, although she looked different in real clothes—rolled her eyes. Her brown hair frizzed around her pimple-speckled face, and her lipstick had smeared at the corners.

The baby made an unhappy noise. The woman picked up an elephant ear. "I only met the one of them." Her eyes slid down Gary's face like egg white running off a freshly egged house. "He ain't so bad."

Vincent slipped out from behind the stroller and took a swaggering sidestep toward the girls. His pointer finger just brushed Jill's cheek. "That's awfully pretty."

"Leave her alone," Gary said. He felt Jordan's hand close on his upper arm.

Vincent's eyes, the color of some National Geographic glacier shoot, rolled toward him. "Such a tough guy." He looked back at Jill. "Little bird told me you're quite the babysitter."

Stacie took a step closer to Jill, who could only nod.

Vincent smiled. "Old lady and I got an anniversary coming up next Wednesday. Sure could use a babysitter."

"Oh, Vinnie." His wife giggled. "You big romantic." She pushed forward, her stroller knocking Gary back a step, pressing herself into Vincent's back. "My man knows how to treat me right," she cooed, lips just a fraction of an inch from his ear.

"Don't you have that thing," Stacie started, but Jill was already saying, "Yeah, I guess I could babysit. I mean, as long as I'm home by 11."

Vincent laughed. "'Cause it's a school night, right?"

David shifted around to Jill's side and put his arm possessively around her waist. "Something like that."

Vincent wagged a finger. "Tsk, tsk." He laughed again. "I'll see you, Fireworks. Wednesday at 6."

He grabbed the handles of the stroller and shoved it forward. The baby gave a little shriek and kicked out its leg. Its pink foot pushed out from the blanket, attached to a leg so chubby and dimpled it looked like it belonged in a baby food ad. Minus the yellow bruises on the calf, of course.

CHAPTER FIFTEEN

GARY: 2018

GARY WAVED BACK at Jim Burns, happily waving goodbye from the front door of John King's makeshift Victorian as Gary shut the car door. He started up the engine and reached for the mp3 player. Soundgarden roared soothingly over him. He'd made it through the rest of the meeting and even managed to make some good notes, but most of his brain had shunted onto a separate track the moment he'd seen that photo of his grandfather.

Grandpa Sheldon hadn't been a bad man, not really. But there'd been a weird, dark intensity to the man that made a kid want to keep well clear of him. Though they must have visited half a dozen times, he could only remember sitting on the floor of his grandfather's trailer house, huddled over his toy trucks in the one patch of light the cracked yellow blinds let in. Had they never eaten dinner there? The old man had died on Gary's first day of second grade. He had to skip Tommy Beaumont's birthday party to go to the funeral.

Gary had never asked his dad why his relationship with his father was so lousy—Gary had never gotten a chance to think about it. Kids rarely spent much energy reflecting on family dynamics. He had two grandparents who loved him and two who died without ever getting to know him, and as a kid, that had been that.

He turned down Soundgarden and glanced over his shoulder. If he sat here wondering about his family, Burns was going to invite him back in for more of his terrible coffee, and they'd already polished off the last of the cookies.

A blue car blocked the parking lot's driveway. Gary pulled out of his parking spot a little, trying to see if anyone was inside the damn thing. A bulky shape sat in the driver's seat.

He tapped the horn in a little trill. Friendly-ish. The car didn't move.

Maybe the driver was really focused on their phone. Gary eased out of the parking spot and turned the car around. The nose of the Camry nearly brushed the other car's passenger door. Gary rolled down the window and leaned out.

"Hey, can you move?"

The driver—a woman, he could see now, middle-aged and surprisingly tall; a big woman who had bulked up in size as she'd bulked up in years—stared back at him. He couldn't read her expression through the glass.

"I'm trying to get out of here, and—"

Her engine revved angrily and the car lurched forward. She didn't even stop at the next intersection, but turned sharply onto 5th Street and cut away south.

Gary shook his head. He wanted to race after her so he could get right up beside her window and flip her off, but he restrained himself. He pulled out of the driveway and drove home sedately, following every traffic rule. He tried not to think about car accidents. He'd seen enough of them for one life.

A white pickup truck sat in front of his house. He parked beside it and then realized his grandmother stood on his front porch, a cardboard box under her arm.

She was a round dumpling of a woman, but her plumpness was the beginning and the end of her grandmotherly attributes. Grandpa gave her the same crisp flat-top haircut she gave him, and she bought all their clothes at the feed store. Grandpa had switched over to overalls at some point when doing up a belt started feeling tedious, but Grandma still wore the same uniform of orange suspenders and plaid shirt that she'd always sported. At some point, she'd gotten the top of her ear pierced, possibly due to a fishing accident, and a silver hoop gleamed against her salt-and-pepper hair. The effect was more piratical than feminine.

He jumped out of the car. "Grams? What are you doing here?"

"Visiting you, you asshole. Can I come inside and pee before I tan your hide?"

He opened his door and pointed her toward the bathroom. "Want some coffee?" he shouted, heading into the kitchen. He brought out the decaf and started measuring out grounds and water.

She appeared in the doorway, drying her palms on her jeans. "You know me too well." She made a circuit of the living room and kitchen. "Not bad. Looks like you're still settling in, though. Maybe that's why you haven't bothered telling me you moved to town."

"I'm sorry, Grams." He looked for an excuse and discarded one after another. "I wanted to tell you, but…"

"Sure." Her face softened a little. "I guess it's probably not easy, moving here. Not after your folks."

"Yeah. And Kim—God, it's crazy. She's in meetings almost every night."

Grams opened a cupboard, then another, and brought out a box of crackers. "She's an important lady these days." She put a cracker in her mouth and held out the box to Gary.

He waved it away. "So I'm learning." He got out mugs. "Where's Gramps?"

"Doctor's office. They're all worried about his cholesterol, so he has to come in once a month for monitoring." She didn't actually make finger quotes around the word "monitoring," but the tone of her voice implied them. "There's no history of heart disease in his entire family. Nobody ever had any of that nonsense—heart disease, diabetes, cancer." She snorted.

"Except me," Gary reminded her.

"Yeah, but yours doesn't count. Spontaneous remission and all."

"I guess." He leaned over and kissed her cheek. She smelled like dish soap and Vaseline.

Grams put down her coffee mug. "I brought you something." She walked out of the kitchen and returned in a moment with the cardboard box. She held it out to him. The flaps had water stains, and the mailing label was for a taxidermy supply place.

He held it for a moment. "What is it?"

"Bunch of your parents' shit. Must have gotten mixed up with your grandpa's work supplies or something. Anyway, I thought you kids might like it. Most of their things got donated while you two were at Tina and Jim's."

"I can't imagine what's in here." He worked loose the flaps. Bright colors winked up at him—a familiar pattern of lurid pinks and purples. "Grandma Sheldon's painting," he said. He had almost forgotten it. The black trawler creeping out to sea looked far spookier than it had in his childhood.

"Better in your house than mine." She knocked back the last of the coffee in her mug. "Well, got to go pick up your grandpa. Thanks for the coffee."

"Thanks for coming by." He wanted to hug her, but the kiss had probably been enough touchy-feely business for her for one day. "I'm sorry I didn't tell you I'd come to town earlier. I don't know. I guess maybe I wasn't sure we'd stick around."

"I wouldn't be surprised if you didn't. And that's okay. This town—well, I'm glad I don't live here." She pounded his shoulder. "I love you, kid." She found her own way outside and didn't bother waving as she got into the truck. Gary watched her drive away.

Then he took the painting out of the box. The colors looked brighter and fiercer and eerier than they had even just a minute ago. Maybe he would send it to Jill.

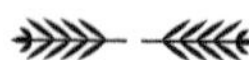

STACIE: 1989

Stacie lay on Jill's bed, their shoulders just touching, their hands squeezed together just tightly enough. The only lights were the strand of Christmas lights Jill had strung above her nightstand. The room still smelled powerfully of nail polish, even though the window was open as far as it went. Outside, the frogs sounded close enough to touch, and every now and then they heard the rustle of leaves or the soft *snick* of a twig as some small creature moved through the brush behind the house. The tiny stream gurgled.

"I can't believe you told that creep you'd babysit for him."

The bedspread rustled beneath Jill as she shifted a little. "I like babies."

"Yeah, but he's probably a drug dealer." Stacie shuddered. "What if his house is like the cabin? Remember that needle that stuck in my shoe? What if that had gone all the way through? I'd probably be addicted to heroin right now."

Jill squeezed her hand tighter. They'd had health class that spring, so Stacie knew exactly what had gone through Jill's brain when she saw that needle sticking out of Stacie's shoe—the same thing that had gone through Stacie's, and it didn't have anything to do with being a drug addict.

Stacie let go of Jill's hand. Tears prickled the edges of her eyelids. She was thinking about health class too. She was one of those dirty, awful people that was going to get AIDS. Not from that stupid needle—although for a second she had imagined it jabbing all the way through her shoe and her sock and into her actual skin—but because of who she was and how weird she was. She shouldn't even be in Jill's house. She should be at home, not touching her best friend's skin and thinking how soft it was.

"Hey," someone whispered, and it wasn't Jill.

Jill got up on her knees. "Wh-who's out there?"

"Me!"

Stacie recognized Jordan's voice. She stood on the bed to see him outside. Jill's window was high enough from the ground the top of his head barely cleared the windowsill. "Grab my hand. And Jill's."

Jill leaned out the window and grabbed Jordan's hand too. They hoisted him up, his shoes scraping up the side of the asphalt-shingled wall. He tumbled over the bottom of the window and knocked them all over in a heap.

Stacie couldn't help giggling, and after a second, Jill joined in.

"I hope my parents didn't hear anything," Jill whispered.

"The way your dad snores?" Stacie asked, and giggled harder.

Jordan's hand closed on her ankle. He was laughing too. It was nice to just lie here like this, laughing, arms and legs all mixed up. It wasn't weird like it had been just a minute ago with Jill. It was cozy. Friendly.

Finally Jordan rolled away and kicked off his shoes. He stretched sideways across the bottom of the bed, looking up at the Patrick Swayze poster Jill had taped up over the paneled ceiling. "My mom went nuts tonight."

Stacie pushed herself up on her elbow. "What do you mean?"

"She had a bad day at work. There's some new guy, I guess. He keeps hassling her about money stuff. I don't know the details." He frowned up at Patrick Swayze, whose nipple showed where his overalls had come undone. "She described him a little, so I have a bad feeling I know who he is."

Jill sat up. "It's Vincent Vernor, isn't it?"

He nodded.

Stacie scooted down so she could reach Jordan's hand. "I don't like it. How is he tangled up in everyone's life? How is he everywhere?"

"What do you mean?" Jill asked.

That's when Stacie remembered she hadn't told Jill. It was the first time she hadn't told Jill about something in her life, and it made her stomach turn over.

"My mom…"

But she couldn't finish. She didn't know why it was easy to tell Jordan what had happened with her mom and Vincent Vernor and the disgusting way her mom had fawned over him. But Jill—Jill had known her mom for years. Had spent the night at their house. Had come to the birthday parties her mom threw for Stacie at the lodge. Had sometimes even called Stacie's mom *Mom*.

"Stacie's mom let him sleep over at their place," Jordan said. "It creeped Stacie out, and I ran into her right afterward, so she told me. She probably just wanted to forget it, right, Stace?"

Jill was shaking her head. "Like he slept on your couch or he slept with your mom? Which is it, Stacie?"

Jordan sat up. "Hey, let's talk about something else." He reached for Jill's hands. "I love your fingernails. Most people just use one color, but you always do something fun."

She must have known he was changing the subject, but she played along. "Thanks."

He made an impish face. "Could you paint my nails like yours?"

She frowned. "Your nails? But you're a boy."

He shrugged. "Why does that matter?"

Stacie rubbed her hand down the curved knobs of his spine. "Because boys who do girl stuff get their asses kicked."

The fun flashed out of his face. Just for a second. And then he forced it back into place. "Toenails, maybe."

"Absolutely," Jill said.

And while she went to get the basket of nail things, Stacie gave Jordan a hug. Up close she could see the dried white lines of tears on his cheeks. Whatever his mom had said or done, it had been bad. Very bad.

Jill leaped onto the bed. "You guys are my best friends," she said. "I mean, I barely know you, Jordan, but you two, Gary, and David—you're not like anybody else I know. I'm going to make you a promise, right here and right now." She held up an emery board with all the seriousness of a Boy Scout making his oath. "I promise that if any of you ever need me, I'll do anything, go anywhere, to be there for you."

Jordan held out his hand, flat as a pancake. "Ditto."

She looked at it for a second, and then slapped her palm down on top of his.

Stacie brought hers down on Jill's. "Double ditto."

They were all smiling.

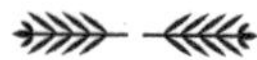

GARY: 2018

Gary had nearly forgotten that tonight Zack's JV team had their first home game. As the day's user of the sole car, he was responsible for acquiring dinner and rounding up gear and making sure he and Zack met Kim at the high school with enough time to bolt their food and let Zack get dressed in her office. Gary had brought a book, but Kim made him take it back to the car. In the last few minutes of the second quarter, a school board member pulled her away for some serious-looking discussion down by the cheerleaders (the JV cheerleading squad looking even more nervous and uncomfortable than the football players), and he pulled his phone from his pocket.

Hey, Jilly Bean. How are things? he typed.

A boy in Myrtle Point's white attempted an interception, skidded on the wet grass, and fell on his butt. Zack leaped over him and kept running. Gary couldn't help whooping. The entire crowd, such as a JV game commanded, cheered along with him. He could almost understand why parents got so worked up about sports.

"Go Big Red!" the woman beside him shrieked.

His phone buzzed. *Better now that work is over.*

Paint anything today? he typed.

At the last moment, a short boy in white slammed into Zack. Zack dropped the ball. The Myrtle Pointer stooped to grab it and sent it flying backward. A buzzer went off, and everyone in the stands, even Myrtle Point's side, groaned. Kingston was crushing the competition 13 to 0, and it was now halftime. The loudspeakers crackled as the announcer switched on the oldies station, and the people around Gary began getting out of their seats. Games like this demanded more snacks.

Kim remained in intense discussion, so he joined the masses in getting to his feet. He thought the bolts in the bleachers may have worked through his butt muscles and dug into the bones. Maybe the booster club was selling seat cushions again. It would be a better use of ten bucks than a tub of waxy nachos and a few gallons of soda.

It took him a minute or two to find the booster club's booth, as it had moved away from the gates to take better advantage of overflow from the concession stand. He picked up two seat cushions—helpfully emblazoned with the dates of every home game for the varsity football team—and got in line to check out. A woman had questions about the washing instructions on the sweatshirts. A man couldn't decide between a bumper sticker and a vinyl window cling. The woman with the cash box talked him into buying both.

A tall man swapped places with the up-selling volunteer, who hurried to refold and neaten the sweatshirts. Gary was nearly up at bat, and Jill still hadn't texted him back. He tapped out a quick series of goofy emojis and then glanced up at the table. The man at the register raised a shark fin-shaped eyebrow.

"Coach Dusseldorf. Good to see you again."

The old man gave a gravelly laugh. "Haven't been a coach in five years, Gary. You can call me Bob."

"Bob." Gary tried to smile, but the word had deformed his face. He couldn't imagine calling Dusseldorf by his first name even in the apocalypse.

Dusseldorf tapped something on the iPad in front of him. "Those are good seat cushions. Well worth the ten bucks." He nodded at the screen. "And we're sure selling more of them since we started taking plastic."

Gary handed him his debit card. "Does anybody carry cash these days?"

"I sure as hell don't." Dusseldorf spun the tablet around so Gary could sign the receipt. "Hey, have you considered joining the booster club?"

"Hadn't thought about it much."

"Your folks were both members. Good people, your mom and dad. Still think about them." The old man held Gary's eyes as if trying to read his soul through his pupils. Gary couldn't help wondering what Dusseldorf saw.

"I guess I'll have to check out a meeting."

"Last Tuesday of every month. We meet at the Dunes Diner, in the banquet room."

A man pushed forward, a key chain in hand. "How much is this?"

Gary stepped out the way. The seat cushions felt sticky and cold in his hands. He walked back to his seat slowly. He'd never known his parents were part of the booster club. Hadn't the Deer Kings kept them busy enough?

The cheerleaders bounded out onto the field, stacking themselves into a wobbly pyramid as he took his seat. Kim came up the stairs, frowning. She didn't seem to see the girls, and she forgot to cheer as the team came back to the bench. Gary reached out and squeezed her hand. She squeezed back hard.

The oldies station crackled off. "And now for a special message from Coach Washburn!"

David strode out to stand beside the cheerleaders, his hand raised in benevolent greeting. A spotlight lit him up like a visiting dignitary.

"Hello, my fellow Kingstonians!"

He waited for the cheering to die down.

"And, of course, our visitors from Myrtle Point." Someone behind Gary snorted. "Thank you all so much for coming out tonight. JV games don't get the turnout the varsity team gets, but you all know how important the junior varsity really is. These boys are Kingston's future. So keep playing hard, boys. I've got my eye on you—especially you, Hunter Kane!" He gave a hearty laugh. "Keep on cheering, folks. And don't forget the good people down at the booster club, raising funds to keep sports great in our schools."

The crowd roared in approval.

"Thank you! Thank you! Now let's play football!"

"Is that normal?" Gary whispered to Kim. She waved a hand to shush him.

A cheerleader turned a flip and the announcer blasted a recording of the school theme song. Gary's pocket buzzed.

I just finished a new painting. I'm kind of scared of it.

He waited a second, searching for the words to comfort his sister. Ever since his folks had died, he'd struggled to talk to her about her work. When they were kids, it was different. It was easy to imagine she was really painting the future. But if she was really upset, she certainly wouldn't appreciate him saying that anything scary in her artwork was the product of her own interpretation. Logical or not, he couldn't bring himself to hurt her.

He took his time typing a response. *It's probably nothing to really worry about. Who knows what your brain is picking up? You'll figure it out soon enough.*

He caught a glimpse of Zack, sitting on the bench now, his helmet between his feet, shifting around to look for Gary and Kim. He waved. Zack waved back, his grin bigger than Gary had possibly ever seen it. The kid seemed to really like football, god damn it. Stupid parties. Stupid Skyler.

His phone buzzed again. He brought up Jill's response: *That's what I'm worried about.*

The words seemed designed to make him uncomfortable. Kim began applauding and he forced his hands together. Whatever had happened on the field, he'd missed it. He had a feeling he'd missed something in his sister's texts too.

CHAPTER SIXTEEN

JILL: 1989

SHE HESITATED ON the edge of the driveway, looking across the grassy field that must have once been the Big House's yard. Someone had planted these two holly trees to frame what had been intended as a path; someone had picked out the floppy rose bush with the yellow flowers and the black-speckled leaves. Once the Big House had been a real home, a nice one even, that someone had tended and cared for and loved.

It had been a rental for a long time, though, and even though her parents wouldn't say a word against the Bermans, Jill knew they were as lazy as landlords could come. She'd only been four or five when they made the move, but she could remember vividly the first day her parents had shown them the cottage. Sometimes she had nightmares about walking through the small dark house and seeing it all over again: the thin layer of mud filling the bottom of the bathtub, the patch of mushrooms blooming from the carpet of what was now Gary's bedroom, the drawer in the kitchen secreting a nest of mummified baby mice. She still dreamed of those tiny little nubs of bone and gray skin, the crystalline wrapper of their eyelids bulging over the black seeds of their infant eyes.

No, anything nice about the Big House or its cottage was the product of her parents' efforts. Hadn't Gary and her dad just gone over to fix the banister at the Big House the last week of school? It wasn't like a banister was some sort of luxury addition to a house. Somebody could have gotten killed going up and down those stairs.

She picked up the tote bag filled with babysitting supplies. She could have been that somebody. . When the Donderos lived in the Big House, she'd babysat all the time. Three-year-old Lisa had been a dream to sit for, and Mrs. Dondero usually paid well. Once Jill had traded a night of babysitting for a box of oil paints, but that had been even better than the usual ten-dollar bill. Mrs. Dondero had been a real kindred spirit. She was the one who told Jill to cut her hair short and enjoy the lightness of her own skin. Jill still wasn't certain what that last part meant, but she missed Mrs. Dondero and her hippie-ish ways.

No one could possibly miss this new woman. Jill had only seen her at Beachfest, but that was more than enough to know Mrs. Vernor was in no way, shape, or form likable. For one thing, she'd married Vincent.

Jill waded through the long grass and up to the front door. She knocked firmly and waited.

"Mrs. Vernor?" she knocked again, harder. She thought she heard music playing, very faintly, from up on the second floor.

With a sigh, she leaned against the wall, looking out at the Big House's enormous orchard. No one had tended the trees in a very long time, and they looked it. One had fallen over sometime that winter and lay miserably on its side, its branches black claws against the weeds. Jill's mom would sometimes walk out and stand at the orchard fence and just shake her head. She hadn't been able to convince the Donderos to let her bring it back to life like she had their own patch of fruit trees. She would certainly never get the Vernors to do anything with them.

The front door gave a groan. Jill spun around to see the frizzy-haired woman, a tiny trickle of blood running out of a sore on her chin.

"Mrs. Vernor? I'm Jill, from next door. Your husband asked me to babysit?"

The woman gave a whoop of laughter. "Husband! That's a good one. We ain't married." She pulled out a packet of cigarettes. "You want one?"

Jill shook her head. "But Mr. Vernor said it was your anniversary."

"Sure. We shacked up two years ago. Don't mean the government gotta know anything about it." The woman belatedly remembered that Jill wanted in, and pulled the door open. "Get your scrawny ass in here."

"Okay." Jill stepped inside. Despite the brightness of the June evening, shadows filled the front room. Jill could barely make out a battered sofa and a coffee table littered with empty pop cans. Jill turned back to the woman. "If you're not Mrs. Vernor, what should I call you?"

She whooped again. "Ain't you a little cutie! Just call me Gwen. Everybody does." She clapped Jill on the shoulder hard enough to buckle Jill's knees. "Honey!" Gwen bellowed. "Babysitter's here! Shake a leg, won't ya?"

Gwen slapped a switch on the wall and a pair of sconces over the fireplace obliged her with a spill of thin light. It refused to clear the gloom in the corners of the room. Gwen leaned closer to the mirror above the mantle. "Damn, I look a fright."

She pulled a tube of lipstick from a pocket and slicked some on. The pink shade did not complement her skin. She kissed the mirror with a smack. "Better, right?"

Jill forced a nod. "Where's the baby?"

"Oh, good question. Let me show you."

Gwen strolled toward the hallway. Jill knew the layout of the Big House well enough to follow along, but she couldn't help crunching through empty bags and plastic cups, and she began to cringe with every step.

"Bathroom," Gwen announced, pushing open the door in the hallway. "Kitchen." She waved into the messy space. "Formula's on the counter, bottles in the sink." She started heading up the stairs.

When the Donderos lived here, the stairway had been lined with photos, but Jill had seen no decoration on any of the walls. At the top of the stairs, someone had bashed a fist-sized hole in the plaster. An empty Snickers wrapper hung out of it.

"Our room," Gwen said, pointing to the door billowing cigarette smoke out a gap. "The brat's in there." She pointed to the second bedroom door, where Lisa had slept. She pointed across the hall to the room Mrs. Dondero had used as an art studio. The door had been taken off its hinges and stood leaning against the wall. "Junk room," she giggled.

Then her face went red and she slapped the bedroom door. "Ain't you ready yet, Vincent?"

He turned to face them, a comb in his hand. He shook it at Gwen, his face twisting. "Don't you yell at me, bitch!"

Then he caught sight of Jill and the anger went sly. "Hello, babysitter."

Gwen kicked the door frame. "Don't you look at that little slut!"

In its room, the baby began to scream. Jill rushed toward the sound.

Empty bags and boxes filled the floor of the room so that the crib looked as if it had been dropped into the middle of the municipal dump. The low stink of dirty diapers hung like fog through the room. Jill stooped over the crib and hoisted the red-faced baby into her arms. If she had to guess, she would have said it was about six months old, just about crawling age. Its yellow pajamas were soaked around the crotch.

Jill looked around for diapers, rags, something. A half-full bag of diapers stuck out from under the crib, so she shoved some trash out of the way and laid the baby in the clear space. Thank God it was just pee. She had no idea how she'd clean up after a dirty one, and from the raw rash around the baby's groin, she wasn't sure the parents had ever bothered.

"Sorry, baby girl," she said. "I wish I had some ointment for you."

She used the clean patches of the pajamas to dry the baby as best she could. She had no idea where another pair of pajamas might be, and the Vernors were still shrieking at each other in the bedroom next door.

The bedroom door pushed open. Gwen stuck her head inside, smiling. "Well, we're out. Gonna catch dinner and a baseball game at the Foxhole, so we ought to be back by about ten. Have a good night."

"Wait—" Jill began, but Gwen had already disappeared. Jill could hear the woman's feet pounding on the stairs, then Vincent shouting at her. An engine fired up outside. Gwen's shrill laughter resounded even over the roar of the Harley.

She carried the baby out of the stinking bedroom and down the stairs. The ground floor might be just as filthy as the second, but at least the dirty dishes and empty packets lying around the kitchen were just ordinary dirty. She felt like she might catch something from just from walking across the dirty blue carpet upstairs.

Down in the kitchen, Jill balanced the baby on her hip while she scrubbed a couple of crusty plastic bottles and a jam jar that she thought probably served as a water glass. She'd never minded cleaning at a babysitting job before, but she was hesitant to touch even the dish sponge, one edge of which looked scorched.

A rap on the back door made her drop the jam jar back into the sink. The baby clawed at her sleeve.

The knock sounded again. "Jill?"

"Jordan?" She rushed to the door and threw it open. "What are you doing here?"

He held up a plastic bag. "Want a corn dog and a Pepsi?"

"Oh, Christ, yes." She paused and made a face. "I'm sorry. Is that not okay?"

He raised an eyebrow. "I offered, didn't I?"

"No, I mean the swearing."

"Oh." He took a can of Pepsi out of the bag and opened it before handing it to her. "You know, my mom wasn't always like this. She went to church on Easter and Christmas, but it was no big deal. Then she lost her job at the mill and went to work for Mr. Schmidt at the gas station. He's real churchy, you know. I think he rubbed off on her."

Jill took a long gulp of the cold, sweet stuff and stifled a burp. The baby reached for the can, making tiny demanding noises. She put the can on the counter and patted the baby's back. "So you're not hung up on all that stuff?"

He dumped a handful of ketchup and mustard packets beside the pop can. "It was okay at first, I guess. But there's nothing good about it now."

She wanted to ask more, but didn't know how. Her parents weren't church people. She'd gone to church with another friend once. It had been boring, and none of the songs made sense. Jordan made himself busy opening his own pop.

She could smell the corn dogs now, hot and sweet and greasy. The baby smacked her little lips, clearly starving. Jill went to the sink and turned on the hot water. "I'll get you some food, kidlet." She had no idea if a baby this size should be eating real food, but Gwen had only mentioned bottles.

"Is she going to get cold with no clothes on?"

Jill scooped some of the formula powder into the bottle and added water from the sink. "I can't find any." She glanced over her shoulder at him while she screwed the nipple on the bottle. "Like, the only thing in her room besides a crib are empty diaper bags."

Jordan squirted mustard on his corn dog. "Maybe they just leave the clothes by the washing machine?"

The baby nearly wrenched the bottle out of Jill's hand. She switched the kid to her other hip and took the second corn dog. "That's a good idea. I think the laundry room is downstairs."

She pointed to the door at the foot of the stairs. Jordan took a step closer to her so their shoulders touched. His shoulder felt much bonier than Gary's.

"I hate basements."

"Me too."

"Let's finish our dogs before we go down there."

Jill swirled ketchup and mustard onto the end of her corn dog and took an enormous bite, relishing the way her mouth filled with salty grease. "Do you think hot dogs are really made with earthworms?"

"Would that be any worse than pig intestines?"

They argued over hot dogs for a few minutes, giving each other a few extra jibes about their condiment usage (Jordan even pretending to cover his eyes while she mixed more ketchup into her ketchup-and-mustard mess), and then fell silent, washing their hands and throwing away the trash. Each of them glanced toward the basement door a half-dozen times while they worked.

Finally, even the baby's bottle was finished. Jordan opened the door. "You ready?"

He flipped the light switch. A single naked light bulb came on at the foot of the stairs. Jill hesitated at the top of the stairs, looking down. She had never gone downstairs while the Donderos had lived here, although she remembered the door standing open and the bracing smell of Surf laundry detergent rushing up the stairs. Her hand went to the pendant at her throat.

"Is that the St. Christopher medallion we found in the cabin?" Jordan asked.

"I shouldn't have taken it, I know," she admitted. "But I like it. I don't even know why."

Jordan gave her a serious look. "Maybe because you could use a protector these days." He slipped past her. "I'll go first."

He grabbed hold of the stair rail and then took a cautious step onto the stairs, watching his feet carefully. Through his worn t-shirt, she could see the outline of his spine, each knob pushing up the soft white fabric.

"Jordan?"

He didn't look up from the stairs. "What?"

She hesitated. He stopped at the foot of the stairs and glanced back at her. "What?" he repeated.

"Why'd you come tonight?"

She had caught up with him. In front of them, clothes had been dumped in a messy pile in front of the washer and dryer. Clean, dirty, there was no way to tell. She saw something tiny and pink and pulled it out of the mess. A nightgown, maybe. Minnie Mouse smiled on the front. It looked clean enough.

He picked up a soft flannel blanket. Something fell out of its folds with a glassy clink.

Jill caught a glimpse of the thing and froze. She had seen something just like it on Calhoun Lake Road—or rather, in the dying woman's car at the accident on Black Lake Road. It was a glass pipe, the bowl blackened and singed.

Jordan nudged the pipe back into the laundry pile and turned to face her.

"Because Vincent Vernor is the creepiest human being on the planet, and I didn't want you to be alone in his house."

"Thanks."

She had to kiss his cheek, then, and even the baby cooed. Maybe the night wasn't going to be so bad.

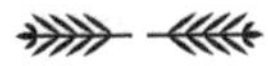

STACIE: 2018

Stacie held up the black blazer, studying it in the mirror. She had liked it when she bought it for an awards banquet, but it was too severe for a teen-focused check presentation ceremony. She stuffed it back in the closet and then flipped through her selection of jackets. Brown tweed. Brown corduroy. Black corduroy. She tried to remember the last time she'd purchased a color and came up blank.

The knock on her front door was loud enough to not only hear in the bedroom but to make her jump and then swear. No buzzer, so it had to be the neighbor. That old biddy had it out for her. Stacie narrowed her eyes as she stomped out to the living room. She wasn't even playing music, for crap's sake.

She threw open the door without even checking the peephole. "What?"

The redhead at the door raised an eyebrow. "Are you always this welcoming, or is it just me?"

"Corinne! I'm so sorry. Did you buzz? I didn't—"

"Some guy with two cases of beer let me in. I presume he's headed to a monster party." Stacie's ex pushed past her, a cardboard file box clearing the way. She'd never set foot in this apartment, but she acted as if she had signed the lease herself. "Couldn't you find anyplace nicer, Stace? This place is a dump."

"I didn't have a lot of time to hunt around, remember?" Stacie folded her arms across her chest.

"Hey, I'm not the one who went down on a junior partner at the company picnic. Or did you forget about that little escapade?"

Guilt squashed Stacie's shoulders. To be honest, she *had* sort of forgotten the event, but only because she'd been mostly hammered on the law office's delicious open bar. Summer meant a lot of drinking—had meant that since she'd first discovered Bartles & Jaymes in the cooler of the Corvallis IGA. She'd been a cashier. It had been all too easy to sneak a sixer every night she closed.

"I'm sorry, Corinne," she whispered.

"It doesn't matter anymore." Corinne put the box down on the couch. Stacie's cat jumped up to inspect the foreign thing. Corinne reached out to his gray back. "Oh, Finch, I've missed you."

"He misses you too." Stacie tried to smile. It hurt, seeing Corinne there on her couch, her long, slim hands moving over the cat's fur. She had such beautiful hands. Such beautiful, supple, talented hands. "I miss you too."

Corinne stood up. She was taller than Stacie by a good five inches, and her posture was better, too, the product of twelve years of ballet training. All of the investments of her privileged, perfect childhood showed when she stood beside Stacie.

And maybe that's why they hadn't worked. How could Corinne ever understand where Stacie had come from or what Stacie had done to pull herself out of there? Corinne had certainly never scrubbed shit off a motel room floor for four dollars an hour.

"You don't miss me, Stacie." Corinne patted Stacie on the shoulder, the pity in her eyes making them shine. "You didn't even really see me while we were together."

Stacie reached for that slim white hand. "What do you mean?"

Corinne pulled away. "I don't know who she was, but whatever she did, you're never going to get over her until you talk to her about it. You can't run away from your heart forever."

She walked out the door then. She didn't even say goodbye.

The rustle of fur against paper reminded Stacie of Finch, still exploring the box on the couch. He had found the picture, of course. No matter how many times Stacie threw it away, it always found its way back to her.

She picked up the chipped wooden frame and stared at the faces. Jordan's floppy bangs. David's tanned face. Gary's grim smile. And then Stacie, all in pinks and greens and yellow, all the colors she refused as an adult, beaming at the camera. Jill had stretched her arms around Stacie's middle and pressed their cheeks together so they could fit in the photo, and she was smiling too. The sun had lit the two of them more brilliantly than the others, and Jill's short curls glowed in the light. They both glowed. Their happiness barely fit in the frame.

Stacie squeezed shut her eyes and remembered the way she'd felt at that moment: incandescent and brilliantly alive. Or at least, brilliantly in love.

CHAPTER SEVENTEEN

GARY: 2018

GARY HAD NEVER had a longer day at work than he did the next day, even counting the terrible summer he'd worked sorting fruit at a maraschino cherry plant. The bleary-eyed mothers with double strollers could not manage to keep their preschoolers from shrieking or knocking books off the shelves. Linda had the gall to claim the little ones were "adorable," and kept forgetting to tidy up the children's section, despite the fact the router for the Wi-Fi demanded Gary's attention every fifteen minutes and the self-check machine would only show the blue screen of death. Not that most of the patrons ever used the damn thing. Every single old man in his Greek fisherman's cap—the most common kind of reader on a Friday morning, for reasons unknown—insisted the machine couldn't read his card. And the old ladies didn't even bother coming up with a lie. They simply liked to stand at the counter and interrogate Gary about his wife's plans for the high school.

And, of course, because this was the most inane and repetitive day of Gary's life, every last one of the patrons had something to say about the upcoming football game. The Bucks wouldn't be playing in Kingston, but that didn't seem to be an issue. At least a quarter of the blue-haired set planned to caravan south to Sutherlin High School Friday afternoon. One of the younger mothers was headed out after story time to spend the night after the game with a doting aunt. The "doting" part was the necessity. No true Bulldogs fan would harbor a Buck Believer the night of the big game, not unless there was real love to cement a blood relationship.

Even the teachers, a group to which Gary tended to ascribe a levelheadedness and bookishness above the ordinary resident, had succumbed to football fever. When he ran into Zack's English teacher after the JV game the night before, she had announced with something like glee that she'd exempted all her classes from homework that day. There was simply too much excitement in the air, she explained, for kids to worry about five-paragraph essays. The Bucks could go all the way, she reminded him. *All the way.*

The tedium of such conversation—and of the football talk after school, and at the dinner table, and at the after-game ice cream social—had grated Gary's supply of sociable behavior down to a mere nubbin. By the time he'd locked up the library Friday night, he wanted nothing more than to crawl into a beer and the pleasant brutality of a first-person shooter. He made his way through a bowl of Kim's delicious chili without snapping or growling, and felt victorious for managing to calmly load the dishwasher despite Zack's decision to whistle as he pre-rinsed.

So it was inevitable that as the family settled into the warmth of their overstuffed sofa and bean bag, the phone would ring. Gary eyed the clock. "Who the hell would be calling our landline at eight pm on a Friday?"

"Maybe it's Gillian." Kim tucked her feet up beneath her. She looked as leery of the phone as he did.

"She only has the cell number."

The phone cut off in mid-chirp as the voicemail activated. Just as Kim reached for her fleece blanket, it began again.

"Jeez." Zack scrambled out of his bean bag. He hoisted the old portable off its wall-mounted cradle by the antenna. "Sheldon residence." He listened for half a second and then his eyes went wide.

Gary paused his game. "Everything okay?"

Zack held out the phone. "Mom, it's for you." He rubbed his ear with his palm.

She stood up to take the phone, her posture gone full professional. "Yes, this is Principal Sheldon." She vanished into the darkened kitchen.

"Loud, huh?"

Zack gave his earlobe one last tug. "Now I understand the expression 'giving someone an earful.'" He plopped down in Kim's spot beside Gary.

Gary studied him a minute. Zack's brown hair, the same unmanageable mop as Gary's, needed either cutting or a hairbrush. From a week of practice in the Indian summer sun, his summer freckles had returned, the dapples adding to his general appearance of a long-legged young deer. He swiped at his nose, and Gary noticed a two-inch-long strip of brown crust across the back of his hand.

"What's that?" Gary tapped the scab.

Zack gave it a glance. "Got stepped on last night. No big deal."

Gary put down the controller. "Hey, when did you and Mom pick up all your football gear? The day you went for your physical?"

The kid bobbed a shoulder, more interested in Kim's pacing in the kitchen than the conversation. "Coach Kane gave me a bunch of stuff Hunter outgrew. And the school said the physical I had for track last spring was good enough."

"Don't you need one every year?"

"Coach Kane says it's the same calendar year, so it counts." He finally spared Gary a glance. "What's with the third degree, Dad?"

"Nothing. Just making sure I hadn't missed anything." And yet something nagged at the back of his mind. "Zack," he began, unsure what to even ask.

Zack's pocket shrieked, and he jumped to his feet. "That's Skyler's ring. I've gotta take this." He hurried toward his room with the phone latched onto his ear.

Gary picked up the controller but did not start up his game. The hand-me-downs, the special rules, the instant success at a new activity. The attention of every boy on the team. It was too familiar. Christ, he needed to call Jill.

Kim came out of the kitchen, crossing her eyes and lolling her tongue clownishly. "That call. Oh my god."

"That good, huh?"

She took the matches off the mantle. "Oh, yes. Please join me on the deck so I may continue."

He thumbed off the console and the TV. "You still haven't picked up a new lighter?"

"Could you get me one? Every time I think about it, there's a school board member at the checkout line, and I have to hide the damn thing behind the tabloids. You think I'm joking, but if you check the *National Enquirers* at Safeway, you'll find three lighters back there." Kim switched on the porch light and found her cigarettes inside the storage bench. "This job, honey. I never guessed it would be like this."

He wisely did not reply.

"You know who was calling? Myron Foster. Do you know Myron? Well, neither do I, but he says he's on the booster club and that he's the mayor's cousin."

"This is Kingston," Gary interjected. "*I'm* probably the mayor's cousin."

"The game isn't even over. The beginning of halftime, and Myron Foster is already so pissed at the coach that he's got to call me up at home." She struck the match and maneuvered it to her cigarette, the flame trembling with her irritation. "The man actually thinks Coach Washburn deserves to be fired because the team was down twenty points in the first half of the game."

On the other side of the glass, the phone began to ring.

"Shit," Kim whispered.

Gary put his arm around her shoulders. Her muscles were so tight his arm might as well have been surrounding a tree. A rock, maybe. "Let it go to voicemail."

"I'm the *principal*, Gary." He'd never seen her smoke like this, each drag burning down an inch of paper. "I'm supposed to make sure the teachers are writing good curriculum and that the kids graduate on time. I didn't know I needed to manage a football team too."

"Let the booster club worry about that crap. Washburn's got a five-year contract, right?"

"Right." The phone rang again. She stubbed out the cigarette and reached for the red pack on the table. "God, my head hurts."

Gary snatched the pack out of her hand. "Those aren't American Spirits."

"What?"

"Why are you smoking Marlboros?"

She made a face. "Why did you buy me Marlboros and leave them on the back porch?"

"I didn't. Wait." He couldn't help glancing out into the woods, now just a black emptiness behind the soft light spilling from the porch. He looked back at her. Her fingers darted toward the cigarettes like hungry birds. "You just found these out here?"

"Yeah, yesterday, I think."

He remembered the figure in the woods, the red cherry of their cigarette glowing in the twilight, and flung the cigarettes into the grass. "Fuck." He kicked the table for good measure. "I saw a guy out by our fence a couple of nights ago. Smoking. I shouted at him, and he must have… Jesus."

Kim wrapped her arms around herself. "You're saying some guy came out of the woods behind our house to just, what? Leave his cigarettes on our patio?"

"Yeah, like a warning. The guy was really big and creepy. Some fucking hillbilly who doesn't give a shit about trespassing." Gary could almost feel the chili crawling back up his throat. "The guy probably sat in our chair and smoked his creepy-ass cigarettes while we slept."

"Jesus, Gary!"

"I'm going to call a contractor tomorrow and get a new fence put in. No way is this happening again."

She burrowed into his side. "Please. Just thinking about this makes me sick."

He smoothed her hair. "I'm sorry I didn't tell you about it. I was hoping it wouldn't matter."

"I know." She kissed his cheek. "Gary? Can you go to the store? I need new cigarettes."

He nearly laughed. Some things stayed steady in life no matter the trouble or fear, and addiction was one of them.

"I'll get you a lighter too."

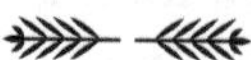

JILL: 1989

The light blazed on, searing Jill's eyelids. For a second she couldn't remember where she was—she was with Jordan, right? It had been so late, and they were cleaning, sweeping up all the mess, and then the baby had been crying, and they sat down to rock her to sleep and then…and then…

She bolted upright, blinking hard as two figures stumbled into the room. The baby began to cry.

"Son of a bitch."

Vincent Vernor stood at the end of the living room, Gwen's arm slung around his shoulder. She was barely upright, her legs wobbling under her, drool spooling down her chin and onto his chest, and as he stared at the two kids on his living room floor, she simply slid to the floor.

"What?" Jordan asked, rubbing his eyes. He reached for Jill as he struggled to sit up.

Vincent's boot shot out and connected with Jordan's side. "Get up, you piece of shit."

Jordan slid back to the floor, clutching his side.

"Leave him alone," Jill said. "He came to help." She got to her feet, anger sparking inside her chest. "And it's like midnight. You owe me extra for being late!" She glared at him, her fists turning to hot angry balls.

Vincent spun to face her. "Oh, you clever little cunt. You think I'm really going to pay you to hang out and fuck your little boyfriend instead of taking care of my kid?"

The skin of his face had gone red everywhere but right around his eyes and nose, like some horrible ski mask of rage. His chest heaved. Jill felt the anger turn cold inside her veins. The baby gave a little squall from the floor, missing Jill's cuddling arms.

She forced up some bravery. "Your baby is just fine, Mr. Vernor. We took good care of her."

Gwen pushed herself to a nearly seated position. "What's going on, Vinnie? Why am I on the floor?"

"Shut up, Gwen."

Jordan got to his feet. "Come on, Jill. We should just go." He held his side, wincing.

Vincent rounded on him, the slap nearly knocking Jordan off his feet. Jill launched herself at the man, driving her fists into his side.

His hand closed on her hair and yanked her backward. "Don't you touch me, you bitch." He grabbed the collar of her shirt and twisted it. His ring dug into her flesh. "I'm gonna teach you and your dirty little boyfriend a lesson."

He was almost panting on the words. Jill kicked at his leg, but his grip on her hair was too strong to resist.

Vincent screamed as Jordan drove the broom handle into the back of his knee. He loosed Jill and stumbled into the couch.

"Run, Jill!" Jordan screamed.

She was already running.

Jordan's hand closed on hers and they raced out the front door, half-leaping down the stairs. The porch light of Jill's house was like a tiny beacon pulling them home.

Behind them, the baby cried, and cried, and cried.

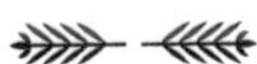

GARY: 2018

Gary woke from nightmares and lay there a long half-hour, willing himself to go back to sleep. Kim's breath came regularly, a metronome of peace, but he could not bring himself to close his eyes. He'd left the light on over the back porch, and its light crept though the bedroom window, staining the ceiling above the bed a faint yellow. Around it, the shadows crept and crawled.

There's nothing there, he told himself. *Be rational.* And yet the words no longer had the power they'd held in Portland. He used to be able to close his eyes and bring up the image of Dr. Monroe, the therapist his Aunt and Uncle Thompson had sent him to while Jill languished at the loony youth farm. Dr. Monroe's gray hair and glasses had filled Gary with a kind of peaceful confidence that no other adult had ever inspired.

But tonight in the dark when he drew up the image of that refined scientist of the mind, that gentleman of logic, that hero of cool thought, it was as if something had crept up behind the doctor and made bunny ears over his balding head. No. Not bunny ears.

Antlers.

Gary got out of bed and went downstairs. His Grandmother Sheldon's painting sat on the mantel like some kind of baleful apocalyptic vision. He rubbed his arms and wished he'd thought to grab his bathrobe. Wrapping the couch afghan around his shoulders, he continued to the kitchen, his breath coming faster as he got closer to the sliding glass door.

It would be out there, the deer-man. He would be out there in the woods, a cigarette in his mouth, waiting and watching Gary. Waiting for what? What could such a creature possibly hope to see in a quiet, bookish middle-aged man?

"It wants you, Gary."

He didn't want to turn around and see who said it, but he had been waiting twenty-five years to hear that voice.

He turned around. "Dad."

His dead father sat on the end of the upholstered booth holding a cup of coffee, just the way he had sat at the kitchen table drinking coffee in real life. Gary could remember getting up at two in the morning and finding his dad just sitting there in the dark, his hands cupped around the Corel mug, his eyes lost in thought. It was the same mug, Gary realized. And where his eyes should have been, there was only the tufted vinyl of the booth.

"Dad," Gary repeated, and this time the tears that had welled up in his eyes streamed down his face. He had spent his entire childhood seeing ghosts and shadows, and the only reason he had refused to see them as an adult was not because he stopped believing or he was afraid to look crazy. He had simply given up waiting for this one to show up.

Gary's father raised his mug as if in a toast. "You turned out great, son. I couldn't be prouder of you."

Gary dropped onto the booth's seat, his legs jellied. "Dad," he said again, stupidly.

"I wish I could explain everything, but I don't think he'll let me." Gary's dad smiled. "You understand, don't you?"

Gary shook his head. The stupidity was passing and turning to rage. He wiped the tears off his face. "Why did you do it?"

His dad took a drink of coffee. Something rustled outside the sliding glass doors.

Gary slammed his fist down on the table. "I was in the fucking hospital, and you went to a Deer Kings party? What kind of father were you?"

The bottom half of his father's face wavered. For a second, Gary had forgotten he was talking to a ghost. Now he pushed himself backward, away from the misty thing that sat across from him. But there was no place to go in the cramped little booth. "Jesus."

"Jesus has nothing to do with it." His dad's face solidified, although the coffee cup vanished. "I didn't understand that until it was too late."

Gary tightened the afghan around himself. "What do you mean?"

The shadows behind his father were moving now, rippling, bulging. Gary's skin crept and crawled. How had he dealt with this when he was a kid? How had he kept from jumping off a bridge or in front of a log truck rather than seeing this shit?

"They could do things," his father said. "The Deer Kings. They helped all of us get through life."

Gary just looked at him. He didn't understand enough to even ask his father the right questions.

"For a price, of course. There was always a price."

His outline was beginning to waver. Out on the back porch, something crashed.

"What did you need help with, Dad?" The back of Gary's neck prickled with sudden heat.

His father stretched out his arm, the hand stretching into a mere wisp of smoke or fog. "You were dying, Gary. Your mother and I would have done anything for you."

Gary slid out of the booth, stumbling to his feet. "What did you do?"

Hammers pounded on the porch. The back of Gary's neck burned. The man in the booth swirled into smoke.

"I'm so sorry," his father said, or perhaps Gary only thought he said, because at that moment something hit the sliding glass door with a horrible clack.

He spun around to see a deer rearing up to bash its hooves against the window, its breath steaming the glass like a dozen angry ghosts.

PART II: Halftime

JILL: 1993

JILL'S HEAD JERKED, snapping her out of sleep. She rubbed her neck. Damn, it was sore. She couldn't remember the last time she'd slept in her own bed. The couch, hospital chairs, the floor: sure. But not her bed. Not since Gary got sick.

She sat up in the awful plastic chair and looked at her brother. The blankets had slid down around his waist, and in the faded hospital gown, he looked more pinched and pale than he had even at home. The IV stand loomed over him, its tube running down into his arm like some kind of sci-fi alien proboscis. She smiled weakly. That was exactly the kind of comparison Gary would have made.

She had to get up.

The kids' ward had private rooms, luckily. She would have hated to bend over and touch her toes with some ancient old guy watching her, his eyes pasted to her ass as she put her foot up on the chair or raised her arms above her head. An old lady would have been just as bad. They were just as critical, just as nit-picky. *Why is your shirt so short, young lady? Does your mother know you're wearing shorts that tight?*

No, her mother did not know what she was wearing right now. Her stupid mother and father had gone out to a Deer Kings meeting last night and now it was seven in the morning on the day their son was supposed to transfer to another hospital, the real one in Eugene, and where the hell were they?

Jill didn't punch the window, but she wanted to. She leaned her head against the glass and stared out at the green hill behind the hospital. The ocean lay just on the other side of it, invisible but always somehow present. A deer came out of the brush and nibbled at the fringe of grass that marked the hospital off from the forest. A young buck, only two points on his rack, the horns reddish in their summer velvet. It was weird to see a buck this close to town, especially so late in the morning. She pressed her palms into the glass, watching him. She didn't like deer. Not anymore.

"Jilly?"

She rushed to Gary's side. "Do you need some water, little guy?" She was already reaching for the water bottle.

He pushed himself up to sitting. "Yeah, thanks."

He actually took the water bottle from her hand. He hadn't been able to do that yesterday. His Adam's apple bobbed as he gulped down more than half the water.

"Hey, take it easy. Lay back down." She reached for the blankets, but he pushed her away.

"I feel different," he said. "I feel good."

Jill frowned at him. "I know you don't want to go to Eugene, but, buddy, you've got to. There's no oncology department here in Kingston."

He shook his head. "No, seriously, Jill. I feel *good*."

The lightest of knocks sounded on the door, and then it swung open. The diminutive woman looked around the room. Maria, that was her name. The nice nurse.

Jill smiled at her. "Good morning."

"Gillian. Glad you're here. Can you come out into the hall?"

"Why?" Gary asked, his voice cracking. "Whatever it is, you can tell me too."

"Jill?" Maria's tone was strained.

Jill couldn't force a smile for her brother. "I'll be back in a minute, Gare Bear."

She couldn't look back at him as she followed the nurse out of the room. The crushing weight of Gary's cancer settled onto her shoulders. She was eighteen now, had been for two weeks, but that didn't mean she wanted to hear whatever Maria had to say. Where the *fuck* were her parents?

"Is there a problem? With the transfer?"

Maria shook her head. "Jill…" She hesitated. This close, Jill could see the lines around the corners of her eyes and mouth. They went deeper, her lips tightening unhappily. "I have bad news about your parents."

Behind the hospital room door, something crashed. Maria reached for the door handle, but it flew open.

Gary stood there in his gown, the IV stand at his feet. His eyes had that sheen Jill remembered from their childhood, that special glow she hadn't seen in years.

"They're dead, aren't they?" he asked. He reached out blindly, his fingers catching on Jill's t-shirt. "Jill, they're dead!"

The dream she'd had sitting in that awful plastic chair crashed back over her, and all the world was pain and blood and the hungry, hungry river.

PART III: Homecoming

The faces of the players were young, but the perfection of their equipment, the gleaming shoes and helmets and the immaculate pants and jerseys, the solemn ritual that was attached to almost everything, made them seem like boys going off to fight a war for the benefit of someone else, unwitting sacrifices to a strange and powerful god.

—H.G. Bissinger, *Friday Night Lights*

Home is the place where when you go there, you have to finally face the thing in the dark.

—Stephen King, *It*

CHAPTER EIGHTEEN

JILL: 2018

JILL MOVED MIGUEL'S arm off her hip and rolled quietly out of bed. Her husband gave a soft snore. Normally the sound of Miguel's breathing filled her with comfort, but after the dream woke her, even his warm presence couldn't shake off the cold, heavy feeling in her gut. For the first time in over ten years, she wanted a cigarette.

She found her bathrobe and opened the bedroom door. Merlin pressed his cold nose into the crook of her knee, concerned. He knew her too well.

"Come on," she whispered, feeling for the plush of his ears and giving them a good rub. The dog followed her out of the bedroom and into the kitchen.

She went to the kettle, but her hand hesitated above it. Insomnia bothered her every few months—a common experience for her age, her doctor liked to reassure her—and usually a cup of Sleepytime Extra got her back to sleep in half an hour or so. But she wasn't sure she *wanted* to go back to sleep. She couldn't remember the dream, but she knew it had been bad, and that it had been about Kingston.

"I don't ever want to go back to Kingston, Merlin."

The golden retriever blinked up at her. She stroked his forehead, studying his wide brown eyes. He could always tell when there was something bothering her.

Jill crouched down, pressing her cheek to the dog's chest, listening to his big dog heart. She could remember listening to her dad's heart like this a few times, trudging out to the kitchen in the middle of the night and finding him sitting at the table, having his midnight cup of coffee. How comforting it always was to leave her bad dreams in her room and go into the good smelling kitchen, her father a sleepy shadow ready to hug her tight. She would cozy into the crook of his arm and breathe in the coffee scent of him. There hadn't been one bad night that she hadn't gotten up to find him already awake. As a kid, she took that for granted, but as an adult, she knew it was some kind of gift.

They all had gifts, the Sheldons. Dad knew when his children were having bad dreams. Gary talked to ghosts. She painted the future. What had been Grandma Sheldon's talent? She had known her parents were going to kill each other, hadn't she? Whatever the extent of her powers, they had almost certainly driven her to the mental hospital.

As had Jill's.

She stood up. Fuck Sleepytime. They didn't keep much booze in the house, but there was an old bottle of tequila above the stove. She got it out, poured a few fingers into a juice glass, and leaned against the counter to sip on it.

Her powers. She'd squashed them down after that summer, hadn't she? She'd mostly stopped painting in high school, at least outside of art class. She'd gotten so busy with all of it—the friends who suddenly found her after years of pretending she didn't exist, her part-time job at the bakery, the steady grind of extracurricular activities, the constant barrage of assignments and tests. It wasn't just that she was too busy to look into the future, it was that she *needed* to be too busy to look into the future. After a summer of painting disasters and talking to the dead, she had needed a long break from being a freak.

And there'd been no one around to tell her she ought to use her gift. Gary was done with the psychic game after what they'd been through that summer; Stacie and Jordan moved; David had vanished into the football team. Their group had been everything to each other those long warm summer weeks, and then like a fire that had run out of fuel, they were gone. Somehow she'd gotten popular in high school, but for all the crowd of friends, she'd never felt anything like the friendship she'd felt with their little pack. No, she'd never been as lonely as she had when she'd been in high school.

The tequila warmed her belly. She hadn't finished her glass, but her limbs felt heavy and stolid, and her upper lip had gone numb. It was good stuff. She didn't know why she didn't drink more often.

She blinked, and her eyelids seem to close for ten minutes. Her hand moved very slowly toward the caddy of pens and pencils beside the sink. There was paper somewhere, but she pressed the pencil's lead right to the countertop. Something was coming. Some emanation of the future was rushing up the track in her brain, stirred by the liquor in her blood. She hadn't expected that. Booze almost never had that effect.

Her vision went black. She didn't panic. She didn't sense the future with her eyes anyway.

Her hand began to move.

She could hear…voices. Excited ones, not angry, not happy. Powerful voices. Like people cheering at a sports event, not because someone scored a point, but because someone told them to. She thought she might hear the *boom-thump* of a percussion section, just faintly. Her heart began to race in her chest, but she couldn't do anything about it. The future was in control, not her.

The black that filled her eyes swirled green, swirled red. That was wrong. There shouldn't be colors. There were never colors.

And then for a second all that existed were colors. The brilliant viridian of turf grass, lit sharp with halogen light. Racing bodies, red and white, smashing together. A figure in the middle of it all, taller than any human ever stood. Its antlers outlined themselves in black across the face of the moon.

Then the voices in her head changed to screams.

For a second she saw the crowd surging around her, smashing, slashing, biting, clawing. A golden-haired cheerleader drove a baton into another girl's eyeball. Jill felt the pencil snap in her fingers. Pain exploded in her chest and her vision filled with red.

She hit the floor hard, her knees protesting as they hit linoleum. Merlin rushed to her side, pressing his nose into her face.

She was crying. Sobbing. Her vision had evaporated, but she couldn't get the scene out of her head, the pain out of her chest. The football game. The crowd gone mad. The deer-man in the middle of it all, his face without expression as blood splattered the pristine green field.

For a moment she just lay there on the floor, clutching the dog's fur. Then she pushed herself to her feet to see what she had drawn. She had never seen her vision unfold before—only seen it later, captured in the static pose of her paintings. If it was tequila that had done this, she was never drinking again.

Graphite smeared the counter in gray streaks, but she hadn't drawn the football field or the insane crowd. It took her a second to make out what she had produced in stylized Gothic letters:

Go Bucks.

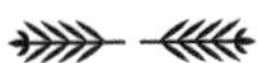

GARY: 2018

The next morning he called out sick to work and felt guilty for it. He knew Shawn would worry the accident had done something irreparable to Gary or Zack; Linda would come in on her day off and then swan around like a martyred superhero. She was convinced she was the best employee the city had ever had, and this would only add to her opinion of herself.

But after the night he'd had, Gary felt too shitty to deal with the public. Who wouldn't feel shitty on only two hours of sleep and a conversation with their dead father? Even after a cup of coffee, his brain felt squishy, so he stopped at Murphy's on his way to the lake. Mrs. Murphy wasn't there, but a shy Latina girl helped him settle on an apple fritter to accompany his extra-large coffee.

He hadn't set out to go to the old house when he got in the car that morning, but he supposed the idea had been simmering in the back of his head since they'd arrived in Kingston. He drove slowly through the old end of town, searching for the turn to Balfour Drive.

Time had squeezed the life out of this part of Kingston. Gary had known the timber industry's demise had hit Kingston hard, but the area near the high school could still pass for an ordinary small American town. People still maintained their two-story ranch houses and their green front yards; tourists still stopped at the diners on Highway 101; the hospital still admitted patients. But you only needed to get a block or two off the highway to see what the town was really like. The Sunfish Trailer Park had once held thirty double-wides—now blackberry vines filled half the property, and the trailers remaining had a glum, abandoned look about them. Across the street, a house sat with its windows boarded up, its blackened roof hacked open in places.

If he hadn't slowed to look at that fire-scorched dump, he would have missed Balfour Drive entirely. Trees overhung the mouth of the narrow road, and brush sprang up almost to the shoulder. The pavement was cracked and pitted. He had to steer around an enormous pothole for fear he'd break an axle.

Stacie's old duplex was still there, the gray paint updated to a modern beige. A sign by the driveway advertised an adult daycare. A stout woman stood on the front porch, her head tracking the Camry as it passed by. Gary waved, but she did not return the gesture.

The road worsened. If the Washburn's trailer remained, there was no sign of it, and the density of the overgrowth made it impossible to even remember where Jordan had lived. Not a single car passed as Gary slowly maneuvered through potholes and broken pavement. If anyone was traveling from Kingston to Calhoun Lake, they were obviously taking Highway 101.

The long slow drive reminded Gary of his journeys up and down this road on bicycle. How many miles had he and Jill put on their bikes every summer, going to and from town? Or even just rambling around the lake or down to the Calhoun Lake Lodge? They'd lived just half a mile down the road from the lodge, and Jill and Stacie must have gone there at least twice a week, not to mention all the times he and Jill stopped in to buy candy or a pop.

He shook his head, wondering. It hadn't seemed like the lake was so far out in the boonies when he'd been a kid. It was only after they moved into town that it began to feel like another world.

Then up ahead he saw it—the lake, quietly winking silver and green at the end of Balfour Drive. Balfour Drive had been the original Highway 101, rerouted for speed around the other side of the state forest, but Calhoun Lake Road connected the old and new. Here where the old highway t-boned into the lake road marked the beginning of Gary's childhood world. He stopped the Camry and looked left, then right, his hands knotted tight on the steering wheel. Leaning forward as he peered right again, he could just make out the heaps of sand that marked the Bureau of Land Management's recreation area. In the summer, the bulldozers would sweep the sand down into a beach to invite the tourists to play, but for now the sand slept above the high-water line.

He looked left again. The curves of the lake wound too tightly to show him how about half a mile in that direction, the lodge had stood, and a little past that, his parents' cottage and the Big House. All he could see were the clumps of trees that leaned out over the steep banks of the great, winding lake—a green snake that filled the narrow valley with its gorged bulk.

He restarted the Camry. This was where it had happened. His mom and dad, totally blitzed after a Deer Kings party, had chosen to breeze through Kingston, skipping over their nice cozy ranch house to careen down Balfour Drive, picking up speed on its relatively straight final stretch before exploding out of the forest and sliding across Calhoun Lake Drive into the lake. Gary had never heard the accident described, but he could picture it in his mind's eye like a David Lynch movie. The car's headlights would have flashed on the double yellow lines, his parents smiling dreamily as for a moment the car hovered in the dark, its forward motion canceling the pull of gravity. They had hung there for a minute or two or maybe an hour, their drunken brains content and happy until the water suddenly rose up and smashed the car with the power of a wrecking ball.

He hadn't realized he was still driving until he couldn't, and he had to pull over to the side of the road and get out, gasping for air.

"Fuck."

He doubled up, the coffee boiling in his gut.

"Shit!"

But he didn't puke. The boiling inside burst out his eyes, hot tears like steam pouring off his cheeks, splattering his Nikes as he choked and coughed and sobbed.

"Fuck!" he shouted. His voice echoed off the hills. He had forgotten what it was like down here by the lake. How close the trees were. How smothering the hills. It was a tiny enclosed world and it had been home until everything cracked in the heat of that final disaster.

And thinking of it, he straightened up and looked around him. There were only a few stretches along Calhoun Lake Road that were wide enough for a car to pull over and someone to get out, and he was surprised it had taken his brain so long to recognize the site of the former Calhoun Lake Lodge. The owners had torn down the ruins of the motel and the restaurant after the fire. They'd promised to rebuild bigger and even better than before. Now a sign, half-swallowed by horse tail weeds and blackberry vines, told him the property was available for redevelopment.

Gary took a cautious step forward. This narrow strip of gravel and weeds was the only open space on the entire lot. Alder and fir fought each other for space where the restaurant had once stood. Ferns crowded over the old sidewalk. There was no way to see through the greenery to the once-vaunted view of the lake. He couldn't even see the cabins, unharmed by the big fire of 1989, because the brush was too thick.

For the first time in a long time—maybe the first time since that awful summer—he let himself miss the lodge. He let himself miss Stacie, and Jordan, and David, and all the time they had spent together here, by the lake. It hurt, of course. He took a deep breath and let himself just feel...bad.

And then he saw movement from the corner of his eye. A tiny thread of darkness, curling up from the ground.

He turned to face it.

All those years of telling himself shadows were just shadows, their movement a misfiring in his brain or a trick of his optic nerve, of telling himself that ghosts were simply the wishful thinking of a hyperactive brain: he pushed all of that away. He looked at the darkness and let himself see it. It moved like smoke, thin wisps of itself rising up from the ground and writhing in the air.

Then Gary closed his eyes and reached out to the coiling shadow with his mind. *Who are you?* he asked it. *Why are you here?*

Shadow whooshed through him like smoke through an open door, rushing to fill the empty places. For a second there was no Gary, only:

Goddamn, I shouldn't have borrowed these heels from Christine. How tiny are her fucking feet, anyway? It's too bad this stupid logger just wants a blow job. Only customer all night, and I can't even get one who will pay for a screw. And what the hell is taking him so long to pay his tab? If he doesn't get out here before I finish my cigarette, I'm going to hitch back into town. My buzz is wearing off.

Gary wrenched his mind free of the girl's voice, stumbling into the car as he struggled. A cold sweat had broken out on his forehead and between his shoulder blades. She had died here. She had died here and no one ever knew. Whoever her last john had been, he'd walked her down the steps to the lake, closed his hands around her neck as she knelt before him, and then he'd simply rolled her body into the lake. It was a deep, dark lake, and no one had been looking for her, not even the girl who had lent her the heels.

She'd been seventeen years old.

He got back in the car and turned on the stereo as loud as it went. Sobs shook his shoulders.

He could cry as long as he wanted—he was never going to get the memory of that girl out of his head.

After a while, he turned down the stereo and found his cell in his pocket. His hands shook as he dialed.

She picked up on the second ring.

"Jill?"

"You're by the lake, aren't you?" The rasp in her voice made it sound like she'd spent the morning screaming.

"Can you come to Kingston? Please?"

"I'll be there tonight."

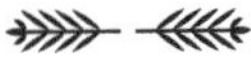

GARY: 1989

They met in the orchard beside the stream, all of them quiet and pale, even David. Jill clung to Jordan and Stacie's hands, barely speaking. This morning, she had stood on the front porch in complete silence as Vincent

Vernor made his little apology to her. He'd pressed an extra twenty-dollar bill into her hand as if that would make up for the things he'd said and done. He'd even had the arrogance to shake their dad's hand and tell him what a terrific babysitter Jill had turned out to be. The whole presentation had made Gary want to vomit.

But his dad had fallen for it. Of course his dad had fallen for it. Would a monster come over first thing in the morning with polished words and a brilliant smile? And how Vincent had smiled. Kindness and charm had oozed off his face like the new mayor at the Founders' Day parade.

"We have to do something," Jordan said. "He's dangerous."

"What can we do?" Jill's voice was barely a whisper. "You should have seen my dad. Everybody buys this guy's shit."

"Not my mom. She knows he's bad." Jordan bit his lip. "But she's too scared to do anything."

Stacie lifted her head. "She should tell the cops," she said. "He's getting her to steal for him, and that's illegal. Plus, he's a drug dealer. You saw him, Jill."

"He sells it to my parents."

Everyone turned to stare at David, but his eyes were fixed on his sneakers. Gary remembered the day at David's house, the way his parents had been so excited to see Vincent. It made sense now.

"They were super fucked up when we lived in Springfield. Things were getting better here." He drove the heel of his shoe into the gravel, spraying rocks into the side of Gary's leg. "Then he showed up."

Jordan patted David's shoulder. "I'm sorry."

David flinched away. "What do you care?"

Jordan's face crumpled. Stacie grabbed his hand and scowled at David.

Jordan took a deep breath. "I don't want my mom to go to jail. She's praying all the time now. All day, all night. She makes me pray with her when I'm around. It's really scary."

David looked up from his feet. "I'm sorry, man."

A weight settled in Gary's gut. He had known Vincent Vernor was trouble the minute he had laid eyes on him. The way the shadows had twisted around him and stroked his shoulders, the way darkness clung to him with love and adoration. He should have stopped Jill from going over there. He should have found a way to convince her. He should have gone with her the way Jordan did.

He closed his eyes. He didn't want to know what would have happened to her if Jordan hadn't clobbered Vincent's knee. He had seen enough movies, read enough books, to know what nearly happened to Jill last night. He had a horrible feeling Vincent would have done something just as bad to Jordan if he'd gotten the chance. It was in his eyes, the cold, slippery way they ran over your body and turned it to meat.

"Should we tell the police about the drugs?" Jill asked. "I mean, before your mom gets in real trouble?"

"No one will believe us," Jordan said, at the same time David blurted out, "It's too risky."

"Risky?" Jill was starting to sound like herself again. "What do you mean?"

David looked like he might cry. "What if he gives up the names of the people he sells to? What am I going to do if my parents go to jail? Live in a foster home? Fuck that!"

"My mom will lie for him," Stacie said. She pulled her knees up to her chest. "I know she would. She was on the phone with him this morning, cooing and chirping."

"That fucking sucks." David shot a mirthless smile at Stacie. "Our parents are idiots."

Jill squeezed the silver pendant she'd been wearing lately. Gary frowned at it. What had their mom said about it? That it symbolized the power of belief? Of hope and will given form?

"I wish there were real saints," Jill said. "Someone magical who would come down and help us." She pulled the medallion out of her shirt and stared at the little figure. "I wish you weren't just a story."

"Well, they're not *just* a story," Jordan said. "I mean, saints start out as real people."

Jill flicked the medallion with her finger. "This guy was a real person?"

"Sure. The church didn't name him a saint until he was dead, though. He had to do a bunch of miraculous things during his life, and then when he died, someone had to check to see if he rotted or not."

"Saints don't rot?" Stacie sounded horrified. "Are they like zombies or something?"

"I don't know. Maybe? Anyway, I wouldn't have thought 'not rotting' was the major definition of a saint, but my mom says it is. She says it's because Catholics are so messed up." He shrugged. "I don't know much more about saints. My mom gets kind of freaked out talking about them."

A shadow twisted in the corner of Gary's eye. He forced his head to turn so he could look at it. Goosebumps rose up all over his body as for the first time he made himself really look at one of those coiling, slithering shadows. But looking at it, he found it no longer terrified him the way spirits used to. How could the ghost of someone dead be as scary as a freak like Vincent Vernor?

The spirit's color went from black to gray. He had never seen that happen before. Was it in response to him? Was it because he wasn't as frightened of it anymore? He thought it might be.

Gary looked back at the circle of friends. He would have never thought he could be friends with someone like David Washburn or Stacie Clinton, but now he would call them his best friends. Vincent Vernor had done that—had pushed together a group of weird kids who lived on the weedy verge of Kingston and made them more than just associates. They were practically family. And he wasn't going to let anything hurt his family.

An idea stirred inside him. Maybe his mom was right that Jill's St. Christopher medallion was just a symbol for people who really wanted something to believe in. But if feelings affected spirits, then maybe feelings and beliefs were stronger than he'd given them credit. He began to pace, thinking about it. In the stories, after all, the saints really did help people. They could do miracles because of the power of their belief. And saints started out just like ordinary people, not ones with special gifts like him and Jill. They just didn't die the same way other people did.

He knew something else that didn't die the right way—something they had just seen at the Eagle Cove campground. His palms went damp with excitement.

"Guys."

Jordan looked up first, then the others, slowly seeing the excitement on Gary's face.

"What if we already know a saint?"

CHAPTER NINETEEN

STACIE: 1989

"WHAT DO YOU mean?" Jill asked.

"The deer," Gary said. "It got hit by that truck, and then it got right up. It looked dead, but it didn't stay dead."

Jordan hugged his arms around himself. "We don't know it was really dead."

"I'm pretty sure it was dead," Gary insisted.

"So what?" David asked. "It's not like it followed us home so we can just ask it to help us."

"No," Jordan said, "but if it was some kind of saint, we could make offerings to it. Light candles and stuff like the Catholics do. We'd need a picture, probably."

"I can make a picture," Jill said.

Stacie looked at Jill. Her eyes were all bright and wide and excited. Stacie couldn't blame her. If lighting a candle in front of a picture of a deer could keep Vincent Vernor from ever showing up on Stacie's doorstep again, she'd do it too.

"I don't know anything about saints," Stacie said, "but I bet if we believe in it enough, it will work. That's how it is in horror stories."

Jill darted back toward the house and returned with her sketchbook. "Look," she said, flipping through the pages. "I've already drawn it about a thousand times. We just have to pick the right picture."

Gary and Stacie leaned toward the sketchbook so quickly their heads collided. Stacie rubbed hers, smiling apologetically at him. He didn't smile back. His eyes had that weird shiny look they got when he had used the Ouija board, only not quite so rainbowy. She wasn't sure he was entirely there.

"This one," Jordan said. He took the sketchbook from Jill and held it up.

She had drawn the stag just the way he had appeared when Stacie first saw him coming out of the woods, the shadows and her imagination making her see it as a very tall man with an enormous deer's head. The hair on Stacie's arms prickled.

"That's how I saw it," Gary whispered. "Before the ghosts got too thick."

"Guys," David said, his voice trembling, "this stuff is too weird. I gotta get out of here."

"No!" Jordan stepped in front of the bigger boy. "Please don't go. I think this is only going to work if we're all in on it."

Jill looked like she might cry. "David, things are only going to get worse for your parents if we don't do something about Vincent Vernor."

The two of them stared at each other a long time. The brightness of their faces, looking into each other's eyes. Stacie had to look away from them. There was no way Jill would ever look at her with that kind of hunger.

Jordan squeezed her hand.

David turned away from Jill and cleared his throat. "Okay, we have our image. What do we do next?"

"We get in a circle," Jordan said. "Holding hands."

Jill moved to Stacie's side and took her free hand. Jordan gave Stacie's hand another squeeze. She could feel the dry skin of his palm prickle against her skin. David reached for Gary and Jill's hands.

"Gary?" Jill asked. "We can't do this without you."

"I know." He took David's hand, and then reached for Jordan's. "All for one, one for all, and all that crap."

"That's the spirit." Stacie stuck her tongue out at him, and he grinned back at her. She felt a little better, seeing him smile like that. He was probably the youngest of them all, and yet somehow he was the leader.

She felt a soft buzzing in her wrists and palms. "Close your eyes," she reminded them.

"Spirits," Gary whispered. "We ask for your assistance tonight."

Stacie could smell the artificial apple of Jill's shampoo. The wind smelled like campfire smoke.

"Fix the image of the deer saint in your minds' eyes," Jordan said. "Try to picture it like we saw it at the campground."

"Deer Saint," Gary said. "Wherever you are, may you hear us in our time of need. Spirits, lend our saint your powers."

The buzzing rose up Stacie's arms. It went into her shoulder blades, down through her ribs. Her heart sped up, as if the buzzing urged it along.

"Deer Saint," she whispered. Behind her eyelids, she could see its figure with perfect clarity. Its horns spread as wide as one of the Sheldons' apple trees. It towered over them, taller than any man. Taller than stupid Vincent Vernor by a good foot.

"Deer Saint," Jill whispered.

"Deer Saint," David and Jordan echoed.

The buzzing rippled down through Stacie's belly, down her thighs, wobbling her knees. Every bit of her body felt newly alive, her skin more sensitive than ever before. She could feel the hairs on Jordan's arms just touching the hairs on her own. Jill's shoulder nearly burned into the flesh of Stacie's upper arm. Her crotch had gone hot and tingly like she was reading one of her mom's romance novels.

"Deer Saint," Gary said, his voice deeper and more solemn than an eleven-year-old's voice should be able to sound.

Something shrieked in the woods behind them. Branches crashed. And then: the bugling of a stag.

Stacie's eyes flew open. The candles' flames leaped up, impossibly high. The moon and stars boiled in the sky. Gary's hair stood up in a cloud around his head. David shook like a man being electrocuted.

But the worst was Jordan's eyes: his eyes were just whites, rolling and trembling in his head.

An enormous shadow passed over them. Something hit the ground with a thud and then bounded off through the orchard. A branch snapped as its horns caught, and for a second, Stacie saw it, the giant deer paused beneath the apple tree. And then it broke free, and it was leaping again, soaring over the fence and onto the driveway.

"The deer saint," Jill breathed.

Jordan dropped to his knees in the gravel. "It was so beautiful. The most beautiful thing I ever saw."

David shuddered. "I think I'm going to be sick."

"So beautiful," Jordan repeated.

"There are so many fucking ghosts out here," Gary said, "that I think I'm going blind."

"Let's go in the house," Jill ordered. "We could all use something to eat."

Stacie had to help Jordan to his feet. His face scorched her skin as he pressed it against her cheek. "Did you see it?" he whispered in her ear. "Did you see how glorious it was?"

"It was pretty neat," she agreed.

"I'm never going to church again," he said, and burst into tears.

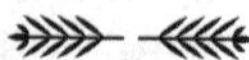

GARY: 2018

He sat in the car, trembling, unready to turn on the engine and return to the road. It had all come back to him here at the ruins of the lodge: the past, his gifts, the darkness. He could see it roiling around beneath the alder seedlings and the Scotch broom. And after nearly thirty years pretending he was normal, pretending there were no shadows moving in the corners of his vision, pretending logic and science and reason ruled his life, well, after thirty years of that, he wasn't sure he knew how to live with this weird shit.

Thank God Jill was coming. He owed her for that—owed her for everything. In high school, she might have swanned around with her popular friends and acted like an ordinary teenager, but she had never turned her back on who she was, not really. Not even when it had gotten her locked up in a mental institution and Gary had acted like she was some kind of embarrassing whack job. After years of being the butt of his jokes, she was still willing to come save his sorry ass.

He didn't deserve such a good sister. He probably never had.

He turned the key in the ignition and eased back onto Calhoun Lake Road. He had never driven this road, he realized. They left Kingston before he got his driver's license, and he'd found ways to never come back.

Gary kept to the speed limit. He might not have driven this road, but he knew it too well. Every corner was wreathed in shadows.

The speedometer dropped five miles below the speed limit, then ten. The road's old familiar turns were just as blind as he remembered, and his palms were wet against the leather steering wheel cover as he approached Skep Rock. He could see the woman from the car accident as if she sat in the passenger seat beside him. *Was a deer*, she whispered in his ear. *A deer!*

Calhoun Lake Road seemed like a strange place to see a deer in mid-afternoon, but the four-legged locusts had overrun the area. No matter how many hunters came every fall, there were always more deer. Deer in the gardens. Deer in the orchards. Deer on the roads. He'd read there were more than a thousand deer-related car accidents in Oregon every year—nearly three a day.

His breath came in shallow gasps now. He forced a deep breath as the car slowly wound around the tremendous curve of Skep Rock. So much blackness. Black mist on the rock side, plumes of black smoke on the lake side. She hadn't been the first to die on this corner, and she hadn't been the last.

Just shut up and take your bottle! a woman shrieked in his head.

A baby wailed over and over and over.

Hot damn, I love a road beer.

Brakes squealed. Rubber scorched.

Come on, baby, kiss me.

Glass shattered.

A deer!

Metal on metal so hard Gary nearly loosed the steering wheel.

He braked and just sat there a second, sweat streaming down his face and pooling in his lower back. He swiped his arm across his face until he could see again, and tapped the accelerator. If a car had come up behind him, he would have been another one of those dead people whispering along the edges of the road.

Then the rock was behind him and the shoulder widened a little, and he breathed a bit easier. He hadn't set out to visit his grandmother when he had called in sick this morning, but now it sounded like a pretty good idea. He should have been out to visit her long before this. It was the road that had kept him from doing it, he knew. The thought of driving down this road had been impossible for Rational Gary to accept.

It was too bad he'd let his fears keep him away. Calhoun Lake was the place where he'd learned to swim, to dive, to water ski, to shotgun beer. He and Jill had spent most of their summers on the lake, even after the lodge burned down. It wasn't until his parents' swan dive that he'd grown afraid of it.

They hadn't been there, he realized. He'd seen plenty of spirits on this drive, but the site where they'd driven into the lake was completely quiet. He thought on that as he put the lake behind him and approached the little village of Aspen Valley.

It looked even shabbier than the outskirts of Kingston. The windows of the old school were boarded up, and moss had overtaken the roof of the volunteer fire department so it nearly blended into the forest. Even the cows he passed picked at the grass as if they were exhausted. Mostly, the road passed between tracts of woods and fields rapidly turning to the brush. He had no idea where all the people had gone. There probably hadn't been that many to begin with. Living in Portland, it had been easy to forget that vast tracts of Oregon sat empty and unpopulated.

The road narrowed. In about half a mile, it would turn to private logging road. He slowed to keep his eyes peeled for the turn to his grandparents' house. He didn't want to miss it, not the way he'd nearly missed Balfour Drive.

He needn't have worried. A brand-new, hand-painted sign announced the address beside a driveway that looked more neatly graveled than it had ever looked when he'd been a kid. The bridge over the little creek had been rebuilt too.

The drive ended in the big turnaround between his grandparents' house and Gramps' workshop. A silver Airstream sat off to one side of the property, and he remembered Grams had rented the site to a couple from Eugene. They came out most weekends, hiking and painting and collecting mushrooms. They were good tenants, and it was probably their money that had graveled the drive.

He felt a prickle of guilt at the thought and pushed it aside. Once they got a grip on Kim's student loans, they'd be able to help out Grams and Gramps.

His grandmother stood on the massive front porch, waving an honest-to-God dishtowel at him. He parked beside her white pickup and got out. Two dogs, one big and black, one small and white, leaped around him, their bodies nearly a blur of movement.

"Zorro, Agnes, leave that boy alone!" Grams strode into their midst, clearing a path with her very willpower. She caught the smallest dog in mid-leap and tucked it under one elbow. "This is a surprise, Gary."

"Is it okay? I mean, is this a bad time?"

"No, no, it's fine. Your grandpa is taking a nap, but he'll be up in an hour or so. You want to come in and have some coffee?"

"Coffee would be great."

Gary followed his grandmother around to the back door, which had been propped open. She waved him into the house, ripe with the smells of tanning chemicals and damp outdoor gear. When he closed the door behind him, the coyote pelt hanging on it wagged its tail. Grandma Templeton gave a mug one last polish with the dish towel and then hung the towel on the nail over the sink. The little white dog jumped around her feet as if spring-powered.

She handed him the mug. "You look like shit, Gary."

"Thanks, Grams."

She poured herself a mug and headed into the front room. A beaver pelt was stretching in front of the piano; an array of deer heads sat on the couch, waiting for someone to pick them up. Gary had never actually sat down inside his grandparents' house, not even once.

Grams looked around the room as if she half-expected a chair to clear itself, and then went out to the front porch. It was an enormous porch, deeper than Gary's living room, and cozier than the actual house. A puzzle sat half-assembled on a coffee table in front of the wicker couch. His grandmother sat down and began sorting pieces into piles based on color. The two dogs climbed up onto the couch and looked at Gary, their tongues lolling. He sat down in the other wicker chair. One of the drainpipes by the porch must have been loose; the rain howled and drummed down the tinny length of it.

"It started raining," Gary said.

"Yep." Grams looked up at him, puzzle piece in hand. Gary thought it might have been part of a rose bush. "What are you doing out here, Gary?"

"I don't know," he admitted. He cupped his hands around his coffee cup. "I just…I don't know."

Grams jumped to her feet. "Son of a bitching drainpipe. I can't hear shit." She went to the porch steps and leaned out. "It's loose."

"Do you want me to do something?"

She waved a hand. "I got it." She pulled a multi-tool out of her pants pocket and scrambled up on the porch railing. "I can see the stupid tie-down. Just gotta tighten it up."

"Grams, that looks slippery. Let me get you a stepladder." Gary stood up.

"I got it!" She leaned out farther, steadying herself on the gutter.

Then her boot skidded on the wet wood.

For a second, she hung there from the gutter, and Gary thought he was going to make it across the porch with enough time to catch her. Then the gutter popped free of the house and she flew backward, out over the rhododendrons.

"Grams!"

Gary raced down the steps. His grandmother lay on the mossy yard, crumpled and still. He dropped to his knees beside her. The ground squished cold beneath his jeans.

"Grams, are you okay?"

She didn't move. He touched her shoulder, but he knew better than to move her in any way. He moved around so he could see her face.

"Grams?"

Was she breathing? He couldn't tell. He leaned closer.

She didn't move. He couldn't feel air moving around her nose and mouth. He stretched out his fingers to her throat.

That's when he noticed the blood. Just a little, under the side of her head.

The dogs nosed around Gary, their tails slapping him in the chest and ribs. The little one nudged Grams' side, whining a little.

"No, God, no."

He touched her throat.

"Please."

He felt nothing beneath her papery skin. Up this close, she looked tiny and small. Where had his hard-ass grandmother gone? She was too damn tough to go like this.

"Please, no!" He had started to cry, and now his shoulders shook. "Somebody help me, please."

A shadow fell across his grandmother's face.

Gary looked up, hopeful, but it was just a deer. A stupid deer.

"Go away," he said, stupidly. He waved at it. "Go on!"

The little white dog whined, louder than it had before. It pressed itself against Gary's side. The big black dog took a hesitant step backward.

"Go on, you stupid dogs. Chase that deer off. Go away!" Gary shouted.

The doe took a step forward. The big dog began to whimper.

Gary opened his mouth, but sound wouldn't come out. There was something strange about this deer, its lack of fear. Even though it was broad daylight, he thought he saw the tapetum flash in its eyes.

It lowered its head until its black-whiskered lips touched his grandmother's head.

Dark mist rose from its muzzle.

Gary couldn't breathe. The dogs had gone silent. The rain pounded harder on the leaves, on his head, on his grandmother's face.

She gave a sudden gasp and rolled onto her back.

The deer took a step back.

"Gary? What the fuck just happened?" she said, her voice thin and small and, for the first time in his life, old.

"Don't move, Grams. I'm calling an ambulance." Gary reached for the cell in his pocket and realized the little white dog had peed itself in fear, soaking his pants. His phone stank, but he pressed it to his ear anyway.

"911. Can I get your address?"

"102468 Calhoun Lake Road," he answered.

There was no sign of the deer, not even a hoof print in the mud.

CHAPTER TWENTY

JILL: 2018

JILL GOT INTO the silver Camry and waited for her brother to settle himself in the driver's side. The last time she'd seen him—in person—was his family's trip to Petaluma two years ago. Then, he'd been full of his usual energy, boiling over with ideas about new books and ways she could expand her gallery. He'd just turned thirty-nine and looked nearly ten years younger. Today, he looked every day of his age, and the thick rims of his glasses did nothing to hide the dark patches beneath his eyes.

"Sorry I couldn't make it here yesterday," she said, cautiously. He didn't meet her eyes as he picked up the thermos tucked between the seats and untwisted the lid. "How's Grams?"

"Good, I guess." He poured coffee into the thermos' cap and held it out to her. "The doctors treated her for bruised ribs and a cut on the side of her head."

"But she was dead." She took the makeshift mug.

"As dead as roadkill." He raised his hand, cutting her off before she could say anything. "Sure, it was a stressful moment. Sure, I could have been wrong about her pulse. But the *way* she was laying there, Gillian. Your neck doesn't go like that unless it's totally fucking broken. And the blood!"

He had told her all of this on the phone Friday night, but it was different hearing it pour out of his mouth on a semi-sunny Sunday afternoon. The Gary who had visited her two years ago would have already spun up a rational explanation for all of this. She'd known things were borked when he had asked her to pack her tarot cards, but she hadn't imagined how broken he would look without all his mental crutches.

She held out the thermos cap. "Do you want me to drive?"

"Oh God, no." He poured more coffee and knocked it back. "If I just sit here, I'll see it again. Or worse, I'll see Dad. So, no. Keeping busy is the only thing holding me together. You should see how clean the house is."

He sealed up the coffee and started the car. Jill let herself look around for the first time since she'd stepped off the airplane at the Southwest Oregon Regional Airport. They used to go shopping out here sometimes, but even in the nineties, the Pony Village Mall had been pretty depressing. She tried to remember the last time she'd been in North Bend and came up empty.

"Dracula."

"What?"

"We went to see *Dracula* at the Egyptian. The Winona Ryder one. You made out with Jason Miller the whole time."

She had to laugh. "Jason Miller? I can't believe he took time away from studying to go out with me. Did you know he's in jail now? Tax fraud."

"He was the smartest kid in your grade too."

"No, that was Ethan Ross. I hear he's teaching high school math somewhere near Seattle."

"Jesus." He was quiet a second. They made the turn onto Highway 101 and began the climb over the great green McCullough Bridge. "This place is haunted, isn't it?"

She looked out over the tidal flats, unsure how to answer.

"I mean, even if our folks hadn't died, it would be haunted by all the boys you ever dated, all the girls I ever kissed. How many of us started at Kingston High in 1991? 105, maybe? They said we were one of the biggest classes the high school ever had. And yet we were down to seventy kids just two years later."

"The cannery closed," she reminded him.

"The cannery closed, and the trees got skinny. The whole place just started drying up and fading away. It won't be long until Kingston is a ghost town, Jill. It already is. It just hasn't realized it yet."

Was he right? She supposed he was. She wiped her sleeve down the window to get a better look at the hills unfolding beside the highway. A lake winked at her, its water thick with lilies and the white shapes of dead trees. If she could have stayed, would she? Would she have wanted to spend her life surrounded by mile after mile of this, trees neither wild nor loved, but merely sprayed and fertilized from airplanes and helicopters? Would she have wanted to drive forty miles to get to the nearest Walmart and eighty to the nearest concert hall? Would she have wanted to fight the mold and mildew every day and spend summer in a damp hoodie?

The view to the west opened for a moment, and she saw a hint of blue ocean. Then they rounded a corner—marked with a yellow deer crossing sign—and were back in forest. The spruce trees grew so close to the road she couldn't see the sky.

Maybe she would have stayed, if she could. If anyone could.

"Jill? Are you paying any attention?"

"Sorry, I was woolgathering. What were you saying?"

"Nothing important. Just talking about Zack. He's at a friend's house this afternoon. He's always at a friend's house. He was never this popular in Portland."

"We were popular in high school, too, remember? You had six girlfriends your freshman year."

They passed a green Prius with California plates.

"Six? No way. Two, maybe."

Despite the ending of the passing lane, a blue Taurus whipped around the green Prius. They weren't quite tailgating, but Jill could still see the red-and-white tassel hanging from their rearview mirror. The girl driving it looked barely old enough to have earned it.

"Better let her pass as soon as we can," Jill complained. Then she remembered Gary's challenge, and held up her pointer finger. "One: Sheri Langstrom." Her middle finger snapped upright. "Two: Donna Waggoner."

"That was just two dates!"

"It counts. Three: Lisa Topping."

"We did *not* date."

"You got to third base with her, dude."

"Only second. Three times. But we never once went on a date."

"You're disgusting."

"That's not what she said." He waggled his eyebrows at her, then glanced in the rearview and noticed the Taurus. "Sheesh. Kids these days have no cool."

They passed the sign for Sandy Lake and rounded a corner. The Sandy Lake straightaway started here, and he slid into the right-hand lane.

Jill glanced over her shoulder. "She's still behind us."

Gary lowered the window and waved for the Taurus to pass. The speedometer's needle dropped a notch, two notches. The Taurus didn't budge.

"What the hell is wrong with this girl?" Gary grumbled.

Jill put her hand on his shoulder. "Try not to worry about it. We can get off in Elk Harbor, look at the beach a little. It's only another ten miles."

Gary sped up. The Taurus did too. It was as if the girl was trying to stay as close to them as possible, a thought that gave Jill the creeps. She reminded herself of all the far more rational explanations for the girl's behavior. She was young, after all. She was probably only half-paying attention to the road as she rocked out to whatever young adults listened to these days.

Jill caught herself sinking down to watch the blue car in her side mirror and forced herself to sit up. "So. Elk Harbor. Definitely."

"Yep." Gary glanced in the mirror again. "She's a surprisingly good driver for an idiot. I mean, she keeps a good distance between us."

He got into the turn lane for Elk Harbor. The blue car came to a stop beside them and the driver rolled down her window.

Jill jabbed at her window's button. "What are you doing? You could cause an accident!"

The girl waved happily. "Hi, Mr. Sheldon! Be careful on the road, okay? We gotta keep you safe!"

A black pickup veered around the Taurus, honking angrily. The girl gave another broad wave and took off.

Gary turned off of the highway, his hands clenched on the steering wheel.

"What the hell is wrong with this town?" Jill wondered.

A deer burst out of the brush on the side of the road and rushed across the street just feet from the Camry.

Gary slammed on the brakes, tires screeching. "Fuck!"

The deer trotted through someone's front yard, unconcerned. The house's door opened, and an older woman rushed out on the porch. She cupped her hands around her mouth. "You all right, Gary?"

Jill reached for Gary's hand and squeezed it as hard as she could. "Dude, I think I'm going to need to stop at the dispensary before we get to your house."

Gary began to laugh. "There aren't any." He laughed louder. "Kingston is a pot-free town, Jilly Bean. Can you believe it?"

He didn't stop laughing, even when the old lady came over to rap on his window and offer him a cup of coffee.

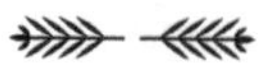

GARY: 1989

Gary woke the morning after the ritual with the feeling that someone had wrapped his brain in steel wool and then proceeded to kick it down a flight of stairs. When he rolled over to check his clock radio, the feeling continued through his joints, with warning grumbles from a similarly mistreated stomach. It seemed impossible that the clock read 9:48, but he could hear the water running in the bathroom, his mom taking a shower before her post-work nap. He tried to remember if she was working graveyard again tonight or if she had the day off, and came up blank.

He forced himself out of bed even though he could have gone for another four or five hours of sleep. He wanted to go out to the orchard and take a good hard look at what they had done. Visit the scene of the crime—but not on an empty stomach. It was hard to remember to eat since he started taking his pills, and if he skipped breakfast, he'd probably forget to eat until dinner.

The kitchen smelled weird without coffee sitting on the burner. He missed his dad. Three weeks was a long time for him to be away. Not for the first time, he wished his parents could just work in the mill or the cannery like normal adults. The anger of it warred with loneliness and made his stomach turn over.

He forced a deep breath and put some bread in the toaster. On second thought, he got out the milk and started heating some on the stove. His mom would be happy if she knew he was getting in the full array of food groups, and he liked making his mom happy. She had a tough enough time, working nights. Some awfully creepy people went to 7-Eleven after everyone else went to bed.

There were plenty of creepy people all over the place, he reminded himself. Vincent Vernor probably never went to 7-Eleven, and he was creepy all day, every day. Gary stirred the milk into some cocoa mix and finished assembling a toasted ham sandwich. He put the milk pan in the sink and filled it with soapy water. He still felt tired, but now he was antsy. Thinking about Vincent Vernor made him want to get outside and breathe clean air. He was supposed to wait half an hour after breakfast before taking his pill, but he took one, chugged the cocoa, and took the sandwich outside.

The candle stumps still stuck out of the gravel, scorched and misshapen after burning through the long ritual. They were so shabby and real today, unlike last night when they, and everything else, including Gary, had gone completely unreal. Or no, not unreal—differently real. He had felt his weird abilities shifting out of himself and spreading through the connected hands of the entire group. For a minute, he had seen the smoky shapes of spirits through David's eyes, crisp and farsighted. He had heard the ghosts' voices through Jordan's ears, super sensitive to the tiny, sibilant sounds in a way Gary's ears had never been. He had felt the sudden urge to pick up a pencil and draw the coiling mist, just as if he was Jill. And Stacie…she had been afraid and thrilled and ready to punch anything that came close to them. He hadn't expected that. She looked so cute and perky, but inside, she was like an angry raccoon.

Gary finished the sandwich and wiped his palms on his shorts. He took another step closer to the gravel heap. The place felt strange today, the air thicker than the air around it, the smells richer, the sounds crisper. He stooped at the edge and scooped up a handful of the small rocks. They buzzed and tingled in his palm.

"What we did blessed you, didn't it?"

He looked around himself, a little embarrassed to be talking to a bunch of rocks. But he could feel the power in them as if they had absorbed some of the…whatever…the five of them had put into their deer saint.

He stood up so fast his knee popped.

He broke into a run, shooting down the spur of their little parking area, out onto the long driveway, over the little bridge. He skidded to a halt beside the dirt track to the barn.

Before stupid Vincent Vernor had showed up, Gary had gone out to the barn two, three, even four times a week to check on the shell. Sometimes he would take a dip in the creek and then stretch out on the grass in front of the barn and read in the sunshine, feeling warm and safe while knowing if he wanted to be scared, he needed only look over his shoulder. The barn, and more importantly, the *shell*, were his. He might not own them, but they owned a part of him, and he needed them more than he needed to feel safe. The day Vincent Vernor had driven him away from the barn, he had gone into a kind of mourning that maybe he was even today feeling.

But no longer. He wasn't sure what this gravel could do, but he had a feeling it would change things.

He crept down the track, keeping as close to the blackberry bushes as he dared. He had the gravel, which he felt pretty sure would protect him, but he also knew Vincent Vernor had a motherfucking machete.

There were no sounds except the soft gurgle of the creek on the far side of the field and the occasional bird. The sun already felt hot on the back of Gary's neck. He crept forward, staying low. Anybody else, he'd assume they were at work, but not Vincent Vernor. He made no assumptions about Vincent.

He stopped at the front corner of the barn. Blackberry vines scrabbled up the side and clawed at Gary's hair as he knelt in the grass. He blew on the handful of gravel.

"Please, Deer Saint. Protect this place. Feels the stones calling to you."

Squeezing his eyes shut, he imagined the gravel landing on the ground and sending up rays of light around the barn like the force fields in a sci-fi novel. He sprinkled a few small bits of stone onto the ground and then murmured a thanks.

A board groaned inside the barn. Gary froze. He didn't even breathe.

There were no further noises, so he scooted along the front of the barn. He wished he didn't have to pass the open doorway, but there was no way to cut down the closer side of the barn; it was just too overgrown with blackberries. He risked a glance around the corner of the barn door.

The darkness inside refused to give way to his quick glance. He held his breath again and took a longer look. There: the crate with the shell. That lump was an old cable spool with a split down the middle. Those lumps over there looked familiar, the same old rusty junk that always lay in the dirt. He thought he saw a few more boxes in the back of the barn than usual, but it was too dark to be sure. Gary darted across the opening and stooped beside the corner to sprinkle a few more gravel bits.

The thump definitely came from inside the barn.

Gary dropped to his knees and pressed his ear to the old siding. What was in there?

The sound of a match striking was perfectly clear and crisp. That first sweet tang of a freshly lit cigarette hit his nose.

He didn't dare walk across the opening of the barn door now. Didn't dare try to cross the field back toward the driveway, either—the big blackberry hedges sealed it up tighter than Tupperware, and anyone looking out from the barn would certainly see him. For a moment, he thought of darting into the tunnel Vincent had hacked out of the brush, but he'd still have to cross the doorway, and even if he made it past that danger, he had no idea where the tunnel went. It couldn't go far. Even if Vincent had cleared the field behind the barn, it would be as tightly hemmed in by brush and the creek as this one.

The creek.

Gary shot a look off to his left. Blackberry brambles crowded up against the banks of the creek in most places, but over the years Gary had beaten his own trail from the barn to the creek. It had grown up a bit since Vincent drove him away from the barn, but it still looked a thousand times less risky than any of Gary's other options.

"What the fuck are you doing here?"

For a moment, Vincent looked as startled as Gary felt. He stood in the doorway of the barn with his cigarette dangling from his lip, wearing a ripped black t-shirt and a pair of jean shorts. Weirdly enough, he held a screen-bottomed drawer in his hand that reminded Gary of his mom's food dehydrator, and it was packed with green leaves.

Gary didn't even think. He threw the last of the gravel in Vincent's face and took off toward the creek. He vaulted a fallen alder tree and landed in a patch of stinging nettle but didn't slow down a bit.

"Come here, you little shit!"

Vincent's hand closed on Gary and spun him around. The man's eyes nearly bulged from his head, the whites streaked red and yellow. He yanked Gary closer.

"You spying on me, brat? You going to rat out my patch to the pigs?"

Gary shook his head wildly. His voice was gone.

Vincent took the cigarette from his mouth. The red cherry glowing at its tip filled the vision of Gary's left eye. "Don't you lie to me."

"I just came to see the shell. That's all."

The cigarette moved, but Gary still felt its heat roving slowly down his cheek, not close enough to burn, but hot enough to scare. If he'd had to pee, he might have wet himself.

Vincent shifted so the length of his body pressed against Gary. The cigarette played down Gary's neck, across his Adam's apple. Vincent pulled Gary more tightly to him. The cigarette's heat was nearly unbearable.

"Hurts, don't it?" Vincent whispered, his breath nearly as hot as the cigarette.

Then something broke loose in Gary's chest, some sudden wash of panic and anger, and he shoved Vincent as hard as he could. The man flailed to stay upright, just for a second, but that second was all Gary needed to spring free. He darted to Vincent's left and then cut back onto the path to the creek.

"You little bastard!"

Gary put a burst of speed into his legs and hit the blackberry hedge at full tilt. The path he'd cut was barely wide enough for him to slip through carefully, and he was not careful. Vines clawed at his hair and face. The branches of an alder sapling slapped at his arms. But he could hear the creek just ahead.

A blackberry vine caught Gary's ankle and nearly tripped him, but he ripped free with a burst of pain in his ankle. He skidded on a stick—*beaver-chewed!*, some normal boyish part of his brain rejoiced—and nearly fell over the edge of the bank. You had to know just the right approach to this little beach or you'd break your neck.

A horrible smashing sound came from the barn. Gary jumped down to the first foothold of sandstone.

"I broke your shell, you little bastard! I'll break you next time!"

Another smash, this time with a hard, porcelain undertone. Gary covered his mouth with his hand. *The shell.*

His eyes filled with tears. If he had finished putting out the gravel, the shell would have been safe. He knew it.

He had failed.

Vincent screamed in rage and something else smashed. Gary scrambled down to the water. It was still high for summertime. He had to wade through nearly chest-deep water at this stretch of the stream. He didn't want to think what it would be like going through the culvert beneath the driveway. The scrapes and scratches covering his body stung in the cold water.

Up on the bank, on the woods side, a branch crunched. He looked up just in time to see a deer unfolding herself from the trampled area where she'd bedded down. Their eyes met for an instant, and then she was gone, just a white flash of tail vanishing through the brush.

Vincent screamed again, but this time he didn't sound angry. He sounded hurt.

Gary grinned and began to wade downstream. Maybe the gravel had done something after all.

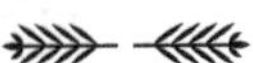

GARY: 2018

It was nice having Jill around.

She had slept through Kim and Zack's morning routine, and he could still hear her snoring quietly in the guest room. They had stayed up talking the way they always did, although the conversation this time was freer than it had been since they were kids. He hadn't realized how many topics had been off the table: mental health, the past, their parents, anything magical or spiritual or weird. The fact they could still even enjoy each other's company while avoiding so much important material showed how close they really were.

He went back downstairs and put the baking sheet of biscuits in the oven. Jilly had loved biscuits and gravy when they were kids, and Gary had recently picked up a recipe for a veggie version she'd love. He already had the gravy ready on the back burner.

In the meantime, he could take care of a bit of business. Last week, he had told Kim he was going to call someone about the fence, but what with everything that had been going on, he'd forgotten. Well, now was the time. He got out the Kingston phone book—feeling more than a little old-fashioned—and dialed the number for the biggest ad in the Yellow Pages. He stirred the gravy as the other line rang. The smell of fennel seed and pepper made his mouth water.

The phone gave a couple more rings. Then: "Chet MacKenzie here."

Gary explained the deer situation and the need for a new fence. Chet listened with a quiet intensity, not even punctuating the conversation with a grunt or a thoughtful *mmn.* Gary might have thought the man had hung up if he hadn't heard the occasional clink and rattle, like someone sorting a sack full of hardware into peanut butter jars. An image flashed in Gary's head: his dad sitting in the garage, doing just that. He blinked it away.

His end of the conversation dwindled into awkward silence.

"I get ya." Chet made some noises for a moment. "Sure, I could do your job. Probably run you fifteen hundred. Two, if your yard's really big."

Gary winced. "It's a pretty small yard. And maybe I could help. Do a little of the work to bring down the cost."

"Yep. That'd do it." Another clinking and rattling. Gary forced his neck muscles to relax. "Problem is, I'm working a pretty big job right now. Won't get done until December at the earliest."

"That's a long time from now."

"I can give you the name of another guy, if you want. His work's okay."

Gary marked a certain note of reluctance in the contractor's voice. It must be galling, giving out a competitor's phone number.

"Yeah, that would be really helpful. We've seen a guy in our backyard, so we're kind of freaked out."

"A trespasser?"

"Yeah, this big creepy asshole. He left his cigarettes on our back porch like some kind of warning."

Chet went quiet. He didn't even rattle.

"Chet? You still there?"

"Oh, yeah. Just getting that number. Sounds like you need a fence sooner rather than later." He read off a phone number. "Name's Mark. MacKenzie. My brother. He can probably squeeze you in soon."

"Thanks, Chet. If I have another project, I'll keep you in mind."

"Did you keep the cigarettes?"

The question caught Gary sideways. "What?"

"Never mind. Just…yeah. Call me if you need anything." The contractor hung up.

Gary frowned at the gravy. Kingston's contracting community seemed odder than most.

His phone buzzed in his hand. A text from Kim: *Three parents have stopped by to complain about the football team's loss.*

He thumbed in a reply: *Those dingdongs!*

Her answer: *Did you see the paper?*

Gary walked out to the paper box and retrieved the weekly rag. The problem screamed from above the fold: "Gig Harbor Courts Keridan Bridge."

His phone buzzed again.

They're already saying it's Coach Washburn's fault, Kim wrote.

He waited for her to explain, but she didn't send a follow-up. He'd watched *Friday Night Lights*, but this kind of football obsession was insane. If this was what being KHS's principal was going to be like, Kim was going to need more than just one cigarette a day.

Gary dropped the paper straight into the recycling cart and headed for the door. A flash of blue made him turn his head. A blue Taurus disappeared around the corner.

The skin on his arms crept up in goosebumps.

CHAPTER TWENTY-ONE

JILL: 1989

DAVID WASN'T ANSWERING his phone and Gary had gone for a run in the woods, so Jill, Jordan, and Stacie tackled graveling the Shell station on their own. First they went to Murphy's to fortify themselves. Jill only had a couple of dollars, but a couple of dollars went a long way at Murphy's, especially if there were day-olds. She pushed open the swinging door and held it for Jordan and Stacie.

They all stood there a long moment in the entryway, just smelling the bakery's wonderful scent. Hot grease and vanilla frosting. A note of maple. The ever-present tang of coffee. Mrs. Murphy looked up from a puzzle book and smiled at them.

"Well, don't just stand there, kiddos. Pick yourself a treat."

They couldn't make themselves hurry to the front counter, though. There was still too much to look at: the pastry case with the pies mounded four or five inches high with cream or meringue. The rack of bread loaves in every style of bread ever baked. The plastic sacks bulging with red-white-and-blue frosted cookies, even though Fourth of July wasn't for another week. A tall Black man set a baking sheet in the window separating the kitchen from the front counter area.

"This batch is ready, Auntie."

Mrs. Murphy picked up the tray like it weighed next to nothing. "Mmmn-mmmn, those smell nice." She brought it to the counter. "There's nothing like a fresh-made donut, is there? Just you sniff."

The smell of those donuts—pershings and cinnamon twists—nearly floated Jill off her feet. It was impossible to feel frightened or worried smelling that vanilla and cinnamon smell.

"Wow," Jordan breathed. "Are they extra because they're just-made?"

"Nope." Mrs. Murphy pulled a little sheet of wax paper out of the box. Her hand floated above a cinnamon twist. "Eighty-five cents, same as always."

Jordan found a dollar in his pocket. "I'll take a cinnamon twist."

Stacie was counting change. "Are chocolate-glazed the same price?"

"Sure are." Mrs. Murphy turned to Jill. "What's calling you, Goldilocks?"

Jill hesitated. She loved pershings more than just about any donut, but if she got a bag of day-olds, she would have enough for her mom and Gary. They were only zebra bars, but they were still good, especially if you warmed in the oven for a minute or two. "I guess I'll take these day-olds." She held out her two dollars.

Mrs. Murphy gave her a sharp look. "Business-minded, aren't you? Good for you, kid."

Jill blinked at her, not sure she'd heard properly. Had anyone ever said anything like that about her? "Head in the clouds," her math teacher had complained this spring. "Daydreamer," her English teacher had said. Her report cards going back to kindergarten were filled with such comments.

"Don't forget your change," Mrs. Murphy reminded them. "And have a nice day."

"Thank you," Jill said. She was smiling wider than she had all summer. "You have a nice day, too, Mrs. Murphy."

She even waved as they walked out the door, and Mrs. Murphy waved back at her. Jill felt as good inside as Murphy's Bakery smelled.

"I can't believe you resisted those pershings," Stacie said. "They're your favorite."

Jordan held out his donut. "You can have a bite of my cinnamon twist. They're kind of like pershings."

"It's okay. I got five donuts for only two bucks." Jill took one out of the bag and tore it in half. It was easy to forget how good a zebra bar could be. They were no pershing, but they were still tender and sweet.

"I don't want to do this," Jordan admitted. "I haven't been to see my mom at work since Vincent Vernor started there. And I really don't want to see him now."

"Me neither," Stacie whispered. She held her donut as if she wasn't sure what to do with it.

Jill gave her a one-armed hug. "It'll be okay. There will be other adults around. It won't be like it was for Gary."

Stacie's expression did not get much more cheerful. Jill dug in her pockets for a handful of the gravel.

"Here. Take some. It'll make you feel better."

"It's warm," Stacie said, surprise in her voice.

"It's been in my pocket," Jill reminded her.

"It's warmer than that." Stacie squeezed the little rocks tighter in her hand. "It kind of buzzes too."

"I want some," Jordan said. He gave his fingers one last lick. "Please."

Jill gave him a handful of gravel too. She felt nothing special when she did, but his eyes widened as he took it.

"This is going to work." Stacie smiled at them. "Come on."

The Shell station was just three blocks from Murphy's. Jill's dad always said the Shell hired the worst mechanics in town and that only an idiot went there instead of Connolly's, but lots of people liked the Shell better. For one, it was cheaper, and for two, Old Man Connolly liked to scold people who forgot about things like changing your oil every 2,000 miles. Jill almost said something and then remembered that Jordan's mom worked there.

"Shit," Jordan whispered.

And Jill saw why: Vincent Vernor's big ugly hog was parked behind the station.

"How close do we need to get to your mom's actual office?" Stacie asked. Her top lip had gone sweaty. It was a warm day, but not that warm.

Jill reached for their hands. "Come on. Let's think about the deer saint. Maybe it will guide us."

She squeezed shut her eyes and brought its image into her head, the tall, wide antlers, the enormous neck. The eyes that flashed in the darkness. The human part of him wasn't any smaller or less scary either. The deer saint was big enough he could pick up Vincent Vernor and throw him across the highway.

She opened her eyes, smiling a little at the thought of Vincent Vernor getting launched fifty yards through traffic. "The outside of the station should be fine," she said. The gravel buzzed in her pocket.

Stacie broke into a run, streaking across the end of the block and darting behind the big white propane tank. No one would see her there, that smart girl.

Jill nodded at Jordan. "Walk up like you belong here. You're just saying hi to your mom."

He stood up a little taller. "I'm just saying hi to my mom."

Jill followed him as casually as any kid running an errand with a friend. She didn't even think about the deer saint. She was just a girl waiting for a friend.

Jordan paused at the front corner of the building and dropped a few gravel bits. Then he opened the door and went inside the gas station.

Jill went around the back where the bathrooms were. "Please, Saint Deer," she whispered, dropping a rock or two with every step. "Please, protect this place."

"You're not a paying customer—you don't get to use the bathrooms."

She stopped, her feet rooted to the ground.

"Hey, kid, you heard me. Get out of here."

She didn't want to turn to face him, but she had to. "I'm just waiting for a friend."

Vincent Vernor's eyes narrowed. "Oh, no fucking way. It's bad enough I have to deal with you shits at home."

Stacie came around from the other side of the station and grabbed Jill's hand. "Let's go."

He looked from Jill to Stacie, and his face went from angry to smirking. "I know you, little girl. I know where you live."

"Let's *go*," Stacie repeated.

"Is there a problem back here?" a man asked, and Jill recognized him as the station's owner. He looked pretty unhappy. "How's that station wagon coming along, Vince?"

"Hey, girls, Mom gave me five bucks," Jordan shouted from the sidewalk. "Let's go!"

"Yeah, get out of here," the station owner growled. "And Vernor, I want that station wagon finished before lunch."

Stacie nearly yanked Jill off her feet running away.

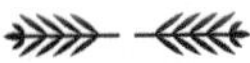

STACIE: 2018

Stacie had opened her eyes in the only slightly musty-smelling motel room and remembered she'd have to drive through Kingston this morning. She'd passed through it on her way down to Coos Bay, of course, but she'd been on a tight schedule, and with a podcast blasting, she'd almost been able to zip through town without noticing. She knew she didn't have the focus to do that a second time. Today she would drive through Kingston and not just look at the town where she'd grown up, but *see* it.

Knowing that, she didn't exactly rush through her morning shower and a breakfast burrito, but she did move quickly. She even took her coffee to-go. She dialed in to the local oldies station and drove the speed limit up Highway 101. Every now and then she rolled down the window. Even when she couldn't see the ocean, she could smell it out there.

The city limits sign arrived before any houses: Kingston, Oregon, population 4,058. She could clearly remember the number being closer to five thousand as a kid. She'd been prepared to feel a lot of things, coming back here, but this weird sadness was not one of them.

She eased into the right-hand lane—it was kind of a surprise that Highway 101 ran four lanes through this one-horse town, but she supposed they got a lot of traffic headed from the coast to the freeway—and let herself gawk. The high school had a new paint job. Someone had bought The Firs motel and renamed it The Waves. Connolly's Autobody had doubled in size. At least someone was doing all right for themselves.

Stacie and her mom had left town before Stacie learned to drive, but she remembered every turn and every slowdown, even the shortcut down Elkay Drive that shaved half a mile off the turn onto Highway 38. She didn't doubt her instincts when she took a left on Fir Drive and pulled up to the pink bakery. Life in Kingston hadn't been all bad, she reminded herself. There had been plenty of sweetness, up to and including trips to Murphy's.

It looked different these days, but she supposed she did too. Someone had hung blue gingham curtains in the window, cuting up the place, and a pair of chainsaw-carved bears flanked the front door. When she pulled the door open, another bear greeted her, a straw hat on its head and brochures in its paws. The old wonderful smell of coffee and hot oil nearly knocked her off her feet.

"Damn, that smells good."

A dark-haired woman pulled her head out of the rotating pie case. "I heard that," she said, shaking her finger. There was a touch of Mexico in her accent, something you never heard in Kingston back in the 1980s. She winked and smiled. "It's the kind of thing we hope we hear." Her smile made dimples spring up around her lips.

If it had been Portland, Stacie would have leaned on the ice cream case and flirted with this girl until the ice cream melted, but there were two tables of old-timers already giving her disapproving looks, and Stacie wasn't an idiot. She glanced at the menu instead of the dimples and raised her eyebrows in shock.

"Espresso? At Murphy's?"

The cutie closed the pie case and went to the register. "You've been here before?"

"I grew up here," Stacie admitted, "but I haven't been to Kingston since I was a kid. Does Mrs. Murphy still own the place?"

"Yep! She went to Coos Bay to do some shopping though. Should I tell her you stopped by?"

The bell above the door chimed. Stacie glanced over her shoulder. A blonde lady had come inside and was standing on the front mat with her eyes closed, making the same blissful face Stacie must have made when she arrived.

Stacie turned back to the register. "Naw, she wouldn't remember me." She bent over the pastry case, studying the varieties. Portland had its fair share of donut places, but none of them could hold a candle to Murphy's—or at least Stacie's memory of Murphy's.

"Excuse me?" The blonde woman had come up to the pastry case. She looked perplexed.

"Oh, I can move," Stacie said. "I haven't started looking at the second case."

The woman stepped closer. "Is your name Stacie Clinton?"

Stacie stared at her, trying to place her face and coming up blank. The blonde had a sort of boho vibe, all long curly hair and loose layers, a look which Stacie thought only worked for twenty-year-olds on Instagram. The woman's freckles and smile lines suggested she was well out of her twenties, and possibly spent a lot of time in the sun. Stacie's age, California-style.

Maybe they had gone to school together back in the day.

"I'm sorry," the woman said. She was looking more familiar by the second, but it was impossible that she could be who Stacie thought she was. "You just reminded me of someone I knew as a kid. Although she would have never worn all black. She wore pink every day."

Stacie took a step backward, prickles rising up on her neck. It *was* her. Somehow, it was really her. "Jill?"

The blonde beamed. "Stacie? It's really you?"

She threw her arms around Stacie's neck, squeezing her so tightly Stacie couldn't have answered if she tried.

From the corner of her eye, she saw an older man stand up, craning his neck to see better. Like he was trying to get a good look at Jill's face.

Stacie patted Jill's back and pulled away. She had about a billion questions, but there was no way she was asking them in front of that creepy asshole. "I've got a little time before I have to get back on the road. Why don't we get coffees and donuts and take a little walk?"

Jill must have seen the old man, because her face changed—just for a second—and then she was smiling again. "That sounds terrific." She turned back to the girl at the register. "I'll take a pershing and a cup of regular coffee. It would be a sin to drink a latte with one of Mrs. Murphy's beautiful donuts."

Stacie put her steel travel mug on the counter. "Regular for me too. And a chocolate-glazed."

Jill smiled at her. "Some things don't change."

Stacie took a quick look behind them. The man had sat down, but he was on his cell phone now. The goosebumps on Stacie's neck were spreading up her hairline and down her arms.

She was in Kingston, and she was scared as hell. She supposed Jill was right: some things don't change.

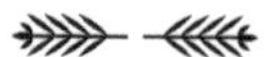

GARY: 1989

Gary and Jill met the others at the lodge for a celebratory lunch, and to give David a handful of the gravel to put around his house. When David walked in the lodge's big front door, his hand on Jordan's shoulder, Gary was glad for the sandwich bag of rocks in his pocket. David looked like he hadn't slept since they had done their ritual, and his hair, which usually did a half-unkempt kind of Keifer Sutherland thing, was flat and greasy.

"You look like crap," Stacie said, bending a fry into her mouth.

"Thanks," he said, sliding into the booth across from her. He took one of the fries. "You look too happy for your own good."

"What's wrong?" Gary asked.

David rolled his eyes. "Nothing."

Jill reached for his hand. "It's not nothing. You look really unhappy."

"Yeah," Jordan agreed.

David's gaze had fixed on Jill's. He hadn't let go of Jill's hand either. Squeezed up beside Stacie in the booth, Gary felt her stiffen into rock. He wasn't sure he liked the thought of Jill getting romantic with David either.

"My parents," David finally said. "They've been to a different party every night, coming back totally wasted. I've never seen them like this, and I've seen them do a lot of stupid shit."

"Crap," Gary said. "Are they hanging out with Vincent Vernor?"

Jill pressed a second hand over David's and squeezed tightly.

David looked from her to Gary. "I don't know. I haven't seen his motorcycle or car around, but that doesn't mean anything."

"Well, take this." Gary pulled the rocks out of his pocket. "We've been putting them places where he might go. I think they'll help the deer saint protect us."

David took the rocks and held them up for a better look. "They're just rocks, right? From your orchard?" He put down the bag and narrowed his eyes. "Don't you think all of this is kind of stupid? What do you think we really did back there, anyway? We're just a bunch of dumb kids who are scared of the local drug dealer."

"You don't mean that," Jordan whispered.

Jill yanked her hands free and pushed herself back in her seat like she wanted to put as much distance between her and David as possible.

Gary just stared at him. One part of Gary wanted to smash his fist into David's nose, while another part sat back and shrugged. Why would David believe in the deer saint? He hadn't been seeing ghosts his whole life. He hadn't been painting visions of the future. He hadn't gone into one of those cabins and found a saint's medallion on the only clean surface in the whole shit- and blood-smeared hell hole. Who the hell was David, anyway? He was just some asshole who hung out with Jordan when he didn't feel like throwing around a football.

"Hallelujah! Hallelujah!"

Coach Dusseldorf burst in the front door of the lodge, singing at top volume.

Everyone turned to stare at him. He had obviously set out to go fishing that morning, but his KHS Bucks cap had been knocked askew and there was a spatter of blood down the front of his fishing vest.

"Hallelujah! Halle-e-lu-u-jaaaaa!"

Stacie's mom intercepted him by the pool table. "Jesus, Coach, what happened?"

He put his arms around her and lifted her off her feet. "I almost died!"

She wriggled out of his grasp and urged him into a chair. "Car accident?"

"Something like that. Can I get a coffee? Fuck, make it a Hamm's. I could use something harder, but you don't have any liquor."

An older couple got up from their table and sat down beside him. "What happened, Coach D?" the man asked.

Stacie's mom brought Dusseldorf the beer and he downed half the glass before putting it down. Gary hadn't noticed the faint red stain around the man's nose and mouth. It must have been a monster nose bleed.

"I was on my way to Eagle Cove," Dusseldorf started, then reached for a napkin and gave his nose a squeeze. "It's a good spot for bass sometimes."

"Nah, you need a boat," the other man said, but his wife jabbed him in the ribs. The cook and another table of what appeared to be fishermen had all come to stand around the coach.

"Anyway, I was driving down Calhoun Lake Road, when this motherfucking Harley, a real big hog, zips around the corner, cutting into my lane. I laid on the horn, but that bastard must have been drunk or stoned or some shit, because he just barrels right at me."

He picked up the beer and finished it. Stacie was gripping Gary's arm so hard he was starting to lose the feeling in his hand.

"I didn't think. I yanked the wheel to the right, and then I realized I was going off the road. Time just froze, you know? The sound of my tires hitting the gravel on the shoulder was about the loudest thing I ever heard." Stacie's mom put down a second Hamm's, and the coach took a quick drink. "This was just ten? Twenty minutes ago? I mean, it's broad daylight and there's no fog or anything."

"Nope, broad daylight," a fisherman agreed.

"Too late to catch bass," the oldest said, and once again his wife jabbed him in the ribs.

"I thought I was dead," Coach Dusseldorf admitted. "I was right there at the head of the lake, where the road's still way high up, and there are all those rocks down there."

"That's what made the lake," the old man interjected. "Rock dam."

"Right," Dusseldorf said, his eyes brightening. "The rock dam! You go off the road and hit that damn thing, and you're not coming out of the drink alive. You're not coming out in one piece, even if you're driving American-made."

"Jesus," Stacie's mom breathed. "I would have pissed myself."

"I almost did! But my pickup hit something before it went off the road."

As one, the assorted listeners leaned in. "What?"

"A deer."

Jordan gasped.

"What?" The cook waved a hand, disbelieving. "That wouldn't stop a truck from going off the road."

Coach Dusseldorf shook his head. "It wasn't any normal kind of deer. It was a giant stag. Taller than my pickup. Standing on its hind legs or something. It just leaped up and stopped my truck with its body. I sat there, staring at it. Staring into its eyes. They were bright, bright green.

You know, like when you catch a glimpse of a deer on the highway at night. Glowing."

Stacie's mom shuddered. "That ain't right."

Half the others were shaking their heads, but half were just blinking at the coach. He was Coach D, after all, not some nutjob or tourist. Coach *D*. He had rebuilt the Bucks into a decent football team after twenty years of being the worst 2A football team in the whole state.

His shoulders began to shake, and he covered his face with his hand. "It was a miracle." He turned his face away so the others couldn't see. "It was a fucking miracle."

Gary felt Stacie's grip loosen on his arm. She leaned into the center of the table. "You all heard him. A giant stag with glowing green eyes."

"Yeah," Jordan whispered. "And what did it save him from? A goddamn black Harley Davidson. If that wasn't Vincent Vernor, I'll eat my t-shirt."

David was still watching Coach Dusseldorf, who was pulling himself together and ordering some pancakes. David turned to look at Gary.

"Give me the goddamn rocks, Gary."

CHAPTER TWENTY-TWO

JILL: 2018

JILL FOLLOWED STACIE out of Murphy's, coffee and donuts in hand. Neither of them said anything as they walked through the parking lot and waited at the corner to cross the highway. The past formed an enormous lump in Jill's throat.

And Stacie—who would have guessed Stacie would turn into this as an adult: black clothes, black eyeliner, black boots, and a black leather wrist cuff. The effect was less goth and more Janeane Garofalo. Stacie took a bite of donut and then rested it on top of her travel mug.

As an empty log truck rattled slowly by, Jill searched for something to say to this stranger. "I like your hair."

It sounded stupid coming out of her mouth, but Stacie brushed her hand over the choppy edges of her bob. "It could use a trim."

"The undercut is still sharp."

They crossed the now-empty road.

"I keep up on it at home." Stacie smiled, a real smile. "Remember how I used to cut our hair?"

They rounded the corner at the post office, headed for the river. They used to walk to the end of town when they were kids, pass by the old shipyard and hang out by the railroad track. Jill's feet still knew the way.

"I had to grow out my hair when you moved. No one in town knew how to cut curly hair."

They walked a few more minutes, the silence less tense between them. Where the trains used to run, a stretch of gravel ran beside the Peshak River. A sign announced the happy news of a rail-to-trail conversion, completed with lottery dollars in Spring, 2010. They paused a second, looking up the empty trail. Jill supposed she shouldn't be surprised the railway was gone. The train hadn't run that often even in the eighties.

"That old guy back at Murphy's was watching us," Stacie said. The gravel crunching underfoot was almost louder than her voice. "He gave me the creeps."

Jill took a bite of her pershing. She had almost forgotten about it. "At least half the population of this town is over sixty-five. That guy was probably worried he'd have a heart attack from looking at us."

Stacie laughed, but her face went serious again in a second. "It's weird, being back in Kingston. I haven't been here since we moved. Not even just to drive through."

"Me neither," Jill admitted. "After my parents died—did you know about my parents?—I couldn't even visit Grams and Gramps. It was too much."

Stacie paused. The trail wound east, paralleling the highway. A thick stand of trees separated the two. They could have been hiking anywhere in the Pacific Northwest: a big, lovely river, tall Douglas firs, graceful alder. Jill had been hiking on a dozen trails with the same configuration. But they weren't on the Clackamas or the Umpqua. They were walking beside the Peshak, and even her bones knew it.

"What was it like after I left? The town, I mean. Jordan kept in touch with David and I. Some of the things David told him were just unbelievable."

Jill strode past Stacie, her eyes on the river and not Stacie's face. There were so many birds out here: cormorants settled on old pilings, ducks and geese swimming close to the riverbank. They swam just six or seven feet beneath her feet, practically touching distance, if the old train embankment hadn't been so steep. She could smell the river, fresh and green and a little bit doggish.

"I didn't really think about it while I was here," Jill admitted. "David and I weren't really friends after he got to high school. He was busy with the jocks, and I was busy with…everyone else. School was great. I mean, the school was *doing* great. The whole town, really. The cheerleading squad went to regionals. The football team won state. The mill got busier, so everyone was making overtime. The library expanded their parking lot."

"Kingston's glory days."

"That's what it seemed like. Everybody was full of town spirit or something. It was totally different from what it was like as kids."

Stacie leaned her elbows on a plaque describing the native bird species. "What the hell happened?"

Jill looked out at the river again. It stretched green and flat, a big empty river with forest clinging to both sides. When they were kids, there were always boats out there, fishing boats, barges, tugs. Now, nothing.

"The fishing and timber industries, I guess." She remembered some of the things Gary had said about the town's quest to land the bridge company. "I sure hope something else comes along to save this town."

Stacie took a drink of her coffee and didn't reply. They started walking again, deeper into the forest. Every now and then Jill heard an engine up on Highway 38, but they were far below it now, the old railroad clinging to the base of the hill, the cars moving up its flanks. She remembered reading that this little finger of land had once held an Indian settlement. While Jill was in high school, archaeologists had come out to dig through the old middens. One of them had made a presentation at an assembly. Jill could still remember the woman's vivid fuchsia dress. Who knew archaeologists wore fuchsia?

"I missed you," Stacie said. "I really, really missed you."

Jill stopped. The corners of her eyes stung. "I wrote you once. You never answered."

Stacie shot her a hot glance and then picked up her pace. "How could I? You were writing about making the cheerleading squad and going out with cute boys. How could I write you back about Corvallis and how my mom was never around and no one would even let me sit with them at lunch?"

"Oh, Stacie, I'm so sorry." Jill reached out to her, but Stacie pushed her away.

"It fucking sucked, Jill. Especially after everything that happened that summer."

Jill had no answer for her. Everything had changed after the lodge burned down. Her dad had gotten a good job, the first good job of maybe his entire life, and they had moved into a house where the plumbing worked all the time and there weren't mildew stains on the walls or mushrooms in the carpet. Her mom stopped working graveyard and started baking cookies, for crap's sake. And if all of this had come at the price of her parents having a social life and all of them being too busy to eat dinner together every night, well then, that was the price. The Sheldons might not have been the richest family in Kingston, but for the first time they had been middle class and they had all had friends, and that had been a *relief*.

She was buoyed by this thought for less than a second before she thought about what Stacie's life must have been like in Corvallis and then she teared up again.

"There's a little path going up the hill," Stacie said. "You can just see it there in the trees."

Jill cleared her throat. "It must lead to the site of the Indian village." She pointed up ahead. "It looks like you might be able to get on it up there."

Stacie pushed back the weedy bush—*spirea*, Jill remembered—beside the trailhead. Someone had wedged two-by-fours into the hillside to form makeshift stairs. "Let's check it out."

Jill half-wondered why, if Stacie was so mad at her, she wanted to keep walking together. But it felt right to follow her up the second path.

"Look." Something hung from one of the alders, swinging from a length of fishing line. Stacie gave it a little tap and sent it swinging. A plastic doll, the kind that came in a Happy Meal. "Creepy."

Jill walked a little faster. The trail wasn't quite wide enough to walk beside Stacie, and she wished it was. "I don't hear any birds."

"We probably scared them off."

"Even the ducks? You'd think they'd be relaxed now that they can't see us."

The trail made a sharp left, running parallel to the former railroad below. This trail looked much older than the gravel path, the ruts of people's footsteps worn deep into the clay subsoil. Jill let her hand brush across the exposed sandstone on her right. Anyplace else, there would have been graffiti.

Stacie paused, stooping to examine a log beside the trail. "Someone cut this with a chainsaw. See? It must have fallen across the trail and someone cleared it."

Jill peered down the bank, where the official trail was still clearly visible. "Why go to all the effort when there's a perfectly good trail just ten yards away?"

"Where does this trail even go?" Stacie wondered.

They kept walking. At one point, Jill noticed another trail, narrow and steep, cutting down the side of the hill. It must have come from the highway. She certainly couldn't imagine trudging down it. It joined their own trail at a point marked with a stack of rocks. She had seen rock stacks at dozens of trailheads, anywhere hippies and hipsters liked to hike, but this one lacked the usual smugness of something designed for Instagram.

Their trail began descending the hill. In a few more steps, she realized the railroad trail was climbing up, the embankment sloping to meet an old railroad trestle. A small creek ran underneath it, snaking down to join the Peshak. Their trail followed the tiny waterway. This had to be Indian Point, that little stretch of rock where archaeologists had studied the ruins of a native village.

A thought struck Jill. "My dad used to come down here."

Jill wasn't sure where the memory came from. It hadn't been there a minute before, but now she could see her father out in the garage, taking a plastic container full of night crawlers out of the mini fridge where he stashed his beer. "He went fishing with his Deer Kings buddies out here. Sometimes my mom went too. I think they were probably partying."

The path made a little turn around the tip of the peninsula, and now they were beside the river. Trees surrounded them on three sides, but this space was open, the ground silt and exposed rock sloping down to a muddy beach. A big rock, as large and flat as a table, stood out from the rest of the beach. In flood state, the Peshak would cover the beach all way up to the tree line.

Someone had built a little fire pit beside the table rock, and a long row of bottles lined its side.

"You could throw a real rager out here," Stacie said, walking toward the fire pit, "and no one would ever know."

Jill nudged a half-burned stick of wood in the ring of rocks. "This looks pretty recent. There aren't even any fallen leaves."

"They could have cleaned up better." Stacie scowled at the bottles. She had a bit of chocolate glaze on her cheek. "Though they were probably wasted. Look—Corona, Heineken, even Jack Daniels."

Jill took a step closer to the table rock. "Some of them aren't even empty."

"Probably full of river water. Or piss." Stacie nudged the Jack Daniels bottle with her boot, toppling it into the sand. The sharp, sweet scent of whiskey overpowered the smells of river and trees.

"Who leaves a fifth of Jack on the beach?" Jill asked. "Unless they're planning to come back and finish it." She turned around, looking for a boat, for another walker, someone. She scanned the flanks of the hill.

That's when she noticed the shelves. "Stacie."

Stacie turned away from the bottles. "What?"

Jill just pointed.

"The fuck is all that?"

Someone had built shelves out there in the trees; nothing fancy, just wide, roughly planed slabs of wood nailed between a pair of alders. They were high enough up from the beach that only a hundred-year flood would touch them.

Jill took an unwilling step closer. The shelves went up and up into the trees, six or seven feet of them, and every inch was crowded with…Jill didn't even have a word for it all. Bottles of liquor in various stages of emptiness. Cartons of cigarettes—all of them Marlboro Reds—some weather-beaten, some nearly new. Two or three cans of Copenhagen. A china doll, its hair matted with moss. Jewelry boxes ranging from ring-sized to tiara-worthy. A Stetson hat with the tag still on it. Somewhere near the top she saw something that made her skin crawl: an RCA-brand VCR just like the one her dad had bought at the Radio Shack in Coos Bay, only to take it back two days later for reasons unclear. She felt with certainty that if she could turn it on, she would find a tape of *Alien³* still paused at the scene she'd left it at.

"They're offerings."

Jill could barely take her eyes off the VCR sitting ten feet above her head, but she finally turned to Stacie, kneeling beside a basket someone had stashed in a sword fern. "What?"

"Offerings. Look—this must have been some little girl's treasure." She held up another china doll, its gown spotted with mildew stains.

There were more baskets, Jill saw now, tucked in between the alders. There were trays, too, pushed into the slope of the hill, holding up watches and old coins and cuff links. Several boxes of chocolates, their pink velour or satin covers bleaching in the sun, rested in the crotches of smaller tree branches, and tiny gadgets, doodads, and gizmos swung on the breeze, suspended by fishing line like a perverse set of Christmas decorations.

"Fuuuuck," Stacie said. She stood up and hit her head on a crystal teardrop swinging at eyebrow height. She flinched away, colliding with the tiny skull of perhaps a cat.

Jill grabbed Stacie's arm. "Offerings to what?"

Stacie pointed to a plastic-shrouded bouquet of roses, the roses inside still perfectly formed. Someone had bought them at 7-11. "I don't know, but those couldn't have been left here very long. They're not even wilting."

"We should get out of here." Jill pulled on Stacie's arm. "And go tell Gary about all this. He saw some weird shit up at the beach. This has to be connected."

"Gary? He's here, too?"

Jill realized she hadn't told Stacie any part of the story that had brought her to Kingston. Was it a coincidence that they were all together again? She was no longer sure.

Something splashed in the creek they'd followed. Stacie jumped at the sound, and Jill felt her legs go to jelly.

"Someone's coming," she whispered.

"We've got to get back to the main trail," Stacie hissed. She scrambled over a concrete statue of a jockey to look up the hill. The ferns and brush were thick here, but the railroad embankment was actually only a short scramble through the brush.

Jill cursed her Dansko clogs as she hurried after Stacie. Moss and dirt fell into the loose backs with every step, and she slipped and skidded, crashing through the brush. Stacie offered her a hand, nearly yanking her up the hill.

Jill could see the trail just a few feet ahead. She risked a glance over her shoulder. Someone was crouching on the beach beside the table rock, holding the now-empty bottle of Jack Daniels up to the light. She couldn't see his face, but he was a big man, wearing the kind of outdoor gear every local probably kept in their closet. An orange deer hunter's cap sat on the beach beside him.

"Faster!" Stacie yelled, and Jill jumped forward, nearly toppling into the split-rail fence of the trail. Her clog slid off her right foot as she swung her leg up and over.

Stacie broke into a run. Jill put a burst of speed into her legs to catch up with her. That man had to know where they'd gone. They'd left a path so clear a toddler could follow it.

The trail sloped down, and now Jill saw the spot where they'd turned onto the other path. She picked up her pace. They were a long way from town if that man caught up with them.

Stacie jumped down the stairs to the gravel trail. "Hurry up!"

Jill kicked off her other Dansko so she could run faster. She lowered her head and charged after Stacie. At the last second, she realized Stacie had stopped in the middle of the path.

It was too late to stop. She hit Stacie so hard they both fell onto the gravel trail. The rock bit into Jill's palms and shins. She jumped to her feet, gasping for air.

"Come on!"

Stacie got to her feet, holding her side. She had lost her travel mug somewhere, and mud and moss streaked her clothes. Jill wondered if she looked as battered as Stacie did. "Look."

There on the informational plaque about native birds, written neatly in fat black Sharpie, someone had left them a message:

WELCOME HOME, JILL.

A duck let out a shriek of alarm, and Jill and Stacie began to run again.

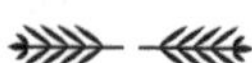

GARY: 2018

Where the hell was Jill? It was only a mile to Murphy's, and she'd been gone over an hour and a half. Gary slipped on his windbreaker and stepped outside. It was one of those perfect days that hit the Oregon coast a few times in September and October, and he almost regretted the windbreaker. He set out for the end of the cul de sac, unsure what he was looking for. He could call, of course. But he felt too antsy to stand around waiting.

He turned onto French Road. The postal truck went past, and the mail carrier waved at him. An older woman brought her black lab out onto her yard and called out a good afternoon. Anyone visiting town would think they had entered the most wholesome, friendly little hamlet in all of Oregon. The hairs on the back of Gary's neck bristled. He wondered if the blue Taurus was somewhere behind him.

A minivan crept by at a snail's pace. He couldn't make out the driver or the passenger. Something crashed inside a garage, and Gary jumped.

"Are you all right, Mr. Sheldon?"

He spun to face the old woman with the black dog. It limped a step closer and then sat down. Its front paw was missing. Gary stared at it, his mouth going dry.

"You don't look well at all, Gary," the woman said, her voice softening. "Maybe you should come inside and lay down."

"What?" He snapped his attention from the dog to her face. She was smiling faintly. Her Kingston Bucks scarf made her throat a broad red slash.

"I'm fine," he said, almost choking. "Just fine."

Tires screeched. A black car pulled over beside them. The old woman's smile vanished.

"Gary!"

Jill stuck her head out the window. "Jump in the back, now." She glanced at the woman. "Oh, hello, Mrs. Keller. Still teaching French?"

The old woman shook her head. "Retired these days. But still a Bucks booster!"

Gary opened the back door of the car. The driver, a woman in the same black as her car, nodded at him. He glanced back at the old woman and three-legged dog. A Bucks pendant swung from the old lab's collar.

The old woman leaned down to look into the passenger window. "Welcome home, Jill."

Jill pulled back inside the window as if the woman had slapped her, the window rushing up before she was even fully inside.

"Fuck this town," the driver growled, punching the gas.

Gary half-fell into the seat, managed to the close the door, and then recognized the ski-slope of the driver's nose. "Stacie?"

She braked at the stop sign hard enough to throw him into Jill's seat.

"Make a right," Jill instructed. "It's the green one at the end of this cul-de-sac."

"It's good to see you again, Gary." Stacie whipped into the driveway with the precision of a stunt car driver. "I just wish it wasn't in Kingston."

He opened the car door and felt in his pocket for his house keys, glancing over his shoulder. No sign of the old woman.

A blue Ford Taurus turned off of French Road.

Gary jammed the key in the lock. He couldn't help checking the street behind them again. Mrs. Keller and her dog appeared at the end of the cul-de-sac, and the woman in the Taurus got out of her car. A bad feeling swept up Gary's spine. He wrenched at the squealing deadbolt. "Let's get inside."

Gary flung himself against the door, locking all three locks. Some of the tension went out of his body. "So what happened?" he asked, turning to Jill. She wasn't wearing any shoes, he realized.

She and Stacie stood in the hallway, unmoving. Just looking through the kitchen and out the sliding glass doors.

A pair of deer stood on the back deck, their noses nearly touching the glass. Their eyes were fixed on Jill and Stacie, huge and dark and damp. Eyes like water, like Calhoun Lake.

"That's not normal for deer, is it?" Jill whispered.

Stacie lunged forward, waving her arms. "Get out of here! Shoo!"

One's ear twitched. The other turned around, flicked its tail, and calmly headed toward the fence line. The first deer huffed a cloud of steam onto the glass, then trotted off after the other.

"Gary," Stacie said, looking indignantly at him, "that deer just shit on your deck."

But Gary couldn't look away from the deer's breath on the glass, a thin fog interrupted by fingerprints and grease smears. Some of the marks joined up to form a shape. It could have been an antler, or two of the letter V.

"Vincent Vernor." He dropped into the vinyl seat of the dining booth.

"What?" Stacie asked. "Why would you say that name?"

But of course it all went back to Vincent Vernor.

CHAPTER TWENTY-THREE

STACIE: 1989

SHE DIDN'T USUALLY wake up when her mom came home from work, but this time she did. Footsteps moved around the kitchen; her mom giggled. Stacie pulled her pillow over her head. Her mom had brought some guy home from the lodge.

She lay beneath her pillow, her face slowly warming the sheet. If only she had stayed asleep. What had she been dreaming about? She'd been with Jill, she could remember that much. They had opened a salon inside the lodge, and women were eating french fries while she cut their hair and Jill filed their nails. It had been a funny dream, but also a little scary, because there had been something outside on the deck, something so big its shadow had made it impossible to see the hair Stacie held in her fingers.

She felt more than heard the door to her mother's bedroom shut, wobbling the walls. At least if they were drunk the next part wouldn't take too long. The framed photo of her grandmother began to jiggle on the far wall.

"Jesus, Mom."

If she'd had headphones, she would have put them on. Shostakovitch, that would cover this up nicely. Or maybe the Melvins. David had given her a new mixtape, and she'd really liked their stuff. It sounded like Kingston, if that made sense.

On the other side of the wall, her mother yelped. Stacie pulled the pillow off her head. Was that kind of sound normal? It didn't sound fun, that was for sure.

The picture frame rattled savagely. Stacie sat up and stared at it. It gave one last, sharp jerk and then went still.

She waited, breathing as quietly as she could. A voice murmured something; her mom sniffled. Stacie balled her hands into fists. What the hell was going on over there?

The voices went silent.

After a minute she laid down again, still listening, but no one spoke. The digits rolled over on her alarm clock: 3:45, 3:46. She had to pee. The clock rolled over again.

Stacie rolled over, trying to convince her bladder it could hold out until morning. She thought about Jordan and Jill and how they had put the deer saint's gravel around the Shell station this afternoon. Would it help? Would anything?

At 3:59, she gave in and sat up. The room next door was silent, and a quick peak under the door showed not a scrap of light. She eased open the door and hurried to the bathroom.

She wouldn't have known what the thing floating in the toilet was if David hadn't pointed one out on the ground behind the Elk Harbor marina. *At least they used a rubber*, he had laughed. It had looked like some transparent sea creature, tossed up beside a stack of fishing nets.

This was one was streaked red.

She dropped the lid and flushed. She couldn't stand the thought of it swirling around beneath her as she peed. It was hard enough to go even knowing it was moving down the pipes, headed out to the water treatment plant on Moore Road. (*Why was it bloody?* her mind whispered to itself, over and over, no matter how hard she tried not to think it.)

She washed her hands twice. She hadn't even touched it, but it didn't matter. She turned the bar of Irish Spring over and over, making thick, green suds and breathing in their clean scent. According to the ads, that's just what Ireland smelled like. Maybe she'd go to Ireland someday. She wished she was there tonight.

Tiptoeing, she headed for her room. The streetlight cast just enough light to let her avoid the pack of cigarettes that had fallen on the floor. Camel, not her mom's brand. She nudged them toward the wall where hopefully they wouldn't be crushed. People got pissed when they couldn't have a cigarette.

Her hand was on the doorknob when her mother's door opened. Stacie turned her head and then froze.

He didn't make any noise as he walked down the hall. It seemed impossible that a man as tall and loud as Vincent Vernor could move with stealth, but that was the case. He walked on the balls of his feet, just like Stacie. His bare legs looked strangely womanly.

"Hello, Stacie."

He kept his voice barely above a whisper. She could only nod. Thank God he was wearing underpants, those stupid tighty-whities that ought to make the whole thing funny. But didn't. There was nothing funny about the way he leaned toward her, nothing funny about the way his hair hung around his face, obscuring the yellow light from the street. There was just darkness, and his breath, hot and foul in her face.

"I saw you at work today, you and your little friends."

She made a sound, maybe a whimper. Her voice wasn't working.

"I don't know what the fuck you were doing, but I hope you weren't trying to mess with me. I showed your little buddy what happens to snot buckets that mess with me. Did he tell you that? I crushed that fucking shell into *dust*."

His hair brushed against her cheek and she shuddered. Her breath was coming in little gasps now, ragged with fear.

"Did you hear your mom and I? You did, didn't you?"

His fingers ran down her cheek, her neck.

"She's gonna have a real hard time sitting down tomorrow, Stacie. You should be extra nice to her."

His hand found her breast and closed on it, hard. Harder. Tears welled up in Stacie's eyes.

He pressed his face so close to hers she could feel the rough skin on his bottom lip. "Don't fuck with me."

He gave her breast one last, excruciating squeeze and took a step backward. "Sleep tight, kid."

She threw open her bedroom door and stumbled inside, sobbing.

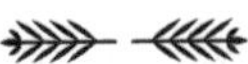

STACIE: 2018

For a long time they just sat in the vinyl booth in Gary's kitchen and said nothing. At first it was a relief, but the quiet grew grating, and there was a distinct strangeness, sitting with two people she barely knew—no, less than *barely*, two people she *did not* know—staring at something as prosaic as a laminate table. She might as well have been sitting at one of her favorite diners, Junior's maybe, or the Twenty-Four Hour Hot Cake House, waiting for the waitress to arrive with a scramble and big side of hash browns. But if she'd been at any of those places, she would have had a little crowd of friends, and it certainly would have been after a long night of drinking, not an afternoon getting chased by weirdos.

Although she felt very much as she would if she had spent the last few hours drinking. Ever since she'd opened the door and seen those stupid deer looking in through the sliding glass doors, things had turned both surreal and mushy. The painting sitting beside the TV in Gary's living room (a painting she remembered from the Sheldons' childhood home) throbbed with the colors of a nasty bruise. The sound of Gary's breathing rasped like a file scraping down an ingrown toenail. Stacie's left eye pulsed quietly to itself, a tiny throb of discomfort that threatened to turn into a migraine.

Gary cleared his throat. "Would anyone like coffee?"

"Fuck yeah." Stacie squeezed shut her eyes. Coffee would help the pounding in her eyeball, wouldn't it?

Jill laid a hand on her arm. Her fingers were warm through Stacie's sleeve. She still smelled good, all these years later, flowers and fruit and something organic. "Are you all right?"

"Nothing a little coffee and some Advil won't help."

Gary had already slid out of the booth and gone to the coffee maker. He brought out a ceramic crock and stopped, scoop in hand. "You know, I didn't want to believe it."

"Believe what?" Stacie asked.

"Any of it. That we'd done séances. That Jill really could paint the future. That we made something out there in the woods that actually did things in the world."

"You were there for all of that," Stacie spat, struggling to her feet. Anger bubbled like lava in her chest. "You saw it happen. How could you not believe in it?"

Jill had gotten to her own feet. She folded her arms over her chest. "Yeah, Gare Bear. Tell us just how you managed to forget all the weird shit of your childhood and how you decided to mock your older sister for believing in all that nonsense."

He jammed the coffee scoop into the canister and shook his finger at her. "I apologized, Jill. I told you what it was like for me, and I *apologized*."

"It still hurt," Jill argued. "You let me feel like shit for years."

"Oh, shut up," Stacie said. Just listening to them sucked the energy from her body. "I don't know what you two were up to the last twenty years, but I know that after that summer, the nightmares never went away. The things we did turned the world upside down for me, and I still don't go out in the woods. Ever."

Jill took a deep breath, as if she expected to rebut something Stacie had said, but then she let it out, her shoulders collapsing on themselves.

"That's one of the reasons I went to California. It's easier down there in the sun."

Stacie gave her a grateful half-smile. "It's easier where there are people."

"Yeah," Gary agreed. He had finished scooping the coffee and now poured in the water. "I didn't really think about it, but yeah. It was one of the reasons I liked living in Portland. It's hard to imagine weirdness when there's a Starbucks around the corner from your house."

Jill laughed. "That's what's wrong with this town. No Starbucks!"

They didn't talk much as they drank their coffee, but the silence no longer felt uncomfortable. Stacie couldn't help glancing from Gary to Jill and back again, comparing their faces to the ones in her head. Jill had lines around her eyes. Gary had gray in his sideburns. Stacie knew time had walked across her own face too. The kids they had been had come to the surface, though. She half-expected Jill to pull out a Bonnie Bell lip smacker and rub it over her bottom lip.

And that lip was still luscious. Stacie had kissed a lot of girls since she left Kingston, but none of them had that delicious a lower lip. None had such honeyed, wild hair either. There'd been one curly-haired blond, but her eyes had been merely green and not a color-changing hazel.

Jill glanced curiously at Stacie, and Stacie felt her cheeks go hot. She quickly wrenched her gaze over to Gary, who was frowning at his phone.

"Everything okay?"

He bobbed a shoulder. "I guess? Zack texted to remind me he's going to a friend's for dinner, and Kim just sent a message saying she has to go to the booster club pizza feed. So I guess it's just us until eight or so."

He looked so crestfallen by the news that Stacie wanted to pat his back, like you would a kid. Instead, she glanced at the clock over the stove. Nearly two in the afternoon. She had planned to be back in the office by four. She should call Kieran and warn them she wouldn't be in today. Get them to check on Finch, too, that furry little pest.

Jill had scooted over in the booth to sit closer to Gary. She murmured something comforting in his ear. Even as kids she had been good at taking care of him. Now she had come all the way up from Petaluma, California, to help him through the weird stuff Kingston was throwing at him.

Stacie went into the living room and pulled out her phone. Maybe the weird Kingston stuff wasn't the same kind of weird that they had lived through that summer, but she had a feeling it was connected somehow, and so she was connected too. The painting glowered at her, its colors more uneasy than ever. The office voicemail picked up.

"I know you're always nagging me to take some time off, Kiernan, so I think you'll be happy when I say that I need to spend a few more days at the coast. Call me if anything big happens, but I'm sure you'll have everything under control." She paused, imagining her assistant's look of utter surprise. "Don't get too excited! I'll be back Thursday. Probably. Please check on my cat."

She hung up the phone and went back to the kitchen. Gary and Jill looked up at her. Something shifted inside her, that anxious feeling that kept her up on summer nights—the one her last therapist said was just an overactive fight or flight instinct. Maybe her therapist was wrong. Maybe her instincts had never been overactive. Maybe she had just been trying to find the right people to fight *for.*

"You said you first figured out there was something weird going on in Kingston when you found the dog's paw at the beach?"

Gary nodded.

"Then we'd better go check it out."

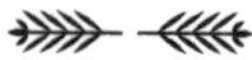

GARY: 2018

Gary directed Stacie toward the beach. She, like him, had never driven in Kingston. Jill had taken driver's ed at Kingston High, but she didn't offer any feedback on their route. He had rarely seen her sit so quietly.

"Does anybody want to get dinner at Pete's-a-Pizza?" Stacie asked. "I'm a stress eater, so I could ravage a pizza."

"Yeah," Gary agreed, although at the moment he couldn't imagine eating anything. "Good idea."

The closer they got to the site, the tighter the muscles got in Gary's neck and shoulders. By the time they'd parked and walked out onto the beach, the muscles in the back of his head had begun to join the fun. He wagged his jaw from side to side to keep from clenching it and then remembered his father doing the same thing.

The past jammed itself into his solar plexus like a fist. How often had he seen his dad pacing around, rolling his shoulders, stretching his jaw? It had been money, always money, that had made his parents so miserable. That had been the best part of his dad's job at the paper mill: no more headaches, no more rolling jaw.

"You okay?" Stacie asked.

He had always given Jordan the credit for being the perceptive one, but Stacie was pretty sharp herself. He forced a smile. "Not bad." He pointed. "It was just past that big log."

The makeshift altar still stood, and the fire pit looked freshly used. Gary wondered if the most recent users had just been roasting marshmallows or if they were practicing horrible rituals.

A man and a woman strolled slowly by, holding hands, laughing. Looking totally normal. But hadn't Mrs. Keller looked totally normal too? She lived in a 1980s split-level and mowed her lawn every weekend. She had a "Bark Less, Wag More" sticker on her bumper. Could anyone that ordinary really cut off their own dog's paw at a beachside ceremony?

Jill studied the stains, wine-dark against the bleached driftwood.

"I can't tell what it is," she admitted. "But it could be blood."

Gary stooped and picked up the red and white packet. "Look."

"Marlboro Reds." Stacie glanced at Jill. "Like all the cigarette cartons at the offering site."

"Yes." Jill's lips tightened. "Let's get out of here."

They hurried back up the beach. No one said anything during the drive. Gary just kept seeing those cigarettes, the same brand as the ones on the deck. The same brand as the one left under his windshield wiper. The same brand his dad had switched to when he started working at the mill.

"They're offerings, right?" Stacie asked. "But why are they making offerings at two different places? Don't people usually leave offerings at sacred sites?"

"What's sacred about Third Beach?" Jill asked.

They turned onto Marina Drive. Boats still filled the old marina, although there were more handsome pleasure boats than fishing vessels, unlike in their childhoods. He remembered that bright day they had come down to the marina to binge on sugar at Beachfest. They had ended the day at Pete's-a-Pizza that day, too, he remembered. They'd had just enough money to share an order of cheesy bread. Well, Stacie'd had just enough money. Gary had scraped his last quarter out of his pocket to help with the tip. He had to scrub lint off its slightly sticky surface.

Maybe it was the lint that helped him remember the gravel. There had been lint on the gravel he'd dropped around the barn the day he decided to bring the deer saint's attention down on the barn.

"Maybe it's not a sacred site at all," he said, musing out loud. "Maybe it's just the southernmost tip of the town."

"What do you mean?" Jill asked.

"You remember how we put the rocks all around the Shell station?"

"And our houses," Stacie reminded him. "To show where the deer saint should protect us."

They had pulled into the parking lot of Pete's-a-Pizza, but no one had opened their door yet. Jill leaned between the two front seats so she could look into Gary's face. "You think these weird offerings are like that? They're building a circle of protection around Kingston?"

"Yeah," Gary said.

"So what do they think is going to protect them?" Stacie asked. She opened her door. No one had an answer for her.

They went inside. The place looked exactly the same, although there were now four kinds of beer on tap that weren't Budweiser. They bought a pitcher of a local IPA and sat down in the back. The faint acrid smell of scorching cornmeal tickled the back of Gary's nose, the same as it had every other visit.

"Donuts. Pizza. I'm eating like a kid today," Stacie complained with a smile.

"Hey, I suggested ordering a salad," Jill reminded her.

The waitress, a buxom redhead in her early twenties, appeared with their cheesy breads. Gary caught Stacie glancing at the woman's retreating backside and wondered what exactly that meant. He assumed plenty of former Kingston High grads had come out of the closet after they had found themselves in more liberal environs, but he hadn't known a single queer kid the entire time he had lived on the coast.

Except for Jordan, of course. He looked at Stacie and wondered if she knew any more about what had happened to Jordan than he or Jill did. She took a bite of cheesy bread and rolled her eyes up with bliss.

He took his own slice of greasy goodness. "I wish Jordan was here."

Stacie put down her bread. "You didn't hear?"

"Didn't hear what?"

She glanced up, but stayed as the waitress hurried toward them, burdened with pizza. When the woman finally left, Stacie sighed. "He died in college."

"What?"

She nodded. "We kept in touch, you know. I never suspected he was in trouble, though. I thought he was just…experimenting? The usual college shit? Then he OD'd."

Jill leaned her head on Stacie's shoulder. "Oh, Stacie. I'm so sorry."

"He was the best of us, wasn't he?" Stacie pressed the heels of her palms into her eyes. "God, let's talk about something else."

They lost themselves in food until they were too stuffed to keep piling it in. But eventually they had to pack up the extra pizza, wipe their mouths, and give their table to another group of customers. Stacie made for the bathroom, and Jill went to the back of the dining room to take in the view. The pizza joint might not be right on the beach, but it had a good enough view of the marina and the jetty, which stuck out at the ocean like a gray tongue. The sun spilled orange across the protected mouth of the harbor.

"It's beautiful," Jill said. "Don't you think so?"

A trawler—the first trawler Gary had seen in years—motored out of the marina, its outriggers raised like antenna. It trudged over the whitecaps marking where the waters of the Peshak hit the ocean, and then turned to run south. In a minute, it would pick up speed, Gary knew, and race to deeper waters. But for the moment, it stood silent and stoic, a black silhouette again the lowering orange sky.

"Jesus," Stacie breathed. "It's the painting from your living room."

Jill's hand closed on Gary's arm. "She's right."

The sun hovered at the edge of the horizon, hot orange in a purple sky. And Gary thought that for a second—no, not even a second—something green flashed inside the sun, the same green that scorched the center of his grandmother's painting. But what made him grab Jill's fingers were the black streaks boiling across the water: the smoke black streaks of the relentless dead.

CHAPTER TWENTY-FOUR

GARY: 2018

GARY SLIPPED INTO bed but didn't pick up the biography cached on the nightstand. Downstairs he could hear the faint murmur of the shower as either Jill or Stacie cleaned up for the night. Kim flushed the toilet of their own bathroom and then scuffed into the bedroom.

"I don't know why you always wear my slippers when you have two much nicer pairs."

She looked down at the disreputable furry things on her feet. They had been rabbits once, two copies of the white, insane rabbit from *Monty Python and the Holy Grail*, a gift from Zack nearly ten years ago. One was missing an eye, and the other's sole had been repaired with duct tape. "These are more comfortable."

She flashed him that irresistible smile she had given him the very first day he met her—at an introductory poli sci study group—and then sat on the bed with a little bounce. "Plus, they're so easy to put on and off." She kicked one of the slippers halfway across the room and then giggled.

He snaked his arm around her middle and pulled her over on her side. "You're so happy tonight." He kissed her neck. "From all your texts, I thought you'd be a lot more stressed out."

She kissed him back, more thoroughly than she had in days. Then she pulled back, her eyes sparkling. "I'm so glad I went to the booster club meeting."

He raised an eyebrow. "Really?"

"Absolutely. You know, Sam Oakley is the president?"

He nuzzled her ear. "No, I had no idea."

"Mmmn-hmmn. She started it up when she moved back to Kingston. I guess some local Elk's Club thing used to organize all the fundraisers back in the day, but they gave up the ghost when the mill closed."

Gary sat up a little. "Yeah, the Deer Kings. My folks were members."

"Oh, cool." She fluffed her pillow. "Anyway, it was great. Sam keeps everything so upbeat. It felt so good to be around such a positive group."

"Okay." He brushed a spot of moisturizer off her cheek. "I guess I'm glad you went, then."

"You silly bear." She leaned over and kissed his forehead. "You should come with me next time, sweetie. You'd be surprised how much better it would make you feel."

Then she reached for the light on her nightstand and turned it off.

He turned off his own light and settled against the pillows, waiting for her to snuggle into the curve of his armpit. Her hair tickled a little against his shoulder. She smelled smokier than usual.

"Are you sure you're okay with Jill and Stacie staying here?"

"Of course, babe! Why wouldn't I? I think it's great you're reconnecting with old friends. And family is important."

He couldn't see her face in the dark, but she sounded enthusiastic. He worked the angle of his arm under her head until he could feel her hair and began playing the strands though his fingertips.

"It's only for a few days. I promise I'll be back to writing next week."

"If it helps you settle in, any amount of time is fine."

He stopped stroking her hair. Hadn't they just had an argument last week about him skipping writing to go running on the beach? When it came to his writing career, Kim had always been his biggest supporter, but she was a stickler for accountability and productivity.

"Are…you sure?"

She kissed his chest. "Yes, you big idiot. In fact, you know what you should do? You should call Coach Washburn. You said you were all friends back when you were kids." She kissed the edge of his areola.

"David Washburn?" The man had barely said hello to him the two times they'd shared the same room. Hell, even in high school they hadn't done more than wave at each other.

"I'll text you his number tomorrow," she whispered, and then her kissing moved from tender little pecks to something hotter, and he forgot all about David Washburn.

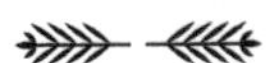

JILL: 1989

Dad called that afternoon, right as Mom was packing her lunch for the night ahead. Jill knew it was him even before her mother said his name: her mother's face lit up brighter than Christmas. Gary nudged her in the ribs, grinning. She grinned back.

They listened in shamelessly. The pet names they usually made gagging faces over sounded comforting after two weeks without hearing them. When Mom beckoned Jill over to the phone, Jill floated more than walked across the kitchen.

"Hi, Dad!"

"Heya, Jilly Bean! How's life treating you?"

He sounded just like he always did, his deep voice so powerful she could feel it vibrating up her ear and into her cheekbone. She sagged against the counter, relaxed for the first time since he left. "Good, Dad. We made a couple of new friends."

"Anybody I know?"

"A couple of really nerdy boys," she said, although "nerdy" hardly seemed the right word for a boy like David. But she had a feeling her dad didn't want to hear her say "a nerdy boy and a troublemaker whose smile makes my teeth tingle."

"Any more troubles with the guy in the Big House?"

There was no point in worrying him, not when they'd gone ahead and taken matters into their own hands. "Nope." And in case her voice sounded weird, she added: "How's Prineville?"

"Pretty boring. I'm getting tired of juniper trees. Can you put your brother on? I don't have too many more quarters."

Jill beckoned Gary over and then hugged her mom. "Wasn't it great talking to Dad?"

Her mother kissed the top of her head. "The best." She looked at the clock. "You can take the casserole out of the oven? It needs about another fifteen minutes."

Jill hugged her mother. She always sounded so worried when she asked these things. "No problem. Gary and I will be fine."

The lines above her mother's nose deepened. "You'll be in bed by midnight?"

"Mom, it's summer vacation."

Her mother sighed. "All right. Well, I love you." She kissed the side of Gary's head in passing, grabbed her lunch box, and set out for the car.

Gary hung up the phone. "I miss Dad."

"Me too."

Jill opened the oven. She didn't know what her mother was talking about; the casserole looked done to her. She got it out. Gary pulled out a pair of plates. Their mother had been working graveyard for the last year and a half. They were very good at getting dinner on the table, pitching in, and helping out.

Gary poured a glass of milk and sat down. His glasses had slid down his nose, giving him the look of a disapproving librarian as Jill brought her own meal to the table. "I have an idea."

"Yeah?"

"I think we should thank the deer saint. I mean, it saved Coach Dusseldorf, right? And when you looked up that other saint in the encyclopedia, it said people leave little offerings to the saints to encourage their assistance."

Jill stabbed a blob of broccoli. It wasn't quite mushy, thankfully. "So how do we thank it?" The broccoli dripped cream of mushroom down her shirtfront as she blew on it.

"We make it an offering."

She thought about the encyclopedia entry and wished it had more pictures. "Like what? We light some candles or something?"

He pushed aside his casserole. "I think it should mean something. The offering. It should be like a sacrifice to give it up."

"Like one of your *Star Wars* toys?"

She expected him to squawk, but he nodded. "Exactly." He stirred his casserole on his plate, sending up a cloud of steam that obscured the lenses of his glasses.

"I'd give up my new fruit salad earrings," she said, slowly, "if it meant getting rid of Vincent Vernor."

He took off his glasses and looked at her, his naked eyes very big. She sometimes forgot they were the same hazel-ish shade as her own, the green flecks showing more when he was happy. They were very brown right now. "I'd give up just about anything to get rid of Vincent Vernor. Especially after what happened to Stacie."

Tuna noodle casserole stuck in Jill's throat, thinking of the call Stacie had made this morning. "Thank God she went to Jordan's house tonight. We have to put gravel around her house tomorrow."

Gary pulled his plate closer and began to eat in small, quick bites. He had been sort of a shoveler before the Ritalin, but he now ate methodically, finishing each quadrant of his plate before moving on to the next. Tonight he chewed about twice as fast as any normal kid had ever chewed tuna and veggies.

She realized she was staring and took a sip of water. "Why the rush?"

"I want to make the offering at sunset. I figure it will take me a little while to get set up too."

He explained his plan for a little ritual involving birthday candles and a chant he had come up with. Jill had to admit it sounded official. More than that, it sounded strangely right. Like it might just work.

They hurried through dishes and then split up, each going to find whatever they needed to sacrifice to the deer saint.

Inside her room, Jill sat down on her bed for a moment. She had suggested the new earrings, but the thought of sacrificing them didn't give her that sense of *rightness* that she'd gotten earlier. She reached for her sketchbook and a pencil and closed her eyes.

The deer saint, she thought. No one had given it that name; everyone had simply called it that, and no one could imagine calling it anything else.

What would a creature like that see as a worthy sacrifice? What could she imbue with all the gratitude she felt, knowing that it was out there keeping people from drowning in the lake and protecting kids from assholes like Vincent Vernor? And what could she give it that would encourage it to work even harder?

She opened her eyes and saw that her hand had been busy while her mind roamed. She had drawn a small dog with buttons for eyes. She threw the notebook onto the bed.

"No."

She jumped to her feet. The earrings would be enough—they were brand new and beautiful and dappled colors onto her neck when the light passed through the dangling plasticine fruits. Jill opened her jewelry box and reached for them.

The St. Christopher medallion lay right beside the new earrings. There was no way a metal face could change its expression, but he did seem to frown at her. She remembered feeling the chain tighten around her neck when Vincent grabbed it and her collar and twisted them in his fist.

She closed the jewelry box and went to her closet.

Her father had brought her the stuffed dog the very first time he had ever gone away for a job. She had missed him endlessly, and the joy she had felt seeing him had only been increased by the yellow plush puppy tucked under his arm. He had almost certainly brought something for Gary, but she had no memory of whatever it had been. Puppy had been her best friend and favorite toy for years after that.

She took the toy dog off the shelf in her closet and went out to find Gary. He was already out in the orchard. She did not comment on the baby quilt by his feet.

They lit the candles and held hands. Gary had not told her what words she should say, but her lips found them easily. She cried when she put Puppy in the circle of birthday candles. To lose it was to lose some important part of herself that she had always assumed she could keep close. Gary sniffled and leaned his head against her shoulder.

"It's for a good cause," he reminded her.

"I know."

The sun's last rays passed from dull rose to thin blue as it sank behind the hills, but neither Jill nor Gary moved. She wasn't sure what she was waiting for. Would the deer saint simply appear? Would it spear their gifts with its giant horns and then race off into the forest, ready to vanquish their enemy? She stood quiet and did not move. She hardly dared to breathe.

The dull roar of a motorcycle engine made them turn around. The air shook with the power of the big, red Harley. If the rider noticed them, he gave no sign.

"That's not Vincent's," Gary said.

The motorcycle turned into the Big House's driveway. Another motor sounded out on the main road, louder and huger. Jill saw a headlight turn off the road, then another, and another. The air shook with motorcycle engines. Jill clapped her hands over her ears.

The motorcyclists parked in front of the Big House, laughing and shouting. A big pickup truck turned down the driveway, Styx blasting out its windows.

"They're having a party," Gary said.

"Let's go inside," Jill said.

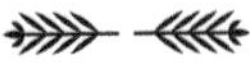

GARY: 2018

Gary got up early to see Kim and Zack off to school. Jill and Stacie slept later, and they each had their own morning rituals—Stacie, a long morning run; Jill, yoga on the back deck. Gary eyed her through the sliding glass door, but there was no sign of deer or more deer crap.

Deer. Jesus. They were supposed to be cute woodsy creatures, but even before they had summoned up the deer saint, he had known they were more dangerous than most people supposed. His mother's car had born an enormous dent on the front side panel where a deer had jumped into it. The deer had stumbled backward and then kept running. They were tough creatures despite the doe eyes.

The doorbell rang.

Gary hesitated. There was no reason not to answer the door, but yet, there was no reason anyone should come by the house. He leaned against the kitchen counter and waited to see if the visitor would ring again.

They did. With a sigh, he trudged to the front door. A wreath he didn't recognize framed the peephole, fresh green boughs bound with red-and-white ribbons. Someone had added a tiny wooden plaque with the words "Go Bucks" burned into the grain. Kim must have picked it up at the booster club meeting.

The doorbell rang again as Gary undid the deadbolt and pulled open the door. He realized in mid-tug that he'd been too distracted by the swag to even look through the stupid peephole. He hoped like hell he wasn't opening the door to a serial killer.

Jim Burns stood on the front porch, beaming happily. "Gary! I hope I'm not waking you."

"No, no, I've been up for hours."

Jim picked up the plastic grocery bag sitting on the step by his feet. "Excellent! I just wanted to drop off these books for you."

Gary took them, but his confusion must have shown.

"Just a few reference books," Jim explained. Even though Gary held the books close to his chest, Jim pushed back the plastic to point out the spines. "This one's a great overview of local history." He tapped a book clad in black buckram. Then a sepia-colored paperback: "This one's got a ton of photos you might enjoy. Most of them are from the historical society, but I think you'll find them inspiring."

Gary noticed the name on the spine. "Did you write that one?"

Jim bobbed his head, beaming. "My baby!" Then he rapped the cover of the smallest of the books. "This is just a copy, but I think you'll like it best. A journal of Abraham Calhoun."

Gary found his interest piqued. "Is that the Calhoun of Calhoun Lake Road?"

"Mmmn-hmmn. He owned everything out there—the mill, the mine, you name it."

The mine. Gary remembered the thick, cold feeling of the spirits haunting the mine, the way they'd clustered in his head, desperate to share their stories. He wasn't sure he wanted to read the personal diary of the man whose business caused all that.

"His sister Lizzie actually wound up marrying John King, so I guess that makes Calhoun one of your relatives. She was one hell of a gal, you know."

Gary tried to stop thinking about the sad, dead miners and their ghosts. He focused on Jim's bright face. "I actually don't know anything about her."

"Oh, golly. One of the mine shafts actually collapsed, did you know that? And she went out there with a shovel to help dig them out. Drove the injured to the hospital in her own wagon too. That's the spirit of service!"

"Wow. I had no idea."

"Yep. She and her husband really took care of Kingston." Jim looked like he might be choking up. He cleared his throat. "Anyway, I just thought you might find the books useful."

"Useful?"

"You know, for your article. About John King?"

"Oh, of course!"

Jim Burns did not look reassured.

Gary felt bad. He had almost forgotten his little volunteer writing assignment. He pushed open the door with his foot. "Do you want to come inside and have some coffee? We could talk more about Lizzie. I'd really like to know more about her."

Jim shook his head. "I can't. My buddy Brian Danse and I are going into Plymouth."

"Plymouth?" Gary couldn't imagine needing anything from the other little town. There was a movie theater, if he remembered correctly. Otherwise, people from Kingston had always gone to Coos Bay or Eugene for whatever their own town couldn't provide.

Jim leaned in, lowering his voice conspiratorially. "I've got a pair of ears on the inside of their chamber of commerce. She'll give me the scuttlebutt on last night's meeting with Keridan Bridge."

Gary wasn't quite sure how to respond. "That's…good?"

Jim pounded him on the shoulder. "Don't worry, my boy. We won't let those bastards steal our bridge deal." His eyes glinted. "I've got an old Navy buddy with an explosives background, you know."

Gary felt even more astonished by this than by the statement that Jim Burns had a spy within the Plymouth Chamber of Commerce. Their meetings at the City Club and the historical society had suggested only that Jim was a history nerd with a sweet tooth. If on the day they met, Gary had gotten even the most vague of hints toward any of these new facets of Jim's personality, Gary would have asked Kim to swap seats.

And Brian Danse was his friend? The police sergeant? What did that mean about the Kingston PD?

Jim clapped his hands and stood up straight. "Keridan Bridge would never settle in a town that let their town hall get blown up." He chuckled. "Well, I'll be seeing you around, Gary. It sure was nice seeing Kim at the booster club meeting last night."

He walked toward his car, still chuckling. Gary stood on the stoop, his hand awkwardly raised in a wave he would have preferred to keep to himself.

Jim stopped at the car's nose and turned around. "Oh, and Gary? You should really hang your booster wreath on the outside of your door."

Gary's tongue stuck to the roof of his mouth.

Jim smiled. "I can get you a wreath hanger if you don't have one."

"No," Gary said, his voice a little choked, at least to his own ears. "I'll pick one up at the hardware store this afternoon."

Jim pumped his fist in the air. "Go Bucks!"

Then he got in his car and pulled out of the driveway. He did stop at the end of the cul-de-sac to roll down his window and ask a question of a jogger coming out of her house. She grabbed a Bucks cap out of the pocket of her fleece vest and pulled it down over her eyes.

CHAPTER TWENTY-FIVE

JILL: 1989

THEY WENT BACK inside, locking the front door behind them. Jill couldn't remember the last time anyone had locked the door. Maybe when they had driven up to Spokane for the Thompson family reunion? That had been three years ago. Jill felt a little silly, turning the little switch on the doorknob, but also quietly comforted.

Another car or two had come down the driveway while Jill and Gary returned to the house, and now a pickup rounded the corner. Jill wasn't sure how many people had gotten out of each vehicle, but the party certainly seemed big enough already. Every light in the Big House burned bright, and someone had set up a fire pit out in the front.

"Mr. Berman isn't going to like that."

The fire flared brighter as if to mock Gary's words.

"What's he going to do? He's in Portland."

Gary sighed. "I know you're right, but it's nice to imagine him kicking Vincent and his awful family out on the curb."

She pushed herself away from the kitchen window and went to the cupboard where her mother kept the cocoa mix. "There aren't any curbs on Balfour Drive."

He stuck out his tongue, then noticed what she was doing. "Cocoa? Will you make me a cup?"

She held up a bag of only somewhat shriveled mini-marshmallows. "Want any of these?"

He nodded. Behind his glasses, his eyes were enormous and dark, the hazel-y brown bits obscuring the other colors. He looked so much like some kind of cuddly little animal—a mouse or a chipmunk, maybe—that she almost wanted to grab him and blow a raspberry on his cheek as she had when he was much littler. She contented herself with adding an extra spoonful of cocoa mix to his cup.

Gary hopped up onto the counter for a better look out the window over the kitchen sink. "I don't know why I'm so scared of this party, but I am."

She turned the burner beneath the kettle up to high. "Do you see anything?" She didn't put any special emphasis on the word *see*, but he knew what she meant.

"I always see things over there. It's an unhappy house."

Jill went to the kitchen sink and laid her hand on her brother's shoulder. He pressed his forehead to the glass.

"The man who built the Big House was a bad man," he said. "He likes to sit in the corners of the house, waiting. I know he can't do anything to me, not dead, but just feeling him watch me is bad enough. Sometimes I see his wife. She would do anything to get away from him, but she's trapped in that house, same as him."

"Poor woman."

He shuddered. "She wasn't so good either."

The kettle gurgled and mumbled to itself, the precursor to an actual boil. Jill turned it off and filled their mugs. The marshmallows bobbed on top, streaming out little clouds of sugar fluff.

When she had been little, their mother made them cocoa all the time. A skinned knee? Time for a cup of cocoa. Got in trouble with the playground monitor? Hot cocoa time. The last year or so, Jill had taken to drinking mostly coffee, but the cocoa reflex remained, and breathing in its gentle sweetness, she was glad she had decided to make it.

She hopped up on the counter to sit by Gary. The cocoa was still too hot to drink, but Gary absently spooned a melted marshmallow into his mouth as he stared out at the neighbor's bonfire.

He gave a little gasp and then choked on the fluff, coughing hard.

"What is it? Are you okay?"

Coughing, he nodded and then pressed his nose to the glass again. "Someone's coming."

"What?" She put down her cocoa.

"Someone's walking across the driveway." He stiffened. "Now they're walking toward our house."

"Shit."

"It's a man."

"Shit!"

Footsteps sounded on the front stairs. Then a knock on the door.

"What do we do?"

Gary shook his head. "Mom says don't open the door to strangers."

"Mrs. Sheldon?" a voice called at the door.

Jill jumped down from the counter. "That's Mike Jones!" She hadn't seen the young man since the day at the lodge, and she only knew him vaguely from a couple of the lodge's annual Super Bowl parties, but she thought he sounded different. Strained, maybe.

"Mrs. Sheldon, can you please help me? I'm hurt."

Gary grabbed her arm as she went to the door. "Don't open it."

"I have to. He's not a stranger, and he's hurt."

She hurried to the door and unlatched it. Mike stood on the porch, his hand pressed to his shoulder. He looked like he might vomit.

"Come in."

He stumbled to the dining room table and fell into a chair. "Where's your mom?" He smelled very strongly of beer.

"At work." Jill folded her arms across her chest, hoping she looked older and tougher than she felt. "What's wrong?"

He moved his hand and she saw the red stain on his shirt, growing steadily.

She took a step backward. "What happened?"

Mike looked down at the blood and made a face like he was going to barf. He squeezed his eyes shut. "Don't fuck with Vincent Vernor."

"Shit," Gary breathed.

"Yeah." The young man forced open his eyes. "Do either of you know anything about first aid?"

Jill shook her head. Mike winced. He looked a lot younger than he had at the lodge Super Bowl party. She remembered he had only graduated last June. "I'll try," she said.

She tried to think of what her mom would do. She supposed the first step was looking at the injury. "Can you take off your shirt?" She looked around for Gary. "Get a washcloth, please? And first-aid stuff. Rubbing alcohol, bandages, that kind of thing."

He gave a quick nod and darted toward the bathroom. Jill turned back to her patient. He made a little hiss as he stripped off his long-sleeved t-shirt.

The cut didn't look like much. Blood stained Mike's pale skin, its source a half-inch long cut beside the tip of his collar bone. Its lips had swollen purple, the skin itself rolling back a little to show the meat below.

She stared at him. "Did Vincent *stab* you?"

"Just a little," he said.

"He stabbed you just a little."

Gary came running from the bathroom, his arms full of the entire medicine cabinet. "There are some guys out there," he warned. "Right now they're just standing under the holly trees, but they look like they could come over here at any minute." He dropped the first-aid stuff on the table.

"Shit," Mike said. "They want his money. I gotta get out of here." He bit his lip.

Jill filled the kettle and wet the washcloth. She wiped down the puffy edges of the cut. Blood seeped from it slowly. "I don't think it's too deep."

"Please hurry," Mike whimpered.

Jill poured a stream of alcohol over the cut and Mike shrieked.

"Holy fuck, are you trying to kill me?"

She blotted the wound. "I have to clean it. What if it gets infected?"

Gary opened the box of Band-Aids and rummaged until he found one of the big ones, the kind good for scraped knees. "This should cover it."

Outside, someone shouted. Mike went paler and swallowed convulsively. "Maybe you kids ought to get out of here for a little bit. Those guys are pretty fucked up."

"What are we going to do? Hide in the woods?" Gary snapped. "Jeez, why did you come to our house?"

Jill sealed down the edges of the bandage.

"Maybe you *should* go hide in the woods," Mike mumbled. He flexed his arm and groaned. "Oh, God, do you have any aspirin or anything?"

Jill reached for the bottle on the table and shook out eight. "There. Now get out of here, and take those goons with you."

He gave a dry laugh. "You think I can control those fuckers?"

Rage surged in Jill's chest, and she jabbed him in the bandage so he gave a cry of pain. "You're the one that knocked on our door! You owe us, asshole."

He got up, his face pale again. "All right."

Gary shoved his bloody shirt at him.

"You're right."

"Damn straight, I'm right." Jill narrowed her eyes at him.

Mike went to the door, still holding his shirt in his fist. "I'm sorry," he said.

"You probably shouldn't use your arm too much," Jill warned him. "And you should see a doctor as soon as you can."

He backed out the door, and Gary rushed to it and relocked it. "Quick," he said. "Let's put a chair under the knob."

"Do you think the deer saint's gravel will help us?"

"I don't know. They're not Vincent Vernor, just his friends." He reached for her hand, staring at the door.

A man shouted, right in their driveway. Jill couldn't tell if it was Mike or one of the others. She rushed to the window. Three men stood in the drive separating the Big House's yard from theirs. Mike walked slowly toward them, his flesh pale as a fish's in the summer starlight.

Gary jumped up on the counter beside her. "I think one of those guys has a gun!"

A crash made the figures in the driveway spin around.

A deer burst out of the orchard. It was enormous, its rack as wide as one of the apple trees, its head taller than any man's on the planet. It barreled out of the Sheldons' yard and into the driveway, slamming into one of the men and sending him flying. The others broke into a run, shrieking. Mike fell onto his knees and clasped his hands like a man praying.

Gary turned to stare at Jill. "The deer saint."

She could only nod. Her brain could only replay the stag's great leap, over and over again.

Gary touched her shoulder. "You should wash your hands."

She looked down and saw the long strip of blood along the side of her hand. She was still holding the alcohol- and blood-soaked washcloth in the other. Something clicked in her head.

Later that night she crept out to the orchard with one of her dad's razor blades. Puppy looked like some abandoned scrap of fabric on the gravel.

"You deserve a real sacrifice, Deer Saint."

She nicked the side of her left hand and pumped her fist until blood dappled the rocks. And when the grass shushed behind her, she wasn't surprised to see Gary.

"I had one of my feelings," he said. "I guess you did too."

He held out his hand for his turn with the blade.

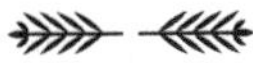

GARY: 2018

Gary walked to the high school to catch the tail end of football practice. The walk felt good; the solitude, better. They had spent most of the afternoon at his grandmother's house, he and Jill watching over the old lady for any signs of wear or damage. It was impossible that anyone could look *well* after a lethal head injury, but not only did Grams seem as healthy as ever, she insisted on baking them a fresh loaf of bread and a batch of cookies.

Stacie had left them for most of the familial gathering to walk down to Eagle Cove. Gary intended to grill her on what the campground was like these days, but not until after dinner and at least two whiskey sodas. Maybe three.

So now Jill and Stacie were reconnecting in his kitchen, making some kind of Indian stew Jill promised that Kim liked. Kim was still at work. Zack was at football practice. No one had seen the blue Taurus all day, and no one had attacked them, welcomed them back to town, or suggested they join the booster club either. It had very nearly been a normal day.

And now Gary was at the field, standing with all the other junior varsity parents at the edge of the track. The football field itself gleamed with green vitality. The grass David Washburn had so carefully weeded to earn french fry money was gone, replaced by pristine AstroTurf Gary couldn't imagine how the school had paid for.

"Hey, Gary," Sam Oakley said, and Gary spun around, startled.

"Sam! I didn't see you." She looked more sober today, her lipstick nearly beige. A Bucks pendant laid on top of the neckline of her blue twinset.

"You seemed quite focused on the wonders of our field."

"How did they afford it?" he blurted, and then remembered she was the president of the booster club.

She did not attack him for impugning the honor of the sports fundraising program. "There was some fundraising, of course," she said. "But rumor has it most of the funds were donated by the family of an alum who died in a car accident. He had a lavish life insurance plan."

"Must have." He looked out at the track. Zack led the group of boys, his head held high and a grin on his face. Gary was no expert, but he thought they were all running a little faster today than the last time he'd been to practice. "Why didn't the family keep the money?"

She shrugged. "It's just a rumor, Gary."

They stood and watched their children for a few quiet moments. Then she turned back to Gary.

"How's Kim holding up?"

He searched for the political answer to that question. "She's enjoying the kids," he said, a bit limply.

She laid her hand on his shoulder. "She really seemed happier after last night's meeting. You should come sometime. It's amazing how good it feels to get together with other parents who are just as concerned about this town's future."

"And our children's future," he added. "I mean, that's the most important role of the booster club, right? Making things better for our kids."

"Sure." She bobbed her head. "But some problems call for a longer term investment than just one kid's time at Kingston High. I want every child in Kingston to get what they need."

"You sound like you should be running for mayor."

"I've thought about it," she said, her expression serious. "I grew up here, just like you did. It's a pretty miraculous place, if people would only try to take care of it. You understand, of course. You're a descendant of John King."

Gary wasn't sure what she meant by that.

"Dad!"

Zack's voice filled Gary with relief. He pulled away from Sam Oakley. "Hey, dude!"

Zack stopped at the edge of the field, kicking up his heels to stretch his quads. "Can Skyler come over for dinner?"

Skyler ran up behind him, smiling shyly. He was a cute kid, Gary thought, even if he wasn't much of a runner. Gary smiled back at him.

"Sure," Gary began, but Sam was shaking her head.

"No, no that's not possible. Remember, Skyler? We've got that dinner with your grandfather."

The boy's face fell. "But we have dinner with Grandpa all the time. I've never been to Zack's house."

Sam folded her arms. She looked much more intimidating that Gary would have imagined. "This is an important dinner, and you know it."

Skyler opened his mouth. Gary decided to intervene.

"It's okay," he said. "My sister's cooking, so dinner will probably be a little weird. Maybe you can come over on Thursday? It's usually spaghetti night."

"Thursday is our game at Coquille," Zack said, his voice hurt.

"Shit," Gary said. "I'm sorry, man. I knew that. We've got the whole schedule on our fridge," he added for Sam's benefit.

"Another day," she said, her lips pinched tight. The only person who didn't look pissed at Gary was Skyler.

The boy was staring at his mother. Gary couldn't quite read his expression, but it didn't look happy.

"Come on," he said, finally, swatting Zack on the back. "Let's go change." The boys headed toward the locker rooms, their shoulders bowed.

Out on the main field, a body hit a practice pad with a resounding *thwack*. Coach Washburn stood on the field lines, old Coach Dusseldorf at his side, talking intensely. Thirty years after they met at Beachfest, David was still hanging out with the old guy. They had to practically be family by now.

"Your dad looks awfully good for his age, doesn't he?" Gary tried to smile at Sam, but her face had retained its irritated expression.

He tried again. "I guess I'll see you around?"

She looked over his shoulder, watching her father. "At the meeting," she said.

"What meeting?"

She glanced back at him. "The town hall meeting at the senior center. It's at 8:00. Kim's speaking."

He had about a hundred more questions, but Zack came running from the locker rooms, damp and happy again, and then Sam was striding away from him, toward her father and Coach Washburn.

STACIE: 1989

Things were subtly different after the night Jill and Gary made their offerings. David's parents stopped going out every night. Jim, the owner of the lodge, took over closing for a couple of weeks so Stacie's mom could spend more time focusing on the lodging reservations side of the business. A wildfire threatened the property in eastern Oregon where Mr. Sheldon was logging, so he came home an entire week early. And Vincent Vernor lost his job as a mechanic at the Shell station, making Jordan's mother so happy she even let him get a library card.

Looking back on the weeks of July, Stacie would say that without a single doubt, they were the finest days of her life. Jordan came over every day for breakfast, and they spent the morning reading and listening to the music David compiled for them. David usually stopped by around lunchtime—his parents might not be spending their days passed out, but that didn't mean they were any good at stocking the fridge—and then they would all ride their bikes to the lake to swim with Jill and Gary.

They took over the beach at the Eagle Cove campground. The

occasional tourist kid tried to join them, but the Balfour Drive crew drove them away without even trying. The events of June, difficult and strange as they were, had left a sort of mark upon them all. They were united closer than family, closer than twins. They had made the deer saint, for crap's sake. They were no longer ordinary mortals.

Some evenings they brought out pencil and paper and tried talking to the spirits the way they had that first trip to Eagle Cove. Gary had to be coerced into such an activity. His usual fee, a peanut butter-chocolate milkshake from the lodge, felt nearly usurious, but between the rest of them, they usually scraped it up. On the times no one had spare pocket money and Gary sat out, nothing happened. The spirits were his domain. The others could share in his powers only if he was willing.

No one asked Jill to look into their future, not after one late night camping in the Sheldons' orchard when David convinced them all to sketch their thirty-year-old selves. Jill had first taken their hands and closed her eyes, and reached out to them with her gifts. After a minute or two, her hands had dropped into her lap. She'd fumbled for a pencil and begun drawing at a breakneck pace.

They had watched her, curious, uncertain what she might be drawing. David was the first to realize something stranger was happening. His gasp could have come straight out of a horror movie, the perfect, sharp inhalation of fear and surprise. They had all stopped looking at Jill, then. They had all looked at David's hand, moving on its own, a pencil held tight in its grasp. It was his right hand, even. David was a leftie.

Then Gary began to draw.

They all drew something that night. Stacie hadn't wanted to, not after David began to scribble, but it didn't matter. Her hand was no longer her own. And while no one had ever agreed on what each of the individual pictures meant—they were barely more than scribbles, as suggestive as tea leaves—Stacie would never forget Jordan's paper. His hand had filled it in completely: one solid mass of gray graphite.

For days she had dreamed about that paper, its surface glossy and yet unimaginably dark. After one of those dreams, she could never go back to sleep. She could only lie in her bed and listen to David's mix tapes.

Outside of the dreams, things were good. They all got tan. Jill made everyone friendship bracelets. Gary taught them how to dive.

Of course it stung to see Jill go off with David sometimes, heading into the woods holding hands. It hurt worse to see them come back smiling and giggly. But Stacie didn't say a word. What could she say? She was Jill's best friend. She owed it to Jill to be happy she had found a boyfriend.

One morning she and Jordan got up and rode their bikes to the library. Gary and Jill were celebrating their mother's birthday at their grandparents' house. David was helping Coach Dusseldorf dig dandelions out of the football field, making twenty-five cents a dandelion root. Jordan had slept over the night before, and Stacie had cut his hair. With his face newly revealed beneath short bangs and her hair knotted back in its scrunchie, they looked surprisingly alike, two brown-eyed, pointed-chinned, serious creatures.

They went into the library, separating to delve into their preferred sections: nonfiction for Jordan, science fiction and fantasy paperbacks for Stacie. She judged the horror content of such volumes by the color of the typeface and the luridness of the monsters. If something was black, gray, or had tentacles, the book probably leaned closer to horror than to sci-fi, especially if the title was written in red.

A library volunteer stopped beside her with a cart full of books to shelve. He might have been anywhere between the age of seventy and a hundred. Stacie thought the fluorescent lights actually passed through his paper-fine skin.

He smiled. "You like horror?"

His voice wasn't as old as his face. She nodded, surprised by his insight. He leaned in, and she noticed the pin on his lapel. It said something about the Deer Kings.

"Have you read any Shirley Jackson?"

Stacie shook her head. A childhood spent being scolded for talking in the library held her tongue.

"I just shelved *The Haunting of Hill House*. Excellent book. Scare your pants off. They keep it in the regular fiction section."

"Like Stephen King."

"Just so."

Stacie moved around the cart full of books waiting for their homes, and the old man squeezed over to make room for her. "Thank you," she said, and he smiled back at her, although for some reason he looked somehow sadder smiling than he had before.

"It's for the good of everyone," he said. Stacie frowned at him, but if he noticed the weirdness of what he had just said, he didn't seem to notice. He turned away, his hand going to a pendant around his neck. He looked worried.

As she and Jordan waited to check out their books, a noise outside commanded their attention. On the other side of the library parking lot, a three-sided glass shelter served as the town's Greyhound bus stop. A woman stood in front, sobbing so hard that as Stacie watched, she was amazed to see the woman's cigarette fall out of her mouth and land on the ground beside the woman's stroller. The woman raised her face to the sky and wailed.

"That's Vincent Vernor's wife," Jordan whispered.

The old man who had advised Stacie to pick up *The Haunting of Hill House* crossed the parking lot, stooped to pick up the cigarette, and gave it back to the woman. They stood talking for a second, and then the man reached into his coat pocket, pulled out his wallet, and removed a few dollars from it.

"Next!" the librarian called. She was Stacie's favorite, a plump cheerful woman who sometimes forgot libraries were about being quiet.

Stacie jumped. "Oh, sorry. I was just watching that nice volunteer. He helped me pick out a book."

The librarian leaned out over the desk so she could see. "That's Harold. Such a nice man. His wife died just about two months ago. I think he's lonely."

The old man patted Mrs. Vernor on the shoulder and then set out for Highway 38. The librarian frowned.

"I wonder where he's going. His car is parked right there." She came around the end of the desk so she could better observe the old man. From their vantage point in the library, they could just make out the intersection of Pearl and Highway 38, although it involved some neck craning.

He stood on the corner, waiting quietly. Stacie heard the soft rattle of a log truck's air brakes coming down the hill.

She remembered the sadness on the man's face and felt an urge to run out to the corner and stop him in his tracks. He deserved more thanks.

He stepped off the curb just as the log truck barreled through the intersection.

CHAPTER TWENTY-SIX

JILL: 2018

SHE WAITED UNTIL Gary was busy with dinner and Stacie was distracted by Zack's PlayStation prowess before going to Gary's office to make the call. All day either Gary or Stacie had been at her side, talking to her, asking her questions, demanding her attention. The relief she felt closing the door on all that was immeasurable. She had forgotten what it was like, living with needy people. Miguel traveled a great deal of the time, and when he was home, he was just there. She could sit with him and paint and never feel any pressure to fill up the silence between them. Sometimes he preferred it that way. He could watch her for hours, he claimed, just enjoying the movement of her hands as she worked.

She took her phone out of her pocket and turned it over in her hands. God, she was nervous. She wished she'd gotten a chance to pop into one of the pot shops she'd seen back in Coos Bay. A little green herb would make the rest of the night a great deal easier.

There was something awkward about being with Stacie. It had started that terrible summer. She had known even as it was happening that some strange barrier was growing between them, but she couldn't quite put her finger on it. Now, nearly thirty years later, she felt like their friendship had been excavated from the layers of their lives, completely intact in every way—good and bad. At some point, Jill was going to have to ask her about what had happened, but she wasn't ready yet. One hard thing at a time.

Jill looked at the lock screen on her phone, but did not enter her pass code. She had asked Kim last night, and her sister-in-law had texted her David's phone number without asking a single question. Jill had only to dial the number and the last of their group—at least the last of the living members—would be reconnected.

She bit her lip.

David.

Her first real boyfriend.

Jill had kissed Michael Swinton in seventh grade. He wasn't the handsomest boy in their class, but he wore a cool Swatch and always squinched his eyes half-shut when he played the clarinet in band concerts. At the first dance she'd gone to at Hewlett Junior High, he had passed her a Dixie cup full of fruit punch. She'd waited until nearly the end of the night, and then, when the nearest chaperone was distracted by a pair of eighth graders with an illicit pack of cigarettes, bumped her lips against his. It would have been unmemorable if it hadn't been her first kiss.

Michael moved to Utah a week later. The kissing experiment had been unsatisfying enough to keep Jill from kissing another boy until that summer, when a boy staying at the BLM campground sat down beside her on the swim float stationed out at the edge of the swimming area. A motorboat rushed past them, sending waves over their feet and legs.

"You're pretty," he said, and they spent the rest of the day swimming and walking together. He kissed her three times—once in the water, twice behind the bathrooms—and then his parents called him to lunch, and she never saw him again.

She didn't bother kissing anyone in eighth grade. No one else in band played with anything like Michael Swinton's verve, and she couldn't stand talking to the others about sports.

Then she met David.

The first time he urged her away from the group, he had put her back to a fir tree and kissed her with a ferocity that made her knees forget how to work. He used his tongue, too, which the other boys had neglected, and he put his hands in her hair, massaging her skin with his fingertips. That was when she realized the power of kissing.

The memory of it forced Jill to take a long, shuddering breath. She was wasting time, and she didn't know why. So David had been a good kisser. That was thirty years ago. She was a middle-aged married woman who had done a great deal of kissing and knew it to be a silly pastime.

Jill unlocked the lock screen and found David's number. She dialed it and waited.

"Hello?" She tried to remember what David had sounded like and failed. The warm baritone could have been anyone's.

"Hello?" the man repeated.

"Yes," Jill said, clearing her throat. "Is this David Washburn?"

A tiny silence. She hoped he didn't think she was some terrifying football fan. Gary had told her about the weirdos who had called Kim. "Yes," he said, grudgingly.

"You probably don't remember me," Jill began, and had to stop and lick her lips. "My name is Jill Sheldon. We were friends in middle school."

His inhalation was ragged. "Jill."

She squeezed her eyes shut. That was just how he had said her name when they walked in the woods, hungry and hopeful. Then she would pull his head down so she could meet his warm, wonderful mouth.

She forced herself to open her eyes and soldier on. "I'm visiting my brother," she said. "He just moved back to Kingston."

"I know, that dumb fuck."

He sounded so angry she pulled the phone away from her ear. When she put the phone back in place, he was talking again.

"Jill? Jill? Are you listening to me?"

"Yes. I just…you got kind of loud."

"I didn't mean to." He sighed. "Look, I can't talk. There's a big meeting I have to go to."

"I know. Gary's wife is speaking at it."

He paused. Out in the living room, she could hear Stacie and Zack laughing. It sounded a lot more enjoyable than this conversation.

"You should go home," he said.

"David, there are things happening in this town. Weird things. And I think they have something to do with that summer."

On his end of the conversation, a horn honked, the small beep of someone locking a car door. He was sitting in his car, she realized, in a parking lot. She could almost picture him like that, watching everyone else arrive for this ultra-important town hall meeting.

"We need to get together and talk," she said. "All of us—you, me, Gary. Stacie's here too."

She heard his door open. "Do yourself a favor, Jill," he said. She could hear other people talking in the background, even a murmur of wind. "Delete my number from your contacts and tell your brother to find his wife a new job."

Tears welled up in her eyes, unexpected, unwelcome. "Why are you being like this?"

"Kingston is a different town these days. And I'm different too."

The call disconnected.

Jill covered her face in her hands. Thirty years and he could still hurt her.

Someone rapped on the door. "Jill? You okay in there?"

"I'm fine, Gary," she called. She picked up her phone, wiped her face on her sleeve. She'd text Miguel. That would cheer her up.

But her hand moved to the mug of pencils sitting beside Gary's computer. She watched it move, not surprised in the least.

Her powers had always been stronger when David was around.

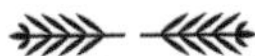

GARY: 2018

Gary wiped the morning drizzle off his glasses and then locked the library door behind himself. He had no idea what Jill and Stacie were going to do with themselves while he was at work; at least he only had a four-hour shift. He went back to the staff room to clock in.

He loved being in the library before it opened. The air inside held an expectant quality, as if the building held its breath, just waiting for the doors to unlock and patrons to require its assistance. He put on his nametag and went out to the main room, smiling a little as he went from computer to computer, powering them on. At the copy machine, he stooped and plugged it in. The library began to fill with the hum and buzz of the information age.

At ten, he flipped the sign and unlocked the doors. Shawn waved and then vanished into his office. An elderly volunteer crept in to tidy the shelves. The clock cruised through the next hour.

In the children's area, story time came and went. A group of homeschool kids arrived with a pair of frumpy chaperones and badgered him with questions about reference books and online resources. The local knitting group settled into the community resource room for their weekly stitch-and-bitch.

The morning moved so smoothly Gary forgot to look at the clock. He added toner to the printer. He unjammed the copy machine. He encouraged a man accessing Pornhub to check out a book of nudes instead.

When Shawn beckoned to Gary from the staff room, he maneuvered his way through a couple of older women catching Pokemon and went behind the desk. The smile on Gary's face faded as he got closer. He had never seen Shawn look so serious. He was even fiddling with something around his neck, a gesture that never failed to remind Gary of Jill and her St. Christopher's medallion. Something stirred in the pit of Gary's stomach.

"Hey, what's up?"

"Your son's friends with Skyler Oakley, isn't he?"

Gary frowned. "They're pretty much inseparable."

Shawn looked like he was going to cry. "The amber alert is going out in a minute. Skyler never made it to school today. He's diabetic, you know. And his mom says he left all his stuff behind."

Gary pushed his knuckles into his lips, certain he was going to throw up.

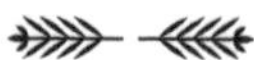

STACIE: 2018

Stacie stood on the deck, her third cup of coffee sending up a plume of steam. Inside, her overnight bag sat beside the front door. Kingston felt no less mysterious, but she had to admit that nothing she could do would crack its shell. It had been a strange place thirty years ago and it was still strange today—just as strange, but more economically depressed.

Maybe she had known that the whole time. Maybe the whole reason she had stayed was just to spend time with Jill and settle her feelings at long last.

Stacie looked over her shoulder. The sliding glass doors lined up with the hallway, which opened onto the big front room. She could just see the tail of Jill's hair flash into view as she bounced up from some invigorating yoga pose.

Stacie's feelings had, in fact, settled. Jill was as straight as the Washington Monument. And while she was still beautiful and her kindness and sweetness made her a perfect cooking companion, Stacie could no longer look at her with the absolute adoration of a first crush.

The front door burst open, and Gary rushed inside, his face wild with misery. Stacie threw open the sliding glass door.

"Hey, what happened?"

Gary flung his work bag on the dining room table. "A kid's gone missing."

Jill had come up behind him. "Oh no."

"What kid?" Stacie asked.

"My son's best friend." Gary grabbed a box of granola bars out of the nearest cupboard and stuffed two in his pocket. "People are gathering at the Dunes Diner to sort into search parties."

Stacie put down her coffee. "We'll help."

"I've got to put on my hiking boots," Gary said, heading into the hall.

Jill took a step closer to Stacie. "I think I drew this," she whispered.

"What?"

She went to the sink and opened the cupboard below. "Last night when I tried to get ahold of David. I didn't want to say anything. At the time I wasn't sure what it meant." She took a folded square of notebook paper out of the recycling bin and handed it to Stacie.

Stacie did not want to unfold it. The back side had a few of Gary's unintelligible scrawls across it—Jill must have just drawn on the nearest scrap of paper she could find. Stacie found herself holding her breath as she uncreased the page.

It took a few seconds for the graphite patches to resolve into shapes. In some places Jill had scrubbed the pencil across the paper with such force she gouged into the fibers; in others, the pencil had barely left a mark. Stacie turned the paper a little, and the darkest area on the page took on the suggestion of an enormous mouth, fringed with sharp teeth. A tiny figure stood beside the mouth, its body contorted in terror.

Stacie wasn't sure how this represented a missing boy. She held it out to Jill, not sure what to say. It obviously meant something to Jill. Her face was drawn, her eyes misty. As their knuckles bumped, a flash of color burst into Stacie's head: oranges, blacks, a dark red.

She pulled her hand away. Only the whites showed in Jill's eyes, and her body had grown strangely rigid.

"Jill? Are you okay?"

A nasty gurgling sound.

Stacie grabbed Jill's shoulders and shook her. "Jill!"

Jill gasped and spluttered, then broke into coughing.

"Jill?" Stacie pounded her on the back. "Are you all right? What happened?"

Jill threw her arms around Stacie, half-collapsing into her. "Oh, Jesus, Stacie, it was so fucked up. There was all this fire. I didn't know what was happening, but the river was right there beside me. I heard a fish jump."

"Did you see the boy?"

Jill pulled away, shaking her head. "I *was* the boy."

Gary reappeared, his face still manic. "I've got to get going."

Stacie waved at him. "We'll be right behind you." She said to Jill: "Get your coat."

CHAPTER TWENTY-SEVEN

GARY: 1989

GARY WALKED TO Stacie's house the next morning. She might have been Jill's best friend, but he felt a certain responsibility for her now that Jill was so busy with David. Seeing someone get mowed down by a forty-ton log truck was too horrible to be stood alone.

He knocked on the Clintons' door and her mom opened. She looked older and more tired than he remembered her looking. She scrunched her cigarette into the corner of her mouth. "What do you want?"

"I'm here to see Stacie, Mrs. Clinton."

She took a long drag on her cigarette. "Jordan's here too."

He had expected that much. Stacie's mom held the door open wide enough for him to squeeze through and then she dropped onto the couch in the living room. "This goddamn summer," she said.

He nodded. Then he knocked on Stacie's door and slipped inside.

She and Jordan were sitting on her bed, the blankets pulled up to their chins. Stacie's eyelids were so pink and swollen she looked like some subterranean creature. Jordan looked only slightly better.

"Hey."

Stacie sniffled. "Hey."

Gary sat down on her bed. "I'm so sorry about yesterday."

"Me, too," she said. "I mean, I didn't know him, but he was a really nice old guy."

"The librarian said he had been a volunteer at the library for ten years," Jordan said. "And he helped with the football team too."

Gary folded his legs underneath him. He found someone's foot under the blanket and gave it a squeeze. "I just wish he hadn't killed himself where you had to see it."

Stacie pushed herself up higher, kicking him in her scramble. "I just wish he hadn't killed himself!"

"It's his life," Gary said. "I mean, it sucks that he felt so bad. But I think sometimes it's okay to kill yourself."

Jordan pulled the blanket up more tightly around his neck. "I've thought about it," he whispered.

Stacie grabbed him. "No. Don't say that."

"But it's true." He pushed her away, but very gently. "Before you guys, I was so lonely. And my mother—" He broke off, shaking his head. "My mother makes me feel lonelier."

Gary reached out to Jordan's shoulder and gripped it. "But you found us."

"David found me."

No one said anything for a minute. The phone rang in the other room.

"Anybody want to go for a walk?" Gary asked. "Or play a game, maybe? We could go back to my house, if you want."

Stacie's door rattled. Her mom stuck her head inside. "Hey, sweetpea? Will you be okay on your own? I've got to go in to work."

Stacie looked up, her eyes too bright. "But it's your day off!"

"Nadine never showed. Probably something with her stupid kids. I'm going to stop by her place and check on her on my way to the lodge." She looked around the room. It would have been impossible for her to miss the tears streaking down Stacie's cheeks, or the general air of seriousness that permeated the space. "Why don't you all come with me? I'll treat you to lunch."

The siren song of free hamburgers was too much. They followed Mrs. Clinton out to the car, although there was none of the usual banter or chit-chat. Gary stared out the window as she drove. Something had changed yesterday, and he couldn't put his finger on it. After the night of Vincent Vernor's party—the night he and Jill had made their offerings to the deer saint and then saw it race out of the driveway—the world had seemed a fine and bright place. He hadn't even seen any ghosts out of the corners of his eyes, not most of the time. But now the road seemed lined with black smoke.

He felt Jordan's fingers close on his, and Gary let him. It might have been a little "faggy" to hold hands with another boy, but it felt too reassuring to touch another human's skin. He had the very pressing desire to jump out of the car and run home to his mother.

She was sleeping, of course. She'd worked the night before.

They drove past the lodge, around the long, horrible curve of Skep

Rock (Gary held his breath and tried not to look outside the car), beyond the little white schoolhouse. They were nearly to his grandparents' house when Mrs. Clinton turned off Calhoun Lake Road and down a long, rutted gravel road. A shack sat off in the middle of a field, its roof sagging almost into a U.

"Nadine lives out here?" Stacie asked.

Her mother said nothing, but turned onto another road, just dirt this time. A log cabin sat at the end of it like it had blown in straight from the 1800s. Gary almost expected Abraham Lincoln to step outside and wave to them.

"Nadine's car is still here," Mrs. Clinton said. She didn't sound happy.

They parked beside the battered old station wagon. Gary thought it might be the oldest car he'd ever seen outside a museum.

They all got out, although Mrs. Clinton shot them a dirty look. "Don't go anywhere," she said. "We have to get to the lodge in a minute."

Stacie just waved to her mom and walked toward the garden on the side of the house. Gary and Jordan hurried to catch up.

Gary's grandparents grew a garden every year, and he often got suckered into weeding it, but Nadine's garden bore about as much resemblance to his grandma's little garden as a blue crayon looked like the sky. Her corn already reached his waist, and the tomato plants overflowed their cages. Flowers overflowed the rows, marigolds and nasturtiums and others he could not name. Leaves of a dozen shades of green, purple, and red burst out of the lettuce patch. A line of sunflowers ran along the back of it all, their centers enormous and dark as they looked up at the sun.

"Who knew Nadine liked plants?" Stacie asked. She squatted low and came up with a strawberry. She bit into it. "Wow."

Gary could not bring himself to poach Nadine's fruit. He brushed his fingers over the fuzzy leaves of the woolly lamb's ear plants and then made his way toward the sunflowers. There were more plants behind them, he realized, big green ones with luxurious leaves.

"Hey, look at these plants," he said. "They look like the ones Vincent was putting in his dehydrator."

Stacie appeared at his elbow. "I think that's pot."

"What?" Jordan pushed a sunflower stalk out of the way. "No way."

She shrugged. "I'm no expert."

Gary couldn't look away from the plants. It would make sense, he thought. Vincent sold other, much stronger drugs. A few pot plants must have been like tomatoes to a guy like that.

Something not-green caught his eye. Something blue. He recognized the familiar shape of Chuck Taylor's.

"Stacie? Does Nadine wear Chucks?"

"What? How the hell should I know what kind of shoes she wears?"

He pushed back a sunflower stalk. "Stay right there."

"What? Why?" Stacie gave a little squawk. He could imagine Jordan grabbing her arm.

Gary kept his eyes fixed on the shoe. There were three drops of black candle wax on the white rubber toe cap. *Please be okay*, he whispered. *Please be okay.*

He didn't see the hoe on the ground until he tripped on it. It was just lying there between the rows of plants and if he hadn't been studying that blue Chuck Taylor so closely, he would have seen it with no problem. The fall hadn't hurt, though. The ground was soft as mashed potatoes.

He pushed himself up from the dirt and looked at his hands. It took him a minute to understand why they were red and not dirt-brown.

Gary turned around to face the others. They had pushed back the sunflower stalks. Of course they had. He stood there, with his hands out in front of him, wishing he could move those damn sunflowers with the power of his mind. If only they hadn't had to see that blue shoe.

All the color went out of Stacie's face. Jordan shoved her toward the house.

"Go get your mom," he said. "Now!"

For the first time in years, Gary found himself crying.

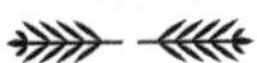

JILL: 2018

Jill followed her group of volunteers past the high school and up Hill Street. Kids were known to hang out up at the cemetery, a deputy had told them, and streets intersecting Hill Street had few streetlights. The deputy hadn't come right out and called it a great spot for a hit and run, but she hadn't needed to. The volunteers had all gone solemn-eyed and serious, and even though they shouted out the boy's name as they made their way up the hill, their shouts sounded subdued.

She peered under a rhododendron bush as if the lost kid might be hiding beneath its branches. After the vision she'd had, she was pretty sure they weren't going to find Skyler lying in a ditch somewhere. He was dead—that much she was certain. She hadn't been able to tell where the murder happened, though. The ring of fire had blinded her, and any ambient sounds had been covered over by the droning chants of the people with the torches.

Jill shuddered. People with torches. It hadn't been just one deranged killer or a tiny group; there had to have been ten or fifteen figures in that circle, plus the actual killer. The boy had been on his side, perspective skewing the person in the middle of the circle into an anonymous black column holding an enormous hunting knife. He hadn't seen their face under their hood. All she knew is that they'd worn a dark-colored rain jacket that didn't look any different from half the jackets on the volunteers around her. She grabbed the rhododendron branch to steady herself. God, the killer could be the woman peering into the end of a culvert on the other side of the street, or the man looking underneath that Chevy Suburban.

"Jill?"

She started so hard she nearly fell into the rhododendron. She turned around, hoping she looked more collected than she felt. "Yes?"

"I didn't mean to startle you." The man standing beside her gave her a tentative smile. "Do you recognize me?"

He was tall, probably a little over six foot, and even in rain gear (she couldn't help noticing his coat was dark blue), obviously athletic. Under a red beanie, his short hair looked a bit more golden than dishwater blond. The regularity of his features would have made him popular with any group of ladies, although Jill preferred men with beards. The smile faded.

"You don't recognize me? Not even after talking last night?"

She took an unwilling step toward him. "David?"

"I can't believe you didn't recognize me."

"No, I knew right off." He had gotten broader and more square-jawed, but the scrappy boy he'd been was still there.

He cleared his throat. "What are you doing here?"

The bulk of the volunteers had passed them by, leaving behind only a few elderly stragglers. Jill stepped out of the rhododendron bush and began walking again. "Looking for the missing kid."

"Skyler Oakley," he said, his voice very quiet. "He wasn't a very good football player."

She didn't know how to respond to that. The road made a right, getting steeper. A pair of volunteers had decided to go off-road, thrashing up the ferny hillside despite the posted "No Trespassing" signs.

"I meant, what are you doing *here*? Kingston?"

She glanced away from the lawsuit waiting to happen. He was looking at her very intently.

"My grandmother had an accident. My brother thought I should come visit."

"Gary Sheldon." He went silent for a minute. "I should have reached out to him when he first arrived in town."

"Yeah, but you didn't."

It was sort of a bitchy thing to say. Jill felt a twinge of conscience, then let it go. David hadn't been their friend since the first day of high school. No; earlier. Since the first day of football practice.

"Do you remember coming up here that summer?"

She hadn't, not until he asked. But they had biked up to the cemetery one day. She had packed a picnic basket. They had sat on John King's grave and talked about their futures while they ate. After they ate, they had made out, probably for hours.

"You said you wanted to be a cop," she remembered.

"And you wanted to illustrate children's books." He chuckled. "How'd that turn out?"

A few volunteers shouted, their voices rolling down the hillside from the cemetery. She peered over the shoulder of the road. The steep flank of Cemetery Hill sloped down into someone's backyard. She could see a trampoline, its safety nets dotted with fallen leaves. No fallen torches or dead kids, though.

"I run a gallery in Petaluma, California," she said. "And I still paint."

"Wow."

She could see the cemetery gates up ahead. They stood open, but she could see the wreaths someone had hung on them, the same red-and-white ribboned variety that Kim had put up on Gary's front door. A cemetery didn't seem like the right spot for a school spirit-themed wreath, but maybe she was just biased.

She remembered then that David's whole career revolved around school spirit and pep rallies. It seemed nearly impossible that the boy she had kissed here on John King's grave would have grown up to be a football coach.

He stopped and faced her. "It's homecoming on Friday."

"Aww, are you asking me to the big dance?"

He shook his head, his face very serious. "I'm asking you to go home."

"What?"

A woman walked by, leaning on a walking stick. She gave David an odd look, and Jill wondered just what they looked like: the big, handsome football coach, the artsy-fartsy beach chick. A soft rain began to fall. Jill pulled up the hood on her jacket.

David stepped in closer. "I still care about you, Jill. I never stopped."

"You had a strange way of showing it."

He looked over his shoulder. Lowered his voice. "I had my reasons. Like I do today. You and Gary were never part of this town the way your parents were. The way I am."

He had taken her hands in his. His fingers were warm and strong, and she found herself leaning toward him. He smelled good, like sandalwood or something. He had always smelled good.

"I know there's something really weird going on in this town. Something bad."

"That's why you should go. You and Gary, both. The things you two can do…" He pressed a kiss on her knuckles, then dropped her hands. "Just go. Tonight, if you can. But definitely before Friday."

"David…"

"Jill! David!"

Jill had always liked her sister-in-law, but she could have gladly thrown her down the side of Cemetery Hill at this moment. She forced a smile onto her face. "Hey, Kim."

"I just came up for a minute to see how the search for Skyler was going." She caught David's eyes and held them. "Have you heard any details, Coach?"

He shook his head mutely.

"Well, that's too bad." Kim turned back to Jill. "Oh. Someone stopped by the school this morning. They found your friend's coffee cup."

She held out Stacie's black travel mug. There was mud smeared on the lid—mud and ash.

Jill could only look at it. It could have been any kind of mud, any kind of ash.

"Jill?" Kim shoved the mug toward her.

When Jill's fingers closed on the mug, she could hear the drone of voices chanting.

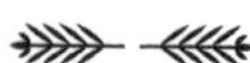

GARY: 2018

Gary hesitated at the edge of the trail. All around him, Lake Mary Elizabeth County Park—the northernmost border of Kingston—rang out with shouts. A pair of kayakers had already set out onto the water, each one planning to circumnavigate the little lake in a different direction. Those who owned hip waders had been directed to the small wetlands on the west side of the lake.

He stepped off the trail, squeezing between salal bushes. For a moment, he all-too-clearly remembered pushing through the sunflower stalks at Nadine's garden, and he shuddered. He hoped like hell they would find Skyler walking in the woods, or hitchhiking up the highway, or waiting at the bus stop in Eugene. But beneath his hopes was that vision of a blue Chuck Taylor sticking out from under a marijuana plant.

"Skyler!" he shouted. "Skyler!"

Maybe he would have felt different if, at the sheriff's office, he hadn't seen Sam sitting there with a blanket around her shoulders, her face blank of all feeling. He had rushed to her side and taken her hand. He couldn't remember just what he'd said, some stupid thing about hope and positive energy.

She had turned her blue eyes toward him. They were totally clear, the whites unstained with the redness of tears. She looked as collected as if she were on her way to deliver a sermon.

"You're all wasting your time," she said. "I told the deputies, but they have to put on a show."

He had backed away from her. The tone of her voice—it was impossible to believe it. So cold. So unfeeling. "What do you mean?"

"He's with his father," she said.

Gary shook his head. "You said Skyler's dad was out of the picture."

"I told them not to bother," she repeated.

An air horn jolted Gary back to the cold damp of the woods. It wasn't raining yet, but the drizzle could still soak through your clothes if you were out long enough.

A woman passed him by, struggling with a big, energetic dog. She caught Gary's eye. "Teenagers run off all the time and they don't do shit," she said. "But when it's Coach D's grandkid, they mobilize the whole town." She gave a big laugh. The dog lifted its leg and sent a steaming stream onto a shore pine. "Go Bucks!"

"Go Bucks," someone murmured in agreement, although Gary could not tell who. They had quite the crowd now, volunteers spilling out across the woods like locusts in a field of grain.

He should go home. It was stupid to be out here, a waste of time. If Sam was right, then Skyler had gone off with his long-lost father and they were probably halfway to Mexico by now. If she wasn't right, well, there were a dozen places a teenage boy was more likely to turn up than the park on the edge of town.

"Gary."

He couldn't have been more surprised to see the man beside his elbow. "David?"

David Washburn smiled weakly. Even in his raincoat and jeans, he somehow gave off an aura of charisma and athleticism. "Ran into your sister. She said you all were helping with the search."

A man stared openly as he passed them, craning his neck to watch the coach deign to speak to the lowly librarian. He almost walked into a tree.

David fell in step with Gary. "Anyway, I just wanted to say that I'm sorry."

"Why?"

"For one, because I know Skyler is a particular friend of your son."

Gary wondered how the hell David knew such a thing, but didn't say anything.

"And for another, because I haven't tried to meet up with you since you came into town. It wasn't kind."

"Well," Gary began. "You've had football," he finished lamely. "You're pretty busy."

"Skyler!" David threw back his head and bellowed. He looked back at Gary. "That's all part of it," he agreed.

"But not all."

They didn't say anything for a minute or two. Gary peered under a fallen log. A scrap of blue caught his eye, but it was only an empty bag of Ruffles and nothing worse.

"Wasn't high school great?" David asked. His smile was perfect. Gary could distinctly remember that David had once had a canine tooth that stuck out, giving his smile a certain goofiness, but the man had clearly put that behind him.

"I guess."

"We were all so popular," David mused. "You always had a girlfriend, and Jill was the homecoming queen senior year."

All of that stuff seemed trivial and stupid now. After his parents died, high school had drifted out of his mind, separated from the rest of his life by an uncrossable chasm.

"Well, you remember." David clapped Gary on the shoulder. "It could be like that again, you know. Zack's already won over the JV team. And you should have seen Kim at the meeting last night. She's the best principal KHS has had in years."

"Oh." Kim hadn't told Gary much about the meeting, other than the fact it focused on the Keridan Bridge Corporation and Plymouth's developing bid for its attention. He had supposed Jim Burns had delivered his spy's information from the Plymouth Chamber of Commerce.

"Anyway," David said, "it's good to see you out here with your community. We need you, Gary. You're John King's last descendent."

Gary stopped to look the man square in the eye. "What the hell are you talking about?" It seemed nearly impossible that this officious asshole could be the boy who once taught him all the words to "In-A-Gadda-Da-Vida," the boy who had begged Gary to help him talk to the spirit of his grandfather.

But David was already turning away. Coach Dusseldorf stood back on the path, his hands on his hips, and David made a beeline for the older man. Gary frowned at them, and Coach D raised his arm in an abbreviated wave.

He was Skyler's grandfather, Gary reminded himself. It made sense that he would be out here.

Gary trudged on. He didn't particularly want to, but no one else had turned back. The rain picked up, adding its own slight muffling to the shouts around him. The other volunteers had spread out in their various directions, and now Gary walked alone, with no one else in eyeshot. The lake and the parking lot were far behind him.

He came to the top of a little rise and stopped to catch his breath. From here, he could see the end of the forest and the beginning of a low strip of dunes. Between their hummocks he could just catch small glimpses of the ocean. Specks moved across the dune tops—fellow volunteers, he presumed. There were a lot of them out there. There had obviously been a great deal of interest in beach searching.

Movement in the corner of his eye made him turn to his right. He had expected another volunteer, maybe even a spirit, but the deer startled him. The doe stood quietly chewing to herself, her eyes fixed on Gary. She did not move when he did, but just watched.

"Hey," he said.

She did not move.

It was hard to be afraid of such a lovely creature. The deer at his house had such an unsettling quality, but she seemed ordinary, natural. He could see the soft white fur lining the inside of her ears and felt a powerful urge to put out his hand to pet her.

The back of his neck felt warm.

He glanced over his shoulder. Nothing. The woods had fallen silent too.

He looked back at the deer. Was she watching him, or was she looking just over his shoulder at something behind him? He spun around.

"Hey, Gary."

He had not seen Vincent Vernor in thirty years, and the last time Gary laid eyes on the man, he had watched him die. But the man standing in front of him was certainly Vincent Vernor. The long blond ponytail, the pale blue eyes, the tattoos creeping out of the blue thermal shirt—they could only have belonged to Vincent.

Gary shut his eyes. He had to be hallucinating.

He opened them to see Vincent standing even closer to him. Gary stumbled backward, his back hitting the warm bulk of the deer. She exhaled huffily.

"It's good to see you remember me." Vincent took a step closer, towering over Gary just as he had thirty years ago. A cigarette seemed to just appear in his hand. He took a long drag and then blew the smoke into Gary's face. "I certainly remember you."

The deer pushed Gary forward. He was bending backward now, struggling to keep his face away from Vincent's. The back of his neck burned terribly.

The smoke cleared enough that Vincent's features reappeared. A strand of blond hair hung lankly by his cheek, a bit of moss caught it in. It was such an ordinary thing to notice, but Gary could not look away from that bit of green fluff.

Vincent's hand came out, seizing Gary's chin. "Why don't you look in my eyes and tell me what you see."

Gary wanted nothing but to stare at that moss, that clean ordinary moss, but his neck muscles were no match for Vincent's strength. Gary's head turned until he was staring into the hollow pits of the man's eyes. Because Vincent's eyes were no longer blue. They were no longer even eyes. They were only coils of black smoke, that smoke that was not smoke, the smoke of the spirits.

And one of them screamed and cried in Skyler's voice.

"You son of a bitch!" Gary shouted.

"Gary?"

Gary turned around, blinking. The air stank of cigarettes. A man stood beside him, his face worried behind his hipster glasses. It took Gary a second to recognize his boss.

"Shawn?"

"Yeah, man. Are you okay?"

Gary looked around the hilltop. There was no deer, and certainly no Vincent Vernor.

"Yeah." He shook himself all over. "I guess my imagination is just running wild."

"They've called off the search," Shawn said. "Someone saw the boy's father down in Medford, so they're pretty sure the boy's down there."

"Sure," Gary said. He gave a sudden, dry sob. "Sure."

"Man, are you okay?" Shawn put an awkward arm around his shoulder.

"I guess I'm just relieved," Gary said. He was crying now, the tears pouring down his face and turning colder than the drizzle.

"They'll bring him home soon," Shawn said, patting his back. "It'll all be okay."

But Gary could not stop hearing the sound of Skyler crying out in pain and fear. Someone had killed his son's friend, and whoever they were, they had the power to stop the search for his body.

CHAPTER TWENTY-EIGHT

GARY: 2018

GARY AND STACIE sat quietly at the kitchen table. A leaf had lodged in her brown bob, but he couldn't bring himself to point it out. The coffee pot gurgled and hissed. How smart of Stacie to start a fresh pot. He didn't crave the caffeine, but after what he'd just seen, he needed the comforting heat and bitterness. Sometimes only coffee could put the soul back in the body.

The front door opened and Jill came in. She looked queasy, and she held a travel mug at arm's length in front of her, as if it contained something awful.

"Is that my travel mug?" Stacie asked.

"Yep."

"But I dropped it in the woods out by that creepy shrine place."

"Yep." Jill tossed the mug in the sink. She didn't sit down at the table, just stood there like she had something to say.

Gary slid down in the booth so he could look up at her more easily. The energy had seeped out of all his joints. "What is it?"

Jill shifted her weight from her left foot to her right. "What do you think happened at that meeting last night?"

He wanted to shrug, but his shoulder didn't have the energy. "They talked about the Keridan Bridge Company, I guess."

She began to pace.

Stacie got up and found the mugs they'd used that morning. She looked down into the sink for a second. "This mug is filthy."

Jill folded her arms around her middle. "Yes." She turned back to look at Gary. "What do you think will happen if the Keridan Bridge Company doesn't come to Kingston?"

He took the cup of coffee Stacie offered him. "Nothing? Just more of the same slow slide into economic depression as ever."

Stacie put a cup of coffee down on Jill's side of the table and then sat down, sipping her own cup. "It's kind of a miracle the town is doing as well as it is," she said. "The fishing industry is dead. The mill closed. Logging is mostly dead. There's not a single major employer left in town."

"And yet a two-bedroom house can go for over $275,000." Gary's laugh sounded hollow.

Jill set her palms on the tabletop, her expression intense. "Remember the first time they talked about closing the cannery?"

He could vaguely remember a month of raised voices and lots of meetings. "Sort of. I know Dad was pretty worried."

"Think harder. Can you remember anything else that happened around that time?"

"Not really. I was pretty focused on school. I had Mrs. Carter for geometry, and she was—" He broke off. "But Mrs. Carter died that November. They said it was a hunting accident."

"Yeah." Jill finally sat down, perching on the edge of the vinyl seat. "Don't you think this town has an awful lot of hunting accidents? And car accidents? And runaways? And even murders?"

"I don't want to play the Devil's advocate here, but Southwest Oregon has always had a significantly higher rate of property crime, drug use, and even general mortality than the rest of the state," Stacie said.

Jill ignored her. "I had a vision," she said. "I think Skyler Oakley was murdered. Wait, that's the wrong word. I think he was *sacrificed.* And I don't think he was the first person who was either."

Gary wished Stacie wasn't blocking his way so he could get out of the booth and stop looking at his sister's face. She sounded crazy. Completely crazy. Except every time she had ever sounded crazy, she had been right.

"I asked it back there and I'll ask now: Who are they making offerings to?" Stacie asked. "People around here are generally Protestants. They don't even light candles for saints."

"Saints," Gary said. He looked from Jill to Stacie. "The deer saint."

"We all made offerings to it," Jill said.

This time Stacie got up from the booth. She went to the kitchen sink and then back, shaking her head. "No."

"Why not?"

"No!" She held up her hands, waving them around her face as if she could double the negation of her head shaking. "We all saw it go into that fire, and then we never saw it again. It finished off Vincent Vernor, and that was its entire reason for existence. It was gone."

Gary's lungs went tight. "I saw him today."

"Who?" Stacie asked.

"Vincent Vernor. Or at least his ghost."

"Fuck!" Stacie kicked the bottom cabinet. "Why didn't you fucking say so, Gary?"

"I…" He tried to take a deep breath. His chest hurt. He took a gulp of coffee. "It was so fucked up. He looked exactly same, except for his eyes. His eyes were…" He trailed off.

Jill put her arm around his shoulder. "His eyes were what?"

"His eyes were just ghost smoke. And…Skyler was in there."

Jill's arm tightened around his shoulder.

Stacie paced back to the kitchen sink, spun around, paced back. "What does that even mean?"

"It ate spirits," Jill said. "We saw it eat Vincent Vernor's."

"I hate this," Stacie said. "I should never have come back to this fucking town." She went to the sink and turned on the water, all the way. "I'm gonna go." She squirted soap onto the dishcloth and slammed the soap bottle back down on the counter. "I've gotta get out of here."

She picked up the mug and took a swipe at its side. "And why is there ash and soot all over my fucking travel mug?"

Jill got up from the booth. "Remember my vision about the boy? People with torches. A big fire. Someone with a knife."

Stacie's head turned slowly until she was looking at Jill. The water rushed from the faucet in a blast of white noise. "A big fire."

"There was a fire pit on Indian Point," Jill reminded them. "And you lost your mug somewhere out there."

Gary shoved his coffee cup across the table as if it was contaminated with the same filth as Stacie's travel mug. "We should go out there. He could still be there, or some sign of him, or…"

Stacie turned off the water. "Somebody already went out there," she said, her voice dull. "I heard them assigning volunteers. Somebody went out there and they didn't find a thing."

Jill licked her lips. "Or else they *did* find something."

"What do you mean?" Gary asked. He thought he knew, but he needed someone else to say it out loud.

"We don't know who all is involved in this," Jill said. "Those volunteers could have been there when they killed Skyler. Anybody could be involved in this. For all we know, the whole town is in on it."

Gary had gotten up without realizing it. "Not the whole town." He pulled his arms around his middle. It was cold here by the sliding glass doors. So cold. "I'm not. Zack's not."

"What about Kim?" Stacie said. "You made it sound like her job hangs on this bridge company deal."

"No," Gary said. "Not Kim. She's couldn't do anything like that."

"She might not know how bad it is," Stacie said. "You can be a part of things without being a part of everything."

Jill made a face. "She was the one who gave me the mug. And she went to that meeting last night. Who knows what that was really about?"

Gary's phone chirped in his pocket. He pulled it out, looking anxiously at the others. "It's Kim."

"What does she say?" Stacie asked.

He read the text out loud: "Going to stop at the market on my way home. Do you need anything?" He texted back a quick "no." Then added a smiley face, which he immediately regretted after sending. He was not the kind of person to add a smiley face to a text unless it served sarcasm.

Stacie frowned. "How long will it take her to get home?"

"Ten minutes, maybe? A few minutes longer if she can't find what she's looking for at the store."

"So we can't go to Indian Point tonight," Stacie said. She turned the water back on and began scrubbing mud off the mug.

"Why not?" Jill asked.

"Because if Kim is a part of this, we can't let her know we've figured out where Skyler was killed." She turned off the water again and glanced at them, her lips pressed tight. "Our lives probably depend on it."

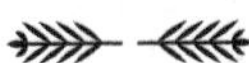

GARY: 1989

John Sheldon put the picnic basket into the car and swung shut the hatchback. "And that's everything," he said, clapping his hands. "Everybody get in and get ready for fun."

Gary folded the passenger seat over and scrambled into the backseat of his mom's little car. It took everyone a minute or two to get settled, and then they pulled out of the driveway. The car's interior filled with the sweetness of coconut suntan lotion. He knew Jill would reapply the stuff once they hit the beach, but she felt her skin required a certain "pre-greasing" to guarantee a good tan. Gary never bothered with the stuff. Like their father, his skin would stay a skim milk shade until it crisped to red, and even after he peeled, the only gold he added to his skin were a few more freckles.

His dad pulled on his beach hat, a disreputable straw thing that had probably been purchased secondhand in the seventies. Gary couldn't remember the last time his father had joined them on a trip to the beach. There had a been a time or two when he was little—he could clearly remember his father patiently teaching him the breaststroke. But in recent years, summers had been filled with travel. It wasn't that the woods around Kingsport were tapped or anything, but that his father preferred the camaraderie of a smaller logging crew, instead of working with the big cheap-skate logging companies. Sometimes Gary wished his father would suck up his principles so they could have family suppers like the old days.

"It sure is beautiful," their mom said as Balfour Drive met Calhoun Lake Road. She sat at the stop sign a few extra minutes, just admiring the view.

A yellow speedboat streaked by, close enough Gary could make out the pink-and-black print of the waterskier's bikini. He couldn't help craning his head to take in the view of her backside. His dad shot him a wink.

Then his mom turned right and Jill gave a happy whoop. "The BLM?"

"I thought we'd make it a real beach day," their dad said.

A sense of relief filled Gary. He had expected a trip to Eagle Cove. There was no day fee at the little campground. But there was no sand either. And only the stinking vault toilet if you had to pee.

Traffic slowed as they approached the entrance to the park. An RV turned in front of the Sheldons' little car, and they had to wait five minutes for the park ranger to explain the campground layout to the RV's balding driver. Gary's dad used the time to tickle his wife. They looked so much younger than usual, Gary thought. A lightness filled the car that he couldn't name.

After paying the entrance fees, they found a parking spot not too far from the water, and Gary carried the picnic basket, walking slowly beside his father while Jill and their mom ran to find them a good place to set up for the day. The picnic tables beneath the trees were marked off with a reserved sign, but that was all right by Gary. He got enough shade at their house.

"You holding up okay?"

"Huh?" He looked up at his father, who had an unusually concerned expression on his face. "Oh, you mean after yesterday. Yeah." He paused. "I didn't sleep too well last night, though."

His father shifted the picnic blanket and umbrella under his elbow.

"You kids have had a hell of a summer."

Gary shrugged. What could he really tell his dad? That their neighbor was a drug dealer and he and his friends had summoned up a saintly protector that may or may not be helping other people around town? With his family's history of nuttiness, he'd be locked up at the Oregon State Mental Hospital before he could say "Salem."

"I didn't sleep so well, myself," his father said. Jill had found an open space on the grass beside a spindly tree. She waved her arms at them to steer them her way. "That fool Vernor was burning stuff in front of his house all night. I think he's gone off his nut since he lost his job and his woman left him."

"Maybe he'll move," Gary said, hope surging through him.

His dad opened the sun umbrella and jabbed its point down into the dirt. "Maybe."

Jill was already slithering out of her street clothes. Her purple one-piece clashed with Gary's orange swim trunks. "Come on, Gary! Let's dive off the dock before there's no room!"

He ripped off his t-shirt and glasses and chased after her. The sun beat down on his hair, warming his skull, and the long, narrow dock pounded under their feet like some enormous drum. This was what summer should be like: sunshine and laughter and water spraying up in his face from his sister's dive. He launched himself off the dock and for a second imagined he was flying.

Then he slid down into the green depths of the lake, chasing the tiny bubbles left by Jill's passage through the water. Tiny leaves scraped his skin as he passed between the strands of lake weed. A tendril caught on his ankle and he had to yank himself free. Smoke boiled in the corner of his vision, and so he squeezed his eyes shut as he twisted toward the surface.

People had died here at the beach: split their heads on rocks, hit their heads on the dock, gotten too drunk and toppled out of their boat. When he burst through the surface of the water, he could taste the smoke of souls saturating the water.

He began to cry.

"Gary? What's wrong?"

The waves from Jill treading water rocked him sideways a little. He pinched snot from his nose and washed it away. "Nothing. Everything. Damn it."

She nudged him toward the dock. They had swum much farther than he had realized, well beyond the chain of floats marking off the swimming area. The water beneath him felt painfully cold.

He swam steadily, ducking under the chain and back toward the shore. He didn't say anything until he could feel sand beneath his feet.

"There's something wrong with this place," he said.

Jill squeegeed water off her face. "What kind of wrong?"

He wasn't sure he had words for it, but he wanted to try. "Remember that first trip to Eagle Cove? The mine?"

She nodded.

He rubbed his arms, even though the sun was still hot. "Things like that happen too often here."

She put her hand on his back. "Things like that happen everywhere."

"Yeah, but something in this place *likes* it when those things happen." He hesitated. He was so close to saying what he wanted, but he wasn't quite there. He took a deep breath. "Do you think we made a mistake, making the deer saint?"

She shook her head so hard water droplets sprang off it. "No! No, we've been helping people. Remember how it saved Coach Dusseldorf? And how it got Vincent Vernor fired? It's protecting everyone in town."

"Not Nadine."

She began wading toward shore. "Yeah, but Nadine was a drug dealer. I don't think the deer saint protects drug dealers."

He remembered the basket he had seen lying on the ground beside Nadine's body. He was sure that had something to do with her death, but what, he didn't know. He followed Jill back to their sun umbrella, his pace half her speed. Had the candles in the basket been used? He thought they had. He remembered Stacie lighting the candles at the ceremony where they'd called up the deer saint, and the breeze raised goosebumps on his naked back.

"Gary, there's chips!" Jill bellowed. He broke into a run.

Their mother made them stand in the grass where they wouldn't drip on the picnic blanket, and passed them each a glass of tea and a cup of chips. She shielded her eyes with her hand as she settled back under the sun umbrella. "Did you two have a nice plunge?"

"It's colder than you'd think out there," Jill said. "A lot colder than it is at Eagle Cove."

Their mother picked up her book. "Well, there's that big drop-off beyond the chain. You shouldn't go out there too far, you know. You could get caught in the current."

"Do lakes have currents?" Jill wondered.

"This one does," their mother said, crunching a chip. "It's caught plenty of boaters and sucked them into the rocks where Matson Creek starts. A lot of people have died over there."

Gary shuddered. He wished he had a hot cup of cocoa and not iced tea.

"Hey, where's Dad?" Jill asked.

Their mother was already focused on her book. "Over there," she said, waving her hand vaguely. "He ran into somebody he knew."

Gary and Jill turned to see if they could spot their dad. He had made his way over to the group of picnic tables beneath the big maple tree, and was now talking to a group of middle-aged men, including Coach Dusseldorf. Their father looked out of place in his swimming trunks and faded t-shirt; everyone else over there was wearing polos or short-sleeved button-downs.

Jill jabbed Gary in the ribs. "Look."

He didn't know how he could have missed it: the flag they'd stuck on a rod and flown beside the center table. It was a white flag with a red border and the sharp black outline of a stag's head. It rippled a little in the breeze off the lake.

"It's the Deer Kings," Jill said.

Coach D offered their dad a cigarette from a red pack. Gary's mouth fell open when his dad took it.

"Dad doesn't smoke, does he, Mom?"

She didn't look up from her book. Gary's skin prickled as the coach lit the cigarette and then glanced toward Gary and Jill. He waved at them lazily. Another man, the best dressed of the group, came over to their father's side and shook his hand. Gary's dad smiled wider than Gary had ever seen him smile.

"I don't like this," Gary said, and Jill squeezed his hand.

CHAPTER TWENTY-NINE

GARY: 2018

GARY WOKE IN the night and could not say what had awakened him. His pillow still supported his head at the right angle; his bladder had no protests; Kim was not snoring. He rolled over onto his back and stared up at the ceiling. He had been dreaming about the hospital again. The skin on the back of his neck stung.

Normally, Gary would get up on nights like this and make a cup of tea or something, but he didn't want to wake Stacie or Jill. He could remember when they had first moved to his Uncle Jim's house, waking in the night and lying there not moving, afraid of every sound. It had taken him a long time to learn what was a normal sound in that house and what should concern him. He would not inflict any of that nervousness on his friend or his sister.

Not that he was sure he could call Stacie his friend. She'd always been closer to Jill than him, and of course, it had been nearly thirty years since he had seen her last, longer than any of the others in their group except Jordan.

The thought sparked a strange squeezing in his chest. He had forgotten—it had seemed so trivial—it hadn't mattered in the least. Except it had.

What had Stacie said about Jordan? That he was the best of the group? Kind of a weird thing to say, except that it was true. He had always been there for whomever needed him most. If someone started an argument, Jordan smoothed it over. If someone got scared, he held their hand. He as much as Vincent Vernor had brought them together that summer.

Then that September, just as school should have been starting,

Jordan's mother had moved them to Coos Bay, where she'd joined a bigger church and gotten a better-paying job. Gary had called Jordan several times that first year, had even gotten together with him on one visit memorable for the sheer quantity of pizza they had devoured. But Gary had gotten busier and busier with friends and school, and Jordan had gotten quieter, and by the time Gary got cancer, he had almost forgotten about Jordan entirely.

But Jordan hadn't forgotten about him. There had been one last call, a call Gary hadn't taken seriously because it was so illogical, and back in Gary's college years he couldn't be bothered with illogical things. He'd been trying like hell to put the past behind him, even if it meant forgetting all about Jordan and their last conversation.

Now he pressed his palm against his mouth hard enough to make his gums complain. He had forgotten a very great deal of 1997—it was the year he had met Kim; the year he had sold his first short story—but here in the dark he could remember that one day of it.

He'd come back from a particularly long run and was getting his shower stuff. Kim was going to meet him for a veggie burger at the student-run cafe; afterward, they were going to an all-night horror movie event in the basement of her dorm. He had high hopes of making out during the boring scenes.

There he'd been, picking up the Head and Shoulders that had somehow fallen out of his shower caddy, when the phone rang. He had answered it immediately; while most of his calls were from Jill, his grandmother did occasionally get a yen to chat, and she could generally be persuaded to send him a couple of bucks.

"Hey," he'd answered the phone. It was a new method he'd been trying.

"Gary? Gary Sheldon?"

The voice at the other end wasn't exactly a stranger's, but it took him a second to place it. "Hey, Jordan! How are things? You in college?"

"Yeah," Jordan said. "Yeah, OSU."

He hadn't sounded sad or upset or anything. He didn't even sound particularly excited to talk to Gary. He could have been calling his dentist.

"So what's new?" Gary asked.

"Gary," Jordan said, and then stopped.

Gary's shirt had begun to stick to his skin in a chilly, clammy sort of way. He sighed.

God, what an asshole he'd been. He had actually fucking sighed.

"What?" he asked, his voice full of all the irritation he could put into it.

"My forestry class went out to the lake last week," Jordan said.

"The lake?" Realization hit him. "Calhoun Lake?"

"It's still there," Jordan whispered.

"Yeah," Gary said, rolling his eyes. "The lake is still there. Big surprise."

"No," Jordan whispered. "*It.* I saw it."

The bottle of Head and Shoulders fell over in the shower caddy. Gary was glad the lid was turquoise and not another, deeper shade of blue. *Stacie, does Nadine wear Chuck Taylor's?* a voice whispered in the back of his head.

"And now I'm dreaming about it," Jordan said.

"I don't want to talk about this anymore," Gary said. "I'm never going back to Kingston, and I don't know what you're talking about."

"Good," Jordan said. "Don't go back. Promise me, Gary—you'll never go back."

"Goodbye, Jordan. And happy Halloween."

Then he'd hung up, and taken his shower, and Kim had let him get to third base on a shabby couch in the back of the movie room. He had thought about what Jordan said exactly once, at the end of *Friday the 13th*, when Jason came up out of the water of the lake, dripping and hideous. It would be like that if he went back to Calhoun Lake, he had thought, and then brushed the thought away. After all, there was no logical reason to ever go back. Dr. Monroe had reassured him: no logical reason.

Gary scrubbed his hands over his face. They came away damp, whether with sweat or tears, he couldn't guess.

He should have made that promise to Jordan—made it, and kept it.

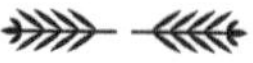

STACIE: 2018

Stacie turned off Highway 38 for the road to the dump and then pulled into the first empty driveway she saw, a weedy track beside a decrepit-looking little house. They sat in the car a second, waiting for the house's owner to come out to the front step and either threaten to shoot them for trespassing or to offer them a welcoming hot drink. To be honest, Stacie wasn't sure which would be more terrifying.

"You sure this is going to work?"

Stacie squeezed Jill's hand. "No. But what other choice do we have?

At least anyone who saw me make the turn off Highway 38 thinks we're heading out to drop off Gary's recycling. With a little luck, they won't be interested in us for a good half-hour or so."

They got out of the car. It wasn't raining, but the clouds had settled in on the hills, filling every ravine and cranny with fog. Stacie felt the damp through her jeans before she'd gone a hundred yards.

"The hardest part is crossing Highway 38 without getting spotted," Jill said.

"Maybe when we were kids," Stacie countered. "This isn't a particularly hot stretch of road these days."

They reached the end of Dump Road and paused behind a scrubby elderberry bush. A pickup roared by.

"Go!" Stacie ordered, breaking into a run. Her skin prickled all over. If a car came, if someone saw them, if the pickup's driver caught a glimpse of them before it rounded the next corner, all of this was for nothing. Despite her fear—or maybe because of it—her body moved so lightly she thought she might just bound over the edge of the hill.

Gravel crunched under her feet as she hit the shoulder of the road, then the squelch of mud. She caught a maple sapling before she slid over the bank.

It was a long way down to the Peshak.

Jill overshot a little, skidding on a sword fern and grabbing a tree to stop herself. "The ground's all torn up over here."

"Volunteers," Stacie reminded her. "They would have made a good show of looking for Skyler, even if they were playing for the other team."

Jill took a cautious step farther down the slope. "God, it's steep."

Stacie was glad for the thick trees between her and the river, but there were still too many rocky places for her to keep looking downhill for more than a few seconds at a time. "Keep moving sideways and we'll hit the trail to Indian Point," she reassured Jill. She risked a glance toward the river and shuddered. Fuck, it was steep over here. "Try not to look down."

Jill moved slowly, grabbing a fern here, a vine maple there. Stacie nearly grabbed the woody branch of a poison oak when she skidded in the muck, but caught some other little plant instead. She'd probably come out of this misadventure covered in hives.

"My husband loves hiking," Jill said. "I think I'll have to skip his next outing."

"How long have you two been married?" Stacie asked. On one hand, it felt inane to talk about anything from their normal lives out here where any second they could slip on a loose stone and tumble three hundred feet into the river. On the other, it was a relief to think about something besides the creepy ass people stalking them around their old hometown, and the fact that they were going to a secret shrine devoted to a supernatural entity they might have made up as children, a site where they believed a high school freshman had been murdered. In fact, Stacie couldn't imagine anything she'd like to think about less than any of those things. Thank God for chit-chat.

"Five years?" Jill said. "Yeah, five years. We were together about six years before that, though. I wasn't sure I wanted to get married. You know, getting the government involved with our private business."

"The government's always involved in your private business. The state wouldn't even let me get married until four years ago."

A twig crunched under Jill's foot. Stacie glanced up and caught a glimpse of the highway guardrail. She hoped like hell that no one up there could see them.

"Yeah, about that," Jill started.

"About what?"

Jill pointed downhill a bit. "Hey, there's the trail. It's just a few yards away." She angled downhill a bit, bending her knees more deeply to balance herself.

"Did you know I was gay?" Stacie asked. "When we were kids?"

Jill shook her head. "No? Maybe? I mean, I knew you weren't like the other girls."

"I was in love with you."

Stacie covered her mouth with her hand. She hadn't meant to say it, of course. Had never meant to say it. Tears rushed up in her eyes and she blinked them away.

Jill looked over her shoulder, her face sad. "I know."

Then something broke loose beneath her feet and she fell, her arms flailing, her legs going out from under her when she hit hard ground. She tumbled end over end down the rough, green slope.

"Jill!"

Stacie ran, or tried to run, but it was so steep, so overgrown. A rock spun out from under her foot and she just barely caught herself, her wrist bending hard as she hit the end of her arm.

"Fuck!"

She found a foothold and steadied herself. Her wrist burned. She didn't think it was broken, maybe not even sprained, but for the moment it hurt to even make a fist. She rubbed the back of her hand and tried to orient herself. The ground here was so rough, so thick with ferns and trees and bushes she couldn't even see Jill.

Someone sniffled, and Stacie turned to her right. "Jill?" she whispered. Please let it be Jill and not some kid-killing psycho.

"Stacie?"

Stacie picked her way over the soft body of a fallen tree. Jill lay just on the other side in a kind of natural hollow, big boulders blocking out the world on three sides. She was sprawled on her back, her legs twisted sideways. Blood streaked her face.

"Oh, shit. Are you okay?"

Jill pushed herself to sitting. "Kind of." She pressed her forearm to her upper lip. "I think I broke my nose." She straightened her leg with a wince. "My knee is kind of fucked up too."

"Shit." Stacie dropped over the edge of the boulder. The ground below squished unpleasantly. In the winter, this must have made a tiny natural pond. She could see a gap between the two biggest boulders where it must have made a little waterfall.

They hadn't brought a first-aid kit, of course. Two idiot city slickers used to hiking on trails in the safety of parks. What else had they forgotten? They'd left a note for Gary, but he wouldn't be off work for another couple of hours.

Stacie pulled off her scarf. "Let me see if I can stabilize your knee any. Can you straighten it?"

Jill obliged with a little hiss. Stacie tightened her scarf around the joint. She took off the sweatshirt she had borrowed from Gary and bundled it around the leg with a couple of sticks too. "I don't know if that will help any," she admitted.

"It feels a little better," Jill said. She grabbed onto a boulder and pulled herself to standing. "Not that I wouldn't kill for some Advil and a pressure bandage. Maybe a joint too."

Stacie picked her way between the two big boulders. The hill had washed out a time or two, and now rocks and detritus sloped sharply all the way down to the river. There was no way Stacie could possibly make her way down a hill this steep and unstable, let alone Jill. She looked around them. She could get back over the boulder she'd jumped down, she was pretty sure. But she doubted Jill could.

"Better make that a couple of joints," Stacie said. She put her hand on Jill's shoulder, and began to make a plan.

CHAPTER THIRTY

STACIE: 1989

IT WAS A Wednesday, Stacie's mom's day off. She asked for Stacie to help her at the grocery store—although most of that "help" seemed to involve choosing between Kellogg's Nut & Honey Crunch and Frosted Flakes—and even bought Stacie a corn dog at the deli counter. Despite this show of generosity, her mom didn't seem particularly cheerful. In fact, she opened the box of ice cream sandwiches before it even made it inside the freezer. Ice cream and the blues went hand in hand, her mom liked to say. Stacie went to the bathroom and scrubbed out the tub, just to stay on her mom's good side.

When she came out of the bathroom, her mom was stretched out on the couch, a Diet Pepsi in one hand, the remote in the other. She turned off the television. "Hey, baby." She smiled up at Stacie.

"Hey, Mom. You feeling okay? I can get you an aspirin if you've got a headache."

"Oh, you are so sweet." Her mother patted Stacie's arm. "Why don't you come sit down with your old mother?"

"Okay."

Her mom sat up so there was room for Stacie to sit beside her. Stacie perched on the edge of the couch. The smell of cleanser had stuck to her hands and wafted around the room.

"Did you just scrub out the tub?"

Stacie nodded.

"Jesus." Her mother rumpled her hair. "I don't deserve a kid as good as you. You know that?"

Stacie studied the toes of her Keds, her cheeks going hot. "I'm not that good."

"You're good." Her mom sighed. "You've had a pretty bad summer, I think."

Stacie snapped her eyes up to look at her. "I've had a lot of fun with the gang. We swim almost every day."

Her mother squeezed the pop can between her palms so that it made a little rhythm. "It would take a lot more than swimming to wash away what you've seen this summer. That cabin. Nadine."

There was no denying those things had been pretty awful. But not as awful as Vincent Vernor. Stacie knew she'd better just keep her mouth shut on that matter. Last night at the lodge, she'd seen her mother give Vincent ten dollars out of the tip jar. When it came to men, her mother was blind, deaf, and stupid.

"Well," she said, realizing her mother was waiting for some kind of response, "those were pretty scary."

Her mother put her arm around Stacie's shoulders, squeezing her into her side. Claustrophobia and kindness fought inside Stacie, and she just barely managed to keep from wriggling free.

"My brave little girl." Her mother's voice had gone thick. She gave a sniff and loosened her grip on Stacie. "Goddamn, I'm lucky to have you."

Then let's run away. Just get in the car and get out of this town. Run and run and run until we don't even remember Kingston, Oregon.

The thought frightened Stacie with its intensity. She wasn't sure where it had come from either. To leave Kingston would mean leaving Gary, David, Jordan. Jill.

She couldn't leave Jill. Not ever. Could she?

"I love you, Mom."

Her mother pulled a pink tissue from the box on the coffee table and honked her nose. "And I love you." Her smile crinkled eyes gone red. "Your birthday is coming up next week. Sweet fifteen!"

"Mom, it's sweet *sixteen*, not sweet fifteen. Nothing sweet happens to anybody when they're fifteen." Stacie stole a sip from the Diet Pepsi.

"Well, something sweet should happen to you. How about a birthday party? We haven't had one of those in forever."

Stacie frowned. "A birthday party? Aren't those for little kids?"

Her mother tucked her legs underneath her, bouncing a little in her seat. "No way! Birthday parties are for every age. It's just nice to get all your friends together and have some nice times. We can invite all your pals—the Sheldon kids, Jordan, that nice boy with the dimples."

"David," Stacie corrected.

"...David with the dimples." Her mother beamed. "We can ask some of the other girls from school if you'd like too. We can have the party at the lodge, so there'd be room for everyone, and I'd turn off the coin box on the jukebox so you kids could play whatever you liked."

Stacie thought it over a second. She couldn't see how a party at the lodge would be so different from their usual hangouts there, but she presumed there would be streamers or balloons or something to give it a nicer atmosphere. Plus, they could probably mark off the whole back section so they wouldn't have to sit with any stinky old fishermen or dirty loggers.

"Okay," she said. "But instead of cake, can we get donuts from Murphy's?"

Smiling and sitting straight, Stacie's mother looked younger than she had when they first got home. She looked happier than Stacie had seen her in months. "Donuts it is."

Stacie clapped her hands with genuine excitement.

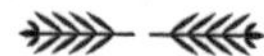

GARY: 2018

The plan Stacie and Gary had drawn up as he finished his shift at the library was to use the emergency fire ladder Gary had purchased at Fred Meyer and then forgotten to install in his bedroom window to help Jill climb up the hill. It wasn't much of a plan, but it wasn't like they could call the police. He had no proof Danse was part of this cult-thing, but if he was buddies with that crazy Jim Burns, it was a strike against him. They were probably both part of Kingston's creepy cult.

He glanced back over his shoulder, wondering if anyone had noticed Stacie's car parked on the shoulder of the road. This process had been awkward enough without being confronted by some whacked-out local.

Jill's hand closed on his, and he pulled back as hard as he could, his arms shaking as she came up over the rock. She lay there gasping.

"Hot damn, my arms hurt," she said.

"We're almost to the top. See? Stacie's up there already." He smiled and hoped it looked sincere enough. *His* arms hurt from pulling her up the damn fire ladder. But he was trying to be stoic about it for her sake. After all, the characters in his novels were always putting themselves through physical hell, and they never complained.

He realized then he was kneeling in a clump of poison oak. Maybe he should change tactics in the damn books. Write what you know, right?

From here on out, his characters were going to complain when he did this kind of shit to them. They would whine about sore muscles and scraped knuckles and having to kneel in a clump of poison oak so they could pull their sister up a goddamn emergency ladder. He could spice up the complaints with juicy descriptions of hives.

Side-by-side, they scrambled up another yard of hill. "Nearly there," he said. "Come on, Jill, you can do it."

"Gary?" Stacie called, but he ignored her.

Jill wobbled and would have fallen backward if Gary hadn't caught her. He gave her butt a hearty shove and she caught the guardrail. Jill's sprained knee hit the top rail and she made a mew of pain. Her left hand lost its grip and for a second, she swung on only one hand, her body crashing back on the gravel at the edge of the road. A rock bounced down and hit Gary in the chin.

Then a man, a very tall, broad man in a blue uniform, grabbed Jill's elbows and pulled her straight up in the air. "Upsy-daisy," Sergeant Brian Danse said.

Gary's heart stopped beating.

Danse hoisted Jill onto the shoulder of the road. "You all right?"

She nodded, her eyes wide.

Danse offered Gary his hand, and Gary had to force himself to take it. "Thanks."

"You want to tell me what you three were doing down there? That's city property, you know. And it's not a park."

Gary could only stare at him. "I, uh…"

"It's my fault," Jill said. "I wanted to take a picture of the river. To paint? I'm a painter."

The officer shook his head. "That was a mighty stupid idea, ma'am."

"I know." She burst into tears. "Oh, God, my leg hurts."

Danse raised an eyebrow at Gary. "Are you going to be able to get this lady some medical attention?"

Gary nodded.

"All right." Danse looked from Stacie to Jill and then back to Gary. "This time I'm not writing any tickets. I know things have been a little…difficult for your family. But I don't want to see any of you trespassing anywhere, ever." He patted Jill's shoulder. "And I don't want to see you anywhere in this town without a knee brace, lady."

Danse walked over to his car, parked neatly beside Stacie's in the little turnout on the side of the highway. The trailhead to Indian Point started just to the left of the nose of his vehicle. If Jill and Stacie hadn't been so insistent on going off-roading, they would have gone down that trail and back up it before Gary had even clocked out at work.

Gary helped Jill to the front seat of Stacie's car. His heart was racing, eighty percent because of the climb, but a solid twenty percent because he had been certain Danse was going to haul them all off in his paddy wagon. The police officer slid into the driver's seat, waved at them, and then turned on his engine. Gary watched him buckle his seat belt, check something on his computer, and then pull out onto the road.

"Jesus, that was awkward," Stacie said. "Jill, you okay over there?"

"Not exactly." Jill turned herself a little, giving her leg a touch more room. "Can I ask for a big favor?"

Gary wondered where "half-carrying you up a forest hill" counted on the favor size-scale, but decided not to be an asshole. He reached between the front seats and squeezed her shoulder. "Sure."

"Can we stop at Murphy's on the way to urgent care?"

"Absolutely," Stacie said. They pulled out onto the highway and drove into town. The highway seemed quieter than ever.

Stacie turned into Murphy's parking lot.

"Shit," Gary said.

A group of four or five teenage boys stood in front of the door, and they didn't look happy. Gary recognized Dirk, that cheapskate football-playing asswipe. Thank God his younger buddy wasn't with him.

"I don't like the looks of this," Stacie said.

Gary opened his door. "I'll go check it out." He schooled his face in his most friendly and nonthreatening expression. "Hey! Are they open?"

A boy turned to face him. Gary didn't recognize him, but he had a varsity letter on his jacket. "Read the sign."

His attitude suggested he was a football player. A Buck's pendant hung from his neck.

Someone had taped up a note on the glass swinging door: "New grandbaby arrived! Closed until further notice."

"Hey!" a boy shouted. "There's someone coming out the side door!"

They moved like a pack, running with the neat, sharp motions of trained athletes. Gary ran after them, his tired and achy body barely moving at half their speed.

"Wait up," he shouted, but it did no good. They closed in on their target, a pint-sized Latina weighed down with garbage bags.

Gary stopped in his tracks, staring. She looked so tiny, surrounded by the big, over-muscled football players. They began to circle her, their movements as economical as wolves'.

"Why are you closed?" one shouted, pushing closer to her.

She gave a little shriek. "Ask the boss lady! I don't know!"

"What's in the bags?" Dirk growled. "I bet they're donuts."

He swiped at the biggest garbage bag. She whipped it out of his grasp.

"Hey, leave her alone!" Gary shouted.

The boys ignored him. "Donuts, donuts," they began to chant.

The shortest of the boys rushed in, snatching the smallest bag. She shouted at him, but he was already ripping it open.

"Donuts, donuts!"

"Donuts! Donuts!"

Toilet paper and dirty paper towels burst out of the bag. The short boy screeched and flung a dirty diaper to the ground.

"It's just garbage," he shouted, but the others were still chanting, still circling. Their red jackets made them one, swirled them into one organism, ugly and angry.

"Donuts! Donuts!"

Dirk grabbed the girl's arm and yanked her up against him. "We. Want. Donuts."

The big black garbage bag dropped out of her grip. She made a horrible sound, the sound of a rabbit with its neck in the coyote's mouth.

Gary shoved forward, pushing the shortest boy out of his way. "Leave her alone."

Dirk bared his teeth. "Or what?"

A boy cackled. "I got 'em! I got the donuts!" He held the big garbage bag triumphantly above his head. "Donuts!" he bellowed. He backed away from the girl, laughing in delight. "Donuts!"

"Fuck yeah!" the shortest boy shouted. He half-scampered after the boy with the big garbage bag, and the others skipped and danced after him.

Dirk glowered at Gary. "You're just lucky you're Gary fucking Sheldon," he said.

Then he strode after the other boys, his hands in his pockets, casual as blue jeans.

Gary looked back at the girl. "Are you okay?"

"No." She wiped away tears. "I was going to take those donuts home. It's my father's birthday."

"I'm sorry." He had no idea how to make it right.

She dropped to her knees, gathering up the trash. Gary got down to help her. The garbage bag was ripped, but they managed to compact most of the trash into the intact bottom.

"I should have listened to Mrs. Murphy," the girl said.

"What do you mean?"

She stood up and tossed the ripped bag into the nearest garbage can. "She said it was a good time to get the hell out of Kingston."

JILL: 1989

Jill was supposed to meet David at noon at the end of their driveway, where her family's oversized mailbox sat beside Vincent Vernor's normal-sized one. He was late.

She checked the mailbox and found it empty. The Donderos had always thought it highly entertaining that their house was twice as big as the Sheldons', but their mailbox almost half as small. The truth was that Jill's dad had replaced their mailbox himself so they didn't have to worry about any packages getting wet. Of course, the only package she could remember their family ever receiving had come when Gary saved up enough box tops to get some kind of collectible cereal bowl. Jill picked a strand of grass and crunched it between her front teeth, trying not to feel impatient. They didn't even have that cereal bowl anymore. Gary had dropped it in the sink while he and Jill were doing dishes, and it had split right down the middle.

Still, it was fun to have such an enormous mailbox. If she wanted to mail a raccoon somewhere, it would easily fit. Maybe even a dog. She began to drum on the hot surface of the silver mailbox, grinning to herself, imagining the stupid things she'd put in the mail and who she'd send them to. A three-layer chocolate cake to her dad's new boss at the mill. A box of rotten eggs to Mrs. Kelly, who taught English at the middle school and French at the high school—for which reason, Jill had signed up for Spanish. A squirrel to Principal Armentrout, who was always cracking peanuts when he circled the playground, probably looking at girl's butts. She remembered the man's watery brown eyes and constant smile and changed her mind. *Definitely* looking at girl's butts.

"Hey, Jill."

She whipped around to face Vincent Vernor. "What are you doing here?"

An unpleasant smile crept across his face. "I live here, don't I?"

Jill wished David had been on time for once in his life. She wished her mom hadn't magically gotten switched to day shift. She wished her dad hadn't decided to work a double.

She looked around. The mailboxes had been planted on the shoulder of Balfour Drive, where the road dropped steeply into the creek. In the other direction, Vincent Vernor. Even if she could get around him, it was a quarter-mile back to their house, and his legs were a lot longer than hers.

Still, she edged sideways, away from the mailboxes. She'd rather jump in the creek and risk breaking her leg than let Vincent Vernor touch her.

The smile widened into a grin. One of his front teeth was newly missing. His hair hung limply around his face, and his skin looked gray. Things had gone very, very badly for Vincent Vernor lately. The thought almost made her smile.

He lunged forward, grabbing her arm. "Something funny, bitch?"

She shook her head. She couldn't talk. His hand ground into the bone of her arm.

"Then why were you laughing at me?" He pulled her closer. His stink of cigarettes and beer nearly choked her. "I know. It's because I lost my job, and my woman and baby just up and left town, and because the police are riding me about fucking Nadine Willis." He gave her a shake. "And that's all your fault, ain't it?"

"No!" She shook her head, harder. "I know you've had some bad luck, Mr. Vernor, but it's just bad luck."

He shook his head, sending tendrils of blond hair flapping around his head. "Oh no. I don't think so. I saw that deer come out of your yard that night. I know you called it."

Jill whimpered.

His eyes widened, as if he saw something horrible she couldn't see. "It's always around. It watches me through the windows of my house. It's everywhere."

"Please let me go," she whispered.

His eyes came back to her face. The pupils looked far too big for anyone standing in the midday sunshine. He scrubbed his thumb across her lips. "You think if I give you to the deer, my luck will go back to normal?"

"Oh, please, no." She gave her arm a sharp yank, but it was no use. His fingers dug in harder. She balled up her fist. She was going to have to punch her way out of this, and she didn't like the odds of that.

Vincent buried his nose in her hair. "You smell so good. It'll like you, I know it will."

She drove her knee into his groin, and when he staggered backward, she slammed her fist into his gut. The air wheezed out of him. She heard it as only a faint whistle, because he had loosed his hold and she was running, her stupid saltwater sandals slap-slapping on the pavement loud enough to make her head hurt.

"Jill!"

She glanced back over her shoulder to see David on his bike, zigzagging around Vincent Vernor, whose face was as red as Hawaiian Punch. He made a sound like a snarl and broke into a run. David's tires spat rocks as he stopped his bike in front of Jill.

"Get on!"

She clambered onto the handlebars and he stood up on the pedals, tall and bright as the sunshine. Vincent Vernor was nearly upon them when David got the bike back up to speed.

The wind tugged and tangled Jill's curls. She had never gone so fast on a bike before, not riding double. It should have been exhilarating.

But when she looked backward, she could see Vincent Vernor standing in the driveway, his hands on his hips, staring after them with pure hatred.

CHAPTER THIRTY-ONE

GARY: 2018

ZACK TOSSED HIS sleeping bag into the trunk of Kim's Camry. Raindrops made his hair sparkle in the front porch light. "I could totally walk, Dad. It's only five blocks to Sam's church."

Gary resisted the fierce, burning desire to pull the boy into his arms and squeeze him until he was a preschooler again. "I don't want you walking alone anywhere in this town. Especially at night."

Zack sighed with the drama only a teenager could produce. "Dad, you know Skyler's dad took him in broad daylight, right? He was on his way to school."

Gary mentally counted to three. He decided to try a new tactic. "Look how much stuff you have. Do you really want to schlep all of that by yourself in the rain? Besides, I promised Hannah I'd bring chips and soda, and she said you needed at least three cases. Three cases of soda! I guess none of you drink water."

Zack snorted. "Dad, half the JV football team is coming, and the youth group is pretty big. We'll need every can of pop you bought." The happiness leaked out of his face. "We're all pretty freaked out, even the kids who don't know Skyler that well."

"He's going to be okay," Gary forced himself to say. "He's with his dad, right?"

"Yeah," Zack said, "but he doesn't even know his dad anymore. And he doesn't have his insulin." Tears sprang up in his eyes. "He could *die*."

This time Gary gave in to impulse and hugged his son. To his surprise, Zack hugged him back even harder. Then they got into the car.

"I'm glad the youth group decided to do this," Gary said, buckling his seat belt. "When Hannah called me at work, I wasn't convinced that a big group sleepover was such a good idea, especially not on a school night. But your mom helped change my mind."

"It would have been our game at Coquille," Zack reminded him. "If the game had to be canceled, then at least we can all be together for Skyler."

The parking lot at the church was so full, cars had spilled out onto the street. A Honda pulled out just as Gary considered whether to park illicitly in the convenience store's lot across the street, and he darted into the place it had abandoned. An enormous pickup had followed him, but instead of looking for a spot, it simply pulled in front of the building and parked in the fire zone.

"What an asshole," Gary grumbled.

A robustly round man wearing head-to-toe camouflage jumped down from his rig and went to the back, loading out a pair of bongos and what looked to be a banner wrapped around a twelve-foot-long pole. He slung the strap for the bongos around his neck and then lost his grip on the banner. It rolled down the slope of the parking lot, stopping at the bumper of Gary's car.

He stared at the bit of banner that had unfurled, the white fabric darkening where the rain stained it. The red border and black ink—he could only make out a bit of it—looked awfully familiar.

"Dad? Are you going to help me carry all this soda?"

Gary glanced over at Zack, who was peering in through the open passenger door. Gary hadn't even heard him get out.

"Yeah. Gosh, I guess I zoned out there."

Zack tucked a case of soda under one arm, his sleeping bag under the other. "Yeah, well, it's not every day you see a redneck playing the bongos."

"Right?"

Gary followed Zack around the side of the church, where teenagers were slowly making their way inside. A young woman, maybe all of twenty years old, stood at the door with Sharpies and name tags. She waved brightly at them.

"Hey, are you Gary and Zack? I was hoping I'd see you tonight."

"Hannah?"

She was already writing up a name tag for Zack, although she misspelled his name. "Yep." She stuck her head in the door and shouted: "Aidan!" She smiled back at Gary. "I'll get the boys to help you with all that pop."

A red-headed boy ran out the door and unloaded Gary's drinks. "Doritos. Solid choice, man." He bobbed his head. "Zack. Glad you made it."

Zack waggled his head in an approximation of waving. "I'd hug you, Dad, but my hands are full. I'll see you tomorrow after school."

"Okay," Gary said, nervousness coloring his voice.

Hannah patted his shoulder reassuringly. "Don't worry, Mr. Sheldon. Once everyone's arrived, I'll lock this door and the one to the upstairs. We'll be perfectly safe—the windows are even barred. And you can pick up Zack's gear tomorrow before the Homecoming Rally."

"Homecoming Rally?"

"Yeah! The boosters have organized a really terrific event. They're gathering upstairs to finalize all the plans, but I hear there will be a bonfire, a pie-eating contest, the whole works. It starts at 6, but I'd try to get to the field by at least 5 for a good seat." She giggled. "We are going to *crush* Plymouth tomorrow night."

"Sure," Gary said. "Okay. Well, keep my son safe."

"Will do, Mr. Sheldon. And go Bucks!"

Gary stuffed his hands in his pockets and turned up the collar of his jacket. It was raining hard now. He was glad he hadn't let Zack walk alone.

The big pickup had moved from the fire zone to hulk beside Gary's car. It took up nearly two parking spaces. Beside an NRA membership sticker, a vinyl decal in the back window read "Kingston Booster Club." Gary was surprised not to see a gun rack anywhere.

He put the key in the Camry's front door and then paused. He was pretty sure the booster club didn't fly a banner. A door slammed and Gary saw Jim Burns running across the parking lot, a plastic folder over his head to keep the bald spot dry.

That was why the banner looked so familiar. He had seen it in photos at the historical society museum: photos of the now-defunct Deer Kings.

Gary looked around. The parking lot was devoid of human life, just cars quietly waiting for their owners to return. The booster club meeting and the teen lock-in must have both started at 7:00. Gary checked his phone. It was 7:08. There could be a few late stragglers, but he was probably safe to snoop around the entrance.

He found himself holding his breath as he opened the church's big glass doors. The strains of a rhythm section came from the nave. The doors had been propped open a little for latecomers. Gary brushed a trickle of rain off his face and went to the door, keeping to one side for invisibility. He could see the Deer Kings banner up on the altar, the black outline of a stag's head identical to the one on the pendants the booster club sold. The pendant his wife wore.

He covered his mouth to stifle any sound, and stuck his head in the gap between the doors.

Every pew was occupied, even packed. Up on the stage beside the altar, a guitarist, an upright bass player, and Bongo Man were cutting loose. Beside them, he saw Linda, the volunteer manager, playing the piano. Sergeant Danse and Dr. Cochran sat side by side. Jim Burns was whispering to Shawn, Gary's boss at the library. Coach Dusseldorf and David Washburn sat in the very first pew, their spines as straight as the pole holding the Deer Kings banner.

As one, they lurched to their feet. The piano belted out the first chords of the Kingston High fight song.

Gary took a step backward. Black mist had begun to gather around the feet of the little rhythm section. It slid up the strings of the upright bass and darkened the tones. Gary's stomach turned over.

Pain, the bass groaned. *Death. Murder.*

How could they not hear it? How could they not notice the whispers of a dozen souls crowding the stage, begging to tell their story? But all the boosters heard were their own voices, raised in roaring, strident song.

The mascot came out on stage, its horns fantastically wide and tall. No stag had ever had a rack like that; it would have caught itself in the trees and died.

Except there had been one stag with horns like that, Gary remembered. One stag, rushing through the undergrowth, rearing up above him like it was an enormous man, a man with a deer's head and smoke for eyes. The back of his neck prickled and stung, hot as fire.

The mascot's eyes glowed blue.

"Shit," Gary breathed.

Sam Oakley's face appeared between the doors. She wore pure white robes and someone had given her a headdress of antlers.

"Would you like to join us, Gary?" she said, smiling.

Every last person in the room turned to stare at him.

"Join us, Gary," they repeated in one unbroken voice. "Join us."

He spun on his heel and raced out of the church.

"Zack!" he bellowed. "Zack!"

He threw himself at the side door. The wood vibrated, not with his blows, but with the noise of music cranked far too loud.

"Zack!" he shouted again, but he knew no one inside heard.

He ran back toward the car. A little crowd had gathered on the front porch of the church. The Camry's engine started with a growl, and his headlights lit up the group, with Sam Oakley at its center. She raised her hand and waved at him, and in the headlights, her eyes flashed the blue glow of a deer's.

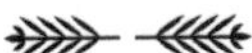

JILL: 1989

Jill slicked on a second layer of Bonne Bell Dr. Pepper and studied the results critically. She needed a haircut pretty desperately, and the summer's trips to the lake had sown a massive crop of freckles across her cheeks and nose. But in general she thought she looked pretty good. Better than most of the girls going into ninth grade, that was for sure.

"Are you ready to go yet?" Gary called through her bedroom door.

Jill ruffled her hair, stuck her tongue out at the curl that refused to fall into place, and looked around for the present she'd just finished wrapping in its hand-drawn paper. "Coming!"

She flung open the door and found Gary still standing there, idly tracing the fading pony sticker she'd applied to the frame during her horse phase. His eyes looked funny, only half-focused, and he blinked at her a second before recognition crept across his face. "You look nice."

She tugged the collar of her new blue-flowered sleeveless blouse. "Thanks. Mom found it on clearance at Sprouse Reitz."

"It's 'Sprouse!' now," he reminded her.

She rolled her eyes. "I will never say that."

He patted the leg of his plaid shorts, which Jill had never seen him wear before. "These came from the same place. I think Mom is trying to make up for all those night shifts." He noticed the rectangle under her arm. "What did you get Stacie?"

"A Stephen King story collection from the Friends of the Library book sale."

He raised his own rectangular package, this one's wrapping from the comics section. "Edgar Allen Poe's complete poems. Same sale."

They chuckled all the way out the front door. Then they both fell silent, their eyes flicking across the driveway to the Big House. Jill found herself holding her breath as she wheeled her bike out of the shed. Was Vincent Vernor over there right now, watching them from one of the upstairs windows? Was he going to pull out on his Harley and cut them off before they got to the end of the driveway? Her palms were sweaty on her handgrips.

"He took off early this morning," Gary said, his voice grim.

"How do you know?"

"I stashed Dad's binoculars on the porch so I can see what's going on over there."

She felt a lot better as she got on her bike. "Thanks, Gary."

His smile wobbled a little. "You're welcome. I just wish he would move. The deer saint's done a pretty good job messing with him, but not good enough."

"Maybe we should do another ritual."

"Maybe."

They came up Balfour Drive and made the left onto Calhoun Lake Road. Speedboats growled loud enough to vibrate Jill's ribcage. She counted four boats just within eyeshot. Despite the morning sunshine, a strip of black clouds hung over the hills, and the air felt thick against Jill's skin. They pulled into the lodge's entrance and had to swerve to miss the long line of cars waiting for the gas pump. It was probably the longest Jill had ever seen at the lodge. Gary jumped off his bike and shoved it into the nearest clump of bushes.

"Sure is busy," Gary noted.

Jill fanned herself with Stacie's gift, trying to dry a little of the sweat before they went inside. "If there's a storm coming, I bet a lot of campers are heading home."

He glanced at the sky. "I hope it holds off until we get home. Or that Mrs. Clinton gives us a ride."

"I think she's working," Jill said. She pointed out Stacie's mother wrestling with the hose on the gas pump.

Mrs. Clinton waved as they walked up to the front door. "Stacie's in the back!"

The inside of the lodge was as busy as the outside. Groups of grizzled older men with fishing vests crowded the booths in the front room. A couple of teenagers stood beside the pool table, leaning on their pool cues with a coolness Jill would never be able to manage. A waitress delivered a stack of pancakes to a family at one of the big tables. At the counter, three mountaineering types were hunched over their eggs and coffee, the lot of them sporting hiking boots with matching red shoelaces. One of them, maybe a college guy with a funny little beard, winked at Jill as she passed them, and her cheeks immediately seared.

"Jill!" Stacie waved from the doorway to the back seating area. Balloons of every color filled the ceiling. Stacie's mom had clearly not stinted on decorations.

She gave Stacie a hug. Stacie scooted to the end of the long booth seat. "Sit by me, Jill."

David looked up from the menu. He'd squeezed into the end of the other seat, but his smile crossed the table and made Jill's cheeks warm up again. "Hey."

"Hi, Jill," a girl said. It took Jill a second to recognize Heather Whately from science class. Something tremendous had happened to her mouse-brown hair, which was now an apricot blonde that she had shaped into two enormous poofs on the sides of her head.

"Wow, Heather, your hair," Jill managed. After a summer interacting solely with their little crowd, she had kind of forgotten how to make small talk. She tried to remember if she even liked Heather. Did Stacie? Had Heather owned a hairbrush before the summer began?

"Hey, Heather. Good to see you." Gary slid into the seat next to the other girl, putting on the smile that let him get away with anything. "Your hair is super cool."

"Thanks, Gary!" Heather's face brightened. She began to recount her adventures in Eugene with her cousin, a beauty student.

"My mom invited her," Stacie whispered. "She remembered we did that science project together and thought we were friends."

Jill stifled a giggle. "That's so your mom."

Stacie jabbed her in the ribs. "Hey, is that a present?"

Jill slid the package down the table. Everyone looked at it expectantly. It was clearly a book, but Jill thought the wrapping paper compensated for any lack of originality.

"Wow, you drew all this?" Stacie pulled the package closer to her, taking in the tiny details. Jill had been working on it for about a week, inking in a tiny forest and then meticulously adding layers of colored pencil. "Is that a griffin? Far out!"

Heather looked at Jill, her eyes enormous. "Did you really draw that?"

"Yeah, Jill's a great artist." Gary slung his arm around Heather's shoulder with the confidence of a boy twice his age. Heather giggled.

Jordan shuffled toward the table. "Hey, guys. Sorry I'm late."

Stacie stretched across Jill to catch Jordan's hands. "I'm so glad you're here!"

Jordan slid into the space beside Jill. "Did you draw that, Jill?" He picked up the package and turned it over to see the back side. "Oh."

"What?" Stacie asked, reaching for the package.

"Jesus, Jill," David hissed. "Why'd you draw that?"

Jill stared at the paper she had on worked so hard for so long. The tiny drawings of animals and plants were gone, scrawled over with ordinary pencil. Her mouth was open. She closed it and licked dry lips.

"I'm sorry," she whispered.

Heather leaned over the table, her hair making her resemble nothing so much as a poodle. "It's just a deer," she said, looking up at them with confusion. "It's kind of a weird pose, but I think it's still neat."

Someone at the counter let out a shout of dismay. Jill caught movement in the corner of her eye, but she was having a hard time looking away from the sketch of the stag she had somehow drawn on the back of Stacie's present. She had no idea when it had happened. Or how.

Not a stag, she thought. *The deer saint.* He stood on his hind legs like a man, his antlers huge and wide. Only he wasn't standing on hind legs, was he? Those were perfectly human legs, human arms. The creature she had drawn—oh, so carefully, so cleanly, so *beautifully*—was half-man, half-stag. Twists of fog or smoke billowed from its nose and eyes.

"It's not smoke," Gary whispered. "It's spirits."

"Oh, fuck," David said, half-rising from his seat.

Everyone turned to see what he was looking at.

The guys at the counter had all gotten to their feet. The crack of flesh against flesh instantly cut through the room's chatter. The bearded guy fell backward into a woman cutting up her daughter's pancake. He clutched his nose.

"You son of a bitch!" he shouted. Blood trickled out from under his hand.

The man who had punched him laughed. He stood out from the hikers like an onion in an apple bin: his blue jean vest, his ropy, tattooed arms, his long blond ponytail. His laugh was a hollow, wild laugh that made the skin on the back of Jill's neck rise up in gooseflesh.

"Vincent Vernor," Jordan breathed.

As if he had heard his name, he turned and stared at the group. A balloon above the table burst, the sound like a gunshot.

He threw back his head and laughed again, the sound rolling on and on, filling the air like poison gas, like smoke, like Gary's ghosts.

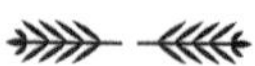

GARY: 2018

Jill went to bed early, knocked out on Vicodin and sore muscles. Stacie took advantage of Zack's absence to play PlayStation. She'd had four whiskey sours after Gary told her about what had happened at the church, though, so her gameplay was a little off.

Kim came home at nine and went straight to the kitchen for a snack. Gary followed her, his skin prickling all over, his stomach achy. He hadn't managed much dinner, and he was on his second whiskey sour. It was making his face feel numb, but it wasn't slowing down his brain any.

"Hey, babe." Kim looked up over the refrigerator door. "You look stressed."

"I got kind of freaked out at the church," he said. He started to explain a little, but he could hear her chuckling behind the door.

She put the mustard and Tofurkey slices on the counter. "Honey, you're just worked up after what happened to Skyler. I've been to the booster club meetings, remember? Yes, they sing the fight song. Of course! Most of them were on one of the sports teams when they were in high school, and this is the closest thing they're going to get to their glory years."

"But it was weird," he maintained. He took a gulp of his drink. "And Sam was there. Shouldn't she be…I don't know…more worried about her kid?"

She kissed him on the nose. "Everyone deals with stress in their own way." She started assembling a half-sandwich, gesticulating with the mustard knife as she spoke. "It's probably too lonely to be at home by herself. Just imagine what it would be like if something happened to Zack and I wasn't in the picture."

"I guess."

"Could you get my cigarettes? I think I'll take this and a drink out on the back deck." Kim popped the tab on one of the half-sized sodas she kept on the bottom shelf and poured it in a cup.

Gary fumbled for the cigarettes in the cupboard, squinting out at the darkness. The package crinkled under his fingertips. "Are you sure you want to go out there?"

He flipped on the outdoors light and peered out the sliding glass doors. The yard was empty, the deck quiet. The rain had stopped sometime since he'd gotten back from the church.

"Come on." She snaked an arm around his waist to unlatch the door. "We'll only be out a minute or two."

He followed her outside. The air felt chilly, damp, and smelled of the sea. He could hear the ocean, just faintly, on the other side of Peshak Head. Kim bit off half of her sandwich in one bite.

"You look hungry."

"Well, Harrison promised dinner, but he only brought a box of fried chicken and a salad. How many times have I told him I'm a vegetarian?"

She huffed air out her nose, exasperated. "The spring budget is still mostly borked, but I think we've gotten some of the kinks worked out. It would help if I could get some of these grants I'm applying for."

He looked over her shoulder, making sure no strange smoker was out in the trees. "Is that what you were doing after dinner? Applying for grants?"

She took a drink of her rum and coke. "What are you looking for out there?" She stepped back so she could rest her shoulder against his. "It's so pretty, isn't it?"

"Yeah, I'll miss the view when we get the bigger fence."

She crinkled her nose. "Are you sure you want to put in a bigger fence? It'll probably cost two or three grand, maybe more. And we only saw the one guy. Isn't this view worth the chance of seeing hikers out in the woods?"

He wished he hadn't left his drink inside on the table. "I guess? And I mean, it's not like the fence guy has called me back."

She slid one hand into his back pocket and then kissed his neck. "I like being able to see into the forest. It's sexy." She slid her lips up his throat, across his neck. Kissed him. Her mouth tasted like molasses.

He pulled back, just a little. "What meeting did you have tonight? After dinner with Harrison?"

She laughed and kissed his chin. The corner of his mouth. "The booster club," she whispered. "And if you had joined us, you wouldn't be nearly so nervous about the whole thing."

He took a step back. "What?"

Kim picked up her cigarettes and drew one out of the pack. "You should really get more involved with the town, Gary. If you just knew some more people, you'd be glad we moved back here. Remember how busy your parents were? They understood how important it was to serve their community."

She lit her cigarette. He realized the pack she held in her hand was red: Marlboro Reds.

"You're going to have such a good time at the booster rally tomorrow," she said. "I can't wait."

CHAPTER THIRTY-TWO

GARY: 2018

GARY CREPT OUT of the house before the sun came up. He was pretty sure Kim had already gotten up and gone for her run, although he couldn't be sure; he had slept in Zack's room that night. She thought it was an affectation of an overly anxious father. He thought it might have been the only thing that kept him sane that long, long night. He couldn't imagine lying beside Kim all night, knowing she'd been in that church with those people. With the Deer Kings, no matter if they called themselves the booster club these days.

The Deer Kings had changed his parents. Gary had always blamed his cancer for his parents' suicide. "They were just too scared to watch me die," he told Kim—and maybe in the Dr. Monroe years, he had even believed that. It was easy to believe things like that in Portland. It was a different world up there. People listened to NPR for their news. They called the cops if their neighbors had a domestic dispute. They expected and demanded that people obey rules, share neatly, and take advantage of every public service available to them.

That just wasn't how it worked in Kingston.

You got your news from the gal slinging drinks in the Kookie Kamel. If you called the cops, you could expect a twenty-minute wait for the officer to make it from whatever they were doing on the other side of town, and that was if it wasn't winter, when a falling tree closed one of the highways every couple of weeks. You drove your own damn self to the hospital. And if someone stole from you, you went to their house and you took it back with your fist or your shotgun.

John Sheldon was a good man, a well-read one, thoughtful and quiet. And when NPR came in on the radio, he loved listening to it. But he was a Kingstonian born and raised, and he never left a fight for another man to finish.

Least of all his son.

So, no, Gary had never really believed his parents had just snapped and abandoned their kids to fend for themselves, not even when Dr. Monroe insisted that was the case. His parents had changed when his dad got the job at the paper mill and got invited to join the Deer Kings. That was when they got worried about community service, and the future of Kingston, and how well Gary and Jill were getting along with the other kids.

Gary stopped reminiscing to unlock the Camry. It was technically Kim's day to use it, but if he was lucky he'd be back before she even got out of the shower. He turned on the engine and hoped the lady in the blue Ford Taurus wasn't around.

What had his dad said when he'd appeared in Gary's dining booth? That the Deer Kings had ways to make life easy, but that it came at a price? Well, the Sheldons' lives had sure gotten easier when Mom and Dad joined the Deer Kings.

And Gary's life had gotten a fuck-ton easier after his parents' drove into the lake. If not easier, then at least longer.

His breath caught in his throat, and he had to fight to keep his attention on the road. They couldn't stay in Kingston, he knew that. Kim was already succumbing to the siren sweetness of the Deer Kings—well, the booster club, but same difference these days, right? And who knew what those bastards would want to keep things nice for her? They had already sacrificed one boy from the JV team. The least athletic boy, of course.

He giggled and clapped his hand over his mouth. Shit, he was losing it. He rolled down the window. Tired. He was just tired, his brain sore from a night of no sleep and too many whiskey sours. He had chugged a cup of coffee after he came up with this little plan, but it wasn't doing much.

The church appeared in the gray light of dawn, and he pulled into the parking lot. A big van sat by the side door. He stared at it dumbly. What the hell were they doing?

Hannah stepped out of the van and waved at the church's side door. A couple of girls darted out, throwing their heads back in laughter.

Gary threw open the car door and rushed to the van. "Hey!"

Hannah looked around, startled, and then smiled at him. "Good mor—"

"Where the hell are you taking these kids?" He grabbed her arm.

She shook him off. "Mr. Sheldon, please. You signed the release form, but let me refresh your memory. This morning is Homecoming Breakfast, where KHS students and faculty alike are treated to an all-you-can-eat pancake breakfast at the school." She tightened her lips. "I find it hard to believe Mrs. Sheldon would approve of your language. Or your behavior."

"Mrs. Sheldon can kiss my—" He broke off, catching sight of Zack. "Zack! Buddy! Why don't you come home for breakfast?"

Zack made an apologetic face at the boy he'd been talking to. He went to Gary's side. "Dad, you're embarrassing me."

Gary grabbed at him, tried to hug him close. "Please just come home. This whole homecoming thing is a mess."

Zack shook him off. "A mess? I think it's fun." He crinkled his nose. "And I think you stink. Didn't you brush your teeth last night?"

"I—"

"Never mind." Zack patted his shoulder. "Dad, I love you, but you should go home and get a shower. I'll see you at the homecoming rally, okay? You can buy me some nachos."

"Zack—"

Zack waved over his shoulder. "Bye, Dad!"

Then he was climbing into the van. The door slammed shut behind him.

Tears made Gary's vision waver. He had a horrible feeling this was the last time he was going to see his son.

Hannah held out a tissue. "It's all right, Mr. Sheldon."

Gary shook his head. "No, you don't understand."

"You'll see Zack tonight," she said, her tone so perky and bright he had to look up at her. She had clasped her hands together, her face beatific. He hadn't noticed the Bucks pendant around her neck before this. It looked bigger than the others, the design edged in red. "We'll *all* see you tonight."

"What?"

She stepped up into the van, and then stuck her head back out the door. "Go Bucks!"

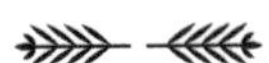

STACIE: 1989

Stacie grabbed Jill's arm. "We've got to get out of here."

Jordan slid out of the booth. "To the back door. Quick."

"Where the *fuck* do you think you're going, you little shits?" Vincent roared.

For a second, there wasn't a single sound in the entire lodge. The ice cream machine stopped churning. No one's fork scritched or scraped. The old fishermen forgot to cough. The boys at the pool table froze, their pool cues stilled in their various poses, even the one half a centimeter from striking the cue ball.

The mom cutting the pancakes broke the silence first. "What the hell is wrong with you?" She jabbed her fork in Vincent's direction, maple syrup dripping off the tines. "You just go on and get!"

He gave her a solid shove. The table gave a lurch. A milk glass toppled over. The baby at the next table began to scream.

Now everyone was shouting. The woman's husband leapt to his feet and launched a punch at Vincent's mocking face. He hit one of the hikers instead, who flung his half-eaten sundae at the man's head. A fisherman tried to tackle Vincent and lost his footing, falling to the floor and gasping with pain. The boys at the pool table threw down their sticks and ran out the back door.

Big Alice, the Saturday cook, ran out of the kitchen and smashed a hiker in the face with a rolling pin. He threw her backward into the kitchen.

Gary began to slide down his seat, his face gray.

"Heather, grab Gary!"

But Heather just scrambled over the top of him, pushing him to the floor. "I want my mom!" she shrieked, and ran for it. She stumbled over the fisherman clutching his chest and fell, her head hitting the corner of the pancake family's table with a sickening crack.

David threw up on the table.

Jordan grabbed Jill's arm. "We can go out the bathroom window."

Stacie's knees didn't want her to stand up. In the main dining room, people were screaming. The pancake mom knelt beside Heather, pressing napkins to Heather's head like she could hold the pieces of Heather's skull together. Blood poured over her hand. The old man on the floor had gone still. Vincent Vernor had another fisherman in a sleeper hold, a fork embedded in the man's eyeball. The fork jiggled and bounced as the man fought for air.

"It's for you!" Vincent roared. "All of this is for you, Stag God!"

The fisherman's boots kicked and shook and then went still.

"Stacie!" David was patting her cheek, then slapping. "Help me with Gary!"

She lurched out of the booth and took hold of Gary's arm. "Come on, buddy." She dragged him out from under the table.

David grabbed his arm and together they hoisted him to his feet. Gary's glasses were nearly sideways on his head. His eyes flickered and he fumbled to get them back into place.

"What?"

He had sparkling confetti stuck to his cheek, Stacie noticed. For years afterward, the sight of the stuff would make her stomach clench.

Glass shattered in the main dining room. David's eyes went wide.

"Run!" he shouted.

They hauled Gary into the boy's bathroom and shoved him out the window into Jordan and Jill's arms. Stacie climbed up on the sink and turned back to give David a hard look.

"What did you see back there?"

Something hit the bathroom door with a splintering sound.

"Deer," he whispered.

He put his hand on her backside and shoved her out the window.

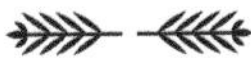

GARY: 2018

Gary turned around in his seat so he could watch Jill struggle into the backseat of Stacie's car. He waited for Stacie to close her door.

"Okay, so here's the plan. We go to the rally, watch out for Coach D and his creepy daughter, find Zack, and then get the hell out of Kingston."

"Good plan," Stacie said.

"What about Kim?" Jill asked. One of her crutches toppled over and bounced off the top of her head. She pushed it out of the way. "What about Kim?" she repeated.

Gary swallowed down a sour taste. "We're leaving with or without Kim."

"Shit," Jill said. She got out her cell phone.

Stacie started the car. "What are you doing?"

Jill raised a finger. "Hi, babe." She paused, listening with a smile.

"Oh, honey, you're the sweetest. I miss you too. Can you put Merlin on?"

"Merlin?" Stacie mouthed at Gary.

"Her dog," he whispered back.

Stacie rolled her eyes and started the car. Gary had loaded the trunk with everything he figured they'd need for a few days—Stacie's overnight bag, Jill's luggage, a bag for himself and Zack—plus passports in case things really got out of hand. But it wouldn't get out of hand, he promised himself. They would go in smiling, find Zack while they pretended to have a good old time, and leave like the very casual people they were.

"Okay, sweetie. I love you bunches and I'll see you very soon." Jill made a kissing sound and hung up.

"Was that your husband or your dog?" Stacie asked.

Jill made a face at her without answering.

They waited at the light for a second. Gary looked at the 22nd Street Market, thinking of all the times he'd gone in to get Kim cigarettes or just to pick up some last-minute mixer for drinks. This was the last time he would ever look at it. They made the right onto Highway 101, passed the Dunes Diner, where he and Kim had yet to try the legendary cherry pie and where he now never would. Everything had that mellow purplish glow of an early autumn sunset. It wasn't even raining.

They turned onto High School Avenue.

"Jesus Christ," Stacie said.

"Wow," said Jill.

Every parking spot on High School was taken. The lot behind the school was filled, with cars double-parked here and there. A few intrepid souls had risked the threat of a parking ticket and squeezed into the bus drop-off site, which was also a fire lane.

Stacie made a left onto a side street and managed to squeeze her car between two minivans. "Glad I have a city car," she mumbled.

Gary had to agree. Kim's Camry wouldn't have fit in that spot.

Jill got her crutches in order and swung herself onto the sidewalk. "I feel weird," she said. "Like we're a Navy Seal team or something."

Gary forced himself to smile. The bowl of tomato soup he'd eaten an hour ago threatened to crawl back up his throat. "Let's go."

Even if Jill hadn't been on crutches, the going would have been slow. More and more people filled the sidewalks the closer they got to the ball field. Smoke rose over the field, spreading its mellow tang liberally over the comers. Already the pep band blasted "Louie, Louie."

At the entrance, Gary flashed his season pass and the guest tickets Kim had picked up for Jill and Stacie. She was here somewhere, he knew. Probably laughing happily with her new booster club friends. He found himself looking for her anyway. Underneath the fear and the nausea, his heart ached. He and Kim had been together nearly twenty years. He had never once considered having an affair. Never once worried about their marriage. And yet tonight he was going to leave her.

And why? Because of this town. Because of something he had created when he was barely twelve years old—something he had made to help a group of innocent kids and that other people had perverted into a monster.

Stacie put her hand on the back of his neck. "Hey, man, breathe. It's going to be okay."

Her palm was cold against the spot burning in the center of his neck. He tried to take a deep breath and felt even his diaphragm shuddering. They stood still like that for a moment, the crowd pushing and shoving around them.

In the concession stand beside them, the popcorn machine grumbled and popped, sending forth its soft warm perfume. A boy, maybe eight or nine, dropped his hot dog and a man blindly walked over the top of it. A pair of teenage girls bumped into Gary, giggling so hard they didn't even notice him. The bonfire at the end of the football field sparked and crackled.

"Welcome, Kingston!" David Washburn's voice burst out of the speakers so loud it made Jill jump and nearly lose her crutches. The crowd roared with approval. "It's so good to see everyone and celebrate what makes our little town great. Good schools, no drugs, great kids, and school spirit!"

Air horns blasted. A cheerleader did a back flip. The crowd was cheering louder than soccer fans at a World Cup.

"Before we bring out your 2018 homecoming court"—he paused for the cheering to abide a little—"let me introduce our fine JV team. They've taken a big hit this week, but these boys are Kingston's finest."

"Zack." Gary shook off Stacie's hand. "Come on, this is our chance."

"I'll wait right there by the field house," Jill said. "I'll keep my eyes out for Coach D and Sam."

They pushed into the flow of the crowd. Shoulders bumped. Knees collided. Gary couldn't believe so many people lived in Kingston these days. David's voice droned on and on, introducing players whose names and roles Gary probably knew from Zack's stories, but who his brain refused to remember. All he could think of was his son.

And there he was, ascending to the little dais set up at the edge of the field. He looked so tall and handsome, his hair the same near-black as Kim's, his smile just like Gary's dad's, the grandfather Zack never got a chance to meet. Gary's eyes misted over. God damn, he was proud of his boy!

Zack crossed the dais and went down the other set of stairs as the Kingston Buck mascot bounded up onto the dais. Coach Washburn gave a happy little laugh and leaned into the microphone.

"Well, what have we here? It's the Kingston Buck, here to lead us in our fight song!"

The pep band blared and the crowd burst into song. The noise was so loud Gary thought he might fall down. He realized he'd lost Stacie in the crowd. He blinked. The crowd had gotten bigger, somehow. Mistier. Dark strands ran between the bodies, coiling and coiling like a mist made of snakes.

"Stacie!" he called, but there was no way anyone was hearing him. He was breathing fast and shallow now.

A hand closed on his arm. He whipped around. "Stacie?"

Shawn from the library smiled at him. "Come on, Gary," he shouted in Gary's ear. "We need your help with a little something."

Gary yanked on his arm, but Shawn wasn't as scrawny as he looked. Another man took Gary's other arm.

"Please don't do this, Shawn!" Gary screamed.

Shawn looked at Gary, his eyes wide. "But, Gary, I have to. It's for the whole town."

The man gripping Gary's right arm tightened his grip. Gary didn't even need to look up at him—way, way up—to know it was Sergeant Brian Danse.

"Go Bucks!" the crowd cheered. "Go Kingston!"

"We are going to just *crush* Plymouth," Danse said in Gary's ear.

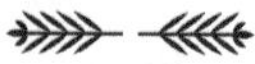

JILL: 2018

She didn't see the men grab Gary, but she saw them lead him onto the field, out to the dais where they had just introduced all those cute little football players, and some weird part of her brain thought, *They can't do anything bad yet, they haven't even introduced the homecoming queen.* She couldn't help laughing at her train of thought. They had already killed a kid, the grandson of their goddamned favorite football coach. She couldn't imagine they'd let a little thing like the introduction of the homecoming court slow down whatever they were going to do to her brother.

Although apparently it was going to, because the stupid deer mascot got off the dais and the thugs stood next to it, and then Kim came out onto the field. She gave Gary a little wave like he was just there to bring her flowers or something, and she climbed up on the dais and shook David's hand. She adjusted the microphone down about four inches.

"Let's give it up for Coach Washburn!"

The crowd roared and stomped. David blew kisses at the audience. They cheered louder. Air horns blasted. Feet stomped. The bleachers shook with pep.

"You're all doing a great job working up that school spirit!" Kim shouted. "That's just what our boys need to beat Plymouth!"

Jill looked around. She couldn't just hop onto the football field on her stupid crutches. Someone would certainly stop her before she even made it a few yards. She wished she knew where Stacie was. Stacie would know what to do.

"Oh, my!" Kim shouted. "What's that out by the end zone? Is that Mayor Sanderson in a 1965 Mustang convertible?"

The crowd roared in approval as the convertible began to slowly roll down the track, the mayor sitting tall and waving. Kim announced the car behind it, which carried one of the homecoming princesses, but Jill was no longer paying attention. She had noticed Stacie at the other end of the field, gripping Zack's arm with obvious firmness.

"Thank goodness," Jill whispered, and began swinging her way toward them. The crowd had mostly gotten into their seats now, so the going was easier. She swerved to avoid a pack of teenagers glued to their phones. Their faces gave her a moment's relief. Maybe everyone else in Kingston was football-crazed and school spirit-obsessed, but at least there were a few normal kids in the place.

"Hey, make a hole! The parade's coming through!" A big man in a Kingston letterman's jacket waved her to the side of the track.

The mayor's convertible nosed past, its engine grumbling lowly to itself. The driver looked over at Jill, grinning. He was wearing a pair of antlers.

She stumbled on the rough ground. When had he put those on? He hadn't been wearing them a moment ago.

Another convertible passed, the princess inside, waving and sobbing. The smell of roses billowed out of the car. A deer sat on the backseat beside the girl's high-heeled shoes.

Jill tried to go faster, but this was the cheerleading team's territory, their bags and pompoms covering every flat surface. She skidded on a duffel bag jacket. A girl squealed.

"Get out of here, lady!"

Jill's crutch caught something else, and for a second she thought she'd topple over, but she caught herself, and then Jill was finally out of that bottleneck. There was Stacie and Zack just ahead. She put some speed into her crutching. If her arms weren't so sore from yesterday's climbing, she would have half-enjoyed herself.

The percussion section began an intense drum roll. Jill staggered into Stacie's side.

"And now the moment you've all been waiting for! Miss 2018 Kingston Homecoming Queen: Danielle Burrows!"

The girl floated up to the dais, her gown trailing behind her. Jill herself had been a homecoming queen, but this girl had a grace and brightness she had never achieved. Her dress had probably cost three times as much as Jill's, too, and that was accounting for inflation.

Danielle went to the microphone. In her heels, she stood a good three inches taller than Kim, and she adjusted the microphone appropriately. She pressed her palms together, kissing her fingertips, overcome with emotion.

"Thank you, Kingston High," she managed.

The crowd leaped to its feet. Air horns screamed.

"Danielle, I love you!" someone shouted.

The girl laughed. "I love you too," she said. Her face went serious. "Now, you and I all know this is a tough time for Kingston. We don't just need to beat Plymouth today in the big game—we need to beat them to that contract with the Keridan Bridge Company. Am I right?"

Whoops and cheers. A boy rushed out on the field, shirtless, his chest painted in red-and-white streaks. He threw a bundle of roses on the stage, and what appeared to be boxer shorts. A sturdy woman began to escort him back to the bleachers.

"We have to find a way to help Gary," Stacie said.

Jill glanced back at the field. The shirtless boy had broken free and was kneeling in front of the dais. Kim had gotten down to talk to him. She looked back at Stacie. "What about Zack? Can he help?"

"I don't know," Stacie said. "He's acting weird."

"Zack?" Jill squeezed closer to her nephew, who stared into empty space like it was more entertaining than the weird activity on the field. "Zack, are you all right?"

"I feel funny," he said. "And everything looks weird too. Misty."

Stacie grabbed Jill's arm. "What the fuck?"

Danielle Burrows had produced a pistol from her bodice. "It's time to give Kingston our all!" she shouted, and the crowd cheered louder than ever. "You know what to do!"

David Washburn burst out of the darkness, running hard. "Jill! You've got to get out of here!" He beckoned them toward the end of the field, toward the bonfire. "This way!"

The crowd broke into the fight song as the homecoming queen blew off the top of her head.

CHAPTER THIRTY-THREE

GARY: 1989

GARY CRUMPLED TO his knees, his stomach heaving. The ancient brown paint of the lodge's back deck flaked under his palms, gritting against the skin. He ground his hands into the wood. Pain felt real. He needed real right now.

Jordan knelt beside him. "Gary, come on. We've got to get out of here."

Gary nodded. "Just let me catch my breath."

In the bathroom behind them, something smashed. "Gary!" Jordan shouted.

David grabbed the back of Gary's shirt, hauling him to his feet. "Fucking run!"

Jill was already climbing over the railing and crashing into the bushes beyond. Gary shook off the strangeness in his head and followed after her.

What had he seen back there? Did he even want to know? The whole room had filled with darkness, mist crawling out of people's eyes, seeping through the walls, boiling in the water glasses. Big Alice's rolling pin had been a solid, swirling mass of spirits.

"This is my fault," he gasped. A blackberry bush slapped his cheek, ripping it open. "This is all my fault."

"Shut up, Gary," David snapped. "Shut up and run!"

Stacie skidded to a stop, nearly colliding with Jordan. "You guys, my mom."

They all stopped. Behind them, a woman screamed in what could only be agony.

Stacie gasped. "That could have been her."

"It's not," Jill said, grabbing her by the shoulders. "Your mom was outside. She can get away." She gave Stacie another shake. "Besides, if there's one thing she'd want, it's for you to get away from all this."

Stacie wiped her nose on her arm. "I'm not leaving her. You guys go on. Get help. I have to find my mom."

She began to run toward the front of the lodge.

Jordan narrowed his eyes. "I'm not leaving her." And then he was off, sprinting faster than anyone had ever seen him.

"Fuck," David said. He spun around and ran after them.

"Gary," Jill whispered. "Don't make me go back there."

He shook his head. "You don't have to. Bike into town. Find someone to help. We'll be right behind you."

She stared at him. "You're going after them?"

"I have to." He took a deep, shuddering breath. "I did something to the spirits when we made the deer saint. I don't know what, but I stirred them up, and now they're different. Dangerous."

"And they're a part of him," she said.

He locked eyes with her. "Did you see this would happen?"

She began to cry. "I didn't think it would be like this. I didn't think anyone would get hurt!"

Gary spun away from his sister and ran after his friends. Thunder rumbled off to the east. He ran faster. The clouds were so thick it was like running in the twilight.

He was running so hard he nearly tripped over his own bike, and he stared at it stupidly for a second before he realized he'd hit the end of the lodge's turn-in. He pushed his way through the thimbleberries and Nootka roses and finally hit gravel.

Stacie's mom lay on the sidewalk by the ice chest, Stacie kneeling beside her, sobbing. Jordan had his arm around her. And David stood in front of them all, his arms spread to make himself bigger.

Vincent Vernor had come out the broken front window. Blood streamed down his neck, and stains of every color soaked his jean vest. His ear hung at an impossible angle.

He spun around. "Gary Sheldon!"

Gary froze.

"I knew you were the one behind it all. The first day I met you, I knew you were a little troublemaker."

Vincent took a step toward him, his eyes so wide the whites seemed to bulge around the icy pupils. A sound gurgled up in his throat that Gary could only barely identify as a chuckle. And for some reason, Gary remembered the happy, laughing man at Beachfest, the one giving his daughter a piece of elephant ear. This man was a shadow of that one.

"You should have left Kingston!" Gary shouted. "That's all we wanted!"

"But I like it here!" Vincent bellowed. "I like it here a lot!"

"Well, we don't like you," a man said from behind Gary. He put his hand on the boy's shoulder. An enormous class ring glinted on his finger. The weight of his hand made Gary's spine sag. The man wore brown boots, hiking boots maybe, the toe of one spattered with black wax.

Just like the toe cap of Nadine's Chucks. Gary's skin broke out in goosebumps. What had Coach D been doing with candles and Nadine's body?

"We don't like drug dealers in this town," the man said.

Gary looked up at Coach Dusseldorf. Coach D drew a cigarette out of the pack of Marlboro Reds in his pocket and lit it. He might as well have been at the bar with his buddies, he was so calm. He took a long pull on the cigarette, and then puffed it out in a cloud. "Go Big Red."

Vincent put out his tongue and lashed it like a snake's. "Fuck off, football."

"David?"

David rushed forward to give Vincent a powerful shove right between the shoulder blades. Vincent stumbled forward, slamming into the concrete hump of the first parking lot.

A girl's voice shrieked, and Gary realized Jill had followed him out of the bushes after all. He grabbed for her hand and squeezed it tight.

Little ribbons of darkness ran up from the ground, swirling around Vincent's body. With a groan, the man pushed himself to his knees. Blood dripped onto the ground from his ear and his newly split lip. He wiped his hand in the blood and raised it overhead.

"Help me, Stag God!"

Coach Dusseldorf took another drag on his cigarette and swung his foot into Vincent's ribs. "The stag demands better offerings, asshole."

Gary's mouth went dry. What did Coach D mean? Was the size of the offering all the deer saint cared about? There was nothing Gary could offer it as big or horrible as a human life.

Smoke billowed out of the ground, rushing up Coach D's legs, swirling around his stomach. He kicked Vincent again, the air rushing from Vincent's lungs.

Stacie's mom got to her feet. "Stop it, Coach! You'll kill him!"

Coach D glanced at her. "That's the point."

Vincent surged to his feet, shoving Coach Dusseldorf to the ground. "Stag God!" he roared.

The coach jumped up and charged Vincent. Vincent's arms wrapped around the coach's ribs, squeezing him tight. They staggered together, first away from the sidewalk, then toward it, then backward toward the gas pumps. Vincent spun them around so he could smash the coach's side into the pump. The machine gave an unhappy chime, and the hose fell free.

"What are we going to do?" David said.

"What are *we* going to do?" Jill shrieked. "What can we do? We're kids." She pointed at the broken window of the lodge, where people were slowly pulling each other to their feet or bandaging wounds or weeping. "We should get some of them to help us."

Coach Dusseldorf roared with pain or anger. He bit into the side of Vincent's face and Vincent lost his grip on the man. Vincent stumbled backward but caught himself and lashed a fist out at the coach. The Marlboro Red shot out of Dusseldorf's mouth.

"Holy shit," Jordan said.

The deer had come.

Gary turned to face them. An entire herd, the small females staring at the men by the gas pumps, their eyes blazing. In their center, the stag stood watching, his antlers impossibly huge.

"Deer Saint!" Gary called. The creature didn't even look his way.

"Stag God!" Vincent cheered.

The gas puddle behind him caught fire. Coach Dusseldorf stumbled away from it, blood running down his chin, his eye swollen.

Stacie's mom shouted something unintelligible and began sprinting for the front door to help the people inside.

"The pumps!" Stacie screamed. "Get away!"

The great stag took a step forward. The mist of a thousand spirits spun around its hooves.

Vincent stretched out bloody palms. "Thank you, Stag God."

The pump behind him went up with a *whoomp* that knocked Gary on his ass. He could only stare at the flames, at the blackness, at the deer saint as it reared up, raking its hooves through the air. It was no longer his, he felt certain. Nothing he could say would mean anything to it.

"Please, Deer Saint," Jordan whispered. "Please."

The stag lunged forward, its hooves striking Vincent in the chest and launching him into the flames. Then the deer saint, too, was engulfed in fire.

The ground shook as the fire hit the underground tank. Flame shot out the roof of the lodge as the gas line sucked fire up through the walls.

The outline of the stag burned brighter. Coach Dusseldorf shielded his face as he stood at the edge of the parking lot, unable, or unwilling, to turn away from the creature that had once saved him from falling into Calhoun Lake.

"He's dead," Jordan said. "Vincent Vernor is dead."

"Stacie?" Mrs. Clinton shouted from the bushes. "Are you all right? Stacie!"

Stacie rushed toward her mother and the people her mother had gotten out of the lodge. "Mom! Mom!"

Flames crawled across the roof of the lodge and up the walls. Metal shrieked inside its frame. And the stag burned brighter, its body going from orange to yellow to white.

In its brightness there wasn't even a tendril of black.

Gary put his arm around Jill and his other around Jordan. "It's gone," he said. "The deer saint is gone."

Jordan pressed his cheek against Gary's, his face wet with tears. Or maybe the tears were Gary's. It was impossible to tell. Even Jill was sobbing.

"We're gonna be all right," Jordan said. "I think we'll really be all right."

GARY: 2018

Up on the dais, the gun went off, and Sergeant Danse let go of Gary's arm to cross himself. "Thank the Stag God," he whispered.

Gary wrenched free of Shawn's hold and took off running. He had no idea where Zack was, where Jill was, or how to even get out of this goddamn ball field, but he wasn't going up on that dais, no how, no way. He swerved around a bare-chested boy rubbing his skin with the splattered brains of the dead homecoming queen.

"Over here!" someone yelled, and Gary saw David Washburn waving his arms as he ran toward him.

Gary put a burst of speed into his legs and thanked the benevolent universe for all the running he'd done in the last ten years. If he made it out of Kingston, he was going to train to run a fucking marathon, and that was a solemn promise.

When Danse tackled him, Gary flew nearly five yards and hit the ground with a two-hundred-and-fifty-pound heap of pain on his back.

The AstroTurf bit into his face.

"No!" David threw himself at Danse, grabbing his ear and wrenching back the man's head. "Get off him!"

"Come now, Coach Washburn," an age-graveled voice said, and Gary knew it was Coach Dusseldorf, even if he couldn't see the man's face. "You know we have a rally to finish."

"Fuck you, Dusseldorf! I've given you and this town my whole life. I'm done!"

The weight shifted off Gary's back, and he rolled onto his side, gasping. Things inside his back shifted and popped. It was going to be a long, long time before he ran any marathons.

"I've got the woman!" someone shouted.

"Jill." David crumpled to his knees. His face twisted. The all-admired football champion and coaching hero mask slid away, leaving behind the scared boy who had once made Gary a sandwich. "Please don't hurt her," he whispered.

Dusseldorf pulled the brim of his KHS cap lower over his eyes. "You know we have to, David. We've talked about this."

"No!"

The hefty assistant coach and another man pulled David to his feet. Danse urged Gary upright, although standing made Gary want to throw up.

He squeezed his eyes shut for a moment. If only he could still take Dr. Monroe's good advice and go back to believing in only the sane and logical things in the world. If only he could open his eyes and see that this was all just a fun local tradition like burning a papier- mâché copy of the visiting team's mascot or celebrating John King's birthday on the first weekend of November. But even with his eyes closed he could smell the blood and hear the screaming and feel the damp touch of a dozen, a hundred, a thousand restless spirits.

He opened his eyes and saw Jill beside him.

"I'm sorry, Gary," Jill said. Her captors had thrown away her crutches, and she staggered as they force-marched her forward. "I tried to get away. This stupid knee."

They were being led toward the dais again. The pep band had switched to "Tequila." Gary could hear the cheerleaders screeching something peppy.

"What do they want with us?" he asked David.

"What do you think?" David said. "You made the fucking thing, Gary. And you're a *Sheldon*."

"That's right." Dusseldorf stood patiently beside the dais stairs.

"Things were so good for us the year the Sheldons sacrificed themselves." He reached out and patted Jill's cheek fondly. "Your parents turned things around for this town. For a while."

Danse shoved Gary up the stairs. Sam Oakley stood beside the microphone wearing the same white robes she had worn last night at the church. Antlers rose from her head, their tines glinting in the stadium lighting. Her sandaled feet stood in a sticky puddle of Danielle Burrow's blood. Black mist circled its edges.

"It really is a beautiful thing, Gary," she said. "You should have seen it when Skyler went."

"You're insane!" he shouted.

She smiled beatifically. "Am I, Gary? Is it insane to want something good for your hometown?"

Gary spat, but the white glob fell short. "My parents didn't sacrifice themselves for this town. They drove into that lake to save *me*."

A finger, hot as fire, touched the back of his neck.

And I did save you, something whispered. *I saved you for this.*

"No," Gary gasped.

The Kingston mascot stepped out from behind David. Its furry face beamed at the crowd.

Sam stepped out of its way. It bent toward the microphone. Tendrils of smoke trickled out its mouth hole.

"Are we going to beat Plymouth tonight?" it bellowed.

"Yes!" the crowd answered.

"Are we going to wipe the field with them?"

"YES!" the crowd roared.

"Then make it happen!"

"Go Bucks!" someone shouted, and then launched himself off the top row of the bleachers. He hit the ground with a wet crunch.

The crowd went wild. Cheerleaders dove onto the track, rolling and clawing and biting at each other. The smallest drove the end of a baton through another girl's eyeball in an explosion of yellow and red. A man ran out onto the football field screaming, chased by a pack of howling teenage boys.

Jill gasped. "It's the lodge all over again."

Gary wanted to answer, but he couldn't breathe. The past was too thick around him. He heard the spirit of a logger scream as he took a chainsaw to the thigh. He heard a woman sob as she swallowed a scoop full of rat poison. He heard two boys begging, pleading not to be taken out to sea.

"There are so many dead people," he managed to whisper. They streamed up from the ground, begging to be heard, to be freed, to be made *whole*, even if it was just for one night. "They gave it so many lives."

There was a horrible crunching to his right and he turned his head to see Jill staring at him, her mouth open as if she had something important to tell him, her eyes enormous and dark. Coach Dusseldorf let go of her head and her neck slumped sideways. They dropped her to the ground.

"Jill!" Gary screamed. "Jill!"

Kim rushed up the stairs. "Wait!" she shouted. "Wait!"

"Oh thank God," Gary breathed. "Kim, help me. They killed Jill!"

Kim dropped to her knees, clutching at Dusseldorf's knees. "I can't find my son. Please. Is he all right? You promised he wouldn't be part of this. You promised."

He laid his hand on her shoulder. The red jewel of his school ring glowed in the light. "Don't worry, Kim. We'll find him. You two are an important part of this town."

She kissed his hand and got to her feet. The knees of her khaki slacks were soaked in blood. "Thank you." She backed away, bowing. "Thank you so much."

"Kim!" Gary shouted after her. "Kim, please! The deer saint only cares how much you give it. It doesn't care about you or this town, just the sacrifices."

But she didn't hear him, or she ignored him, or she no longer cared. Tears streamed down Gary's face. At least Zack would be all right. Whatever that bitch had done to Gary and Jill, at least she still cared about Zack.

Dusseldorf moved to stand in front of David.

"Are you going to kill me, too?" David asked.

"I don't know," Dusseldorf said, and nodded at Sam.

She picked up a baseball bat and brought it down over David's head. His legs went out from under him, and the big men holding him let him fall. He lay still, leaving Gary to face the end alone.

He hoped like hell Stacie had found a way out of this mess.

Gary glared at Coach D and his antlered daughter. "Do it, Sam." He could vaguely hear the strains of "When Ducks Tango" over the sounds of people screaming, and it seemed a terrible song to die to.

The mascot pushed Sam out of the way. Only he wasn't just some kid in a furry suit. Maybe he never was.

The deer saint loomed over Gary, its eyes seeping darkness. Coils of smoky spirits ran from its nose and trickled out of its mouth. Its fur crept and crawled with ghosts. A smell came off it like old cigarettes and stale pee, a smell Gary always associated with the Big House and Vincent

Vernor. And for a second, blue flashed in the thing's eyes—not the blue of a deer's tapetum, but the thin, cold blue of Vincent Vernor's eyes.

It bent down so its smoke-breath rushed into Gary's face.

Remember what I told you?

Gary stared at it, the back of his neck burning.

There in the hospital, I took you from death and I gave you my mark. And I warned you, didn't I?

Gary couldn't stand to look at it another second. He squeezed shut his eyes. "Zack," he whispered. "Oh, Zack, I love you."

You're mine.

And then pain exploded in Gary's chest and his eyes flashed open and for a second all he saw was his father, stretching out his hand.

STACIE: 2018

They drove in silence up Highway 101, tires screeching on the sharper turns. There was no way in hell Stacie was slowing down, not now, not until she got out of the fucking Coastal Mountain range and away from the goddamn sea. Zack sat in the passenger seat, slumped against the window.

They took the turn for Poodle Creek Road far too quickly, but the Florence cops were all asleep or watching their own high school football games. Zack shifted in his seat and rubbed the back of his neck. "My neck hurts. Like a sunburn."

The moon winked off the Siuslaw River to her right. She forced her eyes back to the road. "Sorry. I don't have a first-aid kit."

"Do you have any water?" he said.

"There's coffee in the cupholder. I think."

He took a drink and made a face. "How long has it been there?"

"Since yesterday."

Just saying it made Stacie want to stick her head out the window and vomit. Yesterday they had taken Jill to urgent care for a sprained knee, and now she was dead. Stacie hadn't seen much of what had happened on that football field, but after the homecoming queen shot herself in front of the entire town, she hadn't needed to. She'd looked behind herself and seen them leading Jill up to that dais, and she had known Jill was gone. Her first and best friend, gone.

Stacie gave a shuddering sob and then forced back any more tears. No crying, just driving. Driving. The car's lights flashed on a mileage sign. Only forty miles to Eugene. That was civilization. She could make it that far.

"My parents are dead, aren't they?"

"Yeah," she whispered. She could barely see the road. Tears and exhaustion filmed her eyes. She blinked as hard as she could. If only she could stop for a nap.

Stacie checked the rearview window. There was no one behind her, at least, no one with their lights on. No, she couldn't stop, not even for coffee, not this close to Kingston.

"Where are we going?" Zack asked.

"Away," Stacie said, blinking back tears again. "As far away as we can get."

They drove on through the dark, heavy forest, the highway making hairpins as it wound through the unpeopled hills. Stacie turned up the stereo to fill the silence, and the boy pressed his cheek to the window beside him. For an instant, the headlights flashed in the eyes of a doe that raised her head to watch them pass.

Zack rubbed the back of his neck.

The deer melted into the night like smoke in the rain. Stacie drove faster.

ACKNOWLEDGMENTS

THIS BOOK BEGAN as a short story, and the novel would have never existed without the terrific feedback C.C. Finlay gave me on that piece. So thanks, Charlie! I'm so glad you rejected this one.

Big thanks goes to keen-eyed beta readers Jason LaPier and Nathan Carson, who helped me remember what the '80s were like and also helped me keep all the timelines straight. Nathan, thanks for knowing just what it was like to live in the woods and be a weirdo.

Warm hugs to Emily Hughes and Sadie Hartmann, for all their support and encouragement since this book was announced.

As ever, I couldn't have written this one without the help of my fantastic "writing support group"—Masked Hucksters, you are the very best. And of course, I would never even make it to the keyboard if not for the care, love, and constant support of my wonderful husband John, daughter Fiona, and my giant monster cats.

This one was written in loving memory of James Akre—one inspiring English teacher and a heck of a football coach.

ABOUT THE AUTHOR

WENDY N. WAGNER'S short stories, essays, and poems run the gamut from horror to environmental literature. Her novels include the Locus bestseller *An Oath of Dogs* and two novels for the *Pathfinder* role-playing game. A Hugo award-winning editor of short fiction, she is currently the editor-in-chief of *Nightmare Magazine*. She lives in Oregon with her very understanding family, two large cats, and a Muppet disguised as a dog.

CPSIA information can be obtained
at www.ICGtesting.com
Printed in the USA
LVHW042150171021
700690LV00001B/121

9 781950 305971